Praise for
THE ANNIVERSARY DAY SAGA

... the Anniversary Day Saga could become a milestone in the field.

—*Amazing Stories*

Anniversary Day is an edge-of-the-seat thriller that will keep you turning pages late into the night and it's also really good science fiction. What's not to like?

—*Analog* on *Anniversary Day*

The suspenseful storyline is fast-paced and filled with twists as the hero comes out of retirement to confront his worst nightmare.

—*Midwest Book Reviews* on *Blowback*

Fans of Rusch's Retrieval Artist universe will enjoy the expansion of the Anniversary Day story, with new characters providing more perspectives on its signature events, while newcomers will get a good introduction to the series.

—*Publishers Weekly* on *A Murder of Clones*

This new Retrieval Artist Universe novel is action-packed and continues where *A Murder of Clones* leaves off. These must be read in order to fully appreciate the suspense and mystery that is taking place.

—*RT Book Reviews* on *Search & Recovery*

The Anniversary Day Saga just keeps getting more interesting and more complicated. Each addition is eagerly anticipated and leaves the reader anxious to discover what will happen next, who the bad guys are and what it is they are hoping to achieve.

—*RT Book Reviews* on *The Peyti Crisis*

Praise for
The Retrieval Artist Series

One of the top ten greatest science fiction detectives of all time.

—*io9*

[Miles Flint is] one of 14 great sci-fi and fantasy detectives who out-Sherlock'd Holmes. [Flint] is a candidate for the title of greatest fictional detective of all time.

—*Blastr*

Part *CSI*, part *Blade Runner*, and part hard-boiled gumshoe, the retrieval artist of the series title, one Miles Flint, would be as at home on a foggy San Francisco street in the 1940s as he is in the domed lunar colony of Armstrong City.

—*The Edge Boston*

What links [Miles Flint] to his most memorable literary ancestors is his hard-won ability to perceive the complex nature of morality and live with the burden of his own inevitable failure.

—*Locus*

Instant addiction. You hear about it—maybe you even laugh it off—but you never think it could happen to you. Well, you just haven't run into Miles Flint and the other Retrieval Artists looking for The Disappeared. ...I am hopelessly hooked....

—Lisa DuMond
MEviews.com on *The Disappeared*

An inventive plot and complex, conflicted characters increases the appeal of Kristine Kathryn Rusch's *Extremes*. This futuristic tale breaks new ground as a space police procedural and should appeal to science fiction and mystery fans.

—*RT Book Reveiws* on *Extremes*

Part science fiction, part mystery, and pure enjoyment are the words to describe Kristine Kathryn Rusch's latest Retrieval Artist novel.... This is a strong murder mystery in an outer space storyline.

—*The Best Reviews* on *Consequences*

An exciting, intricately plotted, fast-paced novel. You'll find it difficult to put down.

—*SFRevu* on *Buried Deep*

A science fiction murder mystery by one of the genre's best.... A book with complex characters, an interesting and unpredictable plot, and timeless and universal things to say about the human condition.

—*The Panama News* on *Paloma*

Rusch continues her provocative interplanetary detective series with healthy doses of planet-hopping intrigue, heady legal dilemmas and well-drawn characters.

—*Publishers Weekly* on *Recovery Man*

...the mystery is unpredictable and absorbing and the characters are interesting and sympathetic.

—*Blastr* on *Duplicate Effort*

THE RETRIEVAL ARTIST SERIES:

The Disappeared
Extremes
Consequences
Buried Deep
Paloma
Recovery Man
The Recovery Man's Bargain (Novella)
Duplicate Effort
The Possession of Paavo Deshin (Novella)

The Anniversary Day Saga:

Anniversary Day
Blowback
A Murder of Clones
Search & Recovery
The Peyti Crisis
Vigilantes
Starbase Human
Masterminds

Other Stories:

The Retrieval Artist (Novella)
The Impossibles (A Retrieval Artist Universe Short Story)

The PEYTI CRISIS

A RETRIEVAL ARTIST NOVEL

KRISTINE KATHRYN RUSCH

WMG PUBLISHING

The Peyti Crisis

Book Five of the Anniversary Day Saga

Published 2015 by WMG Publishing
www.wmgpublishing.com

Cover design by Allyson Longueira/WMG Publishing

ISBN-13: 978-1-56146-616-0
ISBN-10: 1-56146-616-6

For Paul B. Higginbotham,
who has supported my writing from the beginning,
and for being one of the best friends ever.

Acknowledgements

The Peyti Crisis started as the third book in what I thought was a trilogy, and then it morphed into the fifth book of an eight-book series. My husband kept me sane through the transition, or at least, as sane as I'll ever be. Thank you, Dean, for talking me down during each and every book of the series.

I also have to thank Annie Reed, Colleen Kuehne and Judy Cashner, who have done their best to keep my errors at bay. (All mistakes are mine.)

Special thanks to Allyson Longueira, who has shepherded this large project with aplomb and who has designed the fantastic covers.

And, last but definitely not least, thanks to all the readers who are traveling with me on this journey. Your enthusiasm has kept me going through each and every word.

Author's Note

Dear Readers,

When one of my regular readers saw the marvelous cover that WMG's Allyson Longueira designed for this book, he also noted the title and asked, "Isn't The Peyti Crisis *a better title for* Blowback?"

Well…no. Because Blowback *is all about the surprise.* The Peyti Crisis *is about the aftermath.*

Before I go any farther with this, let me address those of you who picked this book up because of Allyson's wonderful cover, and have never read a Retrieval Artist novel before. You've jumped into the middle of a long series—which is fine. The series was designed to be jumped into at any point—except for the Anniversary Day Saga books.

The saga is a contained story arc in the middle of the long series. If you want to read the saga, start with Anniversary Day, *then move to* Blowback, A Murder of Clones, Search & Recovery, *and then read this book.*

If you want to read the entire Retrieval Artist series (and you don't have to in order to enjoy the saga), start with The Disappeared.

For those of you who have read Retrieval Artist books before and picked this up, thinking it's the next book after Blowback, *please go back and read* A Murder of Clones *and* Search & Recovery *before starting this book. You'll be glad you did.*

I write out of order, and normally, I assemble my novels after writing all the pieces, rather like a quilter does when she has the fabric cut and the pieces laid out. The Anniversary Day saga is one big story, so having the luxury to finish the books all at once has allowed me to cut and piece this story together as it should go.

The previous two novels took us into the recent (and not-so-recent) past. The Peyti Crisis *starts just after* Blowback *and, indeed, was the book I wrote next—with side trips to Epricomm and a few other short stories (some you'll see upcoming, and some which remain unfinished, written to explain something just to me).*

Initially, though, this book didn't end correctly, but it wasn't until I was midway through Vigilantes *(the next book) that I figured out why. I was trying to add plotlines and characters that you won't see until the last two books in this saga. They don't fit in* The Peyti Crisis, *so I moved them to the places where they belonged, leaving me with some events that needed to be explored* before *I finished* The Peyti Crisis. *I wrote parts of* Search & Recovery *and* Starbase Human *before I revised this book and made it into the volume you have before you.*

Sounds complicated, right? It would be if I were trying to publish only one book a year. But the changes in the publishing industry have allowed me to write and publish the rest of the saga in a short period of time. In consultation with WMG, I decided to publish the last six books in the first six months of 2015.

You don't need a lengthy recap in the beginning, and I don't have to worry that you'll forget what happened from year to year. Plus, it leaves the reading in your hands. You can read all of the books as they appear or save them until July or read one or two in 2015, while reading other things. Your choice, not mine.

I hope you enjoy The Peyti Crisis. *I loved returning to Flint and the gang. I suspect it shows.*

—Kristine Kathryn Rusch
Lincoln City, Oregon
June 14, 2014

The PEYTI CRISIS

A RETRIEVAL ARTIST NOVEL

FIFTY-FIVE YEARS AGO

1

THE VOICE ON HER LINKS, SO FAINT SHE ALMOST DIDN'T HEAR IT.

Jhena, I need you. Oh, God, I need you.

Jhena Andre sat in her tiny office in the back of the administration suite. She was comparing the approved list of names for the morning's trial to the list of names vetted by the Earth Alliance Prison System. She had already compared the approved list to the list vetted through the Human Justice Division. She had five more lists to compare, and then she had to confirm that the DNA associated with the approved list of names for the morning's trial actually belonged to the person with that name.

She had stocked up on coffee: It was going to be a long night.

Jhena, please. Please.

She paused the holographic lists. The same name was highlighted on each. Behind the floating list, she could see the bare wall, the one she'd been told not to decorate since she wouldn't be here long.

Not long had gone from three weeks to six weeks to six months, and now, nearly a year. Somehow PierLuigi Frémont had managed to hire lawyers who actually argued his case, claiming at first that the Earth Alliance had no jurisdiction over events in Abbondiado, and then when his lawyers had lost that, that what happened in Abbondiado had been an internal coup, not a crime against humanity.

The Criminal Court had already tossed out one of the genocide charges, saying that crimes committed on the Frontier did not belong in Earth Alliance Courts. Someone, her boss had said, was afraid of taking this case all the way to the Multicultural Tribunals, and losing.

Jhena....

She finally recognized the voice, and more importantly, she recognized the link. It was her private link, the one she'd only given to friends, and the message was encoded, which was why it seemed faint.

She cursed, and put a hand to her ear, even though she didn't need to, even though she usually made fun of people who did the very same thing.

Didier? She sent back. She knew she sounded timid, but she wasn't sure it was him. Didier Conte was the only person in the entire prison complex who could contact her on her friends link.

Yeah. Please. I need you right now. Bring evidence bags.

Evidence bags? She didn't have access to evidence bags. And then she realized that she did. Extras were stored in the closet just outside her stupid little office, along with a whole bunch of other supplies that this part of the prison needed.

Why? she sent back.

Hurry. And then he signed off.

She stared at the highlighted name, the letters blurring, the image of the person the name belonged to not really registering. Why would Didier need her? Why not call another guard? And why had he signed off so fast?

This was where she usually failed the friendship test. She didn't care what other people needed, especially if they bothered her in the middle of something.

But the something she was in the middle of was extremely tedious, and if Didier's locator was right, he was deep inside the prison, where she only got to go if a supervisor was nearby.

The prison wasn't the most dangerous one Jhena had worked at in her short twenty-one years. That would be a super max on the edge of the Earth Alliance, run by humans but housing all different kinds of aliens who'd broken human laws in various outposts along the way.

She not only couldn't go into certain parts of that prison because she would be fired; she couldn't go because she would die without the proper gear. Not everything was set up on Earth Standard. The Peyti section alone had more toxins in the atmosphere than she had seen since her childhood, when her parents were working for Ultre Corporation.

Her brain skittered away from that memory.

She stood. This was probably her only chance to see PierLuigi Frémont without dozens of guards accompanying him. Didier said that Frémont was charismatic and that made him dangerous, not that it really mattered, since it didn't matter how much the man charmed Jhena. She had no codes, no passkeys, and no DNA recognition that would allow her to open the doors to his cell.

She was quite aware of her place as a lower-level employee of the prison system, one who could be replaced with yet another machine, but wasn't, partly because the law protected certain human jobs against automation, and partly because of the belief that humans could do some work better than machines.

She was grateful for the law, even though she found the belief behind it stupid. But, then, she found a lot of beliefs stupid. She'd learned to be circumspect about it, learned to use those beliefs to her benefit, like now. Even though she hated the tedium, she was getting a hell of a good paycheck, and this job was a stepping stone to better jobs elsewhere in the Earth Alliance System.

All because of a stupid belief.

She grinned, stood, and smoothed her skirt. She wasn't really dressed to go into the prisoner wing. She usually wore pants for that, and a loose-fitting shirt. Because she hadn't wanted to come to work tonight, she had made it a game, deciding to look good for once, even though no one was going to see her.

Now, it seemed, someone was. A mass murderer, by all accounts. A fascinating man. Someone famous.

She left the office, pulling the door closed behind her, and then grabbed a box of evidence bags out of the closet across the hall.

She didn't want Didier to chastise her for not bringing enough bags, so she brought too many.

She tucked the box under her arm, and headed into the high security area. She thought for a brief moment about the cameras that were everywhere, but she didn't know how to shut them off.

If she got in trouble, she would blame Didier, say that he had asked for her help, and she didn't know she wasn't supposed to give it.

But no one around here looked at the camera footage unless there was a problem.

And she hoped that despite his tone, Didier hadn't caused a problem. She hoped he just needed a little bit of help with something.

She hoped she wouldn't pay for this forever.

2

NO HUMAN GUARDS WERE ON DUTY IN THIS PART OF THE PRISON, AT LEAST not this late. The guard station had a full android unit behind the windows. Its yellow eyes tracked Jhena as she slapped her palm against the cool reinforced plastic.

"Didier Conte sent for me," she said as a purely cover-her-ass sentence. She suspected she could have opened the double-latched security entrance all on her own.

But the android recorded everything, just like the security cameras did, and if anyone challenged her presence, she had her words as well as the link contacts to back her up. Unlike so many people, she kept track of every link contact instead of letting it fade into nothingness after a few weeks of time.

She had learned young that it paid to be cautious.

"Proceed," the android said in its gender-neutral voice. The locks thumped, and the door into the decontamination/examination area swung open.

She stepped inside, waving the box of evidence bags as a kind of notice that she had something unusual.

Not that it mattered. Lights changed inside the decontamination/examination area as it checked her. Blue lights for biological hazards, and smuggled diseases; green for contraband goods; and orange for actual weapons. If the system found anything on her, the lights would either become bright yellow to signal possible trouble or bright flaring red for an actual discovery.

Sometimes, when she slept, she dreamed that she was trapped in the decontamination/examination area as the red lights blinked and sirens blared. Guards would find dozens of weapons secreted on her person, or biohazard spread like goo along her clothing.

She always woke from those dreams so terrified that she would have to get up and walk around, hoping the dreams would fade.

Even though she had never carried anything into the prison proper. Even though she had never even *thought* of doing so, except when she stood here, afraid of being caught with something that someone had stashed on her.

The air smelled faintly of ozone, like it always did at this part of the process. Then the lights returned to their low-watt whitish gray intensity, and the doors on the other side hummed open. Three sets of doors, each on a different timer, each opening from a different direction—the first to her right, the second to her left, and the last with the doors sliding up to the ceiling.

Her heart pounded. If she went in there, she couldn't get out without help, no matter how much she wanted to.

She thought of tossing the box of evidence bags into the area, and then letting Didier know that they had arrived without her; he would have to come and get them.

But two things stopped her: his tone, which had been odd, almost secretive; and the chance to see PierLuigi Frémont in what would be his natural environment from now on.

She stepped through the doors, and into the cellblock.

The air was noticeably colder and thinner. The theory was to keep the prisoners so cold that they expended some energy every day just to keep warm. The oxygen content was as low as it could get for human survival so that the prisoners were constantly short of breath.

Every time she stepped in here, she hated it because she always felt momentarily lightheaded. If she stayed too long, she would get nauseous.

She brushed the back of her hand, setting a timer that appeared in the corner of her right eye. The timer was an automatic one for the cell block. If she stayed longer than twenty minutes, the timer would go off.

Twenty-five minutes was her maximum time without some kind of environmental suit in this oxygen-poor environment. That's why she set for twenty minutes: she always gave herself five minutes to escape.

She opened her link to the prison's internal system. *Find Didier Conte*, she sent.

Off-line, came the response, almost immediately.

Her face warmed. Was Didier playing some kind of game with her? Off-line meant that he wasn't in the prison at all.

Her heart started pounding hard, and she suspected it wasn't just because her body was struggling in this environment.

She sent a message across her private link. *The prison system says you're not here, Didier. What are you playing at?*

Nothing, he sent back. *I'll reconnect to the system in a minute. I'm exactly where I should be, okay? Get here now.*

She frowned. He was playing a game of some kind, but she still thought he sounded terrified.

She contacted the prison link system again, not covering her tracks. *I thought Didier Conte was on guard duty tonight. What section was he scheduled for?*

High security, senior prisoner, Frémont. No record of Didier Conte's departure and none of his presence. Would you like to reboot the system?

Not yet, she sent, uncertain how that would play to someone examining her actions much later. But she couldn't really say no to the system (imagining in her mind how that would go over with the bosses: *Why didn't you want to find Conte? Did you know where he was? Weren't you concerned that he had left his post?*) and she couldn't say yes in case Didier really was doing something untoward.

She walked through the corridors, passing a dozen expensive android guards, all of them high security. They were thicker than the average android guard, taller, and made of some shiny black polymer material that hid any access ports. According to the specs, these guards carried a dozen weapons just on their torsos, but she couldn't see any of them.

The guards had no mouths or noses, just those damn big eyes that looked like they could see everything.

They were androids because they theoretically could think for themselves, and they had a very human form, but she never really thought of them as androids. They seemed like a hybrid between the thinking android and the brainless robots that were everywhere outside of the prison system.

In theory, the system couldn't have a brainless contraption anywhere near high-value prisoners. The prisoners might be able to subvert the bot's functions and create everything from a gun to a bomb. In theory, androids wouldn't let that happen, but after the prison riots of twenty years ago, where the androids got turned to the prisoners' sides, the androids were redesigned. No mouths, no noses, no obvious entry points, and absolutely no empathy.

None.

Not for anyone.

Jhena shivered. It seemed colder the farther in she went.

The cellblock was locked down for the night, which meant that each cell had been walled off from the others. Doors darkened, no windows, no access to the outside at all.

In fact, it looked like she was walking past black wall after black wall after black wall, when she had actually passed twenty cells so far.

At the end of this corridor was the specially designed cell that held the highest-value prisoners, who probably would not be permanent guests of this facility. They were supposed to lose their cases, and move to maximum security prisons far away from the Criminal Courts, prisons in the far reaches of the Earth Alliance, prisons that made this one look like a resort in the prettiest place on Planet Earth.

The light around that cell was red, but it wasn't flashing and there were no sirens. Just a deep red light that she should never see this far inside the prison.

"Oh, no." She didn't realize she'd said that out loud until she heard her voice echo off the walls.

A dozen scenarios flashed through her brain: Frémont had somehow co-opted Didier and gotten him to contact her; together, Frémont and Didier would overpower her and make her help them escape; Frémont had *killed* Didier and would get her next—

"Oh, thank God, Jhena." The voice didn't belong to Frémont. It belonged to Didier.

He stepped into the light. He was a burly man, mostly muscle, and his uniform made him look more formidable than the android guards. Although at the moment, he didn't look formidable at all. The red light bathed his bald pate, and put his eyes in shadow. He seemed creepy, almost like a prisoner himself.

"I'm not coming any closer until you tell me what's going on," she said.

"Um, it's better if I don't say. You need to look."

She shook her head. She wasn't getting near that light, particularly now that a smell was reaching her. It was foul—as if someone hadn't cleaned the toilets in this section ever.

"I'm going to throw your evidence bags at you, and then I'm leaving," she said.

"Okay," Didier said, sounding like it wasn't okay. "But then you'll miss your only chance to make a small fortune."

"I'm not helping a mass murderer escape," she said.

"Oh," Didier said. "There's no need to worry about that. Frémont's not going anywhere."

"How do you know that?" she asked.

"I told you," he said. "Take a look."

But shut off your links, he sent through her private link. *All except emergency links.*

She bit her lower lip. She hadn't shut anything down, not yet, and that little request would be recorded. If she complied, it would mean—what? That she had conspired with Didier? Or that she simply didn't know better?

God, she hated second-guessing.

"If you don't join me in fifteen seconds, don't bother," he snapped.

She still couldn't see his face. That worried her.

But she would probably get in trouble just for being here, especially if something had gone wrong. After ten seconds clicked off on the timer she displayed on her right eye, she shut down all the various recording links, then shut down her contact links except for the emergency links.

As she did, the timer in her eye vanished.

Oh, great. She had forgotten the timer was connected to the network. Now she wouldn't know how much time had elapsed. She could probably set another timer with her emergency links, but that would require a jury-rig, which she doubted Didier would give her time for.

She stepped forward.

The red light was actually warm or, at least, warmer than the rest of the corridor had been.

"What the hell's going on?" she asked, trying to ignore the way her stomach flopped at the stench. It felt like a live thing, as if the air itself had sewage molecules, and they were coating her.

Didier nodded at the cell.

She could barely see inside it—the cot that extended from the wall was still out, not recessed like it should have been at this time of day. The toilet didn't look like it had overflowed, but it was hard to see in the deep red light.

Frémont was nowhere in sight. Had Didier let him out? Was Frémont going to attack her?

Her heart rate went up even farther, although she hadn't thought that was even possible.

"Hurry," Didier said.

She looked around. The walls nearby were black from the closed cell doors. She couldn't see any androids at all.

There was, as far as she could tell, no place for Frémont to hide.

Her mouth was dry. She swallowed against it anyway. She couldn't remember ever being this frightened as an adult. As a child, yes, but as an adult—

Her mind skittered away from the thought.

She took another step, and then another, not sure how she was managing to make her feet work. Somehow she was, though.

Somehow.

She peered over that bed, and finally saw Frémont. He was sprawled on the floor, legs twisted, one arm still on the bed, the other extended toward the toilet.

The smell was coming from him, and it was so bad here that her eyes watered.

"What the hell...?" she muttered, but she did so not to be answered, but because she couldn't remain quiet.

Something had dried around his mouth, and there was a lot of liquid on the floor. His face was bloated—or it seemed that way. She couldn't tell if it was a trick of the light.

"What the hell?" she repeated, this time looking at Didier. "Is he dead?"

Didier smiled at her. "Yep," he said. "And we only have a few minutes before the administration finds out."

3

Jhena stood near the entrance to the cell. She stared at PierLuigi Frémont's feet because she didn't want to see any other part of him. Certainly not whatever was causing the stench that seemed to get worse with each passing minute.

She kept a hand over her face, and really wished she had worn an environmental suit. Then, at least, she would be able to breathe fresh air, with the proper amount of oxygen, and she wouldn't be so cold.

"You didn't report his death?" Jhena asked. "My God, do you realize what they'll do—"

"They won't do anything. Not if we act fast." Didier looked like some kind of alien she'd never encountered before with his black guard's uniform reflecting the flaring red emergency light.

With that thing on, wouldn't the authorities know something was wrong?

She let out a small breath, warm against her palm, reminding herself that she and Didier *were* the authorities. At least for the moment.

"Surely, someone will come to check. My links seem to be off," she said. "And you know that triggers terrible alarms. Everyone will come here shortly, and we'll get in trouble—"

"Believe it or not," Didier said with a grin. The red reflected off his teeth, making them seem sharp. "Frémont severed the links, not me."

He couldn't have. Jhena knew that much. Prisoners in Earth Alliance Maximum Security prisons couldn't access systems.

Of course, prisoners couldn't kill themselves either. They didn't have the tools. They didn't have *access* to the tools.

She glanced at Didier. Had he provided Frémont with something that would kill him? She didn't want to know if that was the case. She wasn't going to ask.

She wasn't going to ask anything.

Jhena crouched.

The stench seemed milder down low, or maybe she was just getting used to it. Still, the smell of feces and bodily fluids was so strong that she pinched her nose closed, which then made her breathe through her mouth, which was a mistake. She could taste the smell now, and her stomach turned again.

Frémont must have shut down more than links, because the environmental systems should have cleared out the smell by now, certainly cleared it enough that it wouldn't be so strong that she could almost feel it.

She shivered, and knew it wasn't just because of the cold. Her head ached, and she wondered how long she'd been here.

"Why would he do that?" she asked. "I mean, if he could do that, shouldn't he have tried to escape?"

"Escape where?" Didier asked. "He could have roamed this facility or maybe even made it to the dock, but that's where he'd get caught, and he knew it. He could manipulate systems inside here, maybe just the once. But he couldn't manipulate the entire prison. No one can."

She knew that. She was just so shaken that she hadn't thought it through.

"Besides," Didier said, "he did escape. He died. We can't prosecute him now."

She glanced up at Didier. He still looked odd in the red light, almost as if he were enjoying this.

"Surely the punishment wouldn't have been that bad," she said.

"I don't think it was the punishment he was worried about," Didier said. "He knew he wasn't ever going to get out of prison, and that he would become just another bad guy in a whole universe full of bad guys. This way, his people will still do his bidding—those who are free—and he will always have this doubt connected to him. Did he really do all those things? Or did someone set him up?"

She shook her head, then wished she hadn't. It made her dizzier. She almost put out a hand to catch herself, then thought the better of it.

"Why would he care about that?" she asked. "Wouldn't he rather be alive?"

"This was a man who had people *worship* him." Didier sounded excited. Why would he sound excited? Shouldn't he be worried? "He *liked* that. He believed he was important, and they believed it too."

"Until, what is it called, Abbondiado?"

"See?" Didier said. "You know what happened to him, how he was captured, how things turned on him. You *know* it, and therefore, you think he's important. You don't know that about the other prisoners here."

That wasn't entirely true. There were some Xelen imprisoned in a far wing for eating their human companions on a supply run. If she thought hard, she could come up with a dozen other examples.

But she understood Didier's point. She knew about Frémont. *Everyone* knew about Frémont.

"You think this is important," she said. "I mean, beyond us getting in trouble for his death."

"Oh, we won't," Didier said. "There'll be a big investigation, and everyone will wonder how he got whatever it was that he ingested, and then—"

"He ate something?" she asked.

Didier shrugged. "I'm no coroner. But that pinkish foam around his mouth suggests poison to me."

How he knew the foam was pinkish in this light was beyond her.

"And they can't trace it to us?" she asked.

"Not unless you gave it to him."

She shivered again. She needed to stand up. She was cutting off her own air here—what little air there was.

"I never met him before today," she said, sounding stupid.

"You haven't met him now," Didier said, but he was grinning. "You're not used to the low-oxygen ratios are you?"

"No," she said, and she sounded as sick as she felt. "Can I go?"

"Nope," he said. "I need your help."

"For what?" she asked.

He helped her up, then grabbed some evidence bags from the box.

"You and me," he said. "We got about ten minutes before someone notices something off. I figure the best we can do is five, because I want to jump ahead of this thing. So, we get as much DNA as we can."

"What?" Chills ran down her back. Didier wanted her to *touch* Frémont? What if he wasn't dead? What if he was?

Her stomach did a slow flip.

"Ah, sweet child, do you know why people work in prisons?"

She suspected the answer wasn't as simple as *they need a job*. "Why?"

"Because, if done right, there are a lot of money-making opportunities here."

Somehow she hadn't thought Didier was one of the guards who sold things and made a profit. No prisoner ever flagged Didier as someone who traded on the prison black market. No one ever marked Didier's file for possible illegal activity.

She had thought it was because he was unassailably honest, but she was beginning to realize that maybe he was just unbelievably cautious.

"I don't sell things. I don't want to make money," she said. "I just want out of here."

"We're talking millions," he said.

Her gaze met his. Millions?

"And you wouldn't collect right away, so no one would ever know what you did here. *If* you get busy doing."

Millions. Never getting caught. She was already half a step close to trouble. And she hated it here. She hated it period. Imagine if she were in charge of her own destiny. Imagine if she…

She was lightheaded and not thinking clearly.

But she knew this much: She knew that she would be asked about everything anyway, and the best way to protect herself was to pretend to participate. That way, Didier wouldn't blame her. He'd see her as a co-conspirator.

She could report him after everything was over.

Whatever "over" meant.

4

JHENA'S EYES WERE GETTING USED TO THE FLARING RED LIGHT. EXCEPT THAT as the light increased and decreased, it created shadows in corners. Shadows that looked like they moved.

Maybe they were moving.

Or maybe she was hallucinating from stress and lack of oxygen.

She had a headache. One hand still covered her mouth and nose, but she'd stopped pinching her nostrils, for what good it did her.

Bile rose in the back of her throat. She swallowed hard, hoping she wouldn't vomit right now. She couldn't vomit. She had no idea what Didier would do to her if she did.

"I'm not touching that man," she said. She was looking at Frémont's corpse, its head still hidden from her by the bunk. She thought maybe she saw the foam that Didier had mentioned, although she couldn't be sure.

What she was sure of was that some kind of stain was inching its way toward the only good pair of shoes that she owned.

"I don't want you to touch him," Didier said. "You're strictly the help in this instance."

The...what? She had never heard that phrase before, but it didn't sound good. She didn't like it at all. She took a deep breath, then wished she hadn't, since that foul taste accompanied it.

It didn't matter what Didier wanted. She would be passing out soon, whether he liked it or not.

"Then can I leave?" she asked.

"No." He crouched. "Hand me the bags when I ask for them."

Bags. Evidence bags. Which she was still clutching. Getting her own DNA all over them. DNA, fingerprints, hair, fiber, all kinds of things that would identify her, but not Didier.

Too late now. It was all too late now. She was here, she was involved, and she would betray this son of a bitch before he knew what hit him.

"Oh, hell," he said. "Just give me the damn box."

Had she missed an instruction? It sounded like she had. His irritation suggested it.

Which was good, because his DNA, his prints, his hair and fiber, would be on the box as well.

"DNA," she said. "That's what you want."

It wasn't quite a question, or maybe it was. She struggled to wrap her sluggish mind around what was going on.

"You want to sell DNA?" she asked.

"Something like that." He pulled a scooping tool she hadn't seen before out of one of the many pockets of his uniform, and set to work.

He didn't scrape up the fluids (oh, thank God, because she wasn't sure her stomach could handle it), but he did scrape the skin on the back of Frémont's hands.

Didier put the scrapings inside the first bag. She couldn't see anything, but the bag's exterior changed color, like it was supposed to when something went inside it, going from clear to pale yellow.

Then he reached backward, the bag dangling from his hand.

"Take the damn thing," he snapped.

"And do what?" she asked.

"Hold it until I tell you otherwise. What happened to your brains? Move it."

She took a step closer, careful not to walk in anything, and took the bag. It was warm against her skin.

He didn't look at her. He was touching Frémont's face, swabbing or scooping or doing something to his mouth, eyeballs, nose—

She had to take another deep breath just to keep herself from throwing up. Even though the deep breath was as big a mistake as the previous one. She was so dizzy and nauseous and ill.

He handed her another bag, then another, and another.

She lost count after a while, clutching the bags as if she had gone on a shopping spree gone awry.

Finally, after what seemed like hours, Didier stood up.

"Time's up. We gotta get out of here."

She would have thought that time was up months ago. Years ago.

She thrust the bags at him and he shook his head, putting out his hands.

"You get to keep them," he said.

"But—"

"I'm going to guard the scene like a good prison employee. I've got a handful of empty bags here, just in case someone needs them."

"What am I doing?" She was slurring her words. She sounded drunk. She had Oxygen Deprivation Syndrome, which the prison called ODS. The oxygen was too low. She was not well, at all.

"You're going to stuff those bags back in that box, and get them out of here," he said.

She looked at the bags. They were a different color than the other bags—orange? Maybe yellow. She couldn't tell in this light. If someone (something; some *android*) looked inside the box, they'd see that the bags were full.

"How…?"

"You can take things out of here," he said. "It's bringing things in that they're most worried about."

She knew that was right; it sounded right anyway. She wondered if it really was right.

God, ODS *was* like being drunk. She remembered that from previous times. Earlier times. That was why she had her timer.

Which was shut off.

If only she could think clearly.

"And if you don't get out of here, then they will find the bags," he said.

"What do I do after I get out of here?" she asked.

He grinned. "Exactly what you've been wanting to do all along," he said.

"What's that?" she asked.

"Puke," he said. "Head to the ladies room and puke."

5

JHENA CARRIED THE BOX UNDER HER ARM, AND PRAYED SHE WOULDN'T get caught.

Half a corridor away from the cell, her links came back on. She was supposed to notify everyone else as soon as she reached the entrance to the cell block, and she was supposed to blame ODS on the delay.

If she remembered. If she remembered any of Didier's instructions.

If she didn't pass out.

She was weaving as she walked. Her timer had returned along with the links, and it was blaring all of its alarms. She had run out of time, and if she were actually curious, she could have found out how long ago she had run out of time.

But she wasn't really curious.

She was too sick to be curious.

Too sick to be frightened too, and too sick to be having second or third or eighteenth thoughts. She was going to blame her sickness for her willingness to help Didier, if, of course, he got caught.

Wasn't she going to turn him in?

She couldn't remember her plan.

Just his, which sounded implausible, but she didn't care. Right now, she needed air. Oxygen. Pure oxygen.

And she really needed to puke.

Not just because he said so.

Somehow she remembered to turn on the tracking in her links, helping her find the security post, past all of these blank black walls, behind which were some of the most vicious criminals in the sector. Vicious and impotent, that was what the warden told her when they hired her. Unable to get out, unable to escape, unable to harm anyone ever again.

How in the universe had Frémont managed to get his hands on poison? Or had someone poisoned him? Had someone killed him?

That did happen in here sometimes. In the cold and the low oxygen and the limited contact. Every month or two, someone died. Was murdered. Got stabbed or got their head rammed into a wall. No one could prevent a beating death. Some of these human prisoners knew just the right way to do it, just the right way to kill someone.

Had Didier done that?

If so, how had he kept his hands clean?

She wasn't sure she wanted to know.

She knew too much already.

Somehow, she reached the security area. From the inside, the entrance into the cell block looked like a gauntlet. Windows, android guards, obvious cameras everywhere. Her own features faced her in the security window. She looked gray and unfocused, barely human at all, her dark eyes sunken into her gaunt face.

She placed her palm against the scanner, then leaned in so that it could also take her retinal scan, as well as go over every single security chip she had.

The new position unbalanced her. The world grew black around her, and from a distance, she heard a voice in her own head—her voice, saying from very far away, *Don't faint. Don't faint. Don't faint.*

"Okay," she whispered. She blinked, reminded herself that she was only a few meters away from real air, and looked up.

Two of the android guards were peering at her.

Are you ill? That voice wasn't hers. It belonged to the system. She recognized it. She heard it when the shuttle she took from home docked every morning, when her passes got approved as she tried to enter, when she had to look into the various scanners, sometimes even when she sat down at her desk.

No, she sent. *Not ill. I mean, yes. Oxygen Deprivation Syndrome. I need air. I need to get out of here or I swear to God, I'm going to puke. (I might puke anyway.)*

She wasn't sure she added that last thought to her link or if she just felt it and didn't send it.

Her stomach lurched.

You will have to go through decontamination, the system told her.

The androids were still peering at her, as if they didn't understand what she was doing.

Okay, fine, she sent. *Just get me the hell out of here.*

It wasn't until the first security door slid back with a clang that she worried she had just made the wrong choice. Would decontamination discover the evidence bags of DNA? Would it nullify them? Alter them?

Would that make Didier angry?

She took a deep breath. The air seemed richer here. Maybe it was. She felt a little less dizzy.

She stepped inside the decontamination chamber.

Screw Didier. She didn't work for him. He was probably going to get her in trouble. She was the one who had carried the damn bags in, and she was the one carrying them out filled with stuff. The security monitors were off near the cell. All he had to say was that he had asked for the bags to follow protocol, and she had brought extra so that she could steal DNA.

She set the box on the ground, then braced her hands against the wall as the door to the decontamination chamber closed. She kept her chin up. If she let her head droop, she might pass out.

She closed her eyes anyway.

The first step of decontamination is to see if you have picked up any viruses or contaminates inside. If you are infected, then this system will move to the second step and begin the decontamination procedure. Do you understand?

Yes, she sent back, and didn't add, *Just like I understood the five hundred other times you asked, you damn machine.*

A light passed over her. It wasn't as red as the light in the cell block, but it made her think of that light. She ran her tongue against her teeth. Would the stupid decontamination system pick up stench molecules? The odd smell? The scent of death?

Had Frémont's corpse contaminated her somehow, by shutting off the environmental system? Had whatever poisoned him done so in such a way that she would bring the poison with her? Would the system shut it down?

Her stomach flipped again. *Oh, hurry*, she thought—or maybe she sent—*I'm going to be sick.*

You have no signs of illness, the system told her. *Unless you are speaking colloquially...?*

Yes, dammit, she sent. *I have Oxygen Deprivation Syndrome. I'm going to puke.*

Signs of Oxygen Deprivation Syndrome include elevated heartbeat and nausea. You do not show signs of edema or nosebleed, nothing to indicate that you have severe symptoms that would require medical attention.

I am going to throw up, she repeated. *You need to get me out of here.*

The oxygen levels in this unit are increasing. It will ease your feeling of nausea, although rest is indicated. A medical technician will meet you on the other side.

After I puke, she sent.

If they let her out of here.

You are free of contaminants, the system sent, *and are free to go.*

Thank you, she sent, and hoped to hell the sarcasm got through. She was halfway out the door when she remembered the damn box.

She turned around to get it, making herself dizzy all over again. Black spots formed, and she had to will herself to remain upright.

She crouched, using her knees, not bending over, and grabbed the box. She couldn't leave it here. Not after everything.

She staggered out of the chamber. She was breathing better, and the dizziness was fading somewhat. And so was the nausea. The urge to puke wasn't as extreme.

Still, if she clung to that story, she might get through all the protocols faster.

Another door, an android examining her with its yellow eyes, another watching her, a red sign appearing on its forehead. *You are being surveyed. Your actions may be used in legal proceedings. You have no rights to privacy in this part of the prison.*

She knew that too, but she couldn't take her gaze off those words.

"Yeah, fine," she said. "Got it."

Just in case she had to speak to it. She took a few more steps forward. Through the five remaining layers of security doors and windows, she could see the corridor she needed. She could even see the bathroom.

She focused on it, as if it could save her, her fingers wrapped around the evidence box.

She concentrated on moving forward, on getting out.

She concentrated, until she was finally free.

6

Midway through the loss of her stomach contents, when Jhena remembered to wipe her hand on her shirt before pushing her hair from her face, she also realized she had forgotten to notify the system about Frémont's death. She was still light-headed, still unable to wrap her mind around someone dying alone inside the cell block, and shutting down the system.

Not that she could think much.

She managed to send a message to her immediate supervisor before bending over to puke again.

The bathroom had been clean when she entered. Clean and so much warmer than the cell block. She usually found this bathroom cold and impersonal, with its black and gray non-reflective walls, the wide stalls (which she was so grateful for right now) and the sinks that emerged from beneath the mirrors whenever anyone approached.

She always felt watched here, even if she wasn't, no matter how many times the staff reassured her. The *prisoners* had no privacy, they said, but the staff did. The staff always would.

She had barely made it inside the bathroom before throwing up the first time. She landed on her knees (which she instantly regretted as they got wet). When she was done, she pulled herself up, and hoped she was done.

Then the cleaning bots detached themselves from the wall, little black rounded things scuttling toward her, long hose suction devices deploying toward the remains of the expensive tuna fish lunch she had bought herself before getting on the shuttle for work, and that thought sent her into the nearest stall.

At least she hadn't made as much of a mess there.

All she kept hearing in her mind was Didier's voice, telling her to puke. Well, she had done that. And somehow, she'd managed to keep a grip on the box with the evidence bags.

The notification she had sent her immediate supervisor was cryptic: *Frémont dead in cell. Security shut down. Need assistance.*

And the supervisor hadn't responded—at least not in the few seconds it took Jhena to lose every meal she had ever eaten in her entire life.

She sat down on the cold floor, leaning against the toilet, which flushed automatically, and closed her eyes for just a moment.

Then the sirens went off.

They weren't the escape sirens—those blared, with actual voices coming through the links, warning the staff that some prisoner had managed to slip out of the secure holdings. Since she'd been here, no one had managed to get outside of the cell blocks, to the staff area where she worked, but not for want of trying.

That was what was so impressive about maximum security: notifications started the moment the prisoner failed to follow routine, not the moment some human (or staff member) realized the prisoner had actually disappeared.

It wasn't alert sirens either, the kind that every station had, that called for a total evacuation (of everyone who could evacuate: the prisoners couldn't).

No, these sirens—loud, but not so loud that the dead would awaken—ran for a few minutes, followed by an order inside the links for authorized personnel to hurry to Frémont's cellblock.

She wasn't authorized, but she had been there.

Frémont was dead, and here she was, sitting on a cold bathroom floor, her clothes stained, her left arm still gripping the evidence box with all of the evidence bags containing Frémont's DNA.

If she got caught….

At that moment, her supervisor's image rose in front of her. Markita Duran was tiny, with a round face and rounder eyes, a turned-up nose, and a bow-shaped mouth. Outside of the prison, Jhena had actually heard a man call Duran pretty.

She wasn't pretty. She had a sweet face that hid one of the meanest souls Jhena had ever encountered.

"You're away from your post," Duran's floating head said. She looked awful, superimposed against the stall's open door. The image reflected slightly in the wall of mirrors, but only as a square blocked-out shape, not as a person.

Here it was: Jhena had to think clearly when she was at her absolute worst. Plus she had to keep Duran from noticing the evidence box.

Or did she?

"Yes, I'm away from my post," Jhena said. She wanted to add, *when you throw up, it's better to do it away from your desk*, but this was her supervisor. She didn't dare. "I just threw up. I'd like to take this off visual."

"No," Duran said. "You're holding an evidence box. What's that about?"

Jhena hoped her face didn't show the spike of fear that just went through her. "Didier Conte contacted me through my private links. He couldn't access the network inside the cellblock."

"Then how could he reach you?" Duran asked.

"I don't know," Jhena said miserably. "Maybe because it was my private links—"

"Are you two seeing each other outside of work?" Duran asked. Jhena wanted to check regulations. She wasn't sure if fraternization was allowed. She was convinced friendship was, because in the apartments where they all lived, she'd seen lots of employees talking with each other, and it didn't look like work.

"We know each other." Her voice rasped against her throat. The smell in here was clearing out, and the fresh air of the environmental system felt good on her face. "But we're not dating, if that's what you're asking."

"It was what I was asking," Duran said. "He'll give me the same response?"

"I hope so." Jhena felt miserable, and beneath it, angry. She had just gotten sick, for godsake, and there was a dead man in the cell block and *this* was what Duran cared about?

"You were telling me about the evidence box," Duran said.

"Didier requested it," Jhena said, and leaned her head against the edge of the toilet seat. Not that it mattered. Nanobots had already cleaned that part of the room. They just hadn't touched her, because they needed permission to do so.

She probably shouldn't have used Didier's first name in this conversation. Too late now, though.

"Why did he contact you?" Duran asked.

"Didn't you get my message?" Jhena said. "Maybe I sent it wrong. PierLuigi Frémont is dead. The network was down near the cell, so Didier asked me to come in there. Maybe he tried other guards. I don't know. He probably couldn't reach them. He used my private links."

She wasn't sure how many times she'd have to repeat that last part.

"What has that to do with the evidence box?" Duran asked.

Oh, yeah. God, she was unfocused. It wasn't fair to ask her to lie when her brain wasn't working right.

"Didier asked for it. He was afraid that some of the evidence would get screwed up or something. I left a bunch of bags with him. You need to send someone to help him—"

"We've done that," Duran asked. "Why did you leave him?"

Now she was going to get in trouble for leaving him? How unfair was that?

"It smelled. The environmental system was down too, and the smell was so bad I could taste it. I—" she held up a finger. Her stomach was rolling again. Just the memory of the smell made her feel ill.

She swallowed hard. Her mouth no longer tasted of death. It tasted of stomach acid and tuna fish, and somehow she found that thought comforting.

Her stomach settled.

"Sorry," she said. She sounded as miserable as she felt. "He didn't want me to puke in there. He thought it would contaminate the scene."

To her surprise, Duran smiled. The smile wasn't intimidating or fake. It seemed real and amused. "He was right. It looks like your stomach is sensitive, and we can't have someone like that on the floor."

For a moment, Jhena thought she meant on an actual floor—and she was, and she was going to protest—but then she realized that Duran meant inside the block.

"Forgive me for asking," Jhena said, working hard at controlling her tongue, "but can I go now? I need to take care of myself before getting back to work."

Not that she wanted to go back to work. She wanted Duran to give her the rest of the night off. Of course, Duran wouldn't do that. Duran wasn't that kind.

Besides, there was no one to take Jhena's place. That was why she was working this shift in the first place.

"Use one of those remaining evidence bags for your clothes," Duran said. "Leave it in the forensic units. There's a shower in the guards' locker area that you can use and coveralls if you don't have a change of clothes."

Now Jhena had to follow a script. She hoped she could remember all of it.

"Can't the bots just clean off my clothes?" she asked, and she didn't even have to work at making herself sound plaintive.

"No, this is too delicate," Duran said as quickly as Didier had said she would. "The cleaning bots will destroy as much as they save."

Jhena eyed them. Three of them had gathered in front of the stall door, as if they were sentient and wanted access to her.

She shuddered, even though the room wasn't cold.

"You need to bag the clothes, and leave them here."

"I threw up out here," Jhena said. God, she was whining. "I don't have many clothes, and if I leave any—can't I just take them home?"

Duran frowned just a little. Then she turned away from the camera, her gaze downward a bit. She was doing exactly what Didier had said she would do: she was checking Jhena's progress from the blacked-out security area to the bathroom. She would see that Jhena hadn't thrown up yet. She would see that Jhena hadn't lied—at least about the clothes.

"All right," Duran said after a moment. "Bag them anyway, because I have to check this with my supervisor. But I have a hunch that he won't have a problem."

Jhena suddenly felt very tired. One more hurdle crossed. "Thank you," she said.

"You did good work here, Andre," Duran said. "Difficult situations often show our mettle. Don't worry about your sensitive stomach. You managed to get out of there, and that was good. Now, finish off your shift, and go home. And make sure you drink some fluids."

"Yes, sir. Thank you, sir," Jhena said. She actually felt grateful. It surprised her.

Duran's image had vanished. (Before the thank-yous? Jhena wasn't sure.) Jhena double-checked her links, made sure that she could block the visuals now. If Duran tried to contact her again, then Duran would believe that Jhena was cleaning herself off.

Which she would be.

She would also be taking care of the DNA, like she had promised Didier.

He hadn't lied about the procedures.

She hoped he hadn't lied about anything else.

7

The coveralls made Jhena feel like a different person.

Or, more accurately, they made her feel like the person she'd left behind.

She sat on the bench between the lockers, finger-combing her now-dry hair. She had taken a quick shower because she didn't want to leave the evidence bags alone for very long, even if they were in a guest locker, secured to the chips hidden under her skin. Even after the shower, she still felt like she smelled of vomit: She knew that came from the lining of her nose, and the back of her throat. She had used oral cleansers, and they had helped, just not quite enough.

Her hands were still shaking, and the coveralls weren't helping.

They were blue and white, prison guard regulation clothing, for dirty jobs, and they were made of some scratchy material, as if the designers couldn't find something soft that worked equally well.

The scratchiness, the bagginess, the unfamiliarity reminded her of that night her father had given her to the authorities, with the promise that her aunt would come for her. She'd had no idea what would happen; she'd thought he was gone for good, and that he had lied.

He was gone for good, but he hadn't lied—at least not to her. Her aunt had shown up from Earth, a seven-day journey. By then, Jhena had given up all hope.

And the entire time, she'd been wearing regulation coveralls, because god forbid that any child would feel different from any other child in government care. The long-timers had no special clothing, so Jhena didn't get to wear hers.

She had gotten it back, along with the toys her father had packed for her, but she hadn't had any access to it during those seven days.

Those days had changed her, made her quieter, made her terrified, at least on some level. She certainly never trusted anyone.

Even though she was trusting Didier now.

Kinda. She was at least following his instructions.

Or she would the moment she opened the locker.

You'll be surprised at how simple it will be, Didier had said as he told her what to do after she left the cell block. *You take out the evidence bag, put your clothes in it, then put that bag wherever they want you to. Then you take the box back to storage, with all of the DNA bags inside it. No one will look at it, and I'll clear everything out when I leave.*

She stared at that closed locker door. Black, like everything else in this place; a bit reflective, unlike other parts, probably so someone can check to see if their clothes fit properly without moving to the mirrors; impossible to open without the right code, just like all the other staff areas in the entire prison block.

She swallowed. Her throat hurt. She had actually damaged it. The last time she'd been that sick had been the one and only time she had gotten drunk. Being drunk made her uncomfortable; the loss of control terrified her, instead of liberating her like her friends had promised. And then it had all ended like the last hour had ended, on a bathroom floor, staring down cleaning bots as if they had a mind of their own.

He was using her. That's what her entire mind kept coming back to.

Didier was using her. He might have done so from the very beginning.

He hadn't chatted her up because he found her attractive. When had any man found her attractive? He wasn't needy—that had become clear in the cell block. He had used her, maybe not with Frémont's death in mind, but somehow, with some random future event awaiting both of them. Saving her for just the right moment, which had happened today.

What she couldn't quite figure out was if he would turn her in. She didn't think he would because that would raise too many questions. But he wouldn't be that accommodating either.

He'd spoken of millions. And now that her head cleared, she understood why. He was going to sell the DNA. Crazies always thought that criminal DNA had uses. And some people liked to buy it just because they had a fetish for horrible people like Frémont.

She didn't doubt that there would be millions if Didier figured out a way to monetize Frémont's DNA. She just doubted that there would be millions *for her*.

She would be taking half of the risk, and getting none of the reward.

She would spend the rest of her life in fear if she didn't turn him in, and maybe even in fear if she did turn him in.

After all, she had no idea who Didier was actually working with.

From his calm attitude, he had done this before—and he knew that she hadn't.

She ran her hands through her hair. She couldn't sit here very long. She had no idea how long it would take Didier to get off shift. Probably a long time, considering the debrief.

The sirens had ended while she was in the shower, but the investigation was just beginning. She hadn't been through this before, but she knew the drill. It was in all the procedure manuals.

Whenever something went wrong on a floor, there would be a full-scale investigation, one that could last weeks, maybe even years. The best thing to do, according to the guidelines, was to be honest.

And she doubted she was going to do that. Not unless she did it right now.

Because she needed to turn in Didier right now, or never.

She wished she knew what he was going to do next.

She let out a small sigh. She did know one thing: if he had partners, and they expected millions, and she screwed them of those millions, then they would come after her.

She hadn't been a government orphan for long, but she'd been one long enough to learn how feral humans could be when threatened. It was a lesson she never forgot.

Her entire childhood was a lesson she would never forget.

That decided her. She leaned forward, and used the back of her left hand to unlock the locker. Then she blocked the bottom of the locker with her body as she pulled the door open.

She grabbed one clean evidence bag, put two of the full evidence bags she had carried out for Didier in that clean bag, and then sealed the clean bag. She then took another evidence bag, opened it, and stuffed her filthy pants into it, the stench of vomit making her gag.

She put the bag with the two bags on top of her pants, then stuffed her shirt on top of that, tucking in the sides so that none of it was visible with a single glance. All anyone could see would be her clothing, nothing more.

Her hands were shaking. Her brain stuttered. Her conscience spoke up—not for the first time today—and reminded her of something she already knew.

This was her last chance. Her last chance to be honest, to do the right thing.

Her father had done the right thing—and she had never seen him again.

She sealed the evidence bag, and watched it turn yellow, which meant the seal was active. Then she set it beside her, and took out the box with all those incriminating bags.

If she reported Didier now, the discrepancy between the bags he said he filled and the ones he actually filled might become a matter of record. She could only hope that he hadn't counted the bags he'd used. And if he counted the bags left in the open box, she would tell him that she needed four bags for her clothes.

He might actually believe that.

Or he might expect her to steal a bag or two.

She sat up. Her hands weren't shaking any more.

She had made her decision, and she was acting on it.

Next stop, the storage room to replace the box, just like Didier had instructed.

Then she would finish her shift, go home with her evidence bag of soiled clothes, and leave it in the bottom of her own closet until she figured out what to do with it.

The lightheadedness had returned—not because she was still suffering from ODS, but because she had forgotten to breathe.

She could breathe now.

She was nearly done with her task, and with her shift.

And then she could pretend that this horrible day never ever happened.

NOW

8

Luc Deshin slammed his hand on the lists covering the top of his desk. The lists, nothing more than holograms, split apart into a thousand pieces. When he lifted his fist, the pieces reassembled.

He stood up and turned his back on his entire office.

Dammit.

Just before the second attack on the Moon a week ago, Deshin had met with the Retrieval Artist Miles Flint at the offices of their mutual attorney, Celestine Gonzalez. Deshin had several reasons for meeting with Flint.

The authorities weren't solving the Anniversary Day attacks. From what Deshin could tell, through his usual monitoring of law enforcement, the authorities hadn't a clue about anything. They were going in circles, if they were doing any work at all.

Deshin walked over to the floor-to-ceiling windows in his office. The office had a 360-degree view of the entire city. Armstrong had been lucky on Anniversary Day: the city had lost its mayor, but little else. Nineteen other domes had been attacked, and twelve had had holes blown through them.

Millions of people had died.

Deshin had nearly died, since he had been at a meeting in Yutu City. He'd lost friends and colleagues and security staff—more people than he cared to think about.

Had the attack in Armstrong succeeded, he might have lost his beloved wife Gerda and his amazing son Paavo. And Deshin wouldn't have been able to do anything about it.

He had been too far away.

So he had started to investigate immediately after the attacks, and discovered a hell of a lot more than the so-called authorities had. And what he had discovered unnerved him.

He'd met with Flint because he liked the man and Flint had done him a good turn a while back, actually saving Deshin's family by getting rid of a personal threat.

No matter what Flint thought of Deshin (and Flint made it clear he didn't really like Deshin at all), Deshin respected the hell out of Flint.

That respect got confirmed just last week. All of Deshin's sources confirmed that Flint had helped the Moon's Security Chief, Noelle DeRicci, thwart the second attack—by a group of Peyti lawyers who had been undercover on the Moon for decades. Those lawyers, also clones like the Anniversary Day attackers, had been designed as suicide bombers. They activated on the same day, and would have destroyed more domes and another million lives and everything else.

It was enough to make even the most dug-in businessman want to move off Moon. Only Deshin didn't know any place safer, especially if whoever was masterminding the attacks wasn't aiming at the Moon, but at the Earth Alliance itself.

He blinked and made himself look at the city. He loved this place. Cranes still rose from the area around the first bombing, four years before Anniversary Day, almost hiding the neighborhood housing Dome University. Beyond that was the former slum where he had grown up and where he later invested a fortune buying ancient real estate and turning it into housing for young professionals.

That hadn't even been his first fortune. He had money in dicey places, and he dealt with a lot of shady types.

Hell, he was a shady type, although he'd been trying to clean up his act since he and Gerda adopted Paavo. But some acts weren't so easy to clean. He still had—and used—a lot of connections that he was certain the Armstrong Police Department (the Pre-Anniversary Day Armstrong Police Department, anyway) would have loved to confirm.

He turned slightly, saw the glinting roofs of the homes in his neighborhood. They looked lovely in the slightly red tinge of Dome Daylight which was designed to look like early morning on Earth.

The area where he had made his home wasn't one of those ostentatious upscale neighborhoods that lawyers and politicians and the "upwardly mobile" folks preferred. Nor had he gone for the hectares of land that people like Bernard Magalhães used to show off their wealth.

The Moon was full of empty land; Deshin didn't need to buy large swaths of it to prove he had money. He knew he had money. No one else needed to.

Fortunately, Gerda agreed with him. She hated people who flaunted their wealth. She liked being comfortable. When she spent money, she spent it on things that added to the comfort inside the home rather than impressing anyone who looked at the place from the outside.

Or she spent money on their son. Paavo already had the finest education anyone could buy on the Moon—if only the schools were still open.

Deshin was clenching his fists so tightly that his hands ached. He made himself let go, one finger at a time.

People had died at Paavo's school in the second attack. The order that had come from the United Domes of the Moon Security Office had subjected anyone in the room with a Peyti lawyer to an instant switch to Peyla's environment—which was hostile to humans.

A lot of humans died last week because the bombs the lawyers were wearing only exploded in an Earthlike environment. When the environmental systems shifted, the bombs stopped working.

Millions of lives saved—at the price of thousands.

Deshin understood it. He knew how those calculations worked.

But the events had revived his son's nightmares, just after Paavo was starting to get past the traumas inflicted on him by his biological parents.

And those attacks—the deaths in the Armstrong Wing of the Aristotle Academy—could have been so much worse, if that little conference room where the Peyti lawyers and the human clients had been meeting hadn't been shut off from the rest of the school.

Deshin had lain awake nights, imagining how horribly his son might have died.

Deshin didn't care if he died, but he didn't want his son to die. Paavo wasn't even ten yet. He hadn't even started to live.

And Deshin would do anything to ensure his kid's future.

Deshin returned to his desk. The holographic images of the lists that Flint had sent him still hovered in front of Deshin's chair.

The damn things were useless.

He had asked Flint for lists of the explosives used in the Anniversary Day attacks, thinking—hoping—*believing*—that those lists would have some secret on them, some clue that Deshin would see that the authorities missed.

But Flint had told Deshin last week that the explosives used all across the Moon on Anniversary Day were different, depending on location. Some of the perpetrators used a mix of explosives, others used what was on hand.

And the thwarted attack here in Armstrong would have used some rigged ships in quarantine in the port, which would have destroyed all access to the Moon for large ships.

Deshin had hoped for more. He had *expected* more.

When he had followed the trail left by the zoodeh, the stuff the assassins used to kill various Moon mayors and the governor-general on that same day, he had discovered something chilling.

Most of the zoodeh hadn't come from quarantined ships like the authorities believed, but had already been on the Moon when the zoodeh had joined the list of banned substances.

The traders in zoodeh and similar weapons had sold their zoodeh to the Anniversary Day killers the week or so before the attacks.

And then those traders—to a person—had been murdered.

Deshin poked a finger through the floating holograms of lists and lists and more lists.

The authorities hadn't known about the murders and hadn't tied that loose end together. Last week, Deshin had told Flint to look into it all and hoped that Flint would encourage the Security Chief to start investigating the zoodeh suppliers and the deaths. Because Deshin was sure there was some kind of lead there, but nothing he could pursue without calling attention to himself.

He had expected the lists of explosives to provide the same revelations. But the past five months had turned into one frustrating dead end after another. No trail of murders here, no easily findable link to the Anniversary Day killers.

Just a lot of missing explosives—and not recently missing either. So many explosives had gone missing five years before, when the regulations were looser. Every human household on the Moon could have a tonne of explosives and still hundreds of kilotonnes of missing explosives would been left over.

The very thought chilled him.

And none of that counted all the illegal weapons quarantined in the Port of Armstrong.

What Deshin knew and what he could prove were different. That was why he wanted Flint on board with some of this investigation.

What scared Deshin, though (and until this year, damn near nothing scared Deshin) was this: everything he had found in his post Anniversary Day investigation—*everything*—showed intimate knowledge of the way that the Moon worked, not just in its governmental systems, but also its underworld.

The breadth of information needed to figure out this plan was astonishing—so broad, in fact, that *he* hadn't known some of it until he started looking.

And then last week: new clones, new problems, *Peyti* clones.

Deshin had thought, like everyone else, that this was primarily a human issue—even though he had taunted Flint, and reminded him that there were nonhuman players involved.

But the Peyti involvement, the *Peyti* clones—and the fact that they were planted decades before, and had gone to law school all over the known universe, and had, in fact, practiced law on the Moon for years without ever doing anything wrong—those Peyti clones made Deshin's fear worse.

He couldn't keep quietly investigating.

He couldn't give hints to Flint any more, hoping Flint's contacts would take up the investigation and do it properly.

Last week, before the second attack, Flint had asked Deshin to investigate sources for designer criminal clones based on PierLuigi Frémont. Deshin had agreed, then got sidetracked—as everyone did—by the horrors a few days later.

Now, Deshin needed to do more than investigate the Frémont DNA. He needed to investigate designer criminal clone companies that specialized in multispecies clones. And not fast-grow clones. Slow-grow ones.

He would be putting himself in danger.

But, he reasoned, better him than his family. As long as the threat of another attack hung over the Moon, his family was at great risk.

He could take them out of here—he would talk to Gerda about that—and then he would see what leads he could uncover.

And this time, instead of hinting at them to Flint, Deshin would tell Flint what he found.

Deshin would make sure no attack would destroy the Moon, even if it was the last thing he ever did.

9

Officer Maude Leckie kept her right hand on her laser pistol, and surveyed the train car. All the damn Peyti clones, looking exactly alike, sat in the exact same position, and stared out the windows at the landscape whizzing by.

The bullet train, commandeered by the Security Office of United Domes of the Moon, was going fast, but not fast enough to miss the damage outside the domes. The moment the train zoomed out of Glenn Station, she noted the destroyed buildings of the local manufacturing planet.

Somewhere in this car—Glenn Station's prisoner transport car—sat the Peyti asshole who had sent his colleague to the plant. She had lost a cousin there.

She scanned the car, making eye contact with as many Peyti as she could. The damn things didn't look threatening. They were thin as sticks, with fingers that were too long and eyes that were too big. Their skin was an unhealthy gray.

But the masks they wore that enabled them to survive in an Earth-like environment—those damn things sent a shiver through her. Because this group of asshole lawyer Peyti had weaponized their masks just a week ago, with the idea of killing as many people as possible.

Leckie knew her superiors had checked the masks. She knew some androids had gone over the masks with the various technical tests that only prison android guards could do efficiently.

She knew that these masks had been examined a dozen times each—and she still wanted to rip the damn things off, and toss them out the window onto the Moon's gray surface.

She wanted to see these fuckers die slowly, unable to breathe, their faces turning that weird blue they got when they were "distressed."

She'd turn them blue. She'd make them explode if she could.

It was taking all of her control not to turn her laser pistol on them. She'd flick on the pistol's red sight, and deliberately place the dot on the forehead of the Peyti prisoners, one by one. She wanted them to feel scared, *terrified*, that she was going to kill them slowly.

She'd told her captain she had this impulse and he had just laughed at her.

They're suicide bombers, Leckie, he had said. *They're not going to be scared. They're going to welcome death. Take them to the City of Armstrong. Let them face justice and live with their failures. That will frighten them. That will destroy them. They expect you and your little gun; they don't expect a future filled with incarceration and daily punishment.*

She knew he was right. She knew it deep down, and she had said as much, which was why her captain had sent her as one of the ten human guards designated to shepherd the prisoners to their new home.

But that didn't stop the impulse. She still wanted to kill these creatures. Maybe the pistol wasn't good enough. Maybe she should go after them with her bare hands.

She flexed the fingers of her left hand, imagining them tugging down those stupid old masks, and then wrapping her hand around a scrawny neck, seeing if she could snap it with her grip alone.

She was tired of being frightened, tired of the explosions and the deaths and the uncertainty.

The idea behind bringing these assholes to Armstrong was simple: the cops there would interrogate them and find out what—if anything—was going to happen next.

But anyone with a brain knew that wasn't going to work. These Peyti assholes were lawyers, for god's sake. Lawyers who knew how interrogation worked, who knew how the law worked, who knew what could be done and what couldn't. Suicidal lawyers with enough patience to await attack orders for years.

They would be able to handle impatient cops trying to figure out where the next attack would be. Even the Moon's most experienced interrogators wouldn't be able to crack these nuts. This was a wasted trip, for no good reason.

They should put the Peyti in some crowded room with Peyti atmosphere, confiscate the masks, and then change the atmosphere to Earth Normal. Yeah, the cops would never figure out what prompted these assholes to try to destroy every single dome on the Moon, but the cops wouldn't find out anyway.

And everyone would feel so much better when they were all dead.

She glanced at her colleagues, stationed at various points throughout the car. They were watching the Peyti too, as if the Peyti were doing something interesting. The fact that they all moved the same, they all looked the same, it really bothered her. She wondered if it bothered her colleagues.

She half-wished she were alone on this train with the android guards, stationed at the exits and on platforms outside. The android guards wouldn't care if she shot every single Peyti in the place. The android guards didn't care about anything.

The only reason they weren't shepherding the Peyti to Armstrong was that no one knew if the Peyti had skills enough to compromise the guards. Plus no one knew if these guards were trained to recognize the Peyti lawyers as *lawyers,* not as prisoners.

She'd heard that officials in Armstrong had already reprogrammed their Android guards to accept no Peyti lawyers anywhere in any facility. She'd also heard that Armstrong was closing its port to the Peyti—too damn late, in her opinion.

Someone should have barred the Peyti decades ago.

But that was all dust on the tracks now. Nothing she could do. Nothing anyone could do.

She'd finish her assignment, and head back to Glenn Station, just like she was ordered to do.

And any Peyti there, lawyer or not, non-clone or not, had better stay out of her way.

Because she was done.

No one was going to try to destroy her home again.

And she knew she wasn't alone.

If the authorities couldn't stop these people, she would—one way, or the other. She'd stop them. Whether it was "legal" or not.

10

Bartholomew Nyquist buttoned his last clean shirt. He looked at the pile of laundry at the bottom of his closet and grimaced. He could set the laundry for a quick nanoclean—which got the smells out of everything, but left a residue that always made him crawly, as if the damn nanobots were moving around his skin like a dozen tiny aliens—or he could wash everything later, wasting water, and expending lots of energy.

He ran a hand through his wet hair, and glanced around the darkened bedroom. His apartment was small and cramped, but the building had some amenities. If he wanted to pay the building staff, they would do the laundry for him. Of course, that took organization as well, and he didn't have the mental energy for that.

So he pulled off his clean shirt and set it on a chair, so that the laundry—which smelled of personal funk, sweat, and every stupid person he had encountered in the last week—wouldn't brush against the fabric. Then he carried the pile to the nanobasket, and set the cleaning program to start in four hours.

By then, Noelle DeRicci would be awake.

He glanced at her as he grabbed his shirt. She was sprawled kitty-corner on his narrow bed, her hand on his pillow, her curly black hair covering her face.

She had shown up at his place at two a.m., claiming to need a night off. He hadn't had the heart to tell her that night had passed long ago, and they were into morning now. She had brought real hamburgers, still steaming hot from the expensive meat-place down the block, and waved them at him.

He didn't need a bribe to spend time with her, and he had told her that, but she claimed she needed food.

As gaunt as she was looking, he believed it. He wondered how many meals she had skipped since Anniversary Day. He knew she'd been trying to put her life back in some kind of order, and then a group of Peyti clones had tried to blow up the entire Moon.

She had stopped that by acting quickly and probably illegally, saving millions of lives. Still, the thousands of lives lost weighed on her. She hadn't thought of the locations outside of the domes—the Growing Pits, the mining facilities. The casualties there had been real and heartbreaking, and the press had been reporting on those, as representative of what could have happened to the entire Moon.

This place was jittery—*he* was jittery—expecting another thing to happen each and every moment of each and every day.

He had no idea how DeRicci felt. She was the Chief of Security for the United Domes of the Moon, and after the Anniversary Day attacks, pretty much the only living representative of the United Domes government.

Until just a few years ago, the domes had been independent entities, ruled by their mayors and city councils. A series of crises convinced the Moon's first governor-general, Celia Alfreda, that the Moon needed an overall government to band together for security and other projects. She had pushed that agenda for nearly twenty years before it became real. She served as the first governor-general, only to be assassinated six months ago in the middle of the Anniversary Day attacks.

Since then, the surviving members of the United Domes Council had gone home to their cities to help rebuild, leaving the Security Office and a few other organizations as the only representation of the United

Domes. Everyone seemed to agree that a Moon-based, not a city-based, government was necessary, and with the serial crises mounting, no one wanted to upend the system that was already in place.

Not that there was any legal framework for it. DeRicci was seizing power, and she knew it. It made her deeply uncomfortable, but at the same time, she had no idea where the threats to the Moon were coming from.

And clearly, the threats were to the Moon.

Nyquist wanted to go over to her and brush the hair off her face, but he was afraid to wake her. They had gone to sleep about four a.m., and that four hours was probably the most continual sleep she'd had since the beginning of what the press had started calling the Peyti Crisis began.

He worried about her more than he should have, given the casual nature of their relationship. Her curls were now threaded with gray, she had frown lines on her face, and permanent shadows under her eyes. She wouldn't see a doctor because, he knew, she was afraid the doctor would tell her to slow down.

Since she was the only major United Domes official left standing, she didn't feel like she could slow down.

And Nyquist didn't feel like he could do much to help her.

He could give her a quiet place to sleep. He had convinced her security detail that he could handle anything that might happen, any break-ins or threats from whoever it was that had been attacking the Moon.

So she got what passed for privacy here, and a little bit of time to think about things other than bombings and assassins and mysteries that neither of them could solve with conversation.

He left the bedroom, and went into his small but functional kitchen. Since Anniversary Day, he had stocked up on essentials, and kept the pantry full. He liked to tell himself he did it to make sure DeRicci ate when she came to his place, but if he was honest, he wanted to have supplies in case society broke down completely.

Besides, he found that he liked cooking.

He made himself some coffee, using one of those special blends that Flint kept giving DeRicci. She had a weakness for real Earth food, even though she felt like she should only eat Moon-grown items. But when someone gave her something, she rationalized it by saying it was churlish for her to refuse to use it.

Nyquist had never suggested the obvious: that she could give the food to one of the city's food banks. If he suggested that, she would feel guilty that she hadn't thought of it, and she felt guilty enough about everything already.

He pulled eggs out of the refrigerator, along with some cheese, fresh spinach and tomatoes, and just a bit of oil. He would make two omelets, and leave hers in the warming basket. She could reheat, and while the omelet wouldn't be as good as it was when he scraped it out of the skillet, it would still be better than anything else she would eat all day.

He stirred the eggs, cut the tomatoes, and concentrated, as much as he could, on cooking the perfect omelet. He had cut up some fruit the night before, making DeRicci promise she would eat it before she left. He dished some out for himself.

The cooking calmed him, and he needed calm—not as much as DeRicci did, but more than usual.

Everything at the police department was in chaos. He had a meeting at ten a.m., and he was stalling his arrival. Every detective had to come. Apparently, the chief of the detectives, Andrea Gumiela, was going to assign interrogation partners.

She was determined to break the Peyti clones, and find out not just who created them, but who sent them on these sleeper missions.

There were a million problems with Gumiela's ideas, first among them her refusal to see the scope of the situation. Armstrong's was the only major city dome not damaged in some way by the Anniversary Day attacks. While many of the cities had functioning jails and functioning police departments, the key word was "functioning."

Many of those dome governments had asked Armstrong to take the Peyti prisoners. Armstrong had a first-stop "Reception Center" for prisoners who had been charged with major crimes, but not yet convicted.

The Reception Center was a maximum security facility that was "temporary" for the prisoners, while they were being bound over for trial.

There were only two on the Moon. Armstrong's Reception Center was by far the largest, so it was getting the Peyti prisoners.

Armstrong also had enough interrogation facilities to handle the large wave of prisoners.

What Armstrong didn't have was jurisdiction over the attackers from other domes. Until and unless the interrogations bore fruit, the attacks had to be prosecuted on a local level. There was no Moon-level of jurisdiction. Either the attacks had to be prosecuted by each dome, or they had to be prosecuted by the Earth Alliance itself.

Nyquist scraped his omelet out of the pan, wiped out the pan, and poured the stirred eggs for DeRicci's omelet into the pan. He monitored that while taking bites of his. The omelet was fluffy, the cheese perfectly melted, and the tomatoes just crisp enough to add a sweetness that his omelets usually lacked. He wished he hadn't put in any spinach, and decided not to add it to hers.

Any good lawyer was going to see the problems here. Nyquist had already told Gumiela that the individual domes had to send permission for the Armstrong PD to act in the stead of the other domes, and hope that it would all stand up in whatever court the prosecution ended up in.

Gumiela had countered that her plan was simple: no Armstrong detective would interview a suspect from another dome. If those interviews got done, they'd be done by police detectives from those domes, who had to travel with the prisoners.

That might work as well, but Nyquist wasn't so certain.

Nor was he convinced that anyone would get these Peyti clones to talk. They had all been on the Moon for years, and during that time, all but a handful of them had been practicing attorneys. The one he had corralled had been one of the most important defense attorneys in Armstrong.

Getting these Peyti clones to talk would take a skill set he didn't think most detectives had. He knew he didn't.

He finished his omelet and put it in the sink. Then he left two large notes for DeRicci, one that would float in front of her face the moment she left the bedroom, and the other on the back of the door, telling her that she had enough time for breakfast, since it was cooked, and it would only take her a minute or two to eat it.

He hoped she would take five minutes, but he didn't want to discourage her.

Then he gulped his coffee—a travesty, she would call that—and grabbed his shield, and his weapon.

He had a long day ahead, in what might be a series of long days, maybe even long months.

His biggest worry wasn't so much getting the Peyti clones to talk—he already saw that as close to impossible. His biggest worry was that another group no one had paid attention to would try a third attack.

And he was afraid the third group would learn from their predecessors' mistakes.

He was afraid the third attack would succeed.

11

Luc Deshin did something unusual. He went home only an hour after he arrived at the office.

He needed to. He had to settle something before he could move ahead on his business.

He knew coming home would worry his wife; he also knew that it could not be helped.

He swept through the front door. His home was modest. Most of the money he'd spent on the house he'd spent on security. He kept all the security features up to date, and since the latest attacks, he'd also placed some guards—human guards—outside.

For once, Gerda hadn't objected. She was good in an emergency, but she sometimes needed help, and he hadn't been here for either attack—Anniversary Day or the attack last week. Much as he wanted to be available for his family, he so rarely was.

The house smelled of baking bread, which overlay the usual faint mint scent that Gerda used to calm them all. Gerda had been cooking ever since the Peyti Crisis. She either cooked or organized when she felt helpless.

He preferred the cooking. The organizing sometimes felt compulsive.

He threaded past the living room chairs, which looked like they hadn't been used in weeks, and went into the heart of his home—the kitchen.

His small wife bent over the old-fashioned oven, door open and hot fragrant air wafting into the room. Deshin's son, Paavo, stood beside her, protective gloves on his hands, a streak of flour on his cheek. The evenness of the streak told Deshin that the flour was expensive Earth-made flour, not the Moon flour that most people used.

Gerda was getting fancy. She had been cooking the old-fashioned way for weeks now, not using any of the conveniences he had purchased for her. She had asked for this oven long ago, and he had protested: He hadn't wanted Paavo near anything that could heat up like that.

But Gerda had convinced him, and he had benefitted. He loved the food she made with the slow heating unit.

"Daddy!" Paavo shouted and ran to Deshin. He hit Deshin with a force that rocked him slightly.

His boy, eight now, was no longer so thin that Deshin worried about him. He was getting taller as well. He hadn't hit a growth spurt yet, but it was coming. His face held hints of the adult he would become.

In the two years since Deshin had solved the problem of Paavo's ghosts, the problems that had filtered into the illegal links his biological parents had installed before Disappearing, Paavo had become a steadier, happier child.

He still treated his father as if his father—not his mother—were the center of his world. Deshin constantly braced himself for the day that would change: His memory of growing up and all of the child-rearing experts said at some point in his pre-teen years, Paavo would challenge his father's authority. But that point hadn't come yet.

Paavo looked up at him. The streak of flour was no longer on Paavo's cheek, which meant it was probably on Deshin's clothes.

"Something wrong?" Paavo asked, and his tone held that adultness that had threatened for months now.

Deshin didn't know how to answer that.

Something always was wrong when he arrived home in the middle of the afternoon, but Paavo had meant the question in a particular way. He was asking if something as drastic as Anniversary Day or the Peyti Crisis had occurred.

Deshin's gaze met Gerda's. There were lines on her face that hadn't been there before. She clearly had the same question their son did.

Deshin didn't want to talk about the family's future with Paavo. The boy was brilliant, one of the smartest children ever to attend Aristotle Academy, but he was still very young emotionally. And Deshin never had a good handle on the boy—what he could deal with and what he couldn't.

Deshin had thought that Paavo would have trouble with the Peyti Crisis, particularly since several people—including a student—had died in the United Domes emergency action to stop the Peyti clones. But Paavo had taken that in stride. He was too young to know the student, and somehow he had come to the conclusion that bad things happened everywhere.

The only thing Deshin didn't like about Paavo's attitude was that Paavo also seemed to believe his father would make everything right.

"We haven't heard anything on the news," Gerda said. "Has something happened?"

"Not like that," Deshin said, his hands still on Paavo's back. The boy's muscles had developed now, partly because he had insisted on learning how to be as strong as his father.

Someday, his boy would be as strong as his father and fifty times smarter. His boy would be the most formidable man in Armstrong, maybe in the Alliance—if there was anything left of Armstrong or the Alliance by then.

"Some business has come up," Deshin said. "Paavo, can you let your mother and I—"

"You're going to leave?" Paavo asked, his grip tightening. "Mom's scared and you're going to go away on business?"

Gerda winced, confirming Paavo's words—as if Deshin needed them confirmed. Deshin's heart sank. He knew that Gerda was upset by all that had happened; he hadn't realized that her fears had seeped into the boy as well.

Deshin didn't want to lie to his son, so he told an incomplete truth. "That's not why I'm here."

The actual truth would have been "that's not *exactly* why I'm here," although it was close.

Gerda must have seen the thought cross his face. She tried to get control of her own expression, but didn't seem able to. Instead, she bent down, turned the bread pans around inside the oven, then closed the oven door, her face flushed from the heat. She had done that so she wouldn't have to look at him, so that he wouldn't see her reaction to his news.

"Can you give us a minute, Paavo?" Gerda asked, only her tone brooked no disagreement. She had made it sound like a question, but both the men in her life knew she was commanding Paavo to leave the room.

"I'm old enough—"

"Yes, you are," Deshin said. "But right now, this isn't about age. This is about private things between your parents. Please, let us talk."

Paavo pulled away from him. Gerda half-smiled at Deshin. He never said "please" to anyone except his boy.

He and Gerda had brought him into their lives as a baby, but hadn't formally adopted him until two years ago, fearing legal complications with his Disappeared parents. They ended up having legal complications, just not the ones they expected.

But he was theirs now, and that moment when Deshin thought he might lose the boy, that was the worst moment of his life.

He never expected to be this kind of parent. He thought he would be the father of half a dozen children, coming home to a large laughing household filled with playful athletic kids, not a quiet place with his wife and his brilliant son, thinking the day away.

But early on, Paavo had proven such a difficult child and they had loved him so much they didn't want to lose focus on him when they brought in a different child.

Deshin and Gerda had talked about adopting another child. They felt that it might be good for Paavo now. But that had been just before Anniversary Day.

Anniversary Day changed everything.

Gerda walked to the kitchen door and stood, arms crossed. She watched as Paavo walked into his room and pulled the door closed.

Then she turned to Deshin.

"You can't leave us now. There's going to be another attack. We'll die without you."

He'd never heard his wife sound so terrified. He had married her for her courage as well as her heart. She had stood up to horrible things in their past, and she had defended Paavo like a she-tiger during the crisis with his biological parents.

If Gerda were one of his valued employees or even one of his friends, he would have tried to placate her. But she knew him better than anyone. She knew when he was trying to manipulate her.

He extended his hand toward the table, so that she would sit down. She shook her head slightly, clearly too upset to sit calmly. So he did.

He sat in one of the soft chairs that were such a part of his comfortable home, and stretched out his legs, crossed at the ankle, as if he were relaxing after one of Gerda's marvelous meals.

"I'm not here to talk about my absence," he said.

She frowned. She clearly didn't understand.

"Sit, please," he said.

She did. She sat on the edge of one of the chairs as if she were going to spring up at any moment. Behind her, he could see bowls on the counter. They were filled with fresh-cut vegetables, some meat, and a spice mixture. He had no idea what she was going to make, but he knew it would be good.

"Since the Peyti Crisis, I've been thinking," he said. "Hell, since Anniversary Day. Since I couldn't get home."

"Luc, we've talked about that—"

He held up a hand, silencing her, then instantly regretted it. He didn't want to treat her like staff, but he didn't apologize either.

"Let me, Gerda," he said.

Her lips thinned. She leaned back in the chair like a petulant teenager, and he almost—almost—smiled at the movement.

He'd been married to her long enough to know better than to smile at anything in a serious discussion.

"You remember that Retrieval Artist? Flint?"

She nodded.

"Before the crisis last week, I asked him to get me information on the explosions—what materials were used."

"Luc, you promised you wouldn't get involved." That exasperation again.

He *hadn't* promised. He had dodged. He had believed, after he had traveled to trace the zoodeh, that someone in authority would take over the investigations he was running.

He had hoped it would be Flint, but Deshin was just beginning to realize how stretched everyone was, and how clueless.

He didn't argue with his wife. He couldn't.

"I know you're worried for me," he said. "And—."

"It's not just me," she said. "Paavo is afraid for you. He knows how close you came to dying on Anniversary Day. I don't know how he knows, but he does."

Deshin's cheeks flushed. He hadn't wanted his boy to know, but it was hard to hide information from Paavo. The boy was getting good at ferreting out a lot of things he shouldn't know.

Another sidetrack.

Deshin nodded, working hard to keep his focus on Gerda.

"I've been talking to Flint, and my people have been following the official investigation." Deshin made certain his tone was slow and measured. "They know nothing more than they did six months ago. And yet we all agree on one thing: There will be another attack."

She shook her head. Denial.

"Gerda," he said softly. "You know it too. That was the first thing you and Paavo thought of when you saw me."

She closed her eyes and bowed her head. She wasn't denying anything.

"I used to make fun of people who stayed in war zones," he said quietly. "Especially people who had the money to escape. I wondered what kind of delusion kept them in place."

She raised her head, eyes open now. She was watching him closely.

"Now, I know," he said. "It's a feeling that things just can't get worse. Nothing else can happen. We've been through it all."

That guarded expression had returned to her face. If the circumstances were different, he'd kiss the expression away.

"Gerda," he said, "I'd like you and Paavo to go to Earth until this is all over. Somewhere with fantastic schools, somewhere pretty or with great weather or lots of history. Somewhere that will nurture our son."

"*You* nurture our son," she said.

"I protect our son," Deshin said. "And I've been trying to come up with some place safe for him. There's nowhere on the Moon right now. And you know it."

Gerda stood. She walked over to the counter, and put her hands on two of the bowls as if she were thinking of doing something with them. Only she didn't.

"You'll come with us?" she asked with her back to him. Her posture told him she already knew the answer, and she didn't want to see it on his face before he spoke.

"No," he said.

"Because of *business*." She had never spit the word like that, never made it sound so very hateful, before.

"No," he said.

She whirled. Her face had gone gray.

"Then what?" she asked.

"There's an investigation that only I can do."

"*You?*" She said in that same tone, the one he'd never heard before. "You're going to work with the authorities? *You*?"

It was a sign of how stressed she was, how frightened she was, that she was going to attack him.

He had never seen her like this before.

"Not exactly," he said. "I told you about that Retrieval Artist."

"*He's* working with the authorities," she said.

"Yes," Deshin said. "He wants my help with designer clones."

"What can you do?" She asked. "You never had any respect for people who used them. And you hated it the one time someone planted a clone in our…"

Her voice trailed off. She was clearly beginning to understand.

"These people, they saved our lives," Deshin said. "They stopped the Peyti clones."

"Yes," she said, head down.

"But they have no idea how to investigate the designer clones, and honestly, if they tried, the makers would scatter like the insects that they are. But they won't run from me."

"Won't they know?" she asked. "Won't they suspect you're doing something with the government if you come asking about Peyti clones and PierLuigi Frémont?"

"I won't asked about Peyti clones," he said. "That would tip them off."

Deshin was known for not using aliens in his business.

"But," he continued, "I can ask about Frémont, as long as I have the right kind of bank roll."

"You'd offer to buy…?" her voice trailed off again. "Luc, can't you send some of your people to do this?"

"Maybe," he said. "I'm not sure. But as I was thinking about it, I realized that I would be worrying about you and Paavo the whole time. And I can't, Gerda. I can't be here for you. If something happens on the Moon, we could all die in an instant, even if we're together."

"I'd rather die together," she said softly.

He waited until she looked at him, chin out defiantly.

"You'd condemn Paavo to that?" he asked. "An early death? Or maybe outliving us, and having to survive in the wreckage that would be the Moon."

"Don't put it like that, Luc," Gerda said. "That's not fair."

"The truth isn't always fair," he said.

She glared at him. When she did that, he knew he had moved her. If he didn't push, she would come around.

"How long would we have to be gone?" she asked.

"I don't know," he said.

She swallowed hard, then crossed her arms.

"Will you live through this?" she asked softly.

"I hope so," he said.

"You have to promise me," she said fiercely. "You have to promise me or we won't go without you. I'll make you stay with us. You have to promise me."

He hadn't expected this level of vehemence. It told him just how terrified his wife was underneath her calm façade.

"Gerda," he said gently. "You know I don't make promises I can't keep."

She burst into tears.

He got up and put his arms around her. She felt marvelous, all warm and soft and perfect, his familiar and very strong wife.

He kissed the top of her head.

"I can't live without you," she said into his shirt.

"Of course you can," he said, nuzzling her hair. It smelled of fresh bread. "You just don't want to."

"Damn right," she said. "Don't make me, Luc."

"I don't make you do anything," he said, "except consider Paavo."

She stiffened in his arms. Then she leaned back so she could see his face.

"Bastard," she said, but the word wasn't vehement. It was a capitulation.

"Yeah," he said. "And that's exactly what the Moon needs right now. Bastards like me."

12

Ava Huỳnh stalked down the halls of the Earth Alliance Security Office. She really shouldn't have left her department, Earth Alliance Security Headquarters for the Human Division, but she couldn't remain there any longer.

Someone was going to have to take care of this, and since no one was, she was going to step in. She had thought about it all night, and when she got up, she put on battle clothes.

Not that anyone else would know what those were—her most comfortable outfit, a blue pair of slacks, a matching blue shirt, and her favorite blue shoes—but she knew. And that was what mattered.

That, and the fact that she had been right all along.

She got to the "sky bridge" which connected the Human Investigative Unit and the Joint Investigative Unit, and continued to stomp. If she were going to change her mind, this was where she should have done it, right here, as she crossed out of her jurisdiction to the one she got criticized for consulting all the time.

But she had come here six months ago, and had been shot down, and she had been *right,* dammit. She had believed that humans and aliens should have been *jointly* investigating the Anniversary Day attacks, because—despite what everyone said—the Moon was not just a human place.

It was the gateway into the heart of the Earth Alliance. Earth herself, the very center of the Alliance, the place where it had all begun.

Not to mention the fact that every species traveled to Earth at one point or another, and that meant *every species* traveled to the Moon.

But noooo, Xyven would have none of that. Xyven believed the bombings on the Moon had been a human problem. Xyven had turned down her petition for joint investigatory teams.

And she couldn't help thinking that there might have been more to it.

She had spent all night trying to shed that thought, but she couldn't. She wasn't sure if she was being as bigoted as Xyven had been when he quashed the idea of joint investigations or if she had reason to be suspicious.

And, since she was the kind of woman who didn't even know how to be circumspect, she was going directly to Xyven *first*, even though she probably should have gone farther up the ladder, to the Director of the entire investigative unit—the one that coordinated every single department, human and alien, and the joint department where humans and aliens investigated *together.*

She hated this damn sky bridge. Because there was no sky. She was on the starbase that housed all of the Earth Alliance's Security Division. She thought of the entire thing as a giant spider web, with smaller bases encircling the larger base, and all of them attached by tunnels and "bridges" and all sorts of other walkways and passageways that made it the most confusing place she had ever worked.

At least she had memorized it. So many staff members simply let the maps on the links guide them, which she figured would bite them in the ass one day. What would they do when the systems went down and they had to get from one part of the base to another?

They'd have no idea where to go or how to get there.

But she would.

She slammed her way through Joint Unit's green and silver reception area, past the android receptionist that sent a panicked message to her links:

You do not have an appointment!

She never had appointments, but she knew one day that bipedal thing with the green/gold/blue eyes and the face that tried to shift from one preferred species to another would try to stop her from entering.

If it tried today, she'd—oh, she had no idea what she'd do, but it would be bad.

She ignored the insistent messages, and stomped down the Disty-decorated hall. Because the first director had been Disty, everything was warren-like—small and twisty. Fortunately, she wasn't very tall either. Some of her colleagues couldn't even stand upright here.

A few other android security officers tried to stop her along the way, but she put her security clearance badge as a response to all messages, and that slowed everything down.

Then she reached the rack of environmental suits, and those did stop her. For one brief moment, she thought about returning to her office, and summoning Xyven there.

Of course, he wouldn't come. And then she'd have to go through this all over again.

But it was hard to keep a mad on when she was having to pick through the suits, slide one over her clothes, and find a mask that wasn't too funky.

Somehow she managed to get the stupid suit on and maintain her mood. She hurried down the hall to the Peyti unit, put her gloved hand on the divider, and tapped her personal code into the material. Then she stood still as it did a retinal scan.

The divider opened right away, which surprised her. She would have thought that this week of all weeks Xyven was going to deny her entry.

Maybe he was political enough to realize that if he had refused to see her, she would have gone above his head. Hell, she might even have tried to get him fired.

She still might do that.

She waded through the murk that mimicked the environment on Peyla, the Peyti home world. The atmosphere was thicker here, and even though she couldn't feel it against her skin, the atmosphere still slowed her stomp into Xyven's office.

She managed to arrive at the end of that long corridor just as Xyven's door opened. She half expected him to be standing there, like he had the last several times she barged in, but this time, he wasn't.

She stalked inside.

He stood in front of his human-like desk, amidst the clutter of human, alien, and Peyti furniture that he somehow felt he needed to fill the room.

His arms were at his sides, his thin fingers nearly touching his knees. His face had a mournful expression, which she wouldn't have noticed if he were wearing the usual mask that the Peyti wore in an Earth Normal environment.

I was wrong, he sent her on her links.

Xyven always insisted on a link conversation between colleagues, so that he could save the information.

She was half tempted to yell at the top of her lungs, just so she wasn't following all of his rules.

She took a deep breath of the manufactured air. Damn him. He took control of the conversation before she could even say a word.

Wrong about what? she snapped.

Alien involvement. You were right: It should have been a joint investigation from the start.

She sucked in even more flat air. He had never, in all the years they'd worked together, admitted fault in anything. Never.

She wondered if he did it now to derail her.

Probably.

I'm appalled at the Peyti involvement. Appalled. His skin was a faint blue. *Xivim has already been here to see me. She wanted to send investigators to Peyla, but I asked her to wait until I spoke to you.*

He...what? Huỳnh felt like he had physically pushed her back. She hadn't expected any of this at all.

Why wait? Huỳnh managed.

Because I wasn't sure about the status of your investigations, he sent.

She had over 150 investigators on the Anniversary Day cases, but all were on the Moon.

I don't have anyone on Peyla, she sent. *But I'll send them if we're not doing a joint investigation.*

Obviously, we are now, Xyven sent. *I'm so sorry, Ava. It is my mistake.*

She wanted to ask him if he had decided it was his mistake after he learned what happened on the Moon or after his superior had spoken to him.

Ultimately, though, it wasn't her business.

What was her business was that there would now be a joint investigation.

I know Joint Investigations is your jurisdiction, she sent, *but I'm six months into this. I'm going to coordinate it.*

She didn't ask. She didn't tell him she'd go over his head. She wasn't going to give him that courtesy.

I hoped you would say that, he sent.

She had never seen him be so contrite. She wondered what was behind it, then made herself take a third deep breath. It wasn't her business why he'd had a change of heart.

What was her business was making certain that the Earth Alliance investigation into Anniversary Day and the second attack were conducted properly, and with respect to the investigations her staff had already put months into.

All right, she sent, still feeling off-balance from the lack of a fight. *The sooner we can augment this investigation, the better. I want a meeting within the hour, along with plans from our colleagues in the other departments.*

Done, Xyven sent.

Then he folded his twig-like fingers together and held them just below his chin. She had read about this gesture, but she had never seen it. It represented very deep emotion for a Peyti.

Please, he sent, *accept my deepest apologies. This second attack might be my fault. I did not listen to you. If I had…*

He let the thought trail off, maybe in the hopes that she would step in and utter some platitude about it not being his fault at all.

But she didn't.

We can't change the past, she sent. *But we can do our best to make sure it doesn't repeat for a third time.*

He bowed his head, his skin blue.

I certainly hope so, he sent. *I really do.*

13

DESHIN RETURNED FROM HIS HOUSE WITH A NEW RESOLVE. GERDA HAD taken one problem off of his mind. Now, it was time to focus on making his home—his city—safe once more.

Technically, he shouldn't have set up this next meeting in his office.

But Deshin's usual safe meeting places had been compromised. Some were in the middle of the destroyed areas of domes; others had been in back rooms of buildings where weapons suppliers worked. Not too long ago, he would have asked Ernest Pietres in Crater de Gerlache to broker this meeting somewhere safe.

But Pietres had been one of the Anniversary Day casualties—before Anniversary Day—and even though Deshin now owned a piece of Pietres's store (through more shell corporations than he wanted to think about), he no longer considered it safe.

The only place he considered safe on the Moon was his own office, and even that was an illusion.

But at least it was a place he could protect, a place where he trusted the security. He no longer trusted anywhere else.

He tapped a corner of his desk, bringing up an image of the twenty Anniversary Day clones arriving at the Port of Armstrong. It had become one of the iconic images of Anniversary Day. He had seen it everywhere, a kind of cautionary tale.

He was going to use the image here and now.

But he wasn't going to look at it until he had to.

He ran a hand over his face and walked to his usual spot at the windows. They were made of thick reinforced nanomaterials, materials that three separate structural engineering firms had guaranteed safe—no attack could come through them.

Except, of course, the catastrophic kind. Like the bombing four and a half years ago. Or like Anniversary Day.

He had promised Gerda he would stay as safe as he could. He had also promised her he—or someone on his staff—would contact her with his health update every day.

That had been the only way to convince her and Paavo to leave the Moon.

Deshin had made her promise that she wouldn't tell him where she was going. He didn't want to get kidnapped and have someone pry that information out of him.

He also didn't want it on any net or link, in case someone (or something) wanted to use his family to get to him. What he was going to do in the next few weeks was extremely dangerous—things he hadn't done since he married Gerda—and he didn't want to lose his family by starting out stupid.

He had set up two separate accounts for her, untraceable to Deshin Enterprises, so that she could buy a home for herself and Paavo, as well as enroll him in school, and live in whatever kind of luxury she deemed important.

He had set it all up under her original surname, and explained to Paavo that he had to use a different last name while all of this was going on.

Paavo's response had startled him.

I knew it, his son had said with an excitement that embarrassed Deshin. *I knew you were going to make everything right.*

His boy had jumped right over the fact that the family had to separate to figuring out the reason why the family needed to split up. Paavo understood that Deshin's work might put them in danger, and he seemed to support it wholeheartedly.

Deshin doubted the boy would do that if he knew some of the risks that Deshin would have to take, and some of the horrible things Deshin might have to do, in the name of gathering information, and solving these horrific crimes.

I don't make things right, Deshin had said to Paavo. *I'm just helping in the short term, and I want to make sure you and your mother are safe while I do it. Can you keep her safe?*

Paavo had nodded.

It'll be my sacred duty, he had said with a solemnity that both made Deshin proud and scared the crap out of him. What child said he had a sacred duty? And what child believed he could take on the demons of the universe in his father's absence?

I guess he really is your son, Gerda had said with amusement after Paavo had left the room.

Deshin had shaken his head. *I didn't mean for him to take this so seriously.*

Yes, you did, she had said, and she'd smiled. The smile had been warm, and with it, Deshin had realized he was forgiven for making them leave the Moon.

Apparently Gerda had thought about it and realized, as he had, that it was the best decision for Paavo.

The best decision for her.

And now, Deshin was taking the risks he had planned for.

Deshin sighed and turned away from the window. He faced the image of the twenty men, all of them dead now. The fact that they looked so happy always amazed him.

They were spread out through the crowd at the arrivals area of the Port of Armstrong. People surrounded them, holding hands with children, or walking, heads down, as they hurried to their destinations. Humans, dressed in suits or in casual clothes, carrying tablets or dragging suitcases, looking bored or excited at all of the movement in the port.

Mingled among them were Peyti, with their twig-like bodies and the bulky masks that they wore. He could barely look at them either. He let his gaze skitter away from them, onto the other aliens: a clump of Disty, threading between the legs of humans, looking like children (dangerous children); some Sequev, scurrying along on their eight legs; and two Gyonnese who stood to one side, staring at the arrivals area as if they were waiting for someone else, their whiskers wrapped around their faces as if they didn't want anyone to see their expressions.

Didn't the men see the beings? Hadn't they realized that through their actions, they could have killed everyone in the port?

Deshin took a deep breath and let it out. He needed to calm. He was being sloppy and sentimental. Back when he started up these businesses, he hadn't cared who died.

Of course, he hadn't killed them himself, but he had easily looked the other way. Maybe those men were able to look the other way as well.

Their original certainly had.

There was a lot of argument, scientific and otherwise, argument getting louder and louder since the Anniversary Day attacks, that clones took on traits of the original, that clones were little more than copies of the original.

The laws of the Earth Alliance reflected that. Clones had no legal rights. They were considered property, and only through a complex adoption and/or legitimization program could they actually get full human status.

Deshin only knew a few clones who had ever achieved full human status, and most of them kept their origins secret.

He made himself look at the twenty faces now, forcing himself to see them. Usually he only saw that they were all six feet tall, as muscular as he was, and weirdly blond, pale-skinned, and blue-eyed. Normally the men would have gotten noticed just for their coloring. Those recessive traits were unusual in the known universe, and often a sign that parents believed in genetic purity or some other archaic notion.

Maybe no one noticed that day in Armstrong's port, because the men had already been dismissed as clones. Or maybe it was their mood, which seemed so jovial.

The two men closest to the exit doors were looking at each other and grinning. Two others had their arms draped around each other's shoulders, heads touching. Five of the men were clustered in a group, clearly in the middle of a conversation. One stood in the middle, looking up as if he were trying to see where to go next. The remaining ten were laughing, all of them caught in various poses related to that laugher, mouths and eyes open or closed, hands on stomachs as if holding in the guffaws or hands clasping (or about to clasp) as if they were about to applaud.

The joy offended him the most, since they were all about to leave the port and murder at least one person, and, in some cases, thousands.

Thousands.

Including people he loved.

Somehow, for the next hour or more, he had to control the disgust and anger that he felt. He had to act as if these twenty men were nothing more than tools, tools he wanted. And he had to do so with great calm.

He took another deep breath, then sent a message to his security staff.

Search them. Then send them up.

He was taking a hell of a risk.

He hoped that it would pay off.

14

Rafael Salehi didn't like to get summoned, particularly by his two name partners. Yet that was what had just happened, via the one link that tied all three name partners together and kept their communications completely confidential.

Salehi was a senior partner at a law firm that bore his name. His great-great-great-grandfather had been one of the founding partners, along with at least one great-great-great-grandparent of the other two name partners. If nothing else, the universe could claim that it knew that Schnable, Shishani & Salehi was, and always had been, a family business.

Lately, Salehi had felt trapped by it. He hid in his suite of offices on the fifteenth floor. He'd set the environmental and holographic controls in his private office to mimic one of Earth's deserts—today it was the Mojave, with its orangish mountains and brown landscape. Cacti extended into the distance.

When—if—his mood ever improved, he might have his office mimic the Mojave after a rain. He'd only seen that desert one time in his life and he had been lucky enough to arrive during the week when the desert bloomed. It remained one of the most beautiful, and dramatic, moments of his life.

He kept the office this way to remind himself of other places, places far away from Athena Base where S^3, the nickname everyone used for the firm, made its home. He'd been thinking about leaving the firm—becoming a non-active partner—a year before, but had changed his mind as he started developing a legal theory about the future of clone law.

But, after the debacle six months ago that led to the loss of Rafik Fujita, one of his best transport captains and a good friend, the fight had left Salehi. He was biding his time until he found a way out of this place, a way out of the law.

If only his traitorous mind would allow him to stop thinking about what-ifs.

He kept the temperature in the office at 37 degrees Celsius, the humidity almost non-existent. It kept others out, and helped him stay warm, even though he'd had a lot of trouble lately. He knew that was psychological; he felt guilty for the death of Fujita. Salehi had been the one to notify Fujita's family, and it was a moment he would never forget.

Salehi tugged on his expensive linen shirt, imported from Earth at great expense. He'd bought his khaki shorts in one of the shops nearby that catered to mid-level professionals who planned to go on vacation at a real resort. His sandals were handmade there as well, molded to his feet by a local craftsman rather than artificial nanotechnology.

Most people said they couldn't feel the difference but he could.

He looked at himself, lean and dressed for anywhere but the office, and wondered if he should change before he went to the conference room in Schnable's office suite.

Finally, Salehi decided against changing. He would freeze, but that would give him an excuse to leave.

He really hated being summoned.

He grabbed a floppy brown hat, and wished he had a sweet, senseless brightly colored alcoholic drink complete with chopped fruit along the side, so that he could look even more out of place. He wanted to give the impression that he really didn't care, when deep down, some part of him still gave a damn.

He felt like he owed that much to his family. He had grown up here, playing under his mother's desk, sitting on a miniature replica of his father's favorite work chair while his father finished up depositions, listening to his grandfather badger staff who mistreated clients. Once upon a time, Salehi had loved this place, and part of him still did.

That was the part that he couldn't quite let go.

He opened the door only to find Debra Shishani on the other side of it, hand curled as if she were about to knock. Unlike him, the second named partner in this law firm was dressed like a real lawyer. She wore a black tunic that covered matching black pants, and heels that made her even taller than she usually was. Her brown hair flowed around her shoulders, which accented her angular features.

She narrowed her almond-shaped eyes—the most distinguishing thing about her face—and said, "I came to fetch you."

"I'm coming," he said, sounding petulant even to his own ears. "Although I don't know why you want me. I really don't give a damn about this stuff anymore."

It almost sounded like a lie. Maybe it did sound like a lie. Maybe his ambivalence was evident in his every word.

"You'll care about this," she said. "It's clone law."

He bowed his head, shaking it, surprised at the tears pricking his eyes. Clone law had been what had gotten Fujita killed. Salehi's enthusiasm for clone law had led to the entire case, to the fact that a clone of PierLuigi Frémont had been on board that ship when the Earth Alliance had blown it to smithereens.

"I've given up clone law," Salehi said.

He had given up on clone law so much that when Shishani had suggested a wrongful death suit in the case that might go to the multicultural tribunal, he had said, *You do it.*

She was. Only she made the case about Fujita, not about the clone, which was what Salehi would have done.

"Well, un-give-it-up," she said. "We need you. Come on."

She took his hand. Her fingers were cool around his, her long nails—painted black to match her outfit—brushing against his skin. He let himself be led through the reception area and to the private staircase that went up to Schnable's penthouse suite—if a suite in an office building on a starbase could be called a penthouse.

It did brush against the edges of the base, and the view through the ceiling was of space itself. Or, rather, to be more accurate, of the ships coming in for landing at the various places in this sector.

The constant view of ships and outsiders would have made Salehi nervous. He thought, not for the first time, that he was more suited to the study of the law than the practice of it. He didn't like people, but he loved theory.

With her other hand, Shishani pushed open the door into the conference area. The third partner, Domek Schnable, whom Salehi privately called Schnabby, waited at the head of a long conference table.

Schnable was older than both Shishani and Salehi by many years. Schnable belonged to the generation ahead of them, just younger than their parents, significantly older than Salehi was. Schnable was a short man with a large head and a prominent nose. He liked hats that accented his sharp features and usually wore one inside. On this day, his hat—a wide-brimmed Napoleonic bicorne—rested at the head of the table, marking his place.

As if he needed to. No one ever had to mark a place at this table. Salehi had never seen it full. From the moment he came onboard, only the three of them had been senior partners.

Salehi had heard that back in the day when the firm started, all of the partners met here, but the room had been closed off in his parents' era. In fact the entire penthouse suite had been closed down because the partners at that time argued about who "deserved" it.

The three current senior partners had no such disagreement. Salehi had hated it, and Shishani had wanted a larger suite several floors down.

Schnable took it, and treated it like the spoils of war. He had decorated most of his private office in a military motif—although the motif was more a haphazard mess than anything organized. If an item had a military connection, he wanted it; it didn't matter which military or what the connection was.

Schnable had redone this room in green and gold. The chairs had little epaulets with gold fringe on their backs and the edges of the arms. Those chairs always made Salehi feel like he was sitting down in a nest of spiders.

"Hats off, Raffy," Schnable said. "We have serious business to conduct."

Schnable had called Salehi "Raffy" since he was a boy. Schnable had been part of the firm since Salehi got out of law school. Salehi took off his floppy hat and rolled it in his hands, feeling like a rebellious kid.

Schnable always made him feel like a rebellious kid, and maybe that was why Salehi acted like one. It would explain the looks Salehi got whenever he called Schnable Schnabby, as if he were breaking some important code of behavior.

Salehi sat down, careful not to brush up against the fringe. The chairs were made of fabric and were warmer than his chairs, even in this room with its temperature set at a "normal" 21 degrees.

He sat at the side of the table. Shishani sat at the other head of the table, as she liked to call it. Salehi knew from past experience that Schnable would call that part of the table "the foot."

"Here's the issue," Schnable said, sweeping his stupid hat aside as he sat at his spot at the head of the table. "We got contacted by the Peyti government today."

"What?" Salehi asked, and he looked at Shishani for confirmation.

She raised her eyebrows, made a face that Salehi called her *can you believe it?* face, and folded her hands in front of her.

"You're familiar with what's been happening on the Moon, right?" Schnable asked.

Salehi bit back the answer he wanted to give. Maybe the reason he treated Schnable like a fusty old school teacher was that Schnable treated Salehi like an idiot student.

"They're calling it the Peyti Crisis now," Salehi said, as if he were striving for a good grade. "I'm not sure if that's accurate. I'm hoping that this bombing mania doesn't spread to the rest of the Earth Alliance."

"For all we know, it already has," Schnable said. "Not all societies in the Alliance are as open as ours."

Salehi suppressed a sigh. "Ours," in Schnabby terms meant human society, not Earth Alliance protocols. And humans weren't the most open group in the Earth Alliance. Several other alien cultures had tolerance and communication down to a science.

Still, Salehi decided to let this one pass. Shishani looked at him as if she couldn't believe he had done that. Maybe she hadn't noticed that lately, Salehi had let a lot of Schnabby's stupid remarks pass.

"What do the Peyti want with us?" Salehi asked.

"It seems that your treatises on clone law in the Earth Alliance have attracted their attention," Schnable said.

"Good for them," Salehi said, mostly because he couldn't prevent the sentence from coming out of his mouth. "The Peyti have produced the best lawyers in the Earth Alliance. I'm sure they can make use of my theories."

"That's the issue." Shishani spoke up. Maybe she'd heard the defiance in Salehi's tone, and she didn't want this to devolve into the usual fight. "The Peyti can't get to the Moon. Their ships are being denied entry into the Port of Armstrong. Even Peyti that come on ships from other places are being denied entry."

Salehi stood up, unable to sit with the news. "How come I haven't heard that?"

"You have now." Schnable's tone was smug.

Salehi looked at Shishani in an attempt to remain calm. She opened her hands just a little as if to say, *calm down*. Salehi wasn't mad yet, but dealing with Schnable would make him angry eventually.

Salehi tried another tack. "How did *you* hear about it?"

"I—" Schnable stopped himself and grinned sheepishly. "The Peyti told me."

"I suspect this isn't something the port wants out," Shishani said.

Salehi shook his head. "It's not legal. That port is licensed through the Earth Alliance. Earth Alliance member species cannot be denied entry."

"I doubt they're denying entry to all Peyti," Schnable said. "I'm pretty sure they would find a reason to deny each one."

"We don't know what the reasons are," Shishani said. It didn't seem like this news upset her at all. Schnable just seemed to find it amusing.

It angered Salehi. He hated a lot of things about the Earth Alliance. The fact that it would turn a blind eye to an entire species because of terrible actions of a few disturbed him greatly.

"Can humans get through the Port Of Armstrong?" Salehi asked.

"You know they can," Schnable said. "That's neither here nor there—"

"It is relevant," Salehi said. "Were humans denied entry after Anniversary Day? Because those clones were human."

"Technically," Shishani said, "they weren't human. They're property, and property can be confiscated or sent back to where it came from. I'm sure the port used DNA—"

"You're sure," Salehi glared at Shishani. "And Domek is sure. But neither of you really *know*, do you?"

They didn't answer him, but they both had odd expressions on their faces.

Salehi made a sound of disgust. He didn't care that his partners knew what he thought of them. He used to try to keep his emotions under control, but he didn't now. He didn't care that they seemed to be so blind to injustices.

He made a fist with his right hand, then opened the fist finger by finger, concentrating on the movement before he spoke again.

"Surely," he said in a calmer tone, "there are Peyti lawyers on the Moon who weren't involved in this conspiracy. They can take care of their own on the Moon, right?"

"At the moment, they're under suspicion as well," Shishani said. "Besides, would you want a Peyti lawyer going in front of a judge on the Moon right now? This is a murder case right now or attempted murder. Judges who handle those cases are local, and all local judges lived through Anniversary Day. That'll influence how they react to another mass bombing."

Salehi cursed. He knew Shishani was right. These cases had dozens of issues tied into them: murder, attempted murder, conspiracy, terrorism, treason. And none of those things could be charged against a clone.

The clones' owners would have to be charged, and then the clones would be destroyed. Provided the clones' owners could be found.

If someone got the clones declared to be real Peyti under Earth Alliance law, then each case would go through the Moon's courts separately. Unless someone made this a conspiracy charge.

But there could be no conspiracy with clones, and no conspiracy charge without knowing who the owners were.

Legally, under Earth Alliance law, there were no good choices for punishment. Just a lot of bad ones.

He cursed again.

Schnable grinned at Shishani. "Told you this would fire him up."

She took a deep breath, and gave Salehi a sideways glance, as if he had just caught her conspiring with the enemy. Which, he supposed, he had.

He glared at her. So she turned her chair ever so slightly toward Schnable.

"You said he'd be interested in the Peyti clone issue," she said to Schnable.

"*He* is right here." Salehi gripped the top of his chair. "I've told you before I'm not that interested in practicing law any longer."

Schnable folded his hands in front of him.

"What you said," he said to Salehi in a slow deliberate tone, the tone that won him dozens of cases in court, the one that sent chills through Salehi right now, "is that you can't find your passion for the law any longer, so what's the point. Now, right now, you seem to have quite a bit of passion about the legal case, and we haven't even gotten to the heart of what's happening on the Moon."

Salehi squeezed his fingers on the chair, focusing on the pain as his nails dug into the soft fabric. He repeated softly to himself: *I won't let Schnabby get to me. I won't let Schnabby get to me. I won't let—*

And then he felt himself snap. He called those moments his ah-fuck-it moments, the ones where he threw all caution to the wind. He'd won in court with ah-fuck-it moments, and lost clients with them, and had broken up with girlfriends, a wife or two, and lost half a dozen friends because at some point, he just didn't give a damn.

Or maybe he gave too much of a damn.

He wasn't going to analyze it, particularly when he was in the middle of such a moment.

"You want me to defend a bunch of mass murderers?" Salehi said softly.

"You want a clone law test case," Schnable said. "I want one that will make this firm money. The Government of Peyla will pay all of our expenses and court costs while we organize the defense of several hundred Peyti. We probably won't have to take this to court."

"But if we do, I have to argue that these assholes are *property*, and can't make any decisions for themselves and that one particular person or Peyti or creature is responsible for what happened, and that the property—"

"You could argue that it should be destroyed," Shishani said quietly.

Salehi dug his fingers even deeper into the chair. He felt betrayed. She had talked with Schnabby about this before they had ever brought Salehi in.

They were going after him in a concentrated way, a tag-team, like lawyers on an opposing case.

"Or," Schnable said, "you could force the Earth Alliance to look at what's really going on here. Someone's got to find the mastermind behind these evil attacks."

"You're assuming there is a mastermind," Salehi snapped.

"It's logical," Shishani said. "Someone had to make the clones. Someone had to convince them to infiltrate the Moon."

"And someone had to give them the signal to attack everyone on the same day," Schnable said.

"Hell," Shishani said, "someone had to provide the masks."

Salehi felt the logic of the argument, the appeal of the argument. It was always best, in a court, to have a single villain than it was to have hundreds. The others would plead down, turn against each other, help the prosecution in exchange for reduced sentences, but someone would pay.

But he would be the *defense* attorney. His job would be to make certain that even that horrible mastermind—if there was one—had a fair trial.

He wasn't sure he could do that.

"There are two ways to argue this," Shishani said. "You know that when Peyti lawyers finally arrive, they're going to go with the property argument. They're going to try to get the killers off by declaring them property, and therefore not responsible for their actions."

"If you get them defined as Peyti, as actual members of the Earth Alliance, then they need to be tried like other sentient beings. And this becomes an Earth Alliance case, not a local Moon case." Schnable shrugged. "Sounds interesting no matter how you play it."

"Play," Salehi snapped. "This is not play—"

"You know what I mean," Schnable said.

"What's Peyla's interest in this?" Salehi asked. "Why would the government foot the bill? It'll be hugely expensive."

"That's the first thing I asked," Schnable said. "They've got state's interest. As a species, they're being blamed for this attack. Right now, all of their business interests and all of their personnel are banned from the Moon, even though it's not an official ban."

"There are ways around that," Salehi said. "I'm sure there are a million corporate lawyers working for some Peyti-owned corporation that would love to go after that kind of discrimination."

"And," Schnable said, "you have to remember how Peyti culture works. They believe in the letter of the law. They're the best lawyers in the Earth Alliance, and they're not allowed in the middle of this case. They're feeling discriminated against."

"Who cares?" Salehi said. "Let them deal with it."

"I think they will," Schnable said. "The problem is that if someone doesn't get to the Moon and quickly, then those clones could be destroyed, and along with them, the best opportunity to find out what the hell is going on here."

Salehi narrowed his eyes. "You're trying to make this a *civic* duty for me to handle this damn case?"

"These cases," Schnable said. He didn't seem upset at all. It was as if they were discussing a divorce settlement.

"Right now," Shishani said, "they need a human face on these cases, one who can make an actual difference. If you approach this from the clone law angle—"

"It'll take years," Salehi said.

"Yes, but if you want, when the raw emotions are calmed, you'll be able to hand this case to the Peyti if you like."

"You're just looking at the money," Salehi said to Schnable.

"Of course I am," Schnable said. "You'd be billing Peyla by the hour. Their government has a lot of money, and our firm would get a goodly portion of it, even if you leave after a few months. Maybe you can train someone to take over, if this whole idea of changing clone law doesn't appeal to you."

It did appeal to him, and that made him angry.

And of course, Schnable then tried to press his advantage. He smiled. Schnable should never smile. "You can get an odious law tossed off the Earth Alliance books."

"In exchange for freeing hundreds of killers," Salehi said.

"This is going to take years, Rafael," Shishani said. "You won't ever have to take them to court. By the time the court cases come up, you can retire and go off to your damn desert. You won't get them off."

"But my arguments would be responsible for someone else getting them off," Salehi said.

Shishani stood. She was taller than he was, and she always used that fact to great advantage, especially when she wanted to intimidate him into something.

"You would also change the lives of millions of clones," she said. "You would *improve* their lives. They'd be subject to benefits that they couldn't get before. They'd be able to marry and have children. They wouldn't be subject to archaic laws."

It was a good argument. He could feel it starting to sway him.

"You know how the law works," Schnabby said. "You have to stick your hands in warm smelly crap to remove a hunk of gold."

Shishani, her back to Schnabby, closed her eyes. Salehi bowed his head. He'd almost been convinced, and then Schnabby had opened his big mouth.

The ah-fuck-it moment was lasting longer than usual.

"Think about it," Schnable said. "This case will put us on the map. It'll make you one of the most sought-after attorneys in the sector. Almost immediately, you'll have to be certified to argue in front of the Multi-Cultural Tribunal, and if anyone can do that, you can. Your certification will make us a prestige firm again."

Now, Shishani bowed her head. She knew that these arguments wouldn't work with Salehi.

"Debra's certified," Salehi said.

"But Debra's not an expert in this point of the law," Schnable said. "That's why she went against your wishes and is representing the Fujita family only in that wrongful death suit."

Shishani said, "That's not why—"

"Debra," Schnable said, warningly.

"Don't warn her off, Domek," Salehi said. "She's right. She isn't representing the clone, Trey, because she didn't want to. She didn't really care that he died."

"Not fair, Raphael," Shishani said.

"Fairness and the truth don't often go together," said Salehi.

"Neither do fairness and the law," Schnable said. "But this time, they just might."

Salehi rolled his eyes. Schnable was so bad at manipulation. But it was still having an impact.

Salehi didn't care if the firm made millions. He didn't care if the law firm had prestige.

He cared about making a difference, about doing something right. If he had it to do all over again, he would not go into law. He'd find another profession, one that actually improved lives rather than defended or prosecuted those who costs lives.

Shishani's argument about changing the lives of millions of clones was rattling around in his head.

"Let me think about it," Salehi said.

No one spoke.

But they all knew that he had just agreed to take the case.

15

By the time the group arrived at his office, Luc Deshin had calmed himself. Or, rather, calmed himself as much as he was going to.

He leaned against the front of his desk, legs spread in front of him, crossed at the ankles, his palms resting on the desk's surface. He was staring at the clear wall with its frozen image, and he hoped that the expression on his face was one of intrigue, not disgust.

The three representatives filed in, followed by two of his security guards. The representatives wore black, which Deshin thought clichéd. The woman had long black hair, an angular face, and large eyes.

The man to her left was muscular in a way not common among the space-raised. Deshin suspected that if he looked closer, he would see evidence of enhancements, not actual strength.

The third man was older, his white hair contrasting against a youthful face. But his small eyes seemed both old and wary, and his mouth was set in a thin line.

The woman glared at Deshin's guards, then back at Deshin. "We understood this was a private meeting."

"It is private," he said.

"No guards," she said.

"Then no meeting," he said.

"We agreed—"

"We agreed that I would meet with you privately, nothing more," he said. "In Deshin Enterprises, privately means protecting the Deshin at all costs. Hence, the guards. If you don't like it, get out."

He was taking a risk. The entire meeting could end right now, and he might have to rely on someone else to get the information he wanted.

And honestly, he had no idea who else he could rely on.

Which was why he was doing all of this himself.

The woman studied Deshin as if she were thinking of calling his bluff. Then she looked at the image on the clear wall. She studied the entire office, saw its 360-degree view of the city, and smiled with only half her mouth.

The expression made her seem bitter.

"Well," she said, "I suppose one of us has to take a leap of faith."

As if she were making a sacrifice by letting his guards stay. As if she had risked anything at all.

He had let these people into his empire. He was going to risk his reputation—well, not his reputation, really, but his own sense of self-worth—just to talk with these assholes.

The woman took a few steps toward him, then extended her hand. "Hildegard Iban."

He didn't want to take her hand, but he did. Her palm was dry, her fingers bony. "Luc Deshin."

His guards closed the door and then blocked it with their bodies. The men who had accompanied her shifted nervously.

She tilted her head toward the images on the clear wall. "I see you have the most notorious clones in the universe on your screen."

Deshin smiled slowly, hoping he looked as dangerous as he felt. He let her hand go. "They were the most notorious until last week."

She shrugged. "I'm assuming you don't have a need for alien clones."

He knew how these negotiations went. Probing questions, parried answers, nothing really resolved until the negotiators came to some kind of deal.

If they came to a deal.

"Can you provide alien clones?" he asked, his voice flat.

Her men looked at him sharply, as if they hadn't expected him to ask that. She hadn't bothered to introduce them, which made him think they were her guards.

But he wasn't going to point out that she had guards and she didn't want him to.

"I can't provide anything," she said.

He felt his heart sink. He had reached out to his contacts in the Black Fleet, knowing he was dealing with the devil. Most of Armstrong believed him to be the worst criminal mastermind in the city, even if none of the prosecutors managed to charge him with anything. And, if he were honest with himself, he was a criminal mastermind, just of a different ilk than most people expected of him.

He saw himself as a bit more fair, a bit more humane, than others saw him. He believed in clarity, which there was little of inside of Armstrong. Hell, inside of the Earth Alliance.

And clarity made him see that the Black Fleet did all of those things that people believed he did, and so much worse. The Black Fleet mostly operated outside of the Earth Alliance, in Frontier space and beyond. But they also did business inside the Alliance, usually through proxies.

Iban was unusual; she admitted her Black Fleet connections.

Of course, it was hard for her not to. She was one of the few members of the Black Fleet who had been captured, tried, found guilty, and who had served time in an Earth Alliance prison.

Deshin suspected she had done so because she wanted to work within the Alliance. The Black Fleet, a loosely connected group of pirates (or at least that was how he characterized them to his staff), was more organized than the authorities thought, and a lot more savvy about how to manipulate the system—all of the systems, not just the Earth Alliance's systems.

He'd done some business with other members of the Black Fleet before, and it had always left him feeling unclean.

Like now.

The Black Fleet was clearly fronting for someone. Or maybe they wanted to find out if Deshin himself had contacts in the designer criminal clone community.

He had been led to believe that the Black Fleet controlled the entire designer criminal clones market. He had been misled before, but he had caught the misunderstanding before the person trying to mislead him had gotten into his empire.

He would have to do even more work than usual as he scrubbed the building and his networks of any attempts the Black Fleet made to steal information from his business.

"I don't provide anything directly," she said into his silence, "But I do have contacts."

His shoulders relaxed slightly, even though he felt a great deal of irritation. Of course she had contacts. Of course that was why she was here.

He was off his game; he'd let the images of those damn clone assassins influence his very thoughts.

He longed to shut the image down, but knew he couldn't.

Iban shifted from one foot to the other. Then she glanced around the office, as if she could peer beneath its surface, and didn't like what she could see.

Her gaze finally met his again. "If you want to take this discussion any further, we'll need to mutually agree to shut off all recordings, and shut down our links."

He snorted in derision. He had learned what was behind that trick long ago. The Black Fleet actually recorded the method each business had for link shutdown, so that its operatives could replicate it when they needed to break into the system.

"No," he said.

She raised her eyebrows, obviously surprised. He wondered how many other people took her up on that offer, how deep the Black Fleet's penetration was of every single system inside the Earth Alliance.

"Then we won't talk," she said.

He shrugged. "If we don't talk, you lose millions, maybe a billion or more."

She pouted just a little. "Oh, you play rough."

But her eyes were twinkling. She couldn't hide that. Mention money, and people always became reckless. Even people who thought they were experienced at negotiation.

He shrugged. "My office, my rules."

She made a slight "humph" sound, but he saw that as a victory. She clearly understood, and there was no way she was going stop the negotiation now.

He kept his expression impassive.

"Well," she said. "You're willing to invest a lot of money to—what? Cause chaos?"

And the negotiations continued. She had just conceded a point. Maybe several points.

All the tension left his body, even though he hadn't moved from his position against the desk.

"I didn't say I was going to invest," he said.

She blinked, clearly surprised. "But..."

Then she stopped herself. That single word had revealed her surprise. It cost her. Both of them knew it.

So he decided to pretend he was playing nice. He "explained" himself, which he had been planning to do anyway.

"I don't make money by getting my hands dirty," he said. "The fact that I'm even meeting with you is a risk for me."

That last sounded like a revelation, something he would normally keep secret, even though it wasn't. He wanted her to feel like she had won a point in return.

"Why would this meeting be risky for you?" she asked, taking the bait. "Because we're the Black Fleet? Everyone knows what you are, Deshin."

She meant that as an insult, but he didn't take it that way. Still, he had to be cautious with her. The smile had left her face. Her expression hardened. She finally looked as dangerous as he had heard she was.

"Oh, yes," he said. "I forgot. 'Everyone' is always right. Since you know what I am, and you don't seem to respect that, I see no point in doing business with you. You can leave now."

She opened her mouth, probably to emit another "but." She didn't. She had that much control, at least.

"I'd like to talk with you about this venture that you're proposing," she said. "But it's my policy not to do so with links."

"Yes, you've made that clear." He kept his voice calm, although he was truly beginning to hate this woman. Maybe part of that was the backdrop. It almost looked like she was superimposed over the twenty assassins.

He shrugged again. "You don't want to do business my way. That makes things quite simple for me. I don't need you. You're convenient. I'll find another way to get this project done."

She glanced at the men. One of them—the one with the fake muscles—shrugged. Maybe Deshin had underestimated them. Maybe they were more than bodyguards. Maybe they were the ones in charge, and she was just the spokesperson.

"I suppose I could make an exception for you," she said.

Deshin smiled, even though he knew the look didn't reach his eyes. "Kind of you," he said. "However, in the course of this conversation, I realized that dealing with you is not worth my time."

Her gaze shot to the men again. Two spots of color rose in her cheeks. The money meant something to her. Or maybe his business did.

His reputation—his bad reputation—certainly did.

"We entered the building. People know we came here. People will think we dealt," she said, sounding a bit panicked.

"Yes, I'm sure they will," Deshin said. "And that will add to my much-vaunted reputation. The one you already told me about. I'm sure *everyone* will know that we do business now."

He pushed off the desk, and walked around it, turning his back on her.

"I'm sorry," she said, the words hitching a little. Apparently she didn't say them very often. "We got off on the wrong foot."

He stopped, stared ahead, as if he were thinking about what she had said. Instead, he was feeling a bit surprised that she was as easy to manipulate as she was. These basic negotiation tactics should have been familiar to a weapons' broker.

Maybe "everyone" was so afraid of the Black Fleet that they gave in to her every request.

Or maybe she was playing him.

"I was prepared to have a good-faith discussion with you," he said, as he turned toward her. "Apparently, you don't do business that way. My mistake."

She nodded, then glanced at the men. They started to leave.

Deshin had sounded harsh. He hadn't meant to sound that harsh, but his dislike was showing. Now, he had to pretend to give in. A shudder ran through him that he hoped her partners hadn't seen.

"However," he said, "if you're ready to start over, so am I. Shall we pretend that the first few minutes hadn't happened?"

"They've been recorded," the muscular man said. "We can't pretend anything."

Deshin gave him a withering look. "Is this one of your partners? Because we haven't been introduced. I thought I was dealing with you, Hildegard, and that these were your bodyguards. Correct me if I'm wrong."

He kept his gaze on the other man. That man watched him in return. No bodyguard, then. Someone important. So important, in fact, that they didn't want to introduce him.

Deshin had heard about this with the Black Fleet, that they had nameless negotiators, people who were all the more terrifying because they were impossible to read and know.

Iban glanced at the other man. Her expression hardened, her eyes glazed, telling Deshin that she was concentrating more on communicating through her links than on what was going on around her.

If Deshin had been a slightly different man, he would have smiled. He had gotten her to forget that she was in someone else's office, around someone else's technology.

Technology that was as sophisticated, if not more sophisticated, than the technology of the Black Fleet.

"Ms. Iban?" Deshin said, deciding he had let her lose focus long enough. "Does this man speak for you?"

Her eyes focused on Deshin.

"He's part of my team," she said. "He's—"

"If you're going to make an introduction," Deshin said, "I really don't care. Did you want to talk business or not?"

She gave the man a sideways glance, probably accompanied by yet another chastising link comment, and said, "I thought you weren't interested in working with us."

"You told me that you can get clones," Deshin said, ignoring her challenge. "I'm assuming you mean designer criminal clones."

"Anyone can get designer criminal clones," she said. "You can get them without us, and you have, at least according to the records I saw."

He didn't smile, even though he wanted to. His people had planted that information over a week ago, just for this moment. Before the second attacks on Armstrong, which had given him a bit of concern. He hadn't wanted to be accused of working with clones, at least not from the Armstrong side of things.

So far, the law enforcement community had its hands full, with the attempted bombings. He hoped that by the time they got to a search of the records of people who had asked for designer criminal clones, his name would be scrubbed from the list as if he had never put it there.

"These twenty men," she said, waving a hand at the image, "aren't designer criminal clones, and you know it. I don't appreciate being played, Mr. Deshin."

Oh, he had just begun to play with her. He smiled, just a little.

"I'm not playing you," he lied. "I'm waiting for you to talk with me."

She raised her head, as if he had surprised her. Then she again swept her hand toward the images on that clear wall.

"Those men weren't just grown," she said. "They weren't just 'designed.' They were trained, honed, tested, and ultimately chosen to do that job. They were picked based not just on their physical traits, but also on their willingness to complete the job no matter what."

"A few didn't finish," Deshin said, trying to keep his tone neutral. He was grateful that several were unsuccessful with at least part of their mission; it saved a few lives, albeit not enough.

"A few didn't," she said. "In the field, you never know what a man will do."

"Sounds like an excuse to me," he said.

She raised her chin. He had offended her.

"It's not an excuse. If you want predictable behavior, get an android. See if it can infiltrate the places that these clones infiltrated. Or, for that matter, the Peyti clones. Good Lord, they were embedded in the system for *years*, and no one suspected a thing. That's useful. The fact that there's a bit of a failure rate is to be *expected*, not criticized."

She had a point. A chilling point, but a good one.

"You're sensitive," he said.

"You're critical," she said.

"I'm trying to buy a product," he said, mentally wincing. "Of course I'm going to be critical."

She started to glance at the men again, then stopped herself. She kept her gaze focused on Deshin. "What kind of job is this for?"

"Something similar to the Anniversary Day attacks," he said.

"With humans?" she asked.

"With humans," he said.

"How similar?" she asked.

"I'm not telling you that," he said.

She sighed. "Then I can't help you. Because I need specifics. Otherwise, I can't place an order."

He put his hands on the chair behind his desk, as if he were going to sit down. Instead, he used the desk to shield himself from the view of the three Black Fleet members. He didn't want an involuntary twitch to give anything away.

He didn't say anything. He was beginning to learn that was the best way to handle this woman, because she would keep talking.

And she did.

"I ask for a couple of reasons," she said. "The first is pretty simple. With last week's failed attack, the Moon's authorities are going to monitor clones heavily. There's already legislation being proposed by the Earth

Alliance that would make use of multiple clones of the same individual illegal and subject to huge penalties. The legislation would also allow for what most of us would consider a huge invasion of privacy if those same actions were directed at us."

He hadn't been aware of any legislation. He made a mental note to check up on her sources, to see if she was actually right about this.

"The second reason I'm telling you this is that a group of specialized clones, like those twenty men, don't come cheap, and they certainly aren't something you can order up today for a job next week. Those men were all thirty years in the making, and they were the cream of a very important crop. Hundreds of other clones were rejected for that same job." She crossed her arms. "Anyone who buys clones for a mission like that one will have to pay for a dozen failed clones for every viable clone. And not just a small fee, but creation, maintenance, and training. We're talking a million per clone minimum."

He felt momentarily dizzy, and realized he hadn't taken a breath since she said that. If she was correct about the cost of the clones, then whoever had authorized the first attack on the Moon had easily spent a quarter of a billion on that one attack alone, maybe more.

He shouldn't have been surprised, but he was. That was a lot of money on a malicious event. The kind of money that made him think less of revenge or opportunism, and more about some kind of coup.

Deshin suddenly felt out of his depth. For the first time since he started to pursue this, he wanted to consult with someone. Maybe Miles Flint.

Deshin had been using Flint to his own ends, to find out information and plant seeds to get the official investigation moving, but Deshin also respected Flint.

Flint was one of the few people Deshin had met in the last two decades who couldn't be bought and didn't have an agenda that Deshin could find. People like that were too rare in Deshin's universe; he found he needed them so that he didn't become so cynical that he couldn't function.

All of which made Flint a good person to bounce some of these ideas off of, particularly when it came to coups and other things outside of Deshin's realm.

"Are you still interested, Mr. Deshin?" Iban asked.

Had she seen something cross his face? A bit of a calculation, perhaps? Something a bit more conniving?

If so, he hoped that she misinterpreted it.

"As I said." He kept his voice calm, making sure his words were deliberate. "I'm authorized to spend up to one billion on this project. I'm more concerned about the timing. Do we really have to wait thirty years for the clones?"

"It depends on what you want them for," she said. "There are various human clones of the assassin type that might be perfect for the job. Some of them will be ready in five years, some in ten, and some in twenty. If you want your own clones from an original of your choosing, then you'll have to wait at least twenty-five years, maybe more."

Deshin nodded. "I will need to inspect facilities, talk with other customers, look at the operation, before I ever commit to this kind of money."

"You said you're the middleman," she said. "Why don't you just let me speak to the buyer?"

He gave her a dismissive smile. "No."

"But you're asking me to go through you," she said. "Surely, you can go through me."

"No," he said again.

"Then you can understand why I won't work that way," she said.

He shrugged. "It's pretty simple, Ms. Iban. You are peddling a product. I am representing a buyer who is going to spend more money than you have probably seen in your lifetime. Of course, my buyer will get to inspect the merchandise, speak to previous buyers, and look at the operation. My buyer would be foolhardy not to."

"But—"

"And for obvious reasons," he said, "I will inspect first. My buyer does not want to be known, and if I deem you or your operation untrustworthy, then my buyer will not come out of the shadows. If this doesn't work for you, I'm sure I can find someone else to do business with."

She swallowed hard, then her eyes glazed. Something was happening on her links again.

Deshin had to work to keep his own gaze on her, so that he wouldn't look at the men. He didn't want them to know he had caught on to what they were doing.

"I'll be back in touch with you," she said.

"That's the best you can do?" he asked.

"I need to check—"

"All right," he said. "But be clear on this: while you're checking, I will be looking for someone else to do the job."

"Mr. Deshin, I'm sure—"

"That's all," he said. "I'm sure you can find your own way out."

She frowned ever so slightly, as if she wasn't sure what to make of this conversation. Then she nodded.

"I can," she said. She gestured with her fingers at the men who had accompanied her. "Let's go."

She walked slowly, as if she expected Deshin to stop her. He wasn't going to. His stomach flip-flopped as she walked, and it took all of his strength not to delete the image of those assassins before she even left the room.

She glanced over her shoulder as she stepped through the door, again as if she expected Deshin to stop her. He sat down in the chair, as if he had forgotten her already.

The men followed, then the doors closed behind them.

Make sure you track where they go through the building, Deshin sent to his security staff. *And have someone follow them—discretely—through the city.*

Yes, sir, his head of security sent.

Deshin raised his head, his gaze meeting that of his two guards. *Check for any tracking that they might have set up. I didn't see anything, but it means nothing.*

The guards nodded.

Deshin darkened the screen. He didn't take down the image immediately even though he wanted to.

He was going to find the creators of those sons of bitches. And he was going to stop them, whatever they were doing. And along the way, he was going to exact some revenge.

Just like the people of Armstrong would expect from criminal mastermind Luc Deshin.

Only this time, he knew that the people of Armstrong wouldn't object to anything he did.

16

The train pulled up at Armstrong Department of Correction & Rehabilitation Reception Center. The building was long and wide; a series of buildings, really, the kind of sprawl that had become common outside the domes on the Moon.

The Reception Center was only one of many Armstrong prisons. This one housed the dangerous prisoners who were being bound over for trial in one of Armstrong's local courts. The facility was, in theory, as heavily guarded as Armstrong's super maximum security prison was.

The tracks ended inside Facility One, a grayish building made worse with its layer of Moon dust. Leckie knew the prison officials tried to clean the place, but buildings outside the city with their own private domes to maintain usually didn't have the filtration systems that city domes had.

At least, not the government buildings outside the dome, and certainly not government buildings housing prisoners and undesirables. Leckie wiped a hand over her forehead, and adjusted her helmet downward. It was riot gear, just like her outfit was, although she'd never been part of a prison riot.

She doubted she would be part of one now.

She looked at the rows and rows of Peyti clones that she guarded. They still stared out the window, as if they had a hive mind and they'd received a uniform command to look in the same direction. Although the clones on the other side of the train car were looking out the windows on that side.

The clones' posture disturbed her. She wanted them to do something. She *needed* them to do something.

But the android guards watched her as well. She had realized, halfway from Glenn Station, that the androids weren't there as much for the clone prisoners as they were for guards like her.

Her hand had been on her laser pistol for damn near the entire ride. She'd been on alert, just waiting—hoping—for a moment to use the weapon.

Hell, if there hadn't been android guards with their little see-everything, record-everything eyes, she would have started something herself. She knew she wasn't alone.

Half the guards on this train—half the *human* guards on this train—would have loved an excuse to toss those creatures into the Moon dust alongside the tracks. *Oh, sorry, sir,* she would have said to some investigator upon arrival. *They were trying to flee. Honestly, sir, we didn't do as much as we probably should have to pull them back.*

Fantasies. It was all fantasies now.

She activated her own environmental part of the riot suit, just in case. She felt the temperature around her cool slightly—it had been stuffy on the train. The helmet for her riot gear had lowered, putting a thin barrier between her and everything around her.

That action calmed her a little.

Since she'd brought prisoners here half a dozen times before, turning on the environment and letting the helmet down had become part of her routine. It felt normal to activate the settings, while nothing about this trip had been normal.

She made herself take a deep breath, tasting the stale air in her suit. That too was familiar. She'd learned after her first visit here to turn on the environment before she got off the train.

The authorities at the Reception Center kept the temperatures at the bottom end of human comfort, warm enough that an unsuited human could survive, but cold enough that the survival would be uncomfortable.

Between the chill and the dust-coated air, she preferred to smell the sour stench of a rarely used suit.

Some of her colleagues activated their riot gear as well. Across the car, near the other door, Dunbar Willis adjusted his helmet. The faceplate reflected his eyes. They met hers.

He was just as angry as she was at this assignment—maybe angrier, since his sister had died on Anniversary Day. She had been a first responder. His other sister would have died a week ago, if she hadn't left a meeting to get some coffee for everyone. She was a legal assistant—or had been—until all of this happened. Her firm lost two senior partners and some important associates that day.

Willis nodded at her. Leckie wondered what that meant, if anything. They hadn't planned anything, but then, that didn't always matter. She usually knew how Willis thought.

She made herself look away from him, at the Peyti clones. They continued to stare, as if they had no idea what they were about to experience.

But most of them had been practicing lawyers for years. They knew. They knew they were going to be transferred to this facility, strip searched again, put in some kind of cell with others of their kind, and run through a series of unnecessary procedures in the name of transfer.

They knew it would be rough, and they didn't seem bothered by it.

Of course, why would they? These assholes had tried to blow themselves up, so they probably welcomed discomfort. It probably added to their martyrdom. Or maybe they saw it as an opportunity to die like they were supposed to.

That thought made her heart rate increase. Maybe they expected the guards to attack them, to hurt them, to kill a few of them. Maybe, if she got violent, she would be playing into their fantasies, not her own.

She wondered if she should let Willis know.

Then, she shook off the thought. She didn't even know if regular Peyti had fantasies—and these weren't regular Peyti. They were manufactured creatures. Things.

Dangerous things.

The train came to a complete stop with a whistle of brakes. Whistling brakes happened only in dust-covered areas—in the emptiness of the Moonscape, for example, or in badly maintained domes. She'd never heard it in here.

It made her shudder.

None of the Peyti moved.

She grabbed her rifle, brought it into position, and held it like a lifeline.

"Okay," she said in Standard. She'd be damned if she spoke Peytin to them, even though she knew enough words to get some recalcitrant Peyti off a transport train. "We're disembarking as a unit. You will do as ordered. You will be quiet and mannered and move slowly. You will not cause trouble."

They didn't look at her, which made her even angrier. They kept looking out the damn windows, as if they could see something important.

"Just so you know," she added, "we have a do-not-kill order for you assholes. You act up and try to suicide by guard and we won't be able to kill you. We won't even try. So if you're going to try to achieve that suicide you failed to achieve when your little bombs didn't go off, try to achieve it somewhere else. Got that?"

Where did that speech come from? Willis sent. *I don't remember that order.*

She looked across those turned Peyti heads at him. His head was tilted slightly, making his eyes impossible to read from this distance. A few of the other guards were looking at her as well.

I'm not feeding into their crazy, she sent. *They can kill each other for all that I care, but I'm not doing what they tried to do.*

He moved his head. She couldn't tell if that was a nod or if he was shaking his head. Or if he was just thinking about what she had said.

"All right," she said aloud. "We're going to disembark by row. We will begin with the row at the opposite end of the car from me."

You handle the release, okay? She sent to Willis. *You stand in each row, getting them out.*

She did that because she trusted him, and because she wanted to keep an eye on him.

She said to the damn Peyti, who still weren't looking at her, "When Guard Willis releases your row, you will walk forward and pass me. The android guards will lead you onto the platform where you will be met by the prison's guards. At that moment, you will be in their custody and you will be their responsibility."

None of the Peyti moved. None of the guards did as well. They had all heard this speech before—except for that opening part. She was using the standard procedure, just like she was supposed to do.

Start 'em up, she sent to Willis.

He took a step forward, clutching his laser rifle almost horizontally. It looked like he wanted to use its grip to slam into the Peyti leaving the row on the left, and then swing it around to club the Peyti leaving the row on the right.

She'd seen him fight like that. She knew he was good at it.

"You," he said to the group to his left. "Get out."

The Peyti didn't move.

She sighed. She had known this would happen.

Willis raised his head toward her. *Now what?*

Grab one, she sent.

He picked up the closest Peyti clone by its arm. She could hear the stick-like bones snap across the car.

A couple of the clones winced, and she smiled. Finally, a reaction.

Willis lifted that Peyti clone up.

"You're *clones* and lawyers," he said. "So I really don't need to remind you that I don't have to treat you like full members of the Earth Alliance. I can do what I want, as long as you're still breathing when you get to that prison. Now. *Move*."

He shoved the Peyti clone forward. The clone staggered toward Leckie, clutching his arm. His wide liquid eyes met hers, and she saw pain in them. His features had turned a pale sickly blue.

"Do what Willis says," she said. "You know we would all love to see if every one of your arms makes that same noise when they get snapped."

Now, the Peyti were looking at her. *All* of them. They had been treated like full individuals, *lawyers*, respected members of the community, until now.

They were finally catching a clue that they didn't control this situation.

The Peyti clone next to the empty seat stood, followed by the rest of the Peyti in the row. The others shifted as well. A few moved their arms forward, as if that would protect them from Willis's rough hands.

The injured clone passed her. Others watched him go.

She longed to trip it, but she didn't. She was barely holding herself back.

The others started moving down the aisle. A few of them passed her, and more than one looked at her. She thought she saw shock in their eyes.

They had expected to be killed by the guards but not hurt? Or had they simply not thought about this part at all? They were so used to the respect accorded to lawyers in this culture. The change in treatment was starting to get to them.

Good. They had to realize that their lives would be hell from now on.

She would do everything she could to guarantee that.

17

Miles Flint sat in his home office, pretending to work. He had one lamp on over the antique desk he had bought on a whim. It didn't have screens or any kind of computer link. It was just a piece of furniture—a table with only one space cut out of it for a chair—and he usually enjoyed spending time at it.

Today, it was just a piece of furniture. And the apartment was too damn big for two human beings to share.

The office was on the opposite side of the apartment from the bedrooms. When he and his daughter Talia first looked at the place, he had initially thought that a good arrangement. Now, he hated it.

He had to go through the living room to get to the "personal" side of the apartment.

This place was not just huge, it was embarrassing. He hated showing off his wealth by owning one of the largest penthouse apartments in Armstrong. But he had acquiesced when Talia begged him to get an apartment for the two of them, not the house he had wanted.

Her mother had been kidnapped out of a house in Valhalla Basin, before Flint had even known that Talia existed. That had been the crisis which introduced him to his daughter. She had mostly recovered from it, at least as far as he could tell, but certain things made her dig in her heels.

Staying away from houses had been one.

Making him keep his promise about letting her pick out the apartment had been the other.

She hadn't wanted this apartment because it was showy, but because it had the best security in the city, and because it had bathrooms so large that Flint's real office in Old Armstrong could have fit into just one of them. Talia loved her amenities, or she had until a few days ago.

Now, she didn't seem to love anything.

Flint ran a hand through his blond curls and made himself breathe. He had been a high-level computer programmer, a police officer, a police detective, and a Retrieval Artist. He had dealt with murderers from several species, saved lives, handled harrowing circumstances, and lost a child to an even more harrowing circumstance. His wife had betrayed him, not once, but dozens of times in the cruelest possible ways, and he had survived.

In fact, he had thrived—or he wouldn't be able to afford this place.

What he hadn't been able to do was comfort his daughter after her experience a week ago. She had left her room for meals, where she sat sullenly, staring at the food before she forced herself to eat it.

She wouldn't talk to him. Her lovely copper skin had become sallow, her cheeks chapped, her blue eyes—so like his—red-rimmed.

He knew she'd been crying. When she would finally fall asleep, he would sneak into her room, and see the damp spots on her pillow. Sometimes he even saw a tear leak out of her closed eyes.

She wasn't faking sleep, either. The sadness had followed her into her dreams, giving her no respite.

During the Peyti Crisis, she had been at school. Flint had thought her safe. He had put her in Aristotle Academy, the best school on the Moon, the place where everyone from high-end government officials to the exceedingly wealthy sent their children, both for a good education and for protection against whatever might threaten the families.

But the Peyti clones who had attacked the Moon had been "sleepers," a term that Chief of Security of the Moon, Noelle DeRicci, had started using the day after the Crisis, and one that everyone in the media had picked up. It didn't quite fit: those Peyti clones weren't sleeping. They were taking advantage of their differences and their intellects to ingratiate themselves in human society.

The Peyti were fragile-looking aliens, who wore masks that obscured most of their faces, and enabled them to breathe in a human environment. The masks, it turned out, also masked their identities. Humans had grown accustomed to thinking that all Peyti looked alike, and the Peyti clones had taken advantage of that.

They *had* looked alike. There were hundreds of them, all clones of something quite rare in Peyti culture, a mass murderer who had committed genocide decades before. That wasn't a coincidence, as everyone on the Moon knew.

Flint stood, and slipped his hands in the back pockets of his brown pants. He wore a sweater over them because he'd been cold since this last attack, even though the temperature controls in his apartment hadn't changed in the last week.

He'd been affected by this second attack—hell, he'd been affected by the first attack—but not as badly as Talia.

Talia, who had forbidden him from sitting in the living room. The living room was the center of the apartment, and if he sat there, he could hear her rustling about in her room. He could also hear her sob, or at least, he had heard her on the first day after the attacks.

Then he had gone in and comforted her until she pushed him away. The sobbing had stopped, but the tears hadn't, and he had no idea what to do about it.

He had been consulting with several networked psychologists, mostly people he had known when he worked with the police, and they just told him to give her time.

But his daughter was strong and brilliant, and this kind of collapse was unlike her. She had survived an attack by her mother's kidnappers, and she had survived not just the loss of her house, but the loss of all she had ever known.

Including her identity. Because the great shock for Talia, in addition to learning that her mother had lied to her about pretty much everything, was the fact that Talia was not an original child. She was not a natural-born human being.

She was a clone of Emmeline, Flint's natural daughter, who had died in a day care center when she was an infant. Flint had learned that Talia's mother Rhonda had cloned Emmeline several times for purposes of her own. Most of those clones were older than Talia, whom Rhonda had kept and raised as a natural child, until everything fell apart around her three and a half years ago.

When Flint got Talia, he had adopted her immediately. He had done so for two reasons: He wanted her to feel valued and loved, but he also wanted her to be a legitimate human being in the eyes of the Earth Alliance. His actions had legally declared her a natural human being, even though she had a day of creation document instead of a birth certificate.

The hatred of clones inside the Alliance—and on the Moon especially—had only gotten worse since the Anniversary Day attacks.

Flint hadn't been out in public much since the Peyti Crisis, but he suspected that what had once been acceptable hatred had probably become some kind of vitriol.

For that reason alone, he had been glad his daughter had barely come out of her room—at least on the first day after the attacks. But now, he wanted her beside him. He had vowed, after he had looked one of the Peyti assassins in the eye at Talia's school, that he would make sure that one clone alone would come to justice. What was between him and that Peyti was personal.

But he hadn't been able to deal with that Peyti; he hadn't felt comfortable leaving Talia alone—and he had no one to ask for help. Those he trusted to stay with Talia were busy with their own problems in these days after the crisis.

He walked to the door of his office, hovered there for a moment, then walked back inside. He should have been researching Uzvekmt, the Peyti mass murderer on whom the clones were based, or figuring out what these clone lawyers had worked on throughout their years on the

Moon. He should have been tracing their origins, but he hadn't had the ability to concentrate the way he wanted to.

He could only think of Talia.

His links chirruped, and the sound caught him off-guard. He didn't have an aural setting for his link alarms. He frowned, and examined the link, and realized that it was an inactive private link that he hadn't used for nearly a year.

His frown deepened before he remembered that he had given that link out just recently and only because that link wasn't associated with anyone or anything else.

Luc Deshin.

Flint wasn't sure how he felt about Deshin. Deshin had given him good information about the Anniversary Day attacks before the Peyti Crisis, and they hadn't really spoken since. Deshin's odd little son, Paavo, went to the Aristotle Academy, and both men had seen each other the day of the crisis.

Flint had already been at the school—he had hurried there to save Talia, only to discover her outside a clear barrier. People—humans—had died in that room when the school had changed the room's environment from human to Peyti normal, deactivating the bomb on the Peyti lawyer's face.

Among the dead was a boy whom Talia had claimed she disliked. Only the boy had done something just that day which had confused her, and made her feel guilty about his death at the same time.

Flint had guessed that she was feeling guilty over wishing the boy dead, but she claimed that wasn't it. She said she wasn't mourning the boy, and Flint believed that. But something about the boy's death—about the fact that she had witnessed his death—had triggered this breakdown.

The link chirruped again, and Flint hesitated. Deshin had proven himself trustworthy on the Anniversary Day attacks. He also loved his son, something completely in evidence during the Peyti Crisis. Deshin had swooped into the Academy, gathered Paavo in his arms, and hadn't moved for what seemed like hours. The boy had clung to him, clearly feeling safe.

Flint knew whatever he thought of Deshin and Deshin's various enterprises, that the man was capable of great love.

Flint sighed and sat down on one of the faux leather chairs that Talia had picked out for his office, saying they looked "professional," whatever that meant. He clicked the link on visual, knowing that Deshin would be able to see his face, just like he could see Deshin's.

Deshin appeared from the waist up. Behind him, windows showed the curve of Armstrong's dome over its skyline. The visible part of that skyline included the apartment building where Flint was. Flint wondered if that was a coincidence.

"Mr. Deshin," Flint said as flatly as he could. He didn't want to show any emotion, even though he was certain that his exhaustion showed.

Deshin's square face looked pinched, as if he had eaten something that disagreed with him. He had shadows under his eyes, which surprised Flint. Usually shadows didn't show on men with skin as dark as Deshin's.

"Mr. Flint," Deshin said, nodding just a little. "I need to talk with you in person. It's important."

Flint shook his head. "Let's use the links and trust the encryption."

"No," Deshin said. "We don't dare. I've already arranged our usual meeting location. I'd like to see you there in an hour."

Their usual meeting location, if it could be called that, was the offices of Oberholst, Martinez & Mlsnavek. It turned out that both Flint and Deshin shared an attorney, Celestine Gonzalez. She had handled Talia's adoption and a case involving Deshin's son.

Flint did not want to leave the apartment, not even to go to the law offices for a short time. "I'm not taking orders, Mr. Deshin. I'm in the middle of a family crisis, and I don't want to—"

"Do you remember speaking to me a few days before last week's attack? I have information that may help all of us, and I need to run it by you before I take any other steps."

Flint sighed. He had asked Deshin to use his connections to find out more about the designer criminal clones that had attacked Armstrong on Anniversary Day. The two men hadn't spoken at all since a second set of clones tried to make a second attack.

"Mr. Deshin, you don't need my help on this. You know more about this area than I ever will—"

"Flint, listen." Deshin's eyes had grown hard. "I already spoke to some people, and came across some information that has me—I need to talk with you. You'll see why."

Flint glanced at the door to his office. He couldn't leave Talia. Would she come with him? He wasn't even certain of that.

"I'll do my best," Flint said.

"Best isn't good enough," Deshin said. "You don't want me to be alone on this information. We need both of us on it."

Flint's heart had started pounding. "I can't leave Armstrong right now."

"Not asking you to. I'm asking you to meet me in less than an hour. I will see you there."

Deshin signed off.

Flint stared at the empty spot where Deshin's image had been. Every time Flint interacted with Deshin, he understood why that man had a reputation for ruthlessness. Deshin didn't scare Flint, but something about the man put Flint at attention each time they spoke.

Flint ran his hand through his hair again.

Deshin wouldn't have contacted him if it weren't important. And right now, important took on a whole new meaning. Important might mean the future of the Moon, or even the Earth Alliance itself.

Talia would understand.

She would have to.

18

THE BULLPEN WAS FULL OF DETECTIVES. NYQUIST HATED THE NICKNAME of this part of the First Detective Division, but it was accurate. It was a large meeting area in Armstrong Police Headquarters reserved for times like this, when all detectives needed to be briefed on something.

The ceiling was high, the walls curved, and the floor was littered with built-in platforms that could rise at the touch of a button. The platforms were there for a variety of reasons. The chief of detectives before Gumiela had liked to play with the buttons, so if anyone raised a hand to talk, that person would rise above the group, whether he liked it or not.

Gumiela liked to be the most important person in the room, so she never used that feature. Instead, she used the platforms the way they were intended, to confuse someone who wanted to spy on the proceedings. There would be no way to know—until she arrived—where she'd stand or how she would conduct business.

Like he always did at these things, Nyquist leaned against a back wall, near an exit. He used to arrive early and watch the techs sweep the room for foreign equipment. He stopped doing that when he started seeing holes in their procedures.

The inefficiencies bugged him enough that he would either have to say something, which would then get him involved in the search for outside taps, or he would have to stop watching what happened before everyone else arrived.

He opted to stop watching.

He couldn't fix what he didn't know.

He crossed his arms and tilted his head back, feeling the exhaustion from the night before filling him. He loved his time with DeRicci, even when she was stressed beyond belief, but the lack of sleep, combined with the tension of his job, made him feel worse than usual this morning.

"C'mon," a female voice said beside him. "Don't tell me you of all people aren't sleeping these days. I figured you had balls of steel and could sleep through anything if need be."

Nyquist opened his eyes and looked down. Savita Romey stood beside him, smiling. Her dark eyes met his, and he felt that familiar catch in his heart.

Right after he had spent the night with DeRicci, he would have to see Romey. Spending time with DeRicci didn't stop the attraction from flowing between Nyquist and Romey, deep and fine.

She wore pants so faded he couldn't tell if they had originally been blue or gray. Her shirt was loose, and it took him a moment to realize it had one of the local high school's logos on it. She had sons, and one of them had to be in high school now. The fact she was wearing his shirt meant that the state of her laundry was the same as his.

They had all been worked ragged. She just didn't look it, unless he looked closely.

"Rumor is that they're going to pair us up for interrogations. Want to be my partner, handsome?" she asked.

He wished she hadn't added the "handsome." He would have said yes automatically if she hadn't. They had partnered up twice before, the first time on the Whitford case just before Nyquist nearly died in a Bixian assassins' attack, and the second on Anniversary Day, when they were both supposed to investigate Arek Soseki's murder, before everyone realized that the death wasn't isolated.

"Maybe our partnerships are cursed," he said.

"Or maybe we're in an extraordinary period in Armstrong history, and we need to accept that." She leaned against the wall and crossed her arms, mirroring his position. "I really want someone I can trust, not one of those idiots out there, who think they can do a job, and really can't."

In spite of himself, Nyquist smiled. He liked this woman. He liked her humor, he liked her personality, and he liked her thoroughness. She was the best partner he'd ever had.

Before Anniversary Day, in fact, he'd asked her to partner with him twice. After, everything got screwed up, and he barely saw her.

He barely saw anyone.

"We make a good team," she said, scanning the room. It had filled with detectives—all human, he noted. Half were dressed up, and the other half looked like unmade beds.

He knew, right then, he would only work with an unmade bed. If someone had enough time to dress up for a meeting with the boss—a *group* meeting with the boss—then that person was not busy enough. If someone wasn't busy enough, they simply weren't doing the job.

"You think they'll let us pick who we partner with?" he asked.

"I think they would like anything that makes their lives easier," she said. "Wouldn't you?"

He would love an easier life, at least in theory. Back to the days when criminals were dumb and easy to find. Back when his biggest problem was some ethical dilemma caused by the conflict between some other culture's laws and his own. Back when a Disty Vengeance Killing seemed like a problem instead of something normal.

"I don't think 'easier' is on the menu these days." Nyquist couldn't see where Gumiela was setting up. She hadn't come into the room yet.

But it was getting hotter in here and stuffier. Detectives kept entering, pressing against him as they passed.

Romey bumped him, probably because someone bumped her, and then she did not move away. He probably should have moved away, but he didn't.

"I don't think pre-choosing partners is something they'll disagree with," she said. "Unless you're talking about a different kind of easier?"

He sighed softly. His thoughts had been pretty much the same all morning. That was one of the reasons he was dreading today's meeting.

"I don't care what the brass says," he said softly, thinking as he did so that he should probably have spoken to her on his links. "We're not going to be able to successfully interrogate a bunch of Peyti lawyers."

Romey's entire body was pressed against his. He looked around her, saw that several other detectives pushed against her.

"Oh, I don't know," she said with a grin. "It depends on the rules you choose to follow."

Nyquist frowned at her.

What do you mean? he asked, going with his gut. The rest of this conversation had to be on their private links.

We can interrogate Peyti lawyers, she sent, her grin widening. *Or we can interrogate a bunch of clones.*

He felt a chill. He didn't have to ask her what she meant. He knew.

But she started to explain anyway. *There are no rules for 'interrogating' property. Hell, as long as the property is logged in, we can break it or discard it. We just need to file documentation on what happened to the property.*

His heart was beating hard. He glanced around the room, feeling worried that someone else had heard, and knowing that no one had.

That might be the letter of the law, he sent, *but that's not the* spirit *of the law.*

Oh, God, she sent. *Not that old saw about justice versus legality, right? We don't owe these bastards any kind of justice. Under the law, they have no rights at all.*

She was correct. He knew that, and it scared him. Because if she had thought of it, then dozens of others in the room had as well. Maybe that was what this meeting was about. Maybe it wasn't about picking partners at all.

Or maybe it was.

The chill he felt grew more powerful. Those who objected to the "property" definition would be paired with others who objected, and those who preferred the "property" definition would be paired with like-minded detectives. Those in charge would know, and success would be measured by results.

He leaned his head against the wall.

He also knew which group would get the best results and it wouldn't be the ones who followed the spirit of the law.

You disapprove, Romey sent. *You were there on Anniversary Day. One of these clones tried to kill you—someone you've known for years. And you still disapprove of following the law.*

Nyquist wasn't certain what part of her comment to respond to. He found that he couldn't look at her.

He had respected her. He was attracted to her. He *liked* her.

She was suggesting something wholly repugnant to him. He was having trouble wrapping his mind around her words. Not because of *what* she said—he hadn't thought of what she said, but it didn't surprise him that *someone* in this room had come up with it—but he was surprised at *who* said it to him.

And he was surprised at himself. How could he have misjudged her so badly?

He had to respond. He couldn't keep silent. So he sent, *You're right. Someone I had known for years tried to kill me during the Peyti Crisis. Someone. A person.*

She elbowed him, probably trying to get him to look at her. He didn't want to. He felt childish about it, but he wasn't sure he could face her right now. So he shifted just a bit to his right, moving a little closer to another detective who gave him an odd look.

Nyquist shrugged. He mentally debated moving across the room, when a door opened a few meters from him, and Gumiela's team entered.

The meeting had officially begun.

19

Without the elaborate environmental programs, Salehi's office was distressingly normal. Gray walls, black furniture, whitish-grayish carpet. He had forgotten what the place looked like without the magical, make-believe overlay.

He had designed it this way, so that when he concentrated on work, he would have to *concentrate* on work, and be willing to leave the comfort of his own sanctuary to do whatever needed to be done.

Unfortunately for his potential clients, he had been unwilling to leave his sanctuary these last few years. He had taken less and less work. He hadn't exercised his mind enough. And he'd made stupid pronouncements to the new hires.

His standard speech went something like this: *You'll hit a point when you'll wonder what's the point of defense. You'll feel tainted. You'll think you've sold your soul for a bit of wealth and privilege. That's why you do pro bono work. Or you volunteer for a quarter back at the Impossibles. You'll see the need for defense then. You'll remember it's not just about the guilty. It's also about what's right.*

And then, when half of the hires moved on (and blamed him for their shattered idealism) and the other half became money-grubbing whores, he would say fatuously that no one ever listened to him.

Hell, he didn't even listen to himself.

It's not just about the guilty. It's also about what's right.

Wasn't that what Shishani had just said to him? So what if the Peyti clones had tried to destroy most of the domes on the Moon? They would be treated like *property*, not like Peyti, and that could mean all kinds of disastrous things—for them.

A lesser man would say too damn bad. Or might even decide that they deserved those things. (They probably did.) An even lesser man would take the case for the money. (Screw you, Schnabby, you bastard. *You* defend them if all you want is money.)

But Shishani was right: Salehi could make a difference. A major difference in clone law. Clone law was inherently unfair. Salehi could change it all. Yes, he'd have to go to bed with mass murderers, but he would improve life in the Alliance for millions of very good citizens.

Sometimes good things were built on the backs of very bad events.

Besides, dealing with bad people for good reasons was what he had signed on for, back at the Impossibles. With his pedigree, he could have stepped into a prosecutorial role or he could have gotten on a judgeship track instead of going to the Impossibles. He didn't have school loans, so he didn't have to work them off in the public defender's office.

But he had worked in the worst, most notorious part of the Alliance's judicial system. Not because he was altruistic (okay, he was), but because someone had bet him he couldn't survive that place. Everyone, from his professors to his parents, believed that his delicate upper-class upbringing hadn't prepared him for life in the Impossibles—and it hadn't.

But that upbringing had given him a certain invincibility, a certain sense of what was right. He had needed it in the Impossibles. He was often dealing with clients who had broken a law that they hadn't even realized existed, a law that made no sense to a human being.

The Earth Alliance was built on the idea that local trumped the Alliance—at least when it came to events that happened within a culture. If a human smashed a gold cup on Ostii, the human would be forced to lose an eye for shaming some Ostii God, because the aliens who governed the planet believed that crap, and anyone who went to the planet had to abide by Ostii law.

He always thought of that example because it had been the basis of the first case he lost in the Impossibles. The prosecuting attorney—as green as Salehi was—said after the thirty-second gavel down was over, *Asshole, didn't you take Alien Cultures first year? You should know this stuff.*

Salehi had known it. He somehow hadn't believed until that moment that the Alliance laws protecting local customs applied to actual living beings.

To say learning that was a rude awakening was an understatement.

It certainly wasn't the worst thing he'd seen at the Impossibles, where every judge was horribly overworked, every defense attorney was unable to have an hour to review a case, and all of the legal rulings were stacked against anyone unfortunate enough to walk through those doors.

His clients often hadn't done what was right—at least under the law—but he felt they should have been treated fairly, and they usually weren't, because they were poor, unable to afford any of the amenities that he had, or they didn't understand the various cultures, or they simply weren't smart enough to realize what was happening to them.

He hadn't looked down on them, like so many public defenders had did. He got angry for them. He had *defended* them.

And then he had come here, a firm built on defense. But it was defense for rich people, and he had slowly come to despise that.

Hence his little speech, his attempt at touching the others around him.

His desire to improve the universe around him.

About the time Salehi thought that impossible, Shishani threw his idealism in his face.

You have to defend the worst to protect the best, he had once told a third-year lawyer. That lawyer was now one of the firm's top earners, and on track to make partner.

She had taken the advice.

Salehi had let the problems get to his heart. And he knew this case—these cases—would get to his heart as well.

He wasn't sure he was capable of hardening it enough.

After all, he wouldn't just be dealing with the worst, as he had told that young lawyer. He would be dealing with creatures that had no fellow-feeling, creatures willing to kill for a cause. Or worse, creatures somehow damaged in their creation, creatures deliberately missing something.

He shivered. He hoped the clones were identical to their original, because if they weren't, his case would be ever so much harder.

His case.

He was already thinking of it in a proprietary way.

He rubbed his hands on his bare arms, feeling goose bumps from the so-called normal temperature in his office. He got up, went to the large en suite bathroom/sleeping area he'd had built for the days when he believed he would be really ambitious and work eighteen hour days. He hadn't worked eighteen-hour days in years, but he still had the bed, the bathroom, and the clothes.

He pulled open the closet, seeing an array of high-end suits that someone had been replenishing, probably his legal assistant. Latest styles in the neutrals and light colors that Salehi preferred. He wondered where the old suits had gone. To some charity probably, because that was what he used to mandate.

He grabbed a tan suit with a long coat, and found a pale pink shirt. He changed, pulled back his hair, wondering if he should trim it. How much effort should he put into looking like a lawyer who actually gave a damn?

And when he asked that question of himself, he knew that he had just become a lawyer who gave a damn. If he was going to defend those mass murderers (*attempted*, he corrected himself. Then, because he was horribly out of practice, he corrected himself again. *Alleged*. They were *alleged* conspirators toward mass murder. Or maybe failed assassins for hire. Or something).

Anyway, he already foresaw what a disaster this all could be. Schnabby believed the cases would extend for years, and he was right. No matter how Salehi argued this, he would be arguing for these *alleged* killers for a decade, maybe more.

If the authorities on the Moon treated the *alleged* killers as property and destroyed them before their day in court, then Salehi might be arguing even longer.

He wasn't certain. After all, these were new waters, uncharted and unsung. He would change the law if he succeeded, but he would be using a case (and defendants) so heinous that he wouldn't be lauded for it.

He would be despised.

And strangely enough, that galvanized him even more.

He hadn't become a defense attorney to be liked.

Nor had he become one to be rich. Unlike his colleagues (but not the name partners) he didn't need the money. His family had owned this firm for generations. He had money coming out of his ass. He loathed money. Sometimes he actually believed that cliché that money was the root of all evil.

Hell, Salehi always looked pointedly at Schnabby when spouting that cliché. Because Schnabby, despite inheriting millions in cash not counting the value of all the property and one-third of the firm, always believed that a man could never have enough money.

Salehi had seen Schnabby drool when he talked about the unlimited fees they could charge the Peyti government. Shishani, who liked to claim that she represented the healthy balance between the two men, knew that no client would pay forever, particularly in a heinous case.

But the Peyti, as lawyerly as they were, understood that this case would define not just the Earth Alliance, but the relationship the Peyti had with all members of the Alliance, maybe for decades.

The Peyti needed to get ahead of this case, and they were already years behind.

Salehi was already a week behind, and no matter what he did, he would be another week behind. He couldn't get to the Moon quickly.

He adjusted the sleeves on his suit, then headed back to his desk, finally feeling comfortable for the first time since he shut off the desert program. The clothes, the change in the environment, the cool white light on his desk, made him think like a lawyer again.

He needed injunctions. They could get to the Moon within hours. He needed to enjoin the authorities on the Moon from destroying the clones. He also needed to enjoin them against prosecuting the clones until he and his legal team arrived. He needed to enjoin the authorities from treating the clones as property. Property got placed in storage. Property could be dinged and damaged as part of the treatment in a case. Property wasn't protected, not like living beings were.

His stomach was in knots, not because he was taking this case, but because he was so far behind. Not just in time, but in thought.

He hadn't contemplated any of this stuff for years, if at all.

He would also need injunctions against taking DNA from the so-called conspirators. He needed to prevent the Moon's authorities from interviewing the clones or having any interaction besides the care that they would normally have if they were actual Peyti under the law.

He let out a breath, then rotated his shoulders, listening to them crack. He needed matching injunctions against any authorities in the Earth Alliance, in case the Moon's officials decided to make this one an Alliance case from the start, just to get around what he was doing.

And he needed this all quickly.

He couldn't write these on his own.

If Schnable and Shishani wanted to profit from these cases, then they needed to let him use all of the resources of S^3 to protect these cases until Salehi arrived.

He contacted his partners through the partner link.

I need you, our best attorneys, and our most promising associates in a meeting room right now. Prepare to work all night.

He didn't wait for their answers.

Because he had one more person he had to contact. Only one staff member of S^3 was on the Moon at the moment.

It didn't matter that the staff member was on leave of absence pending a review which (everyone knew) would lead to him stepping down from the firm.

That incident no longer mattered. Even if he wanted to, he wouldn't be able to step down. He actually had experience with the Earth Alliance and with clones, and Salehi needed him.

Salehi contacted his legal assistant on his links.

Find me Torkild Zhu, he sent. *And find him now.*

20

The law offices of Oberholst, Martinez & Mlsnavek looked empty, even though a skeleton staff ran the place. No receptionist guarded the first floor lobby. Instead, someone had set the automated reception protocols.

Luc Deshin didn't have to go through those. He'd cadged a staff chip years ago, although he'd never told anyone at the firm. They knew he came in and out at will, and they pretended they didn't mind.

He knew that the staff, with the exception of a few junior lawyers, were out of the building for the entire day, attending funerals. Most everyone who had died during the Peyti Crisis had been a lawyer or someone connected to a lawyer.

This firm had lost two lawyers who represented the Growing Pits, and were in the middle of an outside-the-dome conference when one of the idiot Peyti clones set off its mask. The explosion had destroyed an outbuilding and killed twenty.

The reason Deshin had insisted Flint come during this hour was because he knew the offices would be empty. Gonzalez had told him so.

She looked defeated. Normally, Celestine Gonzalez was unflappable. A tall woman who had become matronly in the last few years, Gonzalez also had a warm and vicious courtroom presence that Deshin admired.

But this morning, she had seemed smaller, older.

I can't help you, Luc, she had said. *I have this funeral, and then we're going to have a partners meeting this afternoon. The Moon's legal system is in great turmoil right now. Everyone's questioning everything. I don't have time for clandestine meetings between clients of mine who aren't supposed to know each other.*

Normally, she wasn't that harsh with her bluntness. Normally, she pretended that she didn't understand half the things Deshin was doing. Obviously, on this day, she didn't give a damn.

He had thanked her, asked a few questions that sounded sympathetic and weren't, and at the same time, downloaded her calendar for the day while he was talking with her. It was linked to the law firm's calendar, something he would point out in a few weeks, mentioning that confidentiality was easily breached at Oberholst, Martinez & Mlsnavek. That would appall her.

If she could be appalled any more.

Once he got past the automated receptionist, he took the elevator to the proper floor. He didn't care that he would show up on all the surveillance. If anyone asked him—if anyone bothered to look—he would say that he had thought he would have time to see Gonzalez before her meetings.

If someone mentioned Flint, Deshin would say he had no idea why the Retrieval Artist had shown up here. After Flint arrived, they were doing what anyone would do these days—discussing Anniversary Day, the Peyti Crisis, and what it meant for the Moon.

Deshin doubted anyone would challenge him. He brought too much money to this firm, and had for decades.

When he reached the right floor, he exited and waited in what passed for reception here. There was never an actual living being at this reception desk; it had always been automated, and it had always accepted him, whether he had been scheduled or not.

He just wanted to make sure he shepherded Flint through.

Deshin paced while he waited, still turning over his meeting with Iban in his mind. He'd managed to monitor a lot of her link communication, coming up with several names when she consulted via what she thought was a secure connection with the other members of her team.

They hadn't used full names, assuming that each had known who the other was referring to, but that didn't matter to Deshin. He already had staff investigating the connections, hoping he would not have to meet with Iban again and pretend to be interested in buying clones.

Still, he proceeded as if he were going to do business with her. He had several members of his staff follow her to a dilapidated building in Old Armstrong. They had to be careful not to get noticed. They'd tagged off each other, and someone had also included a small fly chip, something barely the size of a fingernail clipping that honed in on a subject and not only tracked it, but recorded it as well.

The chips weren't that sophisticated, and a lot of systems caught and disabled them, which was why he'd actually sent a human team as well.

None of them had been able to get in the building, at least not yet, and he had no idea if they'd been able to set up some kind of internal surveillance. He would find out soon enough, he supposed.

Fifteen minutes after the scheduled appointment time, the elevator opened to reveal Flint. He looked as harried as he had on the link, and Deshin finally saw why.

Flint's daughter—a stunning beauty even at her young age—was a shadow of her usual self. Her blond hair was dark and matted, her skin raw, and her wide mouth actually downturned. She was as tall as her father, but very slim. Her hands were shaking, and when she saw Deshin, she actually flinched.

She looked up at Flint, and Deshin knew they were communicating on their links. He guessed from her expression that Flint hadn't told her who he was meeting, and now she wanted to leave.

Flint put his hand on her shoulder and eased her off the elevator.

His gaze met Deshin's.

"Quiet around here, isn't it," Deshin said. "I've got business down the hall. Excuse me."

He figured Flint would need a moment with his daughter, and need a place to stash her.

Deshin pushed open the door to the conference room. No alarms went off, thanks to his staff chip. Nothing mentioned that he was unauthorized. He kept the lights off, and made sure the recording systems had been deactivated.

Then he settled at the head of the table, and waited.

21

Torkild Zhu sat in an upscale bar in one of the ritziest sections of Armstrong. He preferred ritzy these days. He had had enough of death and destruction. He also liked bars better than any other place in the Universe, upscale in particular.

First, none of his friends came here—or would come here, if he had actual friends.

Second, his ex-fiancée disapproved of bars now that she had become an angel of mercy.

And third, his nearly ex-father-in-law didn't own upscale bars. He owned some downscale bars that catered to the working class, although he would never admit it. Zhu had discovered all of that years ago, when he was looking for reasons not to marry Bernard Magalhães' beloved only daughter, the daughter Zhu had finally dumped on Anniversary Day, maybe fifteen minutes before the attacks.

His timing—on everything—stank. He even became an idealist in his very ritzy law firm about fifteen minutes before that hypocritical supporter of idealism Rafael Salehi decided to give up idealism forever.

They were going to fire Zhu, and at the moment, he didn't care. In fact, he didn't care enough to tender his resignation, although he was certain they expected him to do so.

Instead, he leaned on the highly polished bar, made of real marble imported from some famous building on Earth. Said famous building no longer existed (obviously) and some idiot with too much money decided to ship its various parts to the Moon where things like ancient marble from Earth were exotic and so extravagant that everyone cooed over it.

He was nursing rum of all things, something he'd only had at Magalhães family gatherings, and then only on special occasions. Rum was imported from Earth, and extremely dear. He'd learned, since he decided rum was his drink of choice—just a few days ago, in fact—that it came in a wide variety of expensive types, and he was determined to try them all until his money ran out.

The bartender was helping. The bartender, some guy with shoulders wider than Zhu's car, had to wear a historic costume with a blousy shirt unbuttoned to his naval, wide black breeches, and boots. The cocktail servers wore a variation, only with wide-brimmed hats and feathers.

Pirate costumes, someone had told him, but they looked nothing like the pirates he was familiar with. These costumes had something to do with Earth history, which he wasn't that familiar with—outside of its legal history, and then only the stuff that pertained to the Earth Alliance.

Not that he wanted to think about any of it. He liked the rum. It had a smoothness, a richness with a bit of cinnamon that appealed to him. It wasn't heavy like most beers made with Moon hops. And the rum gave him a good buzz, stronger than he expected the few times he'd gotten off the bar stool to get rid of some liquid.

Of course, like any good human bartender in an expensive place, this one also plied him with alcohol clearers, drinks and gases that made all of the effects of the alcohol disappear. Dive bars without human servers cut off the patrons after a certain amount of money or a certain number of drinks. Androids and bots were very literal about how much humans could drink.

But in high-end bars, they didn't care how much a man drank. They'd sober you up, feed you some food, maybe even give you a cot if needed, then ply you with liquor again.

And they'd do it until the money ran out.

Zhu wasn't sure when his money would run out. He was still getting paid by S^3, even though he knew that wouldn't last forever. He'd already given up his apartment on Athena Base, sold his furniture and his expensive toys, and had been thinking of donating his suits and evening clothes until he discovered the secrets of upscale bars.

He had a hotel room three blocks down from this bar, and he was still charging it to his S^3 expense account. Eventually that would catch up to him too. Eventually S^3 would ask him to reimburse them, and if he was feeling as surly then as he was feeling now, he'd sue them, claiming he'd still been on the payroll and so he was entitled to expenses.

His internal S^3 links chirruped. He waved a hand over his face, as if he could shut them off with his fingers, realized he was drunker than he thought, and grinned at himself.

The bartender, whose name Zhu had already forgotten (and his eyes were too blurry to read the little name tag that floated by the bartender's head), must have recognized the look. He handed Zhu a clearer.

Zhu tried to wave him off, but the bartender insisted.

"If you want more rum…" he said, letting his voice trail off. Or maybe Zhu had already stopped listening.

Because his links chirruped again. Oh, great. S^3 picked this moment to fire him. His life was such a joy.

He was going to ignore them.

He sipped the clearer, which was stronger than any clearer he'd gotten before—or maybe he'd just forgotten. The fog around his brain cleared as the liquid bit the back of his throat. It tasted like cleaning fluid and smelled like menthol mixed with gasoline. His eyes watered, and he sneezed.

An alarm sounded in his head. At first, he thought it the clearer, and then he realized it was his S^3 link. He'd never heard it do that before, but then, he'd never decided to ignore it before either.

He ran a hand over his face, decided to shut off the visual, and answered. *Yeah?*

Who cared about respect, anyway? They had none for him.

A tiny image of Rafael Salehi stood on Zhu's cocktail napkin. So much for shutting off the visual. Then Zhu realized that Salehi was wearing a suit.

Zhu frowned. Were there ghost links? Had something in all the chemicals he'd been consuming activated the archives? Because he didn't think he'd seen Salehi in a suit since the first day he went to the man's office over a decade ago.

Zhu wondered if he could ignore a ghost image.

"You're a mess, Torkild," tiny-suited Salehi said. Zhu couldn't remember Salehi ever saying that to him, not in all the years he'd known the man. "At least you're wearing a suit."

Zhu looked down at himself. He *had* shut off the visual, hadn't he?

"Yes, I can see you," Salehi said. "Your agreement with our firm allows us to override your link settings. Nice bar. Have you just discovered it or did you move in weeks ago?"

Zhu didn't know how to answer him. Zhu didn't want to seem obsequious, but that had been the basis of their relationship for years, and it was a hard habit to break. Zhu also didn't want to be rude to the man, since S^3 was funding not just his bender, but his lifestyle.

"You're in Armstrong, right?" Salehi asked.

"Yes," Zhu said.

The bartender looked at him sharply, and that was when Zhu realized that the bartender couldn't see Salehi.

Zhu asked the bartender, "Is there somewhere private I can go for a business conversation?"

The bartender pointed at a bunch of overgrown ferns. Zhu squinted at them. They were in a box shape, which clearly meant something to someone.

He stood, realized the clearer hadn't fixed whatever the rum had done to his balance, and put a hand on the marble bar. No one else sat on the stools—when did the other customers leave? The place had been unbelievably busy when he arrived. He didn't have to worry about losing his grip as he made his way to the stand of ferns.

He pushed inside them, found a glass booth, complete with a self-serve glass table and an uncomfortable glass stool. He sat down.

Salehi had traveled with him—of course, since Salehi was on his links, not here in person—and now the bastard stood in the middle of the glass table, looking weirdly adult and in control.

"Just fire me already," Zhu said tiredly.

To his surprise, Salehi smiled. "You should be so lucky. I need you on a case."

"Me?" Zhu laughed. "I embarrassed the firm. I lost us our best transport captain. I killed a friend of yours, however inadvertently. And now you want me to handle a case? I suppose it's here on the Moon and you can't get to the venue quickly enough."

"You got it in one, Torkild," Salehi said. "Whatever you think of yourself, you're still a damn good attorney, and one of the smartest men I know."

"You don't flatter people," Zhu said. "So stop playing with me and tell me what's up."

"I need you to make sure a series of injunctions we just sent to all of the authorities on the Moon remain in place," Salehi said.

All that rum Zhu had in his empty stomach sloshed, then rolled. He burped some of it, along with the clearer, and was glad that Salehi wasn't here in person. No one else needed to smell that.

"Injunctions against what?" Zhu asked.

Salehi held up his hands. Zhu recognized the gesture. It meant, *Give me a minute. I'm going to tell you something difficult.*

"I'm ahead of myself," Salehi said. "You're back in the game, Torkild. I need you to open an office in Armstrong. I need some associates, some of the best attorneys you can find—human of course."

"Of course," Zhu said, even though he didn't exactly understand why. S^3 hired attorneys from all species, even though the firm preferred cases involving humans. "What the hell's this about?"

"You'll have a large budget. Make sure these folks are people you can trust."

"You assume I know people here," Zhu said.

"You have connections," Salehi said. "I seem to recall that you know the Magalhães family?"

"I had a messy break-up with the Magalhães family," he said. "They don't like me much."

"Change that," Salehi said. "I'm going to be in Armstrong as soon as I can get there. That'll take—what?—a week? I want the offices up and running by then."

Zhu felt lightheaded. "What's the case?"

"Cases, most likely," Salehi said.

Zhu's stomach sloshed again. The clearer wasn't mixing well with the rum, or maybe his gut knew something his brain hadn't yet figured out.

"What are they?" he asked.

"We're working for Peyla."

It took him a moment to make the connection. Peyla. The Peyti home world. Peyti. S^3 was a firm of defense attorneys.

"Oh, no," he said. "You want me to handle the clones?"

"Injunctions," Salehi said. "They need someone to make sure they're enforced."

"I'm not representing mass murderers," Zhu said.

"Innocent until proven—"

"Oh, hell," Zhu said. "I was *here* for that. All of these guys are guilty. They were all caught with their bomb masks on. Some of the bastards even used them outside the dome. You're far away from this crap, but here, it's a pretty big deal, and I don't have to represent any of them ever. I'll save you the trouble of firing me. I'm quitting."

Salehi smiled, and it was not a nice smile, even tiny. "I had a hunch you'd say that."

Zhu wished he had even more clearer, because if Salehi had already thought of his response, then Salehi had an answer, and even though Salehi liked to present himself as the nice senior partner, he was actually the smartest senior partner, and in legal terms, that also meant the most ruthless when he needed to be.

"Reputation still matters to you, I take it," Salehi said.

Zhu shook his head. "If that were true, I wouldn't be sitting here."

"Then what are you objecting to? You're a *defense* attorney. I glanced over your case files. From a human perspective, you seem very humane. If I take a Disty or a Wygnin point of view, you're one nasty SOB. All nonhumans you went up against would consider you to be as bad as your clients—which, from some of those nonhuman points of view—makes you a mass murderer."

Zhu had heard this argument before, and he had an answer for it. It helped that the answer was even true. "I don't care what nonhumans think."

"Just humans matter, eh?" Salehi asked, and his voice had an edge that Zhu did not like.

"I'm not helping you," Zhu said. "So lay off."

"You're helping," Salehi said. "Enthusiastically. I could threaten you with bankruptcy, with lifelong lawsuits initiated by this firm, breach of contract and anything else that our most creative minds can think of—"

"Have at it," Zhu said tiredly. He'd half expected that anyway after his last case.

"But I think the best thing we can do is release images of you with your most recent client. Maybe even some of your arguments in court, not to mention the fact that you promised Judge Bruchac that she could work in S^3 if she ruled in your client's favor. You bribed a judge to help a clone of PierLuigi Frémont."

"Trey didn't bomb the Moon. He was already incarcerated," Zhu said, and wished he hadn't. He sounded defensive. Salehi knew that he had gotten to Zhu.

"He's a *clone*," Salehi said. "He looked just like the bombers. It won't matter to those nice people on the Moon that you were trying to find out what happened on Anniversary Day. They'll think you conspired with the assassins."

Zhu bit back his protests. He'd heard opposing counsel answer S^3 attorneys who threatened this kind of thing. *That's not true! No one would believe that!* and all those other protests meant nothing in the face of an

S^3 press onslaught. He'd seen reputations destroyed in a weekend. He'd seen cases won without ever going to court, all with the manipulation of images—the right images for the time. It was an S^3 specialty.

They would release images of him with Trey, who was now conveniently dead. Killed by Earth Alliance ships on his way to freedom after decades of false imprisonment. Freedom that Zhu had secured for him, using some tricks of the law, not bribery of a judge. Even though she was willing to listen to him because she thought she'd get a job at S^3 when she retired.

"So what?" Zhu said, trying to sound disinterested. "If I represent the Peyti killers, it's the same thing. I'm consorting with mass murderers. I have no reputation and no life."

"You'll be part of a case that will probably go through all of the Multicultural Tribunals. You might end up being a bad guy to most people on the Moon, but to clones everywhere, you'll be a hero."

"Nice try," Zhu said. "I won't be a hero. The attorneys never are. And they certainly aren't heroes with these kinds of clients, no matter how the law changes or who it benefits."

Salehi shrugged. "So you can be a bad guy and spend the rest of your life defending breach of contract lawsuits with S^3, completely broke and hated throughout the Earth Alliance, or you can be a bad guy and spend the rest of your life arguing clone law and living off your miraculous victory, one that will change the Alliance forever."

"Unless the laws don't change," Zhu said. "You could lose."

"I could," Salehi said. "*We* could. It won't matter. We're charging our full fees to the Peyla government who will support the case for years. You'll be hated and rich or hated and broke. Your choice, Torkild."

Zhu rubbed a hand over his very sore forehead. "Give me twenty-four hours."

"Can't," Salehi said. "I need you at the Armstrong Police Department yesterday. Hell, I needed you there a week ago. And I need you at the United Domes of the Moon Security Office, and maybe even the Earth Alliance offices in Armstrong, right now."

"I can't be three places at once, even if I wanted to," Zhu said.

"I do know that," Salehi said. "Which is why you're hiring staff too."

"Four places at once," Zhu muttered.

"So what's your decision?" Salehi asked.

"I'm not working for you," Zhu said.

Salehi sighed. "You'll regret that," he said, and vanished from the glass tabletop.

22

Come on, Dad, you can't be here for him, Talia sent Flint along his links. She was shaking like a junkie coming down off a high. She hadn't wanted to leave the apartment, but Flint had insisted.

He needed her to come with him, and when he had told her that this meeting had something to do with the attacks, she had reluctantly agreed to accompany him.

The darkened office suites had unnerved her. Honestly, they hadn't made him feel good either, particularly the grilling he had received from the automated reception area. The androgynous voice, which was audible to anyone in the wide space, insisted that the attorneys were out of the building, so no one could receive him.

He insisted that he had an appointment—which he did—and that it had been arranged before he arrived—which it had been—and that the system should simply let him, and his daughter, who was also a client, up to Gonzalez's floor.

The system checked, saw that he had been in the building in the last week, and let him go upstairs, where he would encounter a staff member. But, the system warned him, if no one joined him within the hour, he would have to depart.

He had felt nervous: What if Deshin wasn't here?

Then he realized that if Deshin hadn't arrived, they would simply leave.

Flint's nervousness, however, had affected Talia. Or maybe she was just uncomfortable being outside the apartment.

Or perhaps he was being insensitive, taking her to a law office after a bunch of lawyers had tried to destroy the infrastructure on the Moon.

Deshin hadn't made things any better. Talia had recognized him.

Flint's gaze met hers. They were of a height now, as strange as that seemed to him. But for the first time since he'd known her, she seemed like a frightened child.

I am here for him. He has information that the investigation needs.

Her lips thinned, but to her credit, she didn't look at Deshin. Instead, she let Flint lead her out of the elevator and into the corridor.

Deshin said something about being down the hall. Flint knew he was supposed to follow. He didn't like this situation any more than Talia did. It felt odd.

He didn't really want to be alone with Deshin in a suite of offices that neither of them owned.

Which investigation? Talia asked.

Anniversary Day, Flint sent back, although he wasn't certain. Deshin hadn't specified.

What can he know that you can't? she asked.

A great deal. His contacts are a lot shadier than mine, Flint sent.

She sighed, then glanced down the hall where Deshin had disappeared. *I don't trust him.*

Good, Flint sent. *Because I don't either.*

I'm coming with you, she sent.

I don't think he'll talk to me if you do. Wait here. I'll make certain my links stay active. You can come and get me if you need to.

She bit her upper lip, as if she were trying not to speak up, and then she nodded. Flint didn't wait. He turned and walked down the hall.

All of the doors were closed. The lawyers were gone—to a funeral, the automated reception had told him. He didn't need to ask what the funeral was connected to. For the past few days and the next several, funerals were the biggest business in Armstrong, maybe on the Moon itself.

Even though the Peyti clones hadn't been successful inside any domes, there had been a lot of collateral damage, more than Flint liked to think about, and there had been some deaths outside the domes.

He had ceased paying attention when he realized that Talia was falling apart.

His breath caught when he saw the only room with lights on. It was a conference room. Deshin sat at the head of a long black table, his coat draped over the chair behind him. The exterior windows on the far side had been opaqued, but he left this one clear.

Flint hoped that Talia wouldn't have to come here to find him. This view from the hallway into the conference room might make her regress. Not that she had made a lot of progress. But at least she was out of the apartment, and she wasn't crying.

She had seen Kaleb Lamber die in a conference room filled with lawyers, through a clear barrier. She had tried to pound her way in. Kaleb Lamber had been trying to pound his way out.

She had seen the whole thing, and she had found that more upsetting than anything else she'd witnessed in her short, eventful life.

Flint slipped through the door, then pulled it closed. As he did, he had his personal systems check for active recording devices.

"I'm leaving my links on for my daughter," he said. "I promised her."

"You'll be on your honor then." Deshin did not stand up.

Flint sat down at the other end of the table. "You'll be on yours as well."

Deshin smiled. "We're like old enemies facing a new threat together. We have no choice but to reluctantly trust each other."

Deshin made the moment sound like a grand adventure. Flint didn't see it that way.

"I think reluctantly is the key word," Flint said. "And with that in mind, I'm not going to ask if Celestine knows about this meeting."

"Good," Deshin said with enough emphasis to give Flint the truth anyway. Gonzalez didn't know about the meeting.

Flint tried to suppress his irritation. Gonzalez had been doing them favors the first two times she got them together. And then

Deshin repaid her like this? This sort of bending of the rules was what made him dangerous.

Then Flint felt a tinge of amusement. DeRicci would probably have said the same thing about him.

"What was so important?" he asked Deshin.

Deshin's expression grew serious. Not that he had been smiling before, but he had seemed welcoming, friendly. All of that was gone now.

"This morning," he said, "I met with some people who claim they can lead me to the creator of the clones. These are not designer criminal clones. They're something rarer, and much more expensive."

Flint froze. Here it was: the thing that would cause him to regret working with Deshin. Deshin was going to hit him up for money, even though Deshin was reputed to be worth five times more than Flint.

"How expensive?" Flint asked.

"Minimum, one million per clone," Deshin said. "She told me that the buyer would have to pay for the nonviable as well as the viable."

Flint was glad he hadn't let Talia come here with him. She would have hated the way that Deshin was talking about clones. Hell, Flint hated it, but he couldn't show it.

His daughter was more than a commodity that was "viable" or "non-viable."

And then his own thoughts made him freeze. She was, and so, in some ways were those Frémont clones. They had to feel something, think something. They weren't just "villains."

Deshin had stopped talking, clearly noting that Flint's thoughts had moved away from the discussion.

"Anything you want to share?" Deshin said wryly.

"No," Flint said. "Please continue."

Deshin raised an eyebrow, as if Flint's comment amused him. Then the amused expression left Deshin's face.

"Miles," he said quietly, "if my math is correct, we're talking a quarter of a billion dollars that we could trace just for the Anniversary Day attacks, not counting what happened last week."

It took Flint a moment to understand what Deshin meant. Deshin wasn't talking about borrowing money from Flint to buy a clone. Deshin was talking about the attacks themselves.

Flint frowned, trying to both change his expectation of where the conversation was going and to absorb what Deshin was telling him.

Millions? Per viable clone?

Flint asked, "Does that include the raising and training?"

Deshin opened his hands slightly as if he was confused. "She implied that it did, but I don't know for certain. She claims that she can put me in touch with the people who are creating those clones, but I'll be honest. It'll be dicey, and I'm not sure I want to go that far."

Flint wouldn't either. But that was one reason he had contacted Deshin. He figured Deshin was used to dealing with criminals. Deshin had mocked him for that assumption, but they both knew that it had its basis in fact.

The idea that Deshin felt going into business with the real creator of the clones was too dangerous put Flint on edge.

"So," Flint said, "is this as far as our investigation goes?"

"No," Deshin said. "I didn't mean to imply that. But already we're going in a direction I hadn't expected. I don't have that kind of money, and if I did, I certainly wouldn't invest it in such a long-term scheme, one that would take a minimum of twenty-five years and would have a high degree of failure."

Flint rubbed a hand over his face. Again, Deshin mentioned money, but Flint was too tired—too distracted—to understand if that was a request for a contribution.

"I'm sorry," Flint said, deciding honesty was the only solution. He couldn't do the subtlety dance right now. "I don't quite understand why you contacted me. If you're not done, then what do you need me for?"

Deshin smiled slowly. His eyes narrowed. Flint suddenly felt like the man could see through him.

"I need you for money," Deshin said.

Flint suppressed a sigh. He hadn't wanted to be right.

"We need to track it," Deshin said.

"My money?" Flint asked. "Whatever I give you?"

"No, no," Deshin said, that glint still there. It almost felt like a test, as if he were trying to see if he could mess with Flint.

Clearly, he could. Flint was off his game. Half of his brain was with Talia. Flint felt his cheeks heat. He was actually embarrassed that his thoughts had been so clear.

"Years ago," Deshin was saying, "someone made a huge expenditure on clones. Clones of two different Earth Alliance mass murderers, from two different species. It feels targeted."

"It does," Flint said. They'd discussed part of this before. But not all of it. They had discussed this point before the Peyti Crisis.

He made himself focus, and reminded himself that he didn't have time for personal reactions, for a variety of reasons. Because of Talia in the other room, because Gonzalez and the other lawyers would return soon, and because he had the awful feeling that these attacks were just the beginning of something else—what, he didn't know.

Deshin wanted Flint to understand something, and understanding was coming slowly.

Not that Deshin had explained things clearly.

"We've been acting as if there's a mastermind," Flint said.

Deshin nodded.

"And you're saying there isn't one."

"Not an individual in the sense that one person is financing it, and running it. I think this is a lot bigger." Deshin leaned forward. "The amount of money astonishes me, and that's what got me thinking. You're a hell of a lot smarter than me about systems and stuff. I need a second brain on this before I go any farther. I'll look dumb and obvious if I go in to buy clones of the Frémont variety if the previous purchasers weren't individuals."

Flint leaned back. He finally understood what this meeting was about.

"Obvious," Flint repeated, because on some level, this wasn't obvious to him. "They wouldn't expect you to investigate this for law enforcement. They'd think—"

"They'd expect me to investigate," Deshin said quietly. "I lost a lot of friends on Anniversary Day, and several more a few days ago. Men like me, we're known for exacting revenge."

Flint noted that Deshin didn't say that *he* was noted for exacting revenge. That man was used to making context say a lot while his words admitted nothing.

"You believe they'll know you're not serious about buying clones," Flint said.

"Yes," Deshin said. "And once they know that, they won't treat me well."

Such understatement.

Flint tried not to look surprised. That amount of money, and all that it implied, had frightened Deshin.

Deshin had threaded his hands together, to try to stop himself from twisting them. "I backed off when I realized the price of the clones. I can continue with the meetings, but I'm not sure that'll be of value."

He was right. Flint wasn't certain the sellers of the clones would let Deshin trace anything. They might try to entrap him. He might put himself in danger for no reason.

Flint activated his internal timer. He had been in the conference room for twenty minutes already, and he had arrived late. He had no idea how long Gonzalez and the others would be gone.

But he was interested in this conversation now. He understood the reason for it. He was glad that Deshin had contacted him.

"If there's no mastermind," he said, "what are we looking at?"

"That's what I was hoping we could figure out," Deshin said. "We might not have a lot of time here, but we need to be looking at this all differently."

He'd said that last week, before the Peyti Crisis. He had been right. Maybe if Flint hadn't been so focused on the Frémont clones, he would have already figured out that this attack was too big for one person to pull off.

"Here's what I put together, and I might be wrong." Deshin spread his hands, then flattened them on the table top. Clearly this made him uncomfortable. "Remember, I only have had a few hours to think of this too."

Flint nodded. How had they missed this? It seemed so obvious in retrospect. The cost of doing this scheme would have been outrageous…

Unless there was a mastermind, who somehow owned all of the DNA used, and didn't have to pay for the cloning. Still, any mastermind would have to pay for the raising of the clones and the training.

That all by itself was expensive. And it would require decades of patience.

For what? And for what reason?

"What I figure is this," Deshin said. "There has to be an architect. Or there was an architect at one time. Someone had to have the vision, and someone had to set that vision in motion."

Flint raised his head and really looked at Deshin. Beneath that surface persona, the one who had played that head-game with Flint, was a man who was deeply upset by all he was contemplating. The shadows under Deshin's eyes, which had been visible when they were talking on the links, seemed even deeper now, as if just thinking about these clones made him ill.

"This kind of plan, though," Deshin was saying, "this kind of plan would take a lot of staff to put into motion. And dedicated staff over years. Staff that wouldn't talk. And that sounds, to me, like some kind of organization."

Flint tilted his head. He hadn't thought of that. But then, he was a loner. He had worked for the Armstrong Police Department as well as Space Traffic Control. But he never ran a company filled with people. He never even had his own division when he was in working in computers.

Flint understood these things, but he had never participated in them, which meant that he missed details—things he couldn't really know.

Deshin, on the other hand, had an organization large enough that some called it an empire. Deshin might think that Flint was the smarter of the two men, but when it came to running businesses, Deshin knew a thousand times more than Flint ever would.

"You're thinking this is a corporation?" Flint asked. "That a corporation is attacking the Moon?"

"I don't know," Deshin said. "That's why I'm talking to you. Whatever's attacking us has the money, and the time. Once I figured out the cost, I started thinking about the execution of the attacks. Someone had to put the events of Anniversary Day into motion. Then someone had to initiate the Peyti Crisis. Those lawyers—*lawyers!*—were in place for years and years. They're not programmable like androids. And the masks weren't something that could sit around for months and months."

Flint let out a small breath. He hadn't even thought of the masks. Someone had given the Peyti masks that doubled as bombs. And those masks had looked relatively modern, but Flint had done no investigating since he found Talia in tears at Aristotle Academy.

Oh, he had niggled at it. But he hadn't really concentrated on it.

"This kind of plan—it takes a lot of people, both human and Peyti." Deshin was still twisting his fingers together. He didn't like this either.

The Peyti component should have tipped Flint off. If he had been thinking clearly, which he had not been.

He doubted any human would have come up with the Peyti connection without a reason.

"You don't think they're sending a message?" Flint asked.

"That's what the press has been saying since Anniversary Day," Deshin said, "and it doesn't make sense to me. The message is in the bombings, not in the delivery. At least that's what I'm thinking."

"I thought before the Peyti Crisis that the clones were about distraction," Flint said.

"Look," Deshin said, finally untangling his fingers. "Here's what I'd do. I'd set up the attack. I'd have a backup attack if the first didn't work. Maybe one more failsafe."

Flint leaned forward. They had been in this room for nearly an hour, but he didn't want to leave. He would face Gonzalez if he had to. He would pay her or apologize to her.

Deshin was right: this conversation was important.

"But, if you think about it, the Peyti thing, it's not really a backup." Deshin's gaze met Flint's. "You know what I'm saying?"

Flint felt like he was more than a few hours behind. He felt like he was days behind, months behind, like he didn't have the capability of thinking ahead.

Was that what whoever the architect was had counted on—that the normally smart people on the Moon, the ones who survived, would be so overcome by stress and grief and the very situation that they wouldn't be able to think clearly?

What about the rest of the Earth Alliance?

"Just spell it out for me," Flint said, trying not to sound annoyed. He wasn't annoyed at Deshin. He was annoyed at himself.

"Peyti, they're lawyers, right, most of them? At least on the Moon. And the ones that were the clones, the bulk of them were lawyers, right?"

"Yeah," Flint said.

"So, the bombs go off on Anniversary Day. They destroy the domes. Kill a lot of people. Even a few of these Peyti clones. But think it through. They wear masks."

Flint let out a breath of air. "The destruction of the domes wouldn't have killed them, if they were nowhere near the blast site."

"That's right," Deshin said. "They could breathe. They might even have some of those skin-tight suits that some Peyti have. Maybe they wore them that day under their weirdo suits."

Flint almost smiled at the description. He had always hated seeing Peyti in human suits. It made them look like starving children playing dress up.

He tapped his forefinger against the table.

It felt like his brain was starting to return.

"If the Anniversary Day bombings had been successful, then the survivors would have met with Earth Alliance officials," he said slowly. "Lawyers in particular, because they would have been privy to decisions that the dome governments made."

Deshin leaned his head back. "I hadn't thought of it that way. I just figured that, you know, the surviving bombers would need lawyers, and the Peyti would step in and destroy the bombers."

Flint shook his head. "The bombers died. We caught a few, but that wouldn't have happened if the domes hadn't sectioned."

Deshin's gaze met his. There was something cold in Deshin's eyes, something dangerous. "So the secondary attack—"

"Is also aimed at destroying the Moon." Flint put his hands over his mouth, then realized what he had done. He didn't want to say what he was thinking aloud. "Which is why it wasn't called off."

"Because if the lawyers had succeeded, everyone who was anyone on the Moon would've died."

"And the domes would have blown apart. It *is* a backup plan."

"Which also failed," Deshin said.

Flint nodded. "I've had a feeling that there's another attack coming, but I've been thinking that's partly paranoia."

"I've been worrying about it too," Deshin said. "I don't think it's paranoia."

"But if we're right, then last week's attack wouldn't have been planned as a backup."

"It would have been planned as part of the overall mission," Deshin said.

"Which is...what?" Flint asked. "Destroying the domes on the Moon does...what?"

"We gotta think that through," Deshin said. "You gotta ask, who benefits?"

"That's not what you have to ask first," Flint said, shaking his head. "You have to ask, what gets lost? And more than that. This attack has been planned for decades. So what gets lost now that's exactly the same as what would have gotten lost thirty years ago?"

"Oh, God, Flint, I don't know," Deshin said.

Flint was feeling calmer than he had felt a moment ago. He was starting to get a handle on all of this. It was starting to make sense.

"You were right last week, Deshin," he said. "We're going about this investigation all wrong. We're not looking at the big picture."

"Big picture?" Deshin said with a sardonic grin. "I never thought of a picture this big."

"Well, we're going to have to start," Flint said. "Because focusing on some dome bombings on the Moon is way too small."

"Who thinks that big?" Deshin asked.

"Someone does," Flint said.

"No, no," Deshin said. "I don't mean our architect. I mean, in investigative terms. Who thinks that big?"

Flint frowned, blinked, thought.

There were several branches of Earth Alliance investigators that looked at large-scale issues, but authority was always a problem. Local authority ruled. When the issues got too big, they were already *legal* problems, so the investigation focused on the things that impacted Earth Alliance law, not on truth or what actually happened. Instead the investigations focused on what could be proven, what could be used in Multicultural Tribunals, and what the various cultures could agree on.

Flint had been shaking his head long before he realized he was doing it. Then he forced himself to stop.

Deshin was watching him.

Flint stood up. "If these attacks had gone as planned," he said slowly. "We would have lost the twenty largest domes on the Moon. Millions would have died. The devastation and financial loss would have crippled economies and corporations from here to the edge of the sector."

"But, see, not everyone would have lost money," Deshin said. "Because we need the Moon. It's the gateway to Earth. So corporations that fund construction would've made a lot of money rebuilding the domes."

"Or rebuilding the governments here," Flint said.

"But that's the stuff that no architect can plan," Deshin said. "Money in and out, that can be planned."

"Just like response can be planned," Flint said. "There'd be first responders. Money would flow into the Moon, not just rebuilding money, but money to help the survivors."

"And then some of the survivors would be consultants on what the dead would want."

Flint looked at Deshin. The man said the most ghoulish things with calm certainty.

"And a lot of those survivors would have been Peyti lawyers or represented by Peyti lawyers," Flint said.

"Who would have been in some meetings six months after the destruction, about the time the shock had worn off, the rebuilding had started, and hope was beginning."

"And then thousands—maybe millions—more would have died," Flint said. "This time, it wouldn't have just been Moon officials, but Earth Alliance officials."

"Corporate CEOs," Deshin said.

"Another group of authority figures," Flint said.

"And not just on the Moon," Deshin said. "But throughout the Earth Alliance, because by then, these surviving Peyti lawyers would have been in demand in various places."

Flint's mouth was dry. He peered through the windows down the darkened hallway.

No one had come back yet, so far as he could see.

"The third wave," he said after a moment. "It's not predictable. No one could figure out what would happen after two catastrophic attacks."

"Sure we can," Deshin said with calm certainty. "The third time isn't about investigations or rebuilding the Moon. It's about rebuilding the Earth Alliance itself."

Flint turned around. Deshin's face had gone gray. His eyes were sunken, almost lost.

Flint suspected he looked just as bad.

"We'd give up on the Moon," Flint said softly. "It wouldn't be that important, not in the short term."

Deshin nodded.

"The final attack would be on the Earth Alliance itself," Flint said. "But the Alliance would be prepared."

"You hope it would," Deshin said.

"It doesn't seem right," Flint said. "The attacks are focused on the Moon. The Moon is an understandable target from thirty years out. But the Alliance itself? It would be impossible to figure out how big or small the Alliance would be, what its edges and borders would be."

"What are you saying?" Deshin said.

"I'm not sure we can dismiss a third attack on the Moon," Flint said.

"But it would have to make sense as part of a larger war," Deshin said.

"If this is war," Flint said, "who are we fighting against?"

Deshin shrugged. "Whoever it is has incredible patience."

"Governments have patience," Flint said. "Governments have money."

Deshin stood as well. He also glanced at the hall. Obviously, he was feeling the time pressure too.

"We're still missing something," he said.

"But we've found a lot, thanks to you," Flint said. "You're right. I need to start tracing that money."

"And I'm going to trace the DNA," Deshin said. "But from a completely different angle. I'm not going to be a buyer. I'm going to look for the original seller."

"You think there's only one?" Flint asked.

"It's easier to track the DNA of two mass murderers than it is to track thirty-year-old cloning operations," Deshin said. "I'm going to see what I can find. You keep me informed."

"I will," Flint said. "And thanks."

"For what?" Deshin asked.

Flint smiled at him, just a little. "For getting me focused again."

"We gotta figure out that third attack," Deshin said.

"We will," Flint said. "I'm finally beginning to believe that we will."

23

ZHU DID REGRET TURNING DOWN SALEHI THE MOMENT SALEHI DISAPPEARED from the glass tabletop in the booth at the bar. Zhu hoped the feeling would pass.

He wanted to be the kind of man who could stand up for his principles. He wanted to be the man who said no and meant it, who would travel to hell and back to do what needed to be done. He would be traveling to hell if he took up Salehi on the offer of building a branch of S^3 here. Zhu would spend decades defending those horrible, horrible clones, justifying their acts while trying to keep them out of prison and maybe, just maybe, changing clone law.

And if he succeeded? He would put killers back out on the street.

He staggered out of the booth, waved off the bartender—who was probably going to tell him that his credit chip had been denied—and headed into the bright light of Dome Daylight. He squinted. He had entered the bar in Dome Night. Armstrong always tried to maintain Earth normal days, and they did it by manipulating the dome, something he thought particularly stupid.

But then, he had lived for years in space stations, where no one cared what time of day it was. And they certainly didn't turn up the lights for no apparent reason.

Out here, on the street, cars floating past, people hurrying by to their jobs, some Disty arguing on a street corner, looking like out-of-place children as they waved their long arms, he could smell himself. Sweat, more sweat, and rum, along with an acrid odor from the clearer.

He ran a hand through his hair, felt grease and a tangle, and wondered when he last took a shower.

He put his head down and walked the three blocks back to his hotel, hoping no one at the desk saw him, because they had probably received notice that his company credit had been denied as well.

His legs shook. So did his hands.

He had thousands in savings, but a court case against S^3 would eat that up in days. So would a trip to the Frontier. He had been to the Frontier once, and he had hated it.

He hated alien places—and aliens, truth be told. Which was why he had been so happy at S^3, at least in the beginning. No one cared if his clients were human-only, and no one cared if he refused to partner with some of the nonhuman lawyers.

No one even cared if he argued that alien laws as applied to humans were unfair and unreasonable and inhumane. He was *supposed* to argue that. He had been *good* at arguing that.

He had been a good lawyer.

He had gotten Trey out of prison, for god's sake. A clone of PierLuigi Frémont, held illegally for years. A clone who might have known something important.

It wasn't his fault that S^3 had screwed up.

They were the ones who brought in that transport company, and they were the ones who had let Trey die.

Zhu could have died, if he had gone to get Trey.

He shuddered again, his stomach turning.

He climbed the stairs to his room, afraid to use the elevator. The stairs were black and gold, as fancy as the hotel itself. He could see his reflection in the walls, a too-skinny man with a hollowed-out face, flushed from drink and clearer.

He looked like he had been on a bender. He smelled like he had been on a bender.

He had a choice.

He could go back to work, do his damn job, and save the lives of a bunch of alien murderers, build a law firm in one of the most law firm-heavy cities in the Alliance, and get fat and rich.

Or he could fall further.

This was what he looked like after a few months leave, knowing he would be fired. This was why Berhane had looked at him and said, *You know it's over, Torkild. It's time to let go.*

She hadn't even offered him volunteer work with her foundation. She was doing good works, rebuilding cities, and she hadn't suggested he join her. She knew he wasn't that kind of man.

He wasn't any kind of man.

He was a brain that could pick apart legalities. He was an ego that needed to feel he was important. He could either make a living at his chosen profession, feeling like he was doing something to change the universe in his own small way, or he could die slowly, either from drink or starvation or loneliness.

He sat down on the steps. He hadn't even gone to the next landing. He put his head in his hands.

Wow. He'd managed to stand on principle for not even an hour before realizing how stupid he was being.

He could be weak with money or weak without money.

He was so weak, he opted for the first choice.

He activated his S^3 links.

You son of a bitch, he sent to Salehi. *I'm in.*

24

Flint made a decision halfway home. He turned the car toward his office. He knew that was dicey. He had Talia with him, and he wanted her nowhere near this investigation.

However, if she showed interest in the investigation, he would see that as a step forward. At least then, she wasn't sleeping or staring into space.

He glanced at her. She didn't even seem to have noticed the change of direction.

That was so unlike her. Usually, she was asking him questions the moment he did something different.

She hadn't said a word since they left the meeting with Deshin. Flint had left first, which made him both grateful and uncomfortable. He found himself wondering what Deshin would do when he was alone in the offices.

Then Flint felt that he was being uncharitable.

The man didn't have to come to him. Deshin didn't have to be participating in this investigation at all.

And now, he was going to do something very risky.

Flint could tell that just from the way that Deshin had acted when he talked about investigating the DNA. Flint liked to lie to himself and say that a man like Deshin was used to taking risks. But Flint knew that a man like Deshin took calculated risks.

Flint also knew that Deshin had a family at home, one he loved. Deshin might have taken a lot of personal risks in the past, but he might also have reduced his exposure to personal risk when he had a son.

Flint was doing the same thing. Ever since Talia had come into his life, he took fewer risks—except where she was concerned. In fact, the only times he had been in difficult or life-threatening situations in the past few years had been when he was trying to help (or rescue) Talia.

He glanced at her again. She leaned against the window, eyes closed, her skin slightly gray. At least the tears had stopped. Her nose looked red and sore, and the area around it was raw.

Then the air car bumped as it glided into the dirtier air of the original dome. Flint's office was in Old Armstrong, the oldest part of the city. Many of the buildings here were made of permaplastic, the material that the original colonists used when they built this place. Much of the construction was a combination of old, older, and oldest, some of it dated from the protections put into place when the city started growing.

The city wanted to maintain its historical district, and it made some mistakes as it did so. The laws protected parts of the dome itself—those parts attached to historic buildings—and that meant preserving an environmental system that had been out of date centuries ago.

As a result, Moon dust leaked into this part of the city. The environmental systems in the nearby sections of the dome were as powerful as such systems could get, trying to keep the Moon dust and all the other contaminants out of the rest of the city.

Hence the bump.

Years ago, he had been used to it. Now he was aware of it.

He glanced at Talia again. She didn't even seem to notice.

Even though the dome was on Dome Daylight, it was clearly darker in this part of the city. The old parts of the dome were scratched and cloudy, the buildings dilapidated, and the sidewalks barely worthy of the name.

He lowered the car in his favorite lot. Several other cars were parked in that lot, but they were all covered with a layer of dust. He wondered how many of them had been in that spot since last week, and how many were just plain abandoned.

He had no idea. He hoped that the presence of the little-used vehicles didn't mean that the neighborhood had grown even more dangerous.

He used to love that sense of danger here. That was before he had to bring his teenage daughter with him whenever he went to his office.

The car shut off with a shudder. He wasn't sure he had ever brought this vehicle to his office. The car was relatively new, and he came here less and less.

He did a lot of his work these days in conjunction with the United Domes of the Moon Security Office. All of his focus had been on solving the Anniversary Day attacks. He preferred to use government resources when he was, essentially, doing an unpaid government job.

But he didn't want the resources of the United Domes anywhere near the searches he was about to do. Nor did he want to use his home system for it. Sometimes, he used a non-networked system at the office of the lawyer whose services he used the most, Maxine Van Alen, but he wasn't sure what kind of trouble this search would get him into.

Better to use the office, where he had backups and fail-safes and redundancies. Better to use a place and equipment he could destroy if he had to, should he need to cover his tracks.

He touched Talia's arm and she jumped. She looked frightened when she glanced over at him, just for a moment, before she covered the reaction with that weird implacable expression she'd been trying out since the Peyti Crisis.

He hated the fear. In the past, Talia got frightened—the loss of her mother had scared her—but she had a deep reservoir of courage that Flint loved.

That reservoir seemed to be empty these days.

"We're going to the office," he said.

Talia frowned at him, then wiped a hand over her face. She didn't ask about it. She just nodded, and waited for him to open his door before she opened her own.

The thick air made him cough. He wasn't used to dust particles anymore either, apparently. Two weeks ago, Talia would have laughed at that cough. Today, she didn't even seem to notice.

She pushed her door closed and joined him. He closed his door as well. He wanted to take her hand, but he knew she would pull away.

So he walked across the lot, his feet stirring up even more dust, and reached the sidewalk ahead of her.

She didn't even walk like she used to. She kept her head down, her shoulders hunched forward.

He didn't care how she felt about the show of affection in public. He took her hand as she reached his side, and she didn't even try to shake him off. Her fingers were cold and just a little clammy.

They walked the two blocks to his office. The neighborhood had changed since he last parked here. Three buildings were completely abandoned, the signs hanging above their doors gone. Three more looked like they were going to topple into each other.

He saw no one on the streets, and none of the buildings had lights on. He tried to convince himself that was because of Dome Daylight, but he knew that many places had lights on around the clock because of how dark this neighborhood was.

Talia didn't say anything. He wasn't even sure she noticed that the lawyer's office next door was closed. It looked almost abandoned—the way that an office constantly in use looked when it was suddenly closed.

Flint felt something like despair. He hadn't even liked the lawyer, but he had been a decent attorney. Just not a great one. Flint could afford better.

Had the lawyer been one of the collateral damage casualties of the Peyti Crisis?

Flint didn't have time to investigate that.

He put his hand on the door knob, letting the alarm system identify him through his DNA. The warmth of his hand told the system he was alive; his movements reinforced that; and the fact that he had someone with him alerted the system to making certain that some systems didn't even activate.

The door swung open, and Talia eased in ahead of him.

She glanced over her shoulder at him, and tried to smile. That look, the pathetic half-smile, the attempt to reassure him that she was okay, made him feel even worse.

"At least it smells good in here," she said.

It did too. He hadn't realized that outside smelled faintly of burned rubber. He wondered what was going wrong with the old parts of the dome filtration system now.

He let the door close behind him. The lights came up, not that it would be noticeable from the outside. He hadn't put out his shingle in years. The entire system was instructed to make sure this place looked like it was not a functioning office any more.

Inside, it had been very functional—at least as recently as a few months ago. He had been rebuilding his computer system on Anniversary Day, as well as redesigning the interior. When he'd had a moment after the initial madness calmed down, he'd finished that redesign, with the idea that at some point, he would have to return to work here.

The environmental systems had kept the air clean, the temperature comfortable, and the dust outside of the office.

"What are we doing, Dad?" Talia asked. The question seemed like an effort.

"We're not doing anything," he said. "I've got some things to look up."

"I can help," she said, and she almost sounded interested.

"I know," he said. "Right now, though, the search is a bit dicey, and I need to do it."

She winced. She felt he hadn't trusted her to use the systems in this office since she had nearly exposed her sisters a few years ago. Not that these girls were her actual sisters. They were the other clones from her original, Emmeline.

Those clones were all older than Talia, created at a different time. Flint hadn't been—and still wasn't—sure if they even knew they were clones. Talia hadn't.

And these girls had been adopted by good families throughout the Alliance, so legally, those clones were considered human.

He didn't know how to reassure Talia without bringing up that incident. She had gotten a lot more cautious in the past few years. He wanted to tell her that, but didn't dare.

"I should probably be doing this work at the university or something," Flint said, "but I doubt anyone is in their cafeteria at the moment."

He often used places with excellent networking and fantastic research capabilities, like the Brownie Bar (which he would never go to with Talia beside him) and Dome University's Armstrong Campus so that any weird searches he did would be untraceable to him.

"You think someone would notice?" Talia asked.

"I think we go there later in the week if we need to," he said. "Right now, you and I would get noticed."

That was the curse of looking different from everyone else. His pale skin and curly blond hair always attracted stares. Talia's matching hair got the same attention when the two of them were together.

Now that she was older, and her hair combined with her copper skin and stunningly unusual eyes, she was getting other kinds of stares, the kind of stares a father knew were coming for his daughter, but never wanted to see.

"What are you searching for?" she asked.

"A financial trail," he said.

"I want to help," she said again.

He sighed. "Okay," he said after a moment. "I need you to do a systems check—"

"Da-a-ad." She made that word into three syllables, and then rolled her eyes. He smiled. He had missed the attitude.

"It's important," he said. "I haven't worked here in a long time, and I need to make sure the security—"

"You can do it." She sat down heavily on the floor near the far wall. She brought her legs in so that she was sitting cross-legged, then she leaned the back of her head against the wall. She closed her eyes.

For a moment, Talia had been back. Then he lost her again.

He wanted to try to bring her out, even though he knew it probably wouldn't work.

"It's not make-work," he said. "It's important."

"I know," she said tiredly. "But I'll just screw it up."

Then he realized what he had done wrong. He had said the word 'security.' Security was what had failed to protect that boy in her school. Security had failed to protect almost everyone sitting next to a Peyti clone during the Peyti Crisis, and that failed security had been initiated by the United Domes of the Moon Security Department.

He silently cursed himself. If he got caught or someone came after him because his systems hadn't protected him, Talia would blame herself.

So she protected herself by not even trying.

"I think you'll do fine," he said, and knew it sounded inadequate.

She didn't answer him. She didn't move. He knew the posture.

She was pretending to be asleep.

He sighed, and pulled back the chair near his newly rebuilt system. He had screens all over the office, and several different networked computers. He had some non-networked ones as well, and floating flat screens when he wanted to activate them.

He didn't want to at the moment.

He kept the vocal commands shut down, and he tapped his most powerful system to life. Then he stared at it for a long moment.

He wasn't sure exactly how to start looking for those vast sums of money he and Deshin had talked about.

He wasn't even certain what year to begin in.

He needed to do some background work first. He needed to try to wrap his brain around the scope of the thing that Deshin had presented him, something that should have been obvious to everyone investigating, but hadn't been.

Someone had been planning these attacks for decades. They didn't just buy twenty-some matching clones (in the case of PierLuigi Frémont) or hundreds of them (in the case of the Peyti). They had raised a series of clones with the idea that there would be two attacks, maybe three.

Definitely three.

He leaned his head back, mimicking Talia's posture.

Before he did any investigation here, he needed to get DeRicci on this. He wasn't quite sure how. How did they search for more clones?

And of what? What species? What kind?

Could they legally do that kind of search?

He didn't know.

But he did know that he had to find out.

25

Torkild Zhu was sober. Disgustingly, horribly, sober. He had taken all kinds of clearers. They got rid of the alcohol, the nausea, the headache. They cleared the red out of his eyes, nose, and cheeks (boy, he had been drinking too much), repaired his broken capillaries, and took the puffiness out of his skin.

They would have made him feel good, except that he didn't feel good.

He doubted he would ever feel good again.

He had looked in the metaphorical mirror and had not liked what he had seen.

Of course, what he had seen hadn't gotten him to change his behavior. He knew he never would.

He sat in his hotel room, hands in his hair, scanning the injunctions that Salehi had sent him. Zhu had already run them through his AutoLearn program, but that wasn't the same as reading the documents. Dozens of them, all to be delivered in person. Salehi had already sent them to the various legal arms of the various government agencies.

But all attorneys knew that agencies were great at claiming that legal documents, particularly those sent across great distances, arrived garbled or ruined or not at all.

Zhu had to make sure that the documents got to the right people.

He had wanted to hire some legal assistants to do that, but he couldn't. Not yet. He needed to rent some office space first.

Through his links, he had approached a few law firms here about partnering with S^3, but the two lawyers he had spoken to had begged off before he even got to the meat of the case. Not because they were squeamish about representing the Peyti clones—Zhu hadn't even mentioned that.

Just because anything to do with the Peyti Crisis put the firms in a conflict of interest. They had either lost lawyers to the crisis or they had hired some of the clones who were now under lock and key.

Zhu was finally beginning to understand why the Peyti government had gone to S^3 in the first place. They couldn't hire anyone on the Moon. Every single law firm here was tainted.

He got up, feeling fifty years older than he was. He had changed into the only real suit he had brought with him. It crinkled as he moved—real water silk, the kind that cost a small fortune. It had been a present from Berhane when he graduated from law school, and he hadn't wanted to leave it behind.

He hadn't fit in it after years at S^3, but apparently, he had lost a lot of weight during his little binge. Which made sense, since he was using the alcohol for calories.

The very idea of alcohol made him slightly queasy, and that wasn't because of any clearers or any anti-alcohol nanobots. The way he had behaved the last few weeks disgusted him almost as much as this case did.

Then he corrected himself: these cases, not this case.

He had to wrap his brain around the fact that he was now The Guy Who Had No Soul. He needed to think about his clients and shut off the emotions.

He had to use this as an intellectual challenge.

He checked his appearance in the actual mirror near the door, then finger-combed his hair. He looked good. Amazing what science could do. He made himself smile, then realized that was wrong.

He wasn't going to be the smarmy attorney who smiled his way through a difficult case. He was going to be the *understanding* attorney, who knew how awful his job was, but how necessary it was as well.

The *adult* attorney, the one who regretfully worked against the Alliance's best interest.

Then he shook his head. He couldn't think of this case that way. He couldn't. Because, in reality, this was *for* the Alliance—or at least for all those billions of clones inside the Alliance.

Salehi had been right about that.

Zhu braced himself, and then he left the hotel room. Once he went to the Armstrong Police Department, he couldn't turn back. He was committed.

But he also knew he was fooling himself.

There was no turning back.

He had committed the moment he contacted Salehi.

Zhu represented the Peyti clones, and probably would for the rest of his life.

26

THE MEETING DRONED ON AND THROUGH IT ALL, THE OTHER DETECTIVES listened with a kind of energy that Nyquist had never seen before. Usually in large meetings, his colleagues squirmed. They stared into space, which generally meant they were checking their links or watching the time or maybe even working on an investigation (or playing some kind of game).

If he were chief of detectives, he would shut off all but the emergency links in important meetings. But since he had sometimes been one of the detectives who spent his time working rather than listening, he had never suggested that to Andrea Gumiela.

He had eased away from Savita Romey on the pretext of talking with a friend on the force he hadn't seen for a long time. She should have caught him at that right there; he didn't have many friends on the force, and most people knew that.

But she was like everyone else in the room—eager to have a piece of those Peyti clones.

Gumiela hadn't mentioned the property angle. Nyquist wasn't even certain she thought of it.

She had dealt with a lot of these clones before anyone knew that they were clones. She had known them as high-powered attorneys who came into the offices with agendas. She had to either agree with that agenda (in the case of the prosecutors) or dismiss it somehow (in the case of the defense attorneys).

She probably hadn't realized that much of the room had gone from thinking of the Peyti prisoners as lawyers to thinking of them as clones. As property.

And that would lead to something dangerous.

He did his best not to look over his shoulder at Romey as he eased to the front. When Gumiela stopped speaking, he sent her a message and made certain he caught her eye at the same time.

There's something ugly happening among the detectives, he sent. *Before you approve the interrogation pairs, please give me five minutes of your time.*

Her gaze flitted off his, and for a moment, he thought maybe his message had gone into some kind of queue inside her communications system.

Then she did something he had never seen before: she scanned the room.

He wasn't on a platform. He didn't know what she saw. But whatever it was, it made her lean back almost imperceptivity. If he hadn't been looking for a reaction, he wouldn't have seen it at all.

Then she looked back at him. *You'll have five minutes, Detective,* she sent. *You better make it good.*

27

THE LAST OF THE PEYTI CLONES HAD DISAPPEARED INTO THE SECURITY DOORS at the Reception Center.

Leckie put her fingers under her chin, then swept them forward, a rude gesture that meant anything from *go fuck yourself* to *fuck off and die*. She meant all of those things and so much more.

"Nice," Willis said to her. He still wore his riot suit, but he had deactivated the helmet. "Don't you wish you had magic in those fingertips and you could make them all explode?"

She deactivated her helmet as well. The air on the platform smelled faintly of rubber and some dry dusty thing she'd begun to think of as Peyti sweat.

"I want them to suffer," she said. "I almost wish I could stay here, so that I could snap an arm, like you did, or accidentally stomp on one of their feet."

"I think they should die," Willis said, still looking after them.

The other guards were filing back to the train. Eventually, they'd board it, and ride it back to Glenn Station, and for a brief moment, they would sit in silence, with nothing to do.

Doing nothing made her antsy. She would rather have the stupid clones to focus on than the things she'd seen last week. Or Anniversary Day.

Her hand tightened around the barrel of her laser rifle.

"They should watch each other explode, one by one," Willis said, "and the last guy, he should be spared, so he could live with that memory forever."

"Yeah," she said, but her heart wasn't in it.

Both she and Willis—and everyone else in corrections—assumed these clones had feelings, they had the ability to understand what they had done, and they felt some sense of self-preservation.

And they'd acted on it, after Willis broke an arm. But that was also logic, and she knew how much the Peyti valued logic.

Although there had been nothing logical in their attacks.

She shook her head. "Maybe I'm done with this gig," she said as she took the steps into the train car.

"Prisoner transport?" Willis asked.

"The Moon," she said. "It's not home anymore."

"Ah, c'mon, Maude," he said. "You'll feel different when we get back to the station."

He meant Glenn Station. Parts of it were just fine, and other parts still hadn't recovered from Anniversary Day. From her apartment she could see the attempts at the rebuild, and an exploded Growing Pit outside the city's dome.

She wouldn't feel different when she got back.

Her city would still be damaged.

Her family would still have holes through its heart.

And she didn't know how to deal with any of it.

"Yeah, I'll feel different," she said, and sank into one of the chairs recently vacated by a Peyti clone.

Willis smiled at her. He thought her little crisis was over. But she meant she would feel different forever, and he meant she would feel better.

She doubted there was any better ahead for her.

So it was time to seek different—whatever that meant.

Maybe if things settled down on the Moon, she might actually have time to figure all that out.

28

The platform lowered, and Gumiela's team marched through the throng of detectives. Nyquist scrambled to follow. He had to push past colleagues who were pairing up, saying, "Excuse me, excuse me," by rote. The "excuse mes" got loud when he started shoving, but still no one seemed to notice.

He got to the door that Gumiela went through just before it snicked shut. He put his hand between the frame and the edge of the door, pushing it open, and hurrying inside.

The room off the bullpen was an extension of Gumiela's office. She had quite the setup. It included a full office down the corridor, a larger meeting area, and this thing, attached to the bullpen. Her predecessor had called this the media room, but Gumiela generally met the media on the steps of the police department.

She felt that the department backdrop made everything she said all the more official. Nyquist was always astonished at how Gumiela's insecurities still played out, despite her high rank in the department.

She stopped near the door to the corridor, her black skirt swinging. Her red hair was piled high on the top of her head, wisps falling on either side of her face. The hairstyle made her look younger, and Nyquist remembered his thought about people who had the time to assemble themselves before this meeting.

Then he realized he had not seen Gumiela without makeup and perfect hair in years. This was the Gumiela equivalent of an unmade bed.

Her assistants had already left, probably going to set up the interrogation partnerships as the requests rolled in.

"Make it quick, Bartholomew," Gumiela said, and if he hadn't thought her tired before, he did now. She was exhausted.

"I was talking with some of the other detectives before the meeting," he said, "and I think we might have a problem."

"You mentioned that." She glanced at the door leading to the corridor as if she could escape through it. "What's the problem?"

"They're going to treat the clones like property," Nyquist said.

"So?" Gumiela asked, smoothing her skirt with her right hand. And then her hand stopped moving. Her mouth opened slightly, as she realized what he'd said. "Tell me exactly what you mean."

"Clone law," he said. "If these clones aren't marked, aren't registered, and did not come into city as clones, then—"

"I know clone law," she snapped. "We've already decided to ignore it because we don't have the ability to find their owners, if they do have owners."

"But the law states that they do have owners," Nyquist said, knowing he only had a few minutes of her attention. "Or, if they don't, they're not individuals, they're *abandoned* property. As long as they're logged in and as long as we keep track of them while they're here, we're not responsible for the condition they're found in when their owner is located. *If* their owner is located."

Gumiela cursed, and walked to the other side of the room. She put a hand on her forehead, as if she had the universe's worst headache. Maybe she did.

"Tell me this is only a few rogue operatives," she said, her back to him.

"Maybe it was before you put everyone together in the bullpen," he said. "But I've heard it from a dozen sources so far. Detectives are talking about pairing up according to how they plan to treat their prisoners."

He didn't add that the only person he had had that part of the conversation with had been Romey.

"Son of a bitch," Gumiela said. "I don't want to delay these interrogations further."

"I know, sir," Nyquist said.

"Then you understand what kind of position this puts me in," she said.

"I also know that we're dealing with Peyti here," he said. "They might have thought of this too."

"They were suicide bombers who failed. They wouldn't—" Then she stopped herself and looked at him. "Do you think they'll goad detectives into killing them?"

He hadn't thought of that, but it made sense. Most detectives didn't really know how fragile the Peyti were.

"It's possible," he said. "They're smart, sir. They were high-level lawyers. You can bet they know the nuances of the law better than we do. They also know that breaking property carries a fine, but it's not a felony. No one will get in trouble for doing it."

Gumiela swore a third time. "I didn't need this," she said, but not to him. She was speaking to the air, as if she just needed to vent.

Then her gaze met his. "We're taking in the prisoners from the other domes."

He almost said, *I was listening, sir*, but decided against it. Snark probably wasn't appropriate right now. Besides, she was upset enough already.

"A trainload just arrived from Glenn Station. We're going to need to do *something*, Bartholomew. These clones know who created them, they know who they're working for, and as you said, they're very intelligent. They can't have been programmed," then she raised a hand, as if forestalling a thought, "or, at least, I can't believe they had been programmed. I know several of them. They couldn't have been good lawyers if they were just working by rote, and from everything I've heard so far, *all* of them were good lawyers."

He blinked, feeling a little surprised. Gumiela had been giving this a lot of thought.

"I suppose we can issue some kind of directive." She was speaking more to herself now than to him.

"Or make harming them a crime," he said.

"Oh, that'll play well in the media," she said, then put a hand over her face. "What am I going to do?"

He wasn't sure if she was asking him or just speaking out loud. "You could bind them over for the Alliance to take care of."

"And lose all the information they can give us," she said.

"Do you actually expect a group of trained lawyers who willingly became potential suicide bombers to give up information, no matter how nicely we ask?" he said.

She paused, as if she were considering what to say, and then she shook her head.

"I don't expect it," she said. "But I don't do my job based entirely on my feelings. I have to deal with the expectations of others as well."

And, she was implying, someone higher up in the Armstrong Police Department expected results.

"Then let's figure out a plan," Nyquist said. "Your idea of pairing interrogators was good, but it didn't take into account—"

"The blood-thirstiness of my troops," she said, then sighed. "Which I completely understand."

She tilted her head back for a moment, then looked at him, and gave him a rueful smile. "I've always believed in the law, Bartholomew. I've never understood that vigilante feeling."

"Until now," he said.

She nodded. "It's all I can do to restrain them."

"I know," he said.

"And don't give me that old saw about hurting the Peyti clones makes us as bad as them."

He held up a hand, palm out. "I wasn't planning to. You know my history."

"I do," she said. "That's why I figured you'd understand. And, no offense, I figure if you are appalled at the fact that the division wants to go after the clones in a legal but inappropriate manner, then I should be appalled."

"You should be appalled that you're using me as your moral compass," he said.

This time, her smile was real. "You have to listen to people who've already thought the tough stuff through," she said. Then her smile faded. "It's not going to be easy, corralling the interrogators."

"I know," he said. "But we'll figure out a way."

"I'd rather figure out how to get those damn clones to talk," she said.

"Me, too," he said, wondering if he could find something, anything, to get one of them to speak. "Me, too."

29

THE ELEVATOR DOORS OPENED, AND FLINT STEPPED ONTO THE TOP FLOOR of the United Domes of the Moon Security Building. He extended his hand so that Talia would join him, and so that the elevator door would remain open until she did so.

She looked at him from the back of the elevator, arms wrapped around her stomach as if it hurt. He'd already asked her if it did, and she had said no. She had eaten the lunch he picked up along the way, so he was less concerned about her physical well-being than her emotional one.

The closer the two of them got to this building, the more she shrank into herself. Just once, she'd asked to go home. He didn't want her there without him.

Yes, he was being overprotective, but he didn't know what else to do.

And, if he were honest with himself, he was terrified to leave her alone—not just for what she might do to herself, but because she had nearly died the last time he had.

And if he expanded that self-honesty even more, he had to admit that he was as much of a mess as she was. He had just learned over the years how to keep moving in the face of overwhelming emotion.

She raised her head, giving him what he would once have called "a teenage look," sullen anger mixed with complete contempt. She stared at his hand as if it offended her, then stood up and stalked out of the elevator as if coming here had been her idea.

The hallways here were active—people going in all directions, holding tablets and looking busy.

He rounded the corner and stopped at Rudra Popova's desk. She had gone through a lot since losing her lover on Anniversary Day, but she was working her way through it—or she had been until the Peyti Crisis.

He had no idea how she'd been afterward, since he hadn't come up here at all since finding Talia.

Popova pushed her long black hair away from her face, her dark eyes glinting. She raised her eyebrows in mock surprise.

"Miles Flint," she said. "Fancy seeing you here."

Apparently, DeRicci hadn't told her that he was coming.

Talia hovered just behind him. Popova leaned sideways and grinned. "Hey, Talia."

Talia nodded, but didn't say anything.

Popova's expressive eyebrows went from mock surprise to a very real frown. "You okay?"

"Yeah," Talia said curtly. At least she hadn't snapped, *Why does everyone ask me that?* like she had a few days ago.

Popova's gaze met Flint's, and he could read her questions. He didn't have answers.

"Noelle is expecting me," he said.

"Us," Talia said.

Flint didn't correct her. He knew how vivid her imagination could be. He figured it was better for her to hear his fears and know that the team was expecting something bigger than it was for her to make up things on her own.

He would also have supported her keeping her head down and remaining quiet if that was what she needed.

"I know," Popova said. "I had to clear a bunch of very busy people out of her office."

During the actual Peyti Crisis, a large part of the security staff had been working in DeRicci's gigantic office, partly under the direction of Flint. Then he had realized that Talia was in danger and he had just left.

Apparently, the workstations had remained in the office.

"Thanks," he said to Popova and pushed open the double doors leading into the impressive space.

The view upon entry always took his breath away. Floor-to-ceiling windows overlooking the entire city. The view also worried him: someone could take out DeRicci with just a little effort. He had insisted on reinforced material for the windows. After Anniversary Day, he also insisted that she either rent or confiscate the nearby places where a sniper could target her.

The airspace at this level was restricted as well. No aircars, no drones, no flying aliens, nothing except the protections she had put into place.

That still wouldn't stop a truly determined assassin, but it did take care of the obvious problems.

Talia followed him inside and closed the doors.

Workstations, computers, chairs, tables, all crowded into the vast expanse of floor. Plants—real ones that someone else maintained (because DeRicci just wasn't good at it)—furniture groupings and decorative tables lined the walls, pushed out of the way over a week ago, and never brought back.

DeRicci stood as he entered. She looked thinner and older than she had, or maybe he was just noticing the toll this crisis was taking on everyone.

"Miles," she said, and he thought he heard relief in her voice. Had she felt abandoned? Probably. But she was too classy to say anything about it.

She knew his first priority was—and would remain—Talia.

"You found something?" DeRicci asked.

"Actually, it wasn't me," Flint said as he walked deeper into the office. His usual path was blocked by a chair pulled out from a desk. He slid the chair back in place. "It was Luc Deshin."

DeRicci's lips thinned. She hated that Flint was working with Deshin.

"We've always known this thing was big, Noelle, but he figured out something that makes sense to me." Flint then proceeded to explain the cost of these operations. He added in the timelines, and how long it would have taken to plan everything.

Even Talia paid attention as he spoke. He almost wished she weren't, that she was ready to leave or had left in disgust, because he was going to have to ask DeRicci something about clones that he really didn't want Talia to contemplate.

Still, maybe this would galvanize Talia, bring her back from whatever dark place she had crawled into.

As he spoke, DeRicci rounded her desk and then leaned on it. She looked exhausted, more exhausted than he had ever seen her, and this information didn't seem to be helping.

"What are they trying to do?" she asked. "And who are they?"

"That's the hard question, isn't it?" Flint said. "Deshin believes they're not an individual."

He glanced at Talia. She was sitting on the chair he had moved, hands gripping the arms like it was holding her up.

"He thinks we're at war," Flint said.

"Well, clearly—"

"No, Noelle," he said gently. "Not clearly. This is some kind of planned attack that Deshin believes, and I concur, did not have a criminal motive. It has a political one."

DeRicci frowned.

"They want to get rid of the Moon?" Talia asked.

"That's what we were acting on," DeRicci said, looking at Talia. "Because we were uniting the domes on the Moon, we thought that someone didn't want us to unify the place. All of the attacks have been focused here."

"Right next to Earth," Flint said quietly. "Earth is impossible to get to, very well defended, and quite unified."

"But the Moon isn't any of those things," DeRicci said, "and it really wasn't like that decades ago or whenever they started planning this."

"They," Talia snapped. "How can anyone fight an unknown *they*?"

"We can't," Flint said. "We're trying to find them."

Talia shook her head, as if she didn't believe it.

"Here's what we're thinking," Flint said. "Imagine if the first attack had worked."

"I have," DeRicci said. "Every night when I close my eyes. And it didn't exactly fail, Miles. We lost millions."

"I know." Even talking about Anniversary Day had become a difficult thing, fraught with emotion for everyone involved. "Imagine how many we would have lost if all twenty domes collapsed."

"Then there would have been no reason for the Peyti Crisis," Talia said. She sounded even grumpier than she had before. "I think your criminal friend is wrong, Dad."

"Oh, but there would have," Flint said. "I bet, if we check, all of those lawyers were off-Moon or out of the domes during Anniversary Day."

DeRicci leaned backward on her hands, her eyes narrowed. "We can find that out."

"Do," Flint said. "It'll help."

"So what?" Talia asked.

"The Peyti clones were all high-end lawyers who had been on the Moon for years. They often represented law firms that had clients in government and major Moon-based corporations," Flint said.

DeRicci tapped a finger against her lips. She had started to do that recently when she was thinking.

"They would have been right in the middle of rebuilding plans," she said.

"You're assuming the Alliance would rebuild," Talia said.

"They'd be in talks to rebuild," Flint said. "This is the entrance to Earth. The Alliance needs the port, and it needs Armstrong. The other domes matter less to the Alliance, but they have developed an economic base that makes the Moon what it is. The lawyers would have been helping figure out ways to revive the Moon—or they would have been seeming to."

"And then they would have killed everyone with an interest in rebuilding the Moon," DeRicci said. "Six months after the Moon is devastated, it gets devastated again."

"More than that," Flint said. "Officials who would help with the rebuilding, from Alliance officials to corporate heads, would be in those meetings. The Peyti lawyers would have been very important to the rebuild, as survivors who knew what was going on before the domes collapsed."

"Survivors," DeRicci repeated. Her gaze skittered away, but not before Flint saw bleakness in it. In reality, she was the only major survivor of the United Domes of the Moon's young government. She knew exactly what he was talking about.

"Survivors," Talia said, and for a moment, Flint thought she was agreeing with DeRicci. But Talia's face had gone blank, her eyes fixed.

Flint was beginning to recognize the look. She wasn't in the room at all.

"Talia," he said, and put his hand gently on her shoulder.

She started, then looked up at him, her eyes filling with tears. "I'll be right back," she said, and raced out of the room.

Normally, he would have gone after her. But he knew she couldn't leave the building without him. And he needed to stay here until this conversation was done.

"What was that?" DeRicci asked him.

"I'm beginning to think the Peyti Crisis was some kind of last straw for her," he said. "I don't know what to do about it."

"You have been asking her to handle a huge emotional load," DeRicci said.

Flint almost denied it, but stopped himself. DeRicci was right; he had asked a lot of Talia. "I know," he said gently.

"She's not you, Miles," DeRicci said.

"Or you, Noelle."

DeRicci's smile was sad. "Sometimes you put the emotions away until you have time for them, and hope they respect that distance."

He nodded. He knew that. He glanced at the door. Part of him was very relieved that Talia had left.

"These masterminds had a two-pronged attack," he said, deliberately changing the subject. He would deal with Talia when he left. "Destroy the domes, destroy the people who try to rebuild. The fact that the domes didn't get completely destroyed, and the Earth Alliance wasn't involved in the rebuilding, didn't stop the plan, because I believe that the plan was put in motion decades ago."

"And you think there's more," DeRicci said. "What else could they do to the Moon?"

"I don't think this about the Moon," he said. "This is about the Alliance."

"You think or Deshin thinks?" she asked.

"We both think. But I want to hedge my bets. Just in case I'm wrong, just in case *we're* wrong. If we are, then we should be able to find another group of clones on the Moon, waiting to release some other kind of attack."

DeRicci closed her eyes. She seemed to gather herself. Then she opened her eyes slowly. "You're assuming that they're here now. The Frémont clones weren't. You theorize that the Peyti clones would have been off-Moon if the plan went differently. What makes you think the other clones are here now?"

"Just making certain," Flint said. "If Deshin and I are wrong, then you might find another cluster of clones, based on some mass murderer, here on the Moon."

"And if you're right, we won't find anything?" DeRicci asked.

"If we're right, there might be more clones," Flint said. "But they wouldn't be on the Moon. They'd be scattered throughout the Earth Alliance."

DeRicci frowned. "There's nothing wrong with that. It's not illegal. I'm sure there are all kinds of duplicates of various individuals all over the Alliance."

"I know," Flint said. "The problem gets a lot bigger then. We have to track it through money and DNA and the brokers. But check for me first, all right, Noelle? Search for clones here on the Moon, in unlikely positions, maybe in unlikely species like the Peyti."

DeRicci tapped her lips again. "I'm not sure that's legal, Miles. What we did the day of the Peyti Crisis had exigent circumstances. No one is going to challenge our actions that day. But to do it now, when we don't have any real evidence—"

"What does it matter, Noelle?" Flint asked. "Who will know? And if we're wrong, no one will ever know."

"If you're right, what do we do?" DeRicci asked. "Round them up because they might commit a crime?"

He had thought this through. He hated what he was going to say next. He was so glad Talia wasn't here.

"If they're clones, Noelle, they're property. We can confiscate property that came to the Moon illegally." He spoke very quietly, as if his daughter could hear him through the door. "If they don't identify themselves as clones, then they're breaking a dozen Earth Alliance laws."

"Legally, you're right," DeRicci said, "but I believe that clones are as sentient as anyone else. They're just born differently—"

He wanted to hug her for that; she, like everyone else, had no idea that Talia was a clone.

"—and so, we'd be starting a terrible precedent," DeRicci said. "And what if we're wrong? What if they're harmless? Doing some job they're particularly suited for?"

He shook his head. "I don't like this any more than you do, Noelle. But think of it this way. If some foreign government sent spies into the Alliance, and those spies could be identified with a single search, wouldn't you do it?"

"We don't know this is a foreign government," DeRicci said.

"We don't know that it isn't," Flint said.

She stared at him for a moment. Then she sighed heavily.

"I guess it wouldn't hurt to search," she said.

30

JUST AS NYQUIST WAS ABOUT TO LEAVE THAT STRANGE ROOM ATTACHED to Gumiela's office suite, one of her assistants opened the door from the outside. Gumiela leveled a glance on the assistant that even made Nyquist cringe.

The assistant, to his credit, didn't blink an eye.

"I'm sorry, sir," he said to Gumiela. "I have a lawyer here who won't go away until he sees you. He nearly shoved in on his—"

Then the door opened wider, and a gaunt man wearing a shiny blue suit pushed his way into the room. A waft of spicy cologne followed him, overpowering Nyquist with the scent of cedar mixed with oranges.

Nyquist resisted the urge to put a hand over his nose. He wasn't wearing anything that would allow him to create his own environment, and for the first time in months, he regretted that.

He would go out the other door. "If you'll excuse me, Chief."

She held up a hand, indicating that she wasn't done with him. He held back a sneeze.

"You can see me in my office," she said to the lawyer. His dark hair was slicked back, revealing eyes with pupils that were just a little too large. Either he was nervous, or he had taken a clearer in the past few hours—or both.

Nyquist didn't smell any alcohol, though, although with cologne this strong, it would have been hard to smell anything else.

"No, sir, I can't," the lawyer said. "Time is of the essence here. I already spoke to your bosses upstairs, but I'm going to talk with you as well, since you're the one handling interrogations of the Peyti."

Nyquist had his hand on the doorknob, but he froze. He actually wanted to hear this.

"I'm sure my superiors will contact me," Gumiela said in a tone so frosty that Nyquist was astonished the man hadn't turned into a block of ice.

The lawyer didn't even seem to notice. "And if they don't, then my clients will suffer. So I'm covering all angles."

Gumiela sighed noticeably.

"Fine," she said. "If time is of the essence, then speak quickly."

He bowed slightly, which Nyquist found just a little odd. But then so was the suit, with its long waistcoat and old-fashioned cut, and that overpowering cologne.

"My name is Torkild Zhu," the man said. "I am here, representing all of the clones of Uzvekmt. I have more than two dozen injunctions, which are active immediately."

Nyquist couldn't help himself; he snorted.

"*All* of the clones?" he said. "Aren't we the ambitious little lawyer."

Gumiela shot him an appreciative glance, the edges of her lips turned up in a slight smile. *Well done, Bartholomew*, she sent. *Let's get rid of this creature.*

My pleasure, Nyquist sent.

"Actually, no, I'm not," this Torkild Zhu said. "I just happen to be the Schnable, Shishani and Salehi partner who was unfortunate enough to be on the Moon right now. In case you haven't heard of us, we're a large defense firm. If you have, you might have encountered our nickname instead of our real name. We're—"

"I'm familiar with S-Three," Gumiela said. "What are you doing representing the Peyti clones? They're not even individuals. Property can't hire attorneys."

Nyquist felt surprised that she had used this argument. It made sense, however. She didn't want any legal interference at the moment.

"But other individuals can hire attorneys to act in the interest of property," Zhu said. "To be fair, however, our client—we—are uncertain whether the property laws apply. We seek injunction against any actions you might take involving property laws and clones. We also enjoin you against interrogating the clones of Uzvekmt until the rest of our team arrive. That will take several days. We will be heading to court to find out the rights of these clones and until we have a judge's ruling, you cannot do anything with them."

"Seems you already have a judge in your pocket," Nyquist said. "Otherwise you wouldn't have injunctions."

"Let me see them," Gumiela said. "We're not bound by certain injunctions issued by the Earth Alliance."

"That's right," Zhu said, reaching into his coat. He pulled a small tablet from it. "That's why we have several dozen injunctions here, from judges all over the Alliance, including two that handle cases here in Armstrong. We've enjoined representatives of the Alliance, of the United Domes of the Moon, and of all of the police departments in every dome on the Moon from doing anything except housing the clones until the rest of the team gets here."

"We don't act contingent on lawyers," Gumiela said.

Zhu smiled. He was younger than Nyquist thought. The smile didn't reach the lawyer's eyes. He was nervous. Maybe he wasn't that happy being the representative of so many potential mass murderers.

"I understand that, sir," Zhu said. "Which is why the injunctions are for one month. You may take no action with these clones until the injunctions expire."

She took the tablet from him. Then she glanced at Nyquist.

What the hell? she sent.

Let me, he sent back.

"Obviously, I haven't looked at the injunctions," Nyquist said, "but how do we know that your firm represents these clones?"

"You don't have to worry about it," Zhu said. "The courts have already decided—"

"The courts decided because a famous law firm with some clout asked them to consider this. I think we need to validate the injunctions."

"Go ahead," Zhu said. "But any court you go to will keep the injunctions in place while ruling on their validity. No court would risk removing the injunction while the risk of injury to those clones is so high. Because the consequences to the court—to the judge, actually—would be severe."

"Why don't you just tell us who your client is," Gumiela said.

"The Government of Peyla," Zhu said.

Nyquist exhaled. He hadn't expected that. "The government of an entire planet?"

"Right now, this situation is having a negative impact on the Peyti. Apparently, your port is denying them entry, and you people are refusing to talk with Peyti lawyers of any kind. That's why I'm here. The government of Peyla has an interest, and while all the court cases play out, you are enjoined from acting against that interest."

Sorry, Nyquist sent Gumiela. *It was worth a shot.*

I had hoped we might find out who actually owned the clones, she sent.

You're assuming it's not the government of Peyla, Nyquist sent.

She looked at him with great horror. Zhu watched them both, now realizing they were communicating on their private links.

It couldn't be, she sent.

Nyquist didn't believe in "couldn't" any more. He'd had too many surprises this year already. So he shrugged.

"If you two are finished," Zhu said, "I'll leave you with the injunctions. But do know this: My firm has incredible resources and if you violate the injunctions, not only will you suffer the legal penalties imposed by the various courts, we will sue you."

"For what?" Nyquist asked before stopping himself. "Are you going to value the clones? I can save you some time on that. They have no value. They might be property, but they're worthless property now."

Zhu's smile was smarmy, and this time, his eyes weren't empty. They seemed to be taunting him.

"There're all kinds of ways of measuring damages in a suit," Zhu said. "You've only thought of one out of thousands."

Then he pivoted and left the room. Or, rather, most of him left the room. The cologne remained, and probably would unless someone turned on the environmental scrubbers.

Gumiela closed the door. Then she leaned on it. "How the hell am I going to deal with this?" she asked softly.

Nyquist wasn't even certain she was speaking to him, but he was going to assume she was.

"You look on it as a gift," he said.

She raised her head, and from her expression, he realized that indeed, she hadn't thought of him when she spoke initially.

"A gift?" she asked. "Everyone's after me to get answers. We have to find the next attackers before they hit, and we can't even talk to the attackers we have in custody."

"That's right," Nyquist said. "But now you can find out what kind of interest the Peyti government has in these clones. You're probably closer to solving this than you would have been if all of us interrogated those prisoners."

She shook her head. Then she closed her eyes.

A bulletin came across his links: *Do not proceed with any interrogation. Orders from the top have altered. Wait until we receive new orders before moving forward.*

That was the general announcement that she had just sent. Nyquist supposed she was sending others as well, probably to her lieutenants, making certain they would prevent any action from being taken.

"You said this was a gift."

It took Nyquist a minute to realize she was speaking out loud to him.

He nodded. "You said it. Everyone expects you to get answers, and you know that you can't. You know those lawyers will never talk. You know that what information we would get would be tainted, particularly if some rogue detectives decided to break some property."

She looked at him sideways, as if looking at him full on meant that she would have to agree with everything he said.

"Now, you can blame S-Three or the Peyti government or whoever you want. You can blame your superiors. You can blame the Earth Alliance, or the judges. It's out of your hands."

And, he thought but didn't say, *it probably just saved your career.*

Her cheeks flushed slightly. She looked down. He had a sense she understood what he had just implied.

"Gift is probably the wrong word," she said. "Especially if we get attacked again."

She was ever the politician. But he agreed with that sentiment.

"Still, you're right. It takes some of the pressure off." She sighed and stood up. "Now all I have to do is make sure these injunctions are legitimate. Then I'm going to see if we can investigate S-Three's clients. I really don't want to hand this off to the Earth Alliance, do you?"

"No," he said. "And if you need help looking into things—"

"I will turn to you, Bartholomew. Thank you."

And then she walked out of the room, leaving him alone with the cologne. He felt shaken.

He wasn't even certain he agreed with himself. A gift? Maybe. But it was also a burden. He wanted to catch the perpetrators, and interrogating the Peyti clones would have felt like he was doing something.

He went out the other door, into the now-empty bullpen. That restlessness, that need to do something, made him wonder if he was more of a hypocrite than he realized.

Had he gone in to talk with Gumiela to stop Romey and others like her?

Or had he wanted Gumiela to clarify the rules?

And if she had made it official that no one would get punished for harming the clones, what would he have done?

Nyquist was very glad he would never find out.

31

As Flint left DeRicci's office, he felt like he'd won a Pyrrhic victory. She would use the methods he had developed to find the Peyti clones only a week ago to see if other large groups of clones existed on the Moon. Only it would be a bit worse than the methods he'd used. He had traced the clones of a known mass murderer. DeRicci would be looking for large groups of similar faces, no matter what the species. Then DeRicci would have to determine how many clones of an original were "normal" and how many were "suspicious." Once she deemed them suspicious, she would try to match them to known killers.

Or something. He wasn't sure about the second half of how the search would work.

But he did know this: If DeRicci found anything, her actions might have a negative impact on a lot of individuals as wonderful and innocent as Talia.

At least DeRicci understood that. She was someone he could trust to use the power she had minimally, taking it no farther than she needed to.

The needs were what worried him. Times were extraordinary, and he was enough of a student of history to know that procedures developed in extraordinary times were often misused in ordinary times.

He also knew that DeRicci wouldn't be in charge forever.

But she was in charge at the moment. He had to trust her to do the right thing. Because, as he kept reminding himself, if they didn't figure out where, when, and what that third attack would be, then his concerns about clones and individual rights wouldn't matter at all.

He didn't see Talia. He had expected to find her in one of the chairs littering the reception area where Popova's desk was.

Popova watched him for a moment, as if she were trying to decide something. Then she beckoned him.

He stepped forward, a bit surprised. Popova wasn't the beckoning type.

"Sit for a minute," she said.

"I need to find Talia," he said.

"She's in the bathroom. She'll be there a while."

He felt a surge of panic. "She's sick?"

Popova shook her head. "She's getting herself together again."

Flint glanced toward the restrooms. If Talia was letting other people see how poorly she was doing, then she was in very bad shape indeed.

"Listen," Popova said. "I know someone."

He looked at her. Her cheeks were flushed. The normally unflappable Rudra Popova was flapped.

"There's a therapist I saw after Arek died. I needed someone to talk to." Popova's voice was soft.

Flint remembered how she had been in the days after Anniversary Day. She had been just like Talia, emotions right on the surface, unable to function the way she had before.

Popova was no longer the woman she had been before Anniversary Day, but that day had changed everyone. She was closer to that woman, though, than she had been after Anniversary Day. At that point, DeRicci hadn't been certain if Popova would be able to remain on the job. DeRicci hadn't been certain Popova would ever recover—and neither had Flint.

"Talia needs someone," Popova said, as if she thought Flint were going to contradict her. "She's hit a breaking point and, no offense, you're not the person she can turn to. Neither am I, and I doubt a girl like her has the right kind of friends who can help her through this."

Popova was right; Talia didn't have anyone she could talk to, not about the things that truly disturbed her.

"She and I talked a little," Popova said, glancing at the bathroom door. She clearly didn't want Talia to walk in on them. "She got quiet pretty fast, but not before I could put a few things together."

Flint weaved his fingers so tightly that his hands ached. But he didn't want to show how uncomfortable this conversation made him, not just because he was worried about Talia's mental health, but also because he was worried about her general safety.

Right now, given the climate in Armstrong, he didn't want anyone to figure out that she was a clone.

"She lost her mother, she lost her home, she lost her friends, and she was just rebuilding her life when Anniversary Day happened."

"She handled it all right," Flint said, and realized he sounded defensive.

"She handled it," Popova said, "until she watched a group of people die in front of her at her school. Just like her mother was kidnapped from her home."

Flint nodded. He had known this. But hearing it from someone else made it even harder to deal with.

"And there's something in the middle of all this, something that made her stop talking to me, and start up the tears again." Popova glanced at the bathroom doors one more time. Then she leaned forward and lowered her voice even more. "It was the last straw. If you don't get her help, I'm not sure what will happen."

"I don't know what would help her," Flint said.

"She has secrets," Popova said. "I get that, and they're probably important, given what happened to her mother. But a therapist is bound by confidentiality—"

That didn't mean they would follow it, Flint wanted to say, but didn't. He let Popova go on.

"—and Talia should be safe talking about things she doesn't want the rest of us to know. And that includes you. She's going to have to work this one out on her own."

"She's already worked out too much on her own," Flint said. He had only been able to do so much. Some of it she needed to work out with her mother, but her mother died before the secrets got revealed.

"Exactly," Popova said. "I'm going to give you the name of my therapist. I've already given it to Talia. I want her to present it to you, but if she doesn't do so in a short amount of time, just take her there. She can't go on like this."

"I know," he said, wishing Talia would come out of the bathroom. "Believe me, I know."

FOUR DAYS LATER

32

THE COMPANY'S FASTEST SPACE YACHT FELT MORE LIKE A CARGO SHIP. Even though Rafael Salehi knew that S^3's largest yacht could hold over 150 people comfortably, not counting ship staff, he had never traveled with more than twenty guests on board.

No one here was a guest. No one could even consider being a guest. Everyone had to work.

He left Athena Base with thirty human staff, including lawyers, legal assistants, and researchers. He had picked up a contingent of legal theorists—professors, former judges, and the like—on the way to Peyla. There he had gathered another twenty Peyti attorneys, plus their retinues.

And then there was the staff on the yacht itself. Hired for their discretion and their dedication to service, if he could believe the crap shoveled at him from S^3's personnel department.

Even so, he didn't conduct a lot of conversations where the staff could hear, and he had hired his own expert to make certain that personal areas were not networked, and could not be accessed from the outside in any way.

He felt like he was sneaking into enemy territory, when all he was doing was heading to the Moon.

Part of the Earth Alliance.

Where he had spent his entire life.

He sat in the law library, a large, fully enclosed room that had holographic books on the walls. The books contained non-networked information on the topic listed on the book's cover, sometimes linked to other books or with actual footage of the trials or the rulings. S^3 had a similar room in its research building.

Usually Salehi found all this knowledge, placed in tidy book-like forms, uncomfortable; he preferred to work on the private networked systems. If he were being honest with himself, he had relied too much on AutoLearn the past few years. He'd plug in a legal question, download cases, and then turn on his AutoLearn program.

He'd end up with a vast knowledge of the topic, but the knowledge would be superficial, and often wouldn't last for more than a month. Sometimes, when he used AutoLearn, he wouldn't even remember what the case had been about.

He refused to use AutoLearn on these clone cases—and he had already made it clear to his staff that anyone caught using AutoLearn would be removed from the project and had a good chance of being released from the firm. Some of the legal assistants had hated that, but he had noticed the researchers nodding.

The researchers had told him many times that AutoLearn shouldn't be called AutoLearn at all. In fact, in the research building, the preferred term for AutoLearn was FakeKnowledge.

He thought that sounded as good as any.

No FakeKnowledge here. Only deep research, even deeper discussions, and a lot of theorizing. He actually scheduled everyone's day. They still had three days of travel before they arrived in Armstrong, and he meant to make use of as much of that time as he could.

He'd even scheduled downtime because he knew that study without downtime was as effective as AutoLearn.

Many of the group had meals together, but he only joined them for dinner, and then for only an hour or so. No legal discussions about these cases at the table, only anecdotes, stories, and jokes could be about the law; the rest of the conversation had to be about something else. He didn't care what else, so long as it gave everyone's brains a rest.

This room was reserved for what he privately called the A Team. The best minds of their generation and all that. Really, the best minds he could assemble—not just on clone law, but also on legal theory and courtroom procedures.

He had lawyers on this ship who had argued several cases in front of all of the Multicultural Tribunals. He needed those minds just to keep the team on track. Eventually, he knew, these cases he would be arguing would go in front of one of the Multicultural Tribunals; he just wasn't sure which one.

The thing that made this an Alliance case was the presence of two different kinds of clones—human and Peyti. The fact that both had come from known mass murderers tied his cases together even if he never found who had created the originals.

Right now, the A Team was working on the question of standing. Even though S^3 had been hired to represent the clones, there was some question as to whether or not the clones could appear in court without their owners present.

Since the owners were criminals set on destroying the Moon (at the very least), there was no chance the owners would ever show up in court.

The idea that the clones' actions during the Peyti Crisis had disrupted business for the Peyti Alliance-wide was an argument that the non-legal authorities on the Moon and in the domes might buy, but he wasn't certain any court would accept it.

If he were a judge, he would say that S^3 and the Peyti government did not have standing to defend the clones on any of the charges. S^3 had the ability to argue the unfairness of judging the Peyti according to the behavior of some clones, but not the legality of the clones or their behavior.

He was looking for a way around it, as were two of his assistants, huddled in chairs on opposite sides of the room. These assistants had traveled on the yacht many times and knew that those chairs, with built-in adjustable desks, provided the best places to get serious business done.

There was only one Peyti lawyer in the room, partly because, if Salehi were honest, the Peyti were making everyone nervous right now. The masks obscured most of their faces, and their eyes didn't seem that different from each other's.

He had gotten used to differences in build and skin coloring, as well as the way some of the Peyti held themselves.

He could recognize his co-counsel, Uzvuyiten, anywhere.

Uzvuyiten was one of the oldest Peyti Salehi had ever seen. His gray skin was almost white, the color uneven as if the skin's pigment weren't designed to last as long as Uzvuyiten had. His twig-like fingers were bent at the tips, and nothing he seemed to do could straighten them out.

Salehi had seen some of the other humans on the trip look at Uzvuyiten's fingers and turn away in disgust. Salehi could still remember feeling that way when he had first seen them. The Peyti hand looked almost human until it became clear that the fingers bent in directions no human hand could.

Uzvuyiten's fingers were bent backward, between the last knuckle and the tip on a human finger, about halfway up a human fingernail. To make matters worse, the bent ridge was a bright blue that glowed in the right kind of light.

Shortly after meeting Uzvuyiten for the first time, Salehi had asked him why he hadn't had the fingers repaired. Uzvuyiten had made the odd little choking sound that Salehi would eventually realize was Uzvuyiten's laugh, and said, *They have been repaired.*

Salehi hadn't asked any more. He didn't want to know.

Even without the fingers, though, Uzvuyiten would be recognizable. He wore human suits that were nearly a century old in design. His posture was excellent, making him look like—in the words of Schnabby—the perfect coat hanger.

Uzvuyiten had more personality than any other Peyti that Salehi had ever met, and that personality showed up in every single detail about him.

Even his eyes were unusual. They were moist and blue around the edges, but gray in the center. They seemed almost human, but Salehi wouldn't tell Uzvuyiten that ever, because Uzvuyiten would take that as an insult.

Uzvuyiten had his head bent as he worked on two different screens at the same time, going back and forth between them, marking information down.

One of the first things lawyers learned was not to use their links or any automated networked system to make notes on important cases. Too many attorneys had simply downloaded their opposition's arguments before a big case, then used those arguments to crush the opposition in court.

That restriction made law very writing- and reading-intensive, and somewhat backward, since the rest of the universe could operate at the speed of a thought, but the lawyers and judges and anyone else dealing with confidentiality had to operate with the speed of their fingers.

Uzvuyiten tapped the edge of his long arm on the table, jarring the image that Salehi had been staring at. He hadn't even been sure of what he saw, not because the image was unclear, but because he'd been thinking rather than looking.

"Your arguments are too linear," Uzvuyiten said. "You missed one of the most important arguments of all."

Salehi frowned. He had forgotten this side of working with Uzvuyiten. Uzvuyiten assumed that a conversation they had started three days ago could be continued at any point without providing any context. Uzvuyiten had an eidetic memory, and assumed everyone else did as well. Of course, Salehi didn't. He was smart, but outside-the-box smart. He wasn't traditionally testing-brilliant, which meant that he didn't seem as smart as most of his colleagues from law school.

Although, even factoring out his family money, he was twenty times more successful than anyone he went to school with.

"I'm sure I missed a lot," Salehi said, and was pleased that he didn't sound defensive, just informative. "I slapped nearly a hundred injunctions together in the space of a few hours. I had good help, but the ideas were mine."

"The injunctions are fine," Uzvuyiten said, dismissively. Apparently that wasn't what he had been discussing. "It's that matter of standing."

So they were both thinking about the same thing. Weird.

Salehi didn't comment on that. Instead, he said, "I ignored it mostly, since I didn't know how to deal with it."

He still didn't.

Uzvuyiten kept his gaze on Salehi. Salehi felt like he needed to explain more, which made him uncomfortable.

So now, he did sound defensive. "I figured the courts would listen to us up front, and decide all the pesky minutia later."

Uzvuyiten grunted in acknowledgement. It sounded like he had expected an explanation like that, which made Salehi feel even more defensive.

"If only it were minutia," Uzvuyiten said. "The moment the courts find out that the Peyti government is the client of record, they could throw everything out. And then your grand universe-changing case becomes nothing."

Salehi had thought all this through. It was giving him sleepless nights, making him feel as if he were running a race that he could be disqualified from at any moment.

He had already told Uzvuyiten all the ideas Salehi could find for arguing standing. But it wouldn't hurt to mention the new ones.

"I was thinking that maybe we could argue that since Uzvekmt was caught and imprisoned on Peyla, the Peyti government owned his DNA," Salehi said. "That would make them the owners of record of the clones until we discover the actual owners."

"And if the actual owners are clone brokers or someone from the Black Fleet? Everything gets tossed out," Uzvuyiten said.

Salehi had thought of that too. "Or, everything gets placed on hold while we argue the case we file to reestablish standing."

Uzvuyiten shook his head. That movement always looked unnatural on a Peyti. Salehi felt Peyti shouldn't even try it. But Uzvuyiten had adopted a lot of human mannerisms—and had abandoned just as many.

"You are too trusting," Uzvuyiten said. "You assume the court will put the case on hold. You must always look to the worst case."

Salehi sighed. He thought he had been looking at the worst case. "If you can imagine something we can't fight with another lawsuit, tell me."

"If our cases continually get thrown out for standing," Uzvuyiten said, "then at some point, we will not even be able to file. We will be fighting the wrong battle, maybe for years."

He leaned back and tugged on his mask. Salehi had seen Uzvuyiten do that many times before. It was Uzvuyiten's way of tugging on his chin—a human gesture.

Only now, that gesture made one of the legal assistants cringe. Everyone had seen the images coming from the Moon—the Peyti clones tugging the explosives in their masks. The Crisis was fresh in everyone's minds. Apparently, even in the minds of the lawyers representing the clones.

Uzvuyiten didn't seem to notice the reaction. He also didn't seem to notice that Salehi couldn't quite hide his irritation. He hated having Uzvuyiten explain basic law to him. In fact, Salehi knew better than anyone how easy it was to lose a big case on the smallest of details.

He'd done so more than once in his early career, before he became the kind of lawyer he used to hate—the lawyer who prepared for everything, down to the smallest detail.

"So what did I miss?" Salehi asked, this time with a little heat.

"Unclaimed property," Uzvuyiten said.

Salehi suppressed a smile of irritation. "I didn't miss it. I decided it wasn't relevant. The law says the owners have a month after the property's discovered to claim it. We can't file yet."

"Sure we can," Uzvuyiten said. "All ports examine DNA when someone goes through a decontamination unit."

It was an interesting argument, but it didn't seem viable to Salehi. He said, "The ports are legally bound to keep the DNA private, unless a valid warrant is presented."

Uzvuyiten held up one of his crooked fingers, as a sort of warning. "Ports are also bound by Alliance law to make sure that property remains with its owners. Lost property goes to a specific area of the port. Because lost property can be dangerous in the wrong hands."

Salehi frowned at him. "You're certain?"

He hadn't heard of this.

"Of course I'm certain. But you won't find it in most legal texts. It's actually treaty law. Food, for example, can be an issue. The Ticip'ns must bring their food with them. They eat gases which include things like sarin, which is so lethal when it is airborne that it can kill humans in a few minutes. Yet, Ticip'ns are part of the Earth Alliance, which allows them the right to travel to places where their food is lethal poison. They must control the substance at all times, keep it in a proper container, and only release it in designated areas. If the food—or shall we call it poison?—becomes separated from a Ticip'n in a port, the port must shuffle that property to a safe, designated area, until the property gets reclaimed."

All of the lawyers were watching Uzvuyiten now. Most looked fascinated. A couple glanced at Salehi, as if asking him if this were true.

There was no reason for Uzvuyiten to lie. And if the lawyers wanted to know the truth of what he was saying, they could look it up themselves.

"There is nothing wrong with dangerous property," Uzvuyiten said, a bit dramatically. Apparently, he realized that he now had an audience. "However, all property must be under control of its owners, particularly when traveling outside of its native environment."

Salehi let out a small breath.

"It's clear that the Peyti clones were outside their native environment," one of the junior lawyers said, sounding pleased.

Salehi wasn't willing to be pleased yet. "It's a little more complicated than that. I could easily argue that we have no idea what the native environment is for the clones' owners."

Uzvuyiten waved his hand. "Technicalities that we do not need to foresee."

Salehi resisted the urge to roll his eyes. The conversation had been about technicalities that they *needed* to foresee.

"The key," Uzvuyiten said, "is that lost property shouldn't be allowed to function in society for *decades*."

The staff exchanged glances. Pleased glances from what Salehi saw. But he wasn't pleased. The more he thought about it, the more he realized what a problem this argument was.

Arguing the danger of lost property would harm *all* clones, not help them. They wouldn't be able to travel freely. They would constantly need permission slips or something like it from their owners.

Uzvuyiten looked at him sideways. Once again, Salehi felt like Uzvuyiten knew what he was thinking.

"We are discussing standing," Uzvuyiten said softly. "We need standing first."

He had known what Salehi's arguments were, and Uzvuyiten didn't want Salehi to mention them. Probably a good idea in a crowded room.

"After we have standing, we worry about the consequences of our arguments," Uzvuyiten said softly.

"Seems dangerous to me," Salehi said.

"What we are doing *is* dangerous," Uzvuyiten said. "We are arguing for a group of terrible individuals to save an even larger group of trapped individuals. Or at least you are."

"And you?" Salehi asked.

"I want my freedom back," Uzvuyiten said. "It galls me that we Peyti are no longer welcome within the heart of the Alliance."

"You can sue," one of the junior partners said.

"Our government is. But so far, we cannot prove that the discrimination is anything sanctioned."

And everyone in the room was a good enough lawyer to know that discrimination cases, even those within the Alliance, needed to be against an organization or a person in power. Otherwise, the lawyers would need a long-established pattern of behavior before ever attempting a suit.

Salehi ignored that. He was still focused on what bothered him about the lost property argument.

He said, "Your lost-property argument is, after all, a property argument."

"I'm aware," Uzvuyiten said in a tone that sounded a tad patronizing.

"It bolsters the claim of anyone who wants to interrogate, or torture, or do something worse to those clones."

"No, it doesn't," Uzvuyiten said. "Not at all. Follow me here. It's up to the port to keep track of unclaimed property from the moment the port knows the property is unclaimed. We are not talking about how the clones should be treated now. We're arguing that they should never have been allowed onto the Moon in the first place. One does not follow the other."

Salehi frowned. They would have to argue both cases very carefully. They would need to use different courts first. He could see going against the port, using Alliance Space law. Once they had a ruling from the Space Court, they would be able to go into other courts as the attorneys of record for the clones.

"Okay," he said. "I'll ignore the other ramifications of this argument for the moment. If we use unclaimed property, we sue for Peyla to become the owners of record?"

"No," Uzvuyiten said. "Peyla would claim the property, maybe even buy it at discount rates, after we determine that it is unclaimed, of course."

Salehi let out a small breath. "We're only going to use the unclaimed property argument to gain standing, is that correct?"

"Right now," Uzvuyiten said.

Salehi waited, hoping Uzvuyiten would explain the other arguments.

Of course, he did not.

"Let's just concentrate on standing for the moment," Uzvuyiten said. "Let's set everything else aside."

Salehi suppressed a sigh. He'd had a moment to think now, and he still didn't see how all of this would work.

"I'm still not sure how we could win the unclaimed property argument," he said. "We can't argue that the port knew. These clones are sentient beings. They look like regular Peyti. There is no reason for the port to deny them entrance. If they're anything like the Frémont clones, they have no clone marks."

"That is not our concern," Uzvuyiten said. "You are thinking like an attorney for the port."

"Still," Salehi said. "Information on individuals is private. It can't be accessed. I have no idea how you believe that the port could have known these individuals were clones."

"You forget," Uzvuyiten said. "The port itself has to examine the DNA for nanocontaminants, and it has to examine the body for indications of all kinds of things, including but not limited to, illegal transportation."

"You want to argue that all of the clones were illegally transported?" Salehi asked.

"Yes," Uzvuyiten said. "Their owners are unknown. No one filed documents about the clones. No one has taken responsibility for them *in decades*. Think about it this way. If someone sent actual bombs into the Port of Armstrong, without documentation and without any follow-up, those bombs would have been deactivated and set aside. They also would have been investigated."

"There's no way to claim these clones were the equivalent of bombs," Salehi said.

"No, they were more like ingredients for bombs. They were harmful material that could act on its own. The port already has a quarantine area for harmful material. The clones should have been set aside until their owners found, and their purpose established."

"I don't like this," Salehi said. "Every single free-traveling clone will be subject to increased searches throughout the Alliance if we win this."

"We might not need it," Uzvuyiten said. "Let's hope that we do not. However, we still should file an unclaimed property case in the Space court that handles Armstrong's cases to cover our asses."

Salehi knew Uzvuyiten was right. Salehi knew that they should cover every single angle. It was common for attorneys to use every single argument possible in initial filings to make certain that the contingents were covered if a judge tossed out the important stuff.

"You can do no good for clones in general if you do not have these cases," Uzvuyiten said.

Salehi studied him. That sort of insight was part of what made Uzvuyiten such a good attorney. He knew how to get others to do what he wanted.

Uzvuyiten did not care about clones or clone law. He wanted to prevent the Peyti from becoming permanent second-class citizens.

Salehi had to remember that.

He also had to remember that he had to make a preliminary argument to set up his future argument.

He could twist this unclaimed property argument to his advantage later. No port had the facilities to imprison free-traveling clones until their owners were established. It would take more money and labor than any port had.

Ports already had issues dealing with illegal immigration from a whole variety of planets and cultures. Generally the ports turned those groups away—because they arrived in groups. There were systems to prevent individuals from getting on transports and in other vehicles that traveled to the ports.

There were absolutely no systems in place to prevent clone travel. If he won this argument (if *they* won this argument), then Alliance ports would be filled with untethered clones.

Win an argument, create havoc, state that the havoc was unintended—or maybe even after winning, worry about the havoc.

He had been right after all: This case—these cases—could change everything.

He just wasn't sure the cases would change everything the way he wanted them to.

33

Torkild Zhu hadn't been this busy since his hellish first years as a lawyer. He'd worked 120-hour weeks then, sometimes more, and always felt as if he were behind.

He felt that way now as the only truly official representative of S^3 here on the Moon. Sometimes he found himself cursing his law firm's shortsightedness. It had branch offices all over the Alliance, but none deep in its heart. Most of the branches were located near the Alliance District Courts and the various Multicultural Tribunals. Most of the branches concentrated on appeals or big cases, or gave the attorneys a home away from home.

Like this place was supposed to be.

He now had access to S^3's virtually unlimited accounts, so that he could establish that base, order furniture, and hire staff from lawyers to security. S^3 On The Moon, as he was calling the offices, would need a lot of security, if the response he was getting from potential employees was any indication.

The very idea that they would be working with the Peyti clones made most people stomp out of here in anger.

Zhu had stopped mentioning it after the third potential hire, but he knew that he couldn't hide it from everyone. They would need to know. He didn't want people stomping out *after* they'd filled out their documentation.

He stood in the middle of the office space he'd rented. It was on the middle floor of a fairly nondescript building near the edge of Old Armstrong. He didn't have a budget, which was good, because the rents in this city for large amounts of office space were astronomical. Even so, he couldn't find much that suited the firm's needs.

Salehi had been clear: he wanted a base of operations for now, one that would last a few months at most. By then, he expected that the firm's real estate broker would arrive from wherever the hell she was and she would pick out (or build) the perfect offices.

Until that moment, Zhu hadn't known that S^3 had someone in charge of real estate, although it made sense. Just like it made sense that the firm had various investment brokers to handle not just the firm's money, but the multitudinous client estates and accounts that the firm handled.

He rarely thought of the size of S^3, but now he was deep in the middle of it, and it truly overwhelmed him.

The space he'd rented took the entire floor. It had a lot of offices, blocked off from the others, and they all had windows, but the views were of the scratchy old parts of the dome. It looked like someone had taken knives to the interior of the dome, then coated it with yellow paint, and then tried to scrape it all off.

The rental agent who had brokered the office transaction had spent most of her time impressing on Zhu that the environmental system was up to handling the Moon dust, which freaked him out. Moon dust belonged *outside* the dome, not inside. As she nattered on, he'd actually looked up the Moon dust problem on his links, and saw that it was endemic to certain parts of Armstrong.

The only places he could find to rent immediately were all in or near those parts.

The rest of the places needed repair, many of them because they were the site—just a week ago—of incidents that composed the Peyti Crisis. A lot of businesses had closed or were opting to move out of those locations.

If Salehi had waited a month, then there would have been a surfeit of rentals on the market. But Salehi wanted a base of operations by the time he arrived, and that was about three days from now.

Zhu intended to have the place furnished, staffed, spit-and-polished, and as perfect as he could get it.

All while he was handling questions about the injunctions.

He spent half his days on his links with the heads of various police departments, asking him (off the record of course) if he truly intended to prosecute anyone who violated the injunctions.

Of course we do, he would tell them, frowning for emphasis. He knew he didn't look that tough, but he had to try. He needed the injunctions to hold until Salehi got here.

Zhu had held more meetings than he ever wanted to. He'd talked to port officials, alliance officials, and representatives of various law enforcement communities in Armstrong. He hadn't talked with the Chief of Moon Security, but only because he had pleaded flunkiness.

I'm the lawyer S³ *hired to set up its base here,* he'd told the chief's assistant truthfully. *My boss will be here in just a few days. I suggest you hold your questions for him, since I'd just have to work through him anyway.*

She had agreed. He'd only seen her once, a striking woman with long black hair and intelligent dark eyes. There was an air of sadness to her that he found appealing, although he wasn't entirely sure why.

She had given him the sense that the Security Office was so busy that waiting a few days meant absolutely nothing, and might even be a relief. He was happy to see someone busier than himself—although he wasn't entirely sure how that was possible.

The furniture had arrived about an hour ago, and right now, the offices were filled with androids, bots, and burly humans lugging gigantic desks and chairs up the service elevator.

The biggest items, like the conference tables, grew in place using some kind of nano-something or other. He hadn't entirely understood how that worked, never having bought furniture on this scale before, and he didn't really care.

All he knew was that the furniture people needed to keep an employee on hand for the next thirty-six hours to supervise the various growing tables and chairs.

He didn't mind. There was no proprietary information in any of the offices where the furniture needed to grow, and at the moment, there were no other lawyers with whom he was sharing information. The furniture guy couldn't hack into their systems even if he wanted to, because at the moment, there was nothing to hack.

Salehi probably wouldn't approve. Hell, an office manager probably wouldn't approve.

But Zhu was here alone, and he had no backup. He had three different office managers coming back for a second interview later in the afternoon. He'd investigated their backgrounds and got rid of half the good applicants right there. Maybe once one of them was on board, his life would get easier.

Even though he doubted it.

He spun around the lobby—or what would be the lobby—as the furniture people and their androids slid the groupings into place. He had just completed an agreement with a janitorial service, and they would start the following morning.

That service he'd had to vet, and vet heavily (using company resources) because the bots and cleaners would have access to everything.

The minute it became clear to the entire Moon that S^3 represented the clones, this place would be under constant attack.

The elevator door opened. He headed toward it, feeling more anticipation than he should have. In fifteen minutes, a group of newly minted lawyers sent up from a headhunter on Earth were scheduled to arrive.

Zhu had been looking forward to seeing them. They didn't have the concerns Moon-based lawyers did, nor did they have the experiences of both the Peyti Crisis and Anniversary Day. In just a few short days, he was beginning to realize how very important that was.

Not to mention the fact that lawyers were at a premium now. Every law firm on the Moon was interviewing new lawyers, because they had lost several—not just the Peyti lawyers, but the lawyers who had accompanied them on whatever case was underway when the Peyti environment kicked in.

Zhu was competing with reputable firms, firms that weren't asking the lawyers to represent the Peyti clones, and so far he was losing out.

This new group was his best chance of hiring qualified attorneys in the past two days.

But only one person stood in front of the elevator, back to him. He paused, confused, not certain what he was seeing. Small and slight, with black hair so short that only the elegant curve of the neck told him he was looking at a woman.

She turned, and his breath caught.

Berhane.

34

NYQUIST CLUTCHED THE BAG OF BURGERS TO HIS CHEST LIKE A WOUNDED child as he exited the elevator in the United Domes of the Moon Security Office. He half-wished he hadn't brought the food now. He'd never had a bag of food searched so thoroughly before.

He hoped to hell whoever had been handling his burger had clean hands.

It had seemed like such a good idea, bringing food to DeRicci and Popova, since they were stuck at work again. He was feeling at loose ends since the injunctions got confirmed. He had other cases, but they faded in importance to interrogating the Peyti Crisis clones. Even though he'd been worried about his fellow detectives using the wrong interrogation methods, he wasn't happy that the interrogations had been cut off.

Even though he had called that a gift when he spoke to Gumiela, he wasn't sure he had meant it. Every day they failed to get information was a day that they fell farther and farther behind.

He pasted a smile on his face as he stepped in front of Popova's desk. She had her long hair pulled back into some kind of bun, held in place with long pointed black sticks—stylish, yes, but dangerous. He wondered if those sticks had been searched when Popova had come to work this morning.

"Rudra," he said, setting the bag on her desk. "I bring dinner."

He almost told her that the guards downstairs had run dinner through several scanners after pawing the buns and patties. Then Nyquist changed his mind. If he told her, she might not eat it, and both Popova and DeRicci needed food more than they needed something else to worry about.

Popova smiled at him. "Smells good, Bartholomew," she said. "I don't know when I last had hot food."

"Bartholomew sees it as his duty to feed me." DeRicci spoke from behind him.

He turned.

She looked even more tired than she had the night before. Her features were drawn, her eyes disappearing into their sockets. Last night, when she arrived at his apartment, he'd given her the leftovers from his unusually healthy dinner, and then sent her to bed—without him.

She had only gotten four hours of sleep, but that had been at least two more hours than she would have gotten if she had gone home. And probably four more hours than she would have gotten if she had stayed here.

He wanted to harangue her for living on sleep blockers and artificial wakefulness drugs, but he didn't dare. Better to feed her and try to manipulate her into resting. That way, she wouldn't avoid him. If he started nagging her, he was truly worried that she would stop talking to him out of sheer self-protection.

He smiled at her. He had missed her.

"I need something useful to do since that stupid law firm tied our hands," he said.

"S-Three," Popova said. "I wish I had never heard of them."

"We have more than enough to do without worrying about the Peyti clones," DeRicci said, frowning at Popova over Nyquist's shoulder.

"Yeah," he said, "that's something I want to talk with you about."

"Bring that yummy food into my lair," DeRicci said. "I'm not sure how much longer I can withstand that wonderful smell."

He took the bag with him as DeRicci led him into the office.

He wasn't quite prepared for it. He'd been here many times, but it always seemed organized. Now there were pieces of desks and chairs in the wrong place. The plants had been moved, and DeRicci's desk was mounded with all kinds of detritus—some of which, he realized, were shirts and pants. She'd been changing clothes here, possibly on the nights she had nothing to wear at his place.

She grabbed some water bottles from a nearby fridge—that was new as well—and set them on the table in the center of the room. Then she eased into one of the chairs.

"Theoretically, I shouldn't talk to you about what we're doing," she said tiredly. "But there's no one left to yell at me for breaking rules that aren't even codified into law yet. So, Bartholomew, what do you want to ask?"

He wanted to hold her. She was so sad and she hadn't dealt with any of those softer emotions yet. But she kept giving herself away with phrases like the one she just used: *There's no one left to yell at me*. She had hated the restrictions before, and now, she missed them.

Or rather, she missed the people who had imposed them.

If he were less charitable, he would say she missed having something to push against, but he knew that wasn't entirely the problem. She used to say that she wanted to be the person in charge, but now that she was, it was eating her up from the inside out.

Or maybe that was just the nature of the entire crisis.

He took the two burgers out of the bag. He'd also indulged and bought French fries made the old-fashioned way, in oil, with salt and sugar. He knew that DeRicci loved the things, and he also knew they were the most unhealthy thing he could find.

But he didn't care. Food was food. And the restaurant he'd bought this at used only the best ingredients for its meals—as if good grease made the food healthier.

"I was wondering if you need another investigator," Nyquist said.

"Because S-Three tied your hands?" DeRicci asked.

He nodded.

"I'm sure you have other cases," she said, adjusting the bun on her burger. She seemed to know that the guards downstairs had messed with the food, and apparently it didn't bother her.

"I do," he said. "But an unsolved murder from seven months ago seems a lot less important than solving millions of attempted murders less than two weeks old."

She gave him a weak smile. "Well, when you put it that way," she said.

She took a bite out of the burger, and closed her eyes. She made a sound he thought she only made in bed.

"You know," he said after a minute, "you have a staff. Someone could bring you food on a regular basis."

He regretted the words the moment he spoke them. But DeRicci just opened her eyes and smiled at him.

"Then I wouldn't get to see you," she said.

He adjusted the pieces of his burger. The bun was hot. The bag had kept everything just-cooked-fresh, even though the guards had tampered with the food.

"If you brought me on," he said, "I'd double as your food-provider."

She smiled, but the look didn't go to her eyes. Something he had said disturbed her. "I thought you were working with Miles on the side," she said.

"I thought so too," Nyquist said, "but I haven't heard from him since the Peyti Crisis."

"Did you contact him?" DeRicci asked.

"I left a few non-urgent messages for him," Nyquist said, "in the last few days. I actually thought I'd be busy until those injunctions."

She nodded. "Miles was here. He's got problems with Talia."

"Serious ones?" Nyquist asked.

DeRicci shrugged. Nyquist wasn't sure if that meant that Flint's problems *were* serious or that she didn't want to tell Nyquist because she felt that he had no right to know.

He really didn't.

"I think you should keep working with him," DeRicci said.

Nyquist felt his heart sink. "I'd hoped—"

"I know, Bartholomew, but I can't request you, and I'm juggling so much here."

"I can take some of that off you," he said.

"Can you?" she asked, looking at him. "Because most of what I need done is United Domes political stuff, and you're no more qualified than I am."

He felt his heart sink further. "If anything, I'm less qualified. You're doing a great job."

"No, I'm not," she said. "Since I've become head of security for the Moon, we've suffered two devastating attacks. I'm sure there are more on the way. I just can't find the perpetrators. I can't figure out what's going to happen. I can't *foresee* them any more than I could foresee the Peyti Crisis."

"But you saved lives," Nyquist said.

"Did I?" she asked. "Or is that just the lie we tell ourselves to make it all better? Are we sure those Peyti clones would have set off the bombs? Are we really?"

"I am," Nyquist said. He remembered standing outside the interrogation room in which he had locked Uzvaan, one of the Peyti lawyers, someone he had known for decades. Their gazes had met through the window, and Uzvaan had removed the bomb from his mask, trying to activate it.

Nyquist still saw that moment in his sleep. Only in those dreams, he was inside the room, and the environmental controls hadn't shifted to Peyti normal, and as Uzvaan pulled his mask apart, Nyquist knew he was going to die, and there was nothing he could do about it.

"You're sweet, Bartholomew." Her tone was dismissive. She thought he had told her she had saved lives to make her feel better.

"And you're tired, Noelle," he said with a bit more bite than he intended, "or you'd remember that one of the lives you saved was mine."

She stared at him. Then she frowned ever so slightly. "I hadn't thought of that."

"That you saved me?" he said. "I told you that—"

"No." She waved what was left of her burger. "That you actually had a reason to see—what was his name? The Peyti lawyer?"

"Uzvaan," Nyquist said. "His name is Uzvaan."

"You had a reason to see him that day," DeRicci said. "That's how you were able to isolate him."

"I lied to him, Noelle. I told him I had information on his client, Ursula Palmette." Palmette had been involved in the assassinations on Anniversary Day. She had supplied the materials used in at least one assassination—or so Nyquist believed.

Flint's sources believed the materials came from somewhere else, but that never explained why Palmette was going to try to set off her own makeshift bomb at the port when Nyquist caught her.

"But this Uzvaan had a client, and he needed to see you," DeRicci said.

"He used it as an excuse to come to the precinct," Nyquist said. "He was probably excited about how many people he could kill."

Nyquist's words were clipped. He could hear the anger in his own voice. He usually kept that anger down, but the fact that Uzvaan—whom he had known for years—had been willing to kill him so very easily infuriated him.

"You can't interrogate any of the Peyti clones about the crisis, right?" DeRicci said.

"Yeah," Nyquist said.

"But they are lawyers," shc said.

He stared at her.

"They haven't been disbarred—at least, not yet. They haven't been taken off cases. We've been reacting to their actions and what the clones turned out to be, but we haven't removed them from anything."

"S-Three would say we're playing games here," Nyquist said.

DeRicci set her burger down. "Of course we are, Bartholomew. That's what the law is all about. It's about games. S-Three is going to be playing games with us. They just caught us off-guard, is all. They'll twist language and ideas and anything else they can to protect their clients. We'll fight back in the courts by saying that these clones have no right to an attorney, and we'll meet each challenge with another. Each challenge will be all about words and interpretations of the law, but even while we're doing that, life goes on. Like you said."

"I did?" Nyquist's head was spinning. He set his burger down, remembering to put it on top of the warming bag so that the burger remained hot.

"You did," she said. "You said you still had cases, but who cares about them in the face of the Peyti Crisis."

He nodded.

"Start caring," she said. "Palmette is one of your cases, and it ties to Uzvaan. I'm sure there are others, with other lawyers involved."

He let out a breath.

"Okay, let's take this a bit slower," he said. "I was a little relieved that the injunctions came down, because my colleagues aren't in a cautious mood."

"Meaning?"

"Meaning they believe that destroying property is allowed under the law," he said.

"See?" DeRicci said, apparently not shocked. Had she thought of this too? "Twisting the rules to make them work. We're all going to be doing it."

"You don't care that they were going to harm the clones?"

"Not for the clones' sake," DeRicci said.

Nyquist felt his world shift. DeRicci, of all people, should have cared. She wasn't like Romey. She knew—

"But," DeRicci added, apparently not noticing his distress, "I don't want to lose a single one of those bastards. Because we don't know which one will talk to us. And with that many clones, that many *opportunities*, one of them will talk. Maybe that one is Uzvaan."

"He's tough," Nyquist said.

"And smart, I'll bet," DeRicci said.

"Of course," Nyquist said.

"So he'll know that they're going to be coming for him, with everything they have."

"He's a failed suicide bomber, Noelle. He's not going to care about his own safety."

She took another bite of the burger, chewed. Thought. Then she nodded. "It's a dilemma, granted, but I doubt it's insurmountable. You're assuming that he wanted to die."

"Yes, I am," Nyquist said. "Because he did."

"No," she said. "He might have believed it was his *duty* to die. He might have believed in the cause, whatever that cause is. He might have had other reasons to take his own life, reasons that no longer exist."

Nyquist shook his head. "I doubt he'll talk to me for any reason."

"He's smart," DeRicci said. "He knows he's lost. He knows—"

"He doesn't, though," Nyquist said. "He doesn't know he's lost. If there is a third attack coming, then all he has to do is wait."

She finished her burger, then licked off her fingers. He watched her, wondering if she even realized how quickly she had eaten, the way that it showed how ravenous she was.

"And if he doesn't wait," DeRicci said, "if he makes a deal with you, if he's even willing to *talk* to you, then we'll know that he no longer believes in the cause."

"We can't make that assumption," Nyquist said. "Because he might not know there is a third attack."

"He might not," DeRicci said. "Or he might assume the attack has failed."

"He's a lawyer, Noelle. Even if he wants to talk to me, he'll want something in exchange."

She nodded. "I already thought of that. We can give him immunity."

"*Immunity*?" Nyquist asked. "From what?"

"Treatment as a clone," she said, and Nyquist let out a breath of air. He had thought that she would give Uzvaan immunity from prosecution, period.

"That might make things worse for him," Nyquist said.

"That might allow him to live a long life," DeRicci said. "As a full-individual, he'll be able to appeal. As a clone, he can be destroyed at any moment."

Nyquist thought for a moment. "I can't offer him anything, Noelle," he said. "I can't talk to him about the Peyti Crisis."

"So, offer him a deal if he talks about Palmette," DeRicci said. "What is the standing of a clone lawyer? He's not subject to laws for individuals. He's property. So all that confidentiality, all of those protections afforded a normal lawyer, he wouldn't have—"

"We don't want to go there, Noelle," Nyquist said quietly. "We have decades of cases that would have to be retried if we win that particular argument. All of those cases in which the lawyers' work would be declared null and void."

"We don't have any Peyti prosecutors in Armstrong, Bartholomew," DeRicci said. "There's no prosecutorial misconduct. I'm not a lawyer, but I'll bet we could get some judge to sign off on a review of the cases, and say that's enough. Because there's nothing in Armstrong law that says we need to have a real lawyer *defending* something. There are laws against prosecutorial misconduct, but not on the type of representation that a defendant must have, as long as the defendant got a competent representative."

The burger didn't look appealing, but the fries suddenly did. Nyquist grabbed some, and ate, tasting grease, salt, and sugar. *Enjoying* the grease, salt, and sugar.

"That's a real risk, Noelle," he said. "It's not an argument that just anyone could make."

So many of his colleagues had tossed out subtlety after the attacks.

"No," she said. "But you could. And maybe you could get Uzvaan to talk."

"So many maybes," Nyquist said.

"So many opportunities," DeRicci said, and smiled.

Nyquist smiled back. What she was suggesting was crazy. But crazy in a way that might help them.

If he could keep his anger under control. If he could manipulate Uzvaan. If Uzvaan knew anything useful.

If, if, if.

Nyquist knew what DeRicci would say next. She would tell him to try.

Because, when it came down to it, he had nothing to lose.

35

ZHU STOOD IN THE CENTER OF WHAT WOULD BE THE RECEPTION AREA OF S^3 On The Moon, and stared at the woman he never thought he would talk to again.

Berhane Magalhães, his former fiancée, whom he'd dumped with his usual exquisite timing. He had left her inside the terminal in the Port of Armstrong just before the news of the Anniversary Day attacks broke. She lost friends, and family members, and he hadn't been able to comfort her.

Not that she had really needed comforting. It seemed like Anniversary Day had revealed the inner Berhane, the one he hadn't known existed.

She came from one of the Moon's richest families, and instead of sitting back and letting her money take care of all the problems, she worked for a variety of organizations, doing her best to help victims of Anniversary Day. And then she had started a foundation of her own. All of her work was hands-on. He supposed she was also donating more than time, but he didn't know.

He had barely spoken to her since that day, and when he had, the conversations left him feeling inadequate.

"Berhane?" His voice sounded strangled.

She turned. Her face had become angular, as if she had lost weight or gained gravitas or something. He had never seen her hair so short. It accented her features. She lost some conventional beauty and gained a luminosity that he hadn't thought possible.

When her gaze found his, she frowned.

"Tell me it's not true, Torkild," she said, without saying hello.

His stomach clenched. He knew what she was talking about, but he pretended that he didn't.

"Hello to you too," he said. "Welcome to the new offices of S-Three On The Moon. I'm setting them up. If you or your father know of any large property for sale—"

"We certainly wouldn't sell it to S-Three," she said. "Not if the rumors are true."

He made himself smile, even though his stomach actively hurt now. Funny how before Anniversary Day he couldn't have cared what this woman thought of him, and now her opinion mattered more than he wanted to admit.

"I've been so busy, I don't have time for rumors," he said.

"You're representing the *murderers?* How could you, Torkild?"

He almost took refuge in that most lawyerly of tricks, arguing with her word choice. *They're not murderers, Berhane, until they're found guilty.* Or, he could have said, *They're not really murderers, Berhane. They only attempted murder. Those who succeeded died.*

But he caught all the words before they flooded out of him. His cheeks warmed and he wished he could control that. Normally, he could, but apparently Berhane had found another way in.

"I'm S-Three's representative on the Moon," he said in his *let's humor Berhane* voice, a voice he never ever used with anyone else. "The only reason I'm doing all this is because I'm the only partner on the Moon. Luck of the draw and all that."

"You're not denying it. You're representing those murderers." She blinked. Her eyes looked moist. Was she going to come up to his new office suite and *cry*?

That pissed him off. That was the old Berhane, the one who got her way through manipulation and tears.

"I'm starting a branch of the firm," he said. "That does mean I'm handling some matters while I wait for the actual attorneys of record to show up, but that's all, Berhane. I—"

"You're *lying*," she said. "I always knew when you were lying, even when you thought I didn't. You can't do this, Torkild. You can't represent them. They're monsters."

The lawyer answers, so rote, rose up first. *Everyone's entitled to a defense, Berhane.* But he suppressed that too, and then protected his links so he didn't accidentally send those answers to her that way.

"You came up here to yell at me, Berhane?" he asked quietly.

"I came up here so you could tell me it was all a vicious lie," she said. "And it's not, is it?"

He sighed. "What do you want from me, Berhane? We're not engaged anymore."

"Let me hire you away," she said. "Shut this all down. Become a victim's advocate. We can use lawyers with vision. You'll be able to argue for people who've lost everything."

His shoulders slumped. If only she had offered him that a few days ago, he would have considered it. He had actually asked her for a job when he got here, and she had said no.

He wondered if she remembered. He suspected she did.

"What'll you pay, Berhane?"

"Is this really about money?" she asked.

He thought, *Of course it's about money, Berhane. Don't you know me?* and struggled to keep that thought to himself as well.

"Berhane?" he asked.

She frowned. That disapproving expression that had covered her face so many times in the past. He recognized it, and then he would try to placate it. Now, he didn't want to.

She said, "The organizations that represent the victims, we don't have a lot of money."

He knew that. He had known that when he asked the question. But he wanted her on the defensive now.

"So," he said, "pay for it with family funds."

If she did that, if she paid him commensurate with the money he would get from S^3 over the next ten years, then maybe he would consider working for her.

Her lips thinned. She whirled away from him and walked to the window.

He'd hit a sore spot. And as he was getting over his shock, he realized he was also getting mad. She had attacked him.

He was going to attack back.

"Your father doesn't approve of what you're doing, does he?" Zhu said.

"It's not about my father," she said.

Liar, he wanted to say. *It's always about your father.*

"Did he cut you off?" Zhu asked.

"No," she said, arms crossed.

Zhu recognized the posture. He wasn't to ask any more questions. She would lose control if he did. And he didn't want her to cry in front of him. That had happened more times than he could count, and he really didn't want to suffer through it again.

"So, he put you on an allowance?" Zhu asked.

"Why is this suddenly about me?" she asked, turning around to face him. Her skin was beet red, her eyes wet. "You're defending murderers."

He was. And, oddly, that was the job he had signed on for. He had decided to be a defense attorney years ago, knowing he might defend awful criminals.

And knowing it would make him rich.

"What do you want from me, Berhane?" Zhu asked quietly.

"Everyone knows we were engaged, Torkild. They sent me up here to call you off."

"We're not engaged any longer, Berhane," he said less gently than he probably should have. "Why did anyone think I would listen to you now?"

They both knew the rest of that sentence. *When I didn't listen to you before*, was what he should have added if he really wanted to hurt her.

He didn't. He respected what she had been doing. He admired it. He wished he could be like her, but he wasn't. He never would be.

"They tried to destroy the *Moon*, Torkild," she said. "How can you defend that?"

His back stiffened. He actually felt himself growing stronger. It didn't matter that he had asked himself these questions. What mattered was that *she* was questioning him, and she had no right to do so.

She was crystalizing how he felt—about the cases, about himself, about S^3.

"I'm going to handle these cases like I'd handle any other case," he said with as much dignity as he could muster.

"Don't give me that crap about everyone being entitled to a defense. You know better," she said. "Monsters don't get a defense."

"We're a society of laws, Berhane," he said, maintaining that dignity. He was rather shocked that he was no longer using his humor-Berhane voice. Now he was actually talking to her like she was an equal, something he probably hadn't done in years.

"That's crap, and you know it," she said. "If it were true, we wouldn't have Disappeareds, we wouldn't have—"

"People who Disappear are breaking the law," Zhu said. "There's a lot to dislike in the Alliance system, but there's a lot to like. We get along with thousands of alien species. We have cultural exchanges and economic cooperation because of this 'crap' you're talking about. That means, sometimes, you have to abide by laws you don't believe in. It also means that sometimes you have to make sure that a group of bad individuals get the best treatment possible under the law."

"You can't believe that," she said, in a near-whisper.

Oh, God, he thought. *Here come the tears.*

"You know," he said, "I actually do."

He sounded surprised. He *was* surprised. After the death of Trey, Zhu had let himself believe all the horrible things everyone had ever said of him—that he was in the law only for the money, that he didn't belong anywhere, that he was a screw-up of the first order, that he didn't believe in anything.

But he did believe. He had always believed in rules and order and law. He knew, deep down, that without them, governments couldn't survive.

Governments were a fiction, after all. They were a fiction that individuals agreed to abide by, and the moment an individual didn't abide by those rules, then there had to be punishments or other individuals would join. There would be chaos, governments would collapse, and he would be living in a universe that he didn't like.

That idealism that Salehi had tried to nurture in him, the one Salehi had tapped when he got Zhu to agree to represent Trey in the first place, that idealism was still there, under the cynicism, the lies about money, the lies about his personal strength.

If anyone could turn Zhu against this mission, it was Berhane. He really admired her now. He admired the victims' advocacy she was doing; he admired the work she was doing in cleaning up the mess left by Anniversary Day.

She had become an amazing woman, and he had never thought she could. She was standing on her own, and he thought that tremendous. There was something about her that reminded him of their early days, of the woman she might have been, without the toxic influence of her father.

Without the toxic influence of Zhu himself.

"You're not going to change your mind," Berhane said, as if he had stunned her.

"No," he said softly. "I'm not."

"You're doing this for the money," she said. "If I can get Daddy to pay you to leave here, will you do that?"

Zhu thought about it; he really did. He checked in with himself. He glanced around the office, and thought about how he'd feel.

He could almost see it—the money, the apartment, the stupid silk suits. The feeling of emptiness.

He could almost taste the alcohol on his tongue.

"Working with victims, they need defense too. They don't have anything right now. Two of the biggest insurance companies handling civic organizations have gone bankrupt, and that means that two of the domes won't be able to compensate victims for the dome's lack of action—"

"What?" Zhu asked, frowning. "The domes didn't act? Are you talking about Anniversary Day?"

"Yes," she said. "I am. It's too soon to see what kind of excuses the authorities will have for the Peyti Crisis. Not catching these clones immediately, not realizing they were clones, I mean, Torkild, the responsibility—"

"The law states that an organization is only liable when a future event is both foreseeable and preventable," Zhu said.

She looked at him. "Who *are* you?"

"Blame goes to the clones and whoever created them," Zhu said. "Innocent people suffered. It was awful for everyone. But you can't make the wrong people pay."

"The city governments *are* responsible," she said. "It's their job to protect us."

"And they did the best they could," he said softly. "Berhane, you have to account for failure. Not everything can be successful."

"Like you are," she snapped. "You just want to be rich. You want to be at the top of your stupid game, whatever that means. You don't care about other people's lives."

He let the words hang between them. She was breathing hard, as if spitting out those thoughts had cost her too much effort.

"Berhane," he said softly. "If S-Three succeeds in its defense of these clones, it will improve millions of lives."

"So that's the lie you tell yourself," she said. "That you're doing this for the public good."

"You're telling me that some lives are worthwhile and others aren't? The Peyti clones are individuals, Berhane. All normally raised clones are. They are the same as the originals, except under the law. How is that right?"

"They should die for what they did," Berhane said, her face squinched up. He had never seen her like this.

"If they were Peyti," he said, "they would receive the appropriate punishment. But they're clones. They can be destroyed in their sleep."

"So?" she asked.

"So, isn't a long punishment better? Something that would give them time to reflect—"

"No," she said. "I don't care what happens to them. And neither should you, Torkild."

He stared at her. Who was this woman? She used to say that he should have compassion for everyone, including the aliens whose cultures were so different that he couldn't understand them. He had never thought of Berhane as bloodthirsty, certainly not as dismissive of the rights of others as she was being now.

"Berhane," he said softly, "I care about the law."

"At the expense of real people, Torkild," she said. "Stop thinking about theory, and start thinking about lives damaged and lost. Start thinking about *repercussions*, for once, instead of yourself and how famous you'll become. You won't be famous doing this. You'll be *in*famous. Do you know how awful that will be? Do you have any idea—"

"Awful?" he asked. "For me? Or for my former fiancée?"

"How dare you," she said. "*I'm* doing good work, no thanks to you or my father, and you're getting in the way. Both of you are. And you're ruining lives. Just ruining them. Don't you see that?"

Zhu took a deep breath. They could argue about this forever. He thought it no coincidence that she was comparing him to her father.

Zhu was treating her—he had *always* treated her—like her father had. Dismissive, difficult, emotional, as if she counted for nothing.

She had just been arm-candy for him, never an equal. And now she was demanding equality and he was giving it to her, but not in the way that she wanted.

He would never be what she wanted, and she would never be what he wanted. He understood that. In calmer moments, she probably knew it as well.

"Berhane," he said.

"Don't use that tone with me," she snapped. So she did know, deep down, how fraught their relationship had been.

"Berhane," he said again, not changing his tone. "You are doing good work."

"You always talk to me—what?" She blinked at him, looking young and startled and vulnerable. "What did you just say?"

"You're doing *great* work. Things that I never would have expected of anyone. You're changing the Moon all by yourself," he said. "You're making the kind of difference that so many people say they want to make and never do. It's wonderful."

Her frown grew deeper. "But?"

He shook his head. "No 'but.' None. You're amazing."

She swallowed hard. He could see her bracing herself for whatever was going to come next.

"So join us," she said after a moment.

"You know that wouldn't work," he said. "We're fighting now. We've been together half an hour and we're at each other's throats. I'm not made to do the kind of work you do. I *like* theory. I don't like individuals much. I'm really good at what I do. So are you."

"And we're on opposite sides," she said quietly.

He shook his head. "Weirdly, we're on the same side. We're both trying to preserve our way of life here, and repair the damage that's been done. Deep down, I don't understand what you do or how you can do it. I know you don't understand me."

"And who you're working for," she said.

"I'm working for S-Three," he said.

"Your clients," she said. "I'm talking about your clients."

"S-Three's client is the Government of Peyla," he said, and watched her eyes widen in surprise. "This Crisis is ruining their place in the Alliance. They need our help."

"Why didn't you say that?" she asked.

"Because," he said. "The help begins by representing the clones. Then we work from there."

"But they have lawyers, right? The Peyti Government?"

"No Peyti is being allowed on the Moon, and no Peyti lawyer has a job since the Crisis," he said.

She made an odd grunting sound, kind of an agreement mixed with humph. "I'm supposed to care about that, aren't I? I'm supposed to say that it's a shame, and the Peyti aren't all alike. But how do we know that, Torkild?"

"The same way we know that we're nothing like the clones of Pier-Luigi Frémont," he said.

"It's not the same," she said.

He resisted the urge to close his eyes against her words. It was exactly the same. And if she weren't so locked into her position, she would see that.

"It's time you leave, Berhane," he said.

"And we'll agree to disagree," she said.

"No," he said. "We're not going to agree on anything. I don't think we should see each other at all anymore."

Her gaze narrowed. "Why not?"

Because what we used to have in common was our self-absorption, he thought. *And we're changing. We're not those people anymore. But we're still self-absorbed. I think my way is better. You think your way is better. We're probably both wrong.*

"Because," he said, "I'm not your fiancé anymore. You have no ties to me. What I do is what I do, and what you do is what you do. Tell your so-called friends that. Tell them we broke up because I was a prick. I was, too, and I'm sorry about that. Tell them I can't be influenced—and neither can you. Tell them S-Three will do what it does, and nothing will change that. Tell them to focus on their work, and not mine."

"You don't know these people," she said. "You don't—"

"I do know them," he said. "Maybe not them as individuals, but I know their type. And I know who you and I are, Berhane. Let's declare this relationship over once and for all."

Her breath caught, then she nodded. His heart twisted. *This* was the break-up. The real one. And it wasn't mean or dispirited. It was the kind that two people who had nothing in common except an initial attraction should have had in the first place.

He leaned forward and kissed her forehead. "Good-bye Berhane," he said, and walked away.

36

FLINT TRIED NOT TO PACE. HE FIDGETED ON THE SOFT BLUE COUCH IN THE waiting area, clenching and unclenching his fists. He'd tried every relaxation trick he knew except finding some relaxation program through his links.

He even counted his breaths, trying to focus, but he kept staring at the door on the far wall. The door was fake blond wood—at least, he assumed that it was fake. He couldn't imagine that a group of therapists made enough money to afford a real wood door.

He had come to the Armstrong Comfort Center on the strength of Popova's recommendation. He hated the place's name, because he worried that it promised more than it could give. Plus, he wasn't certain comfort was what Talia needed.

He had left her with Popova, without telling either of them where he was going. He knew the Security Office was safe. Popova would provide Talia with a sympathetic ear and maybe find something for her to do.

He hadn't told Talia he was coming here. He knew that Popova had broached the subject with Talia before, and he had asked Popova to discuss it with her again. Not to tell Talia to get help, but just to let Talia know that strong women sought help now and then.

He couldn't say it without sounding patronizing. Or worried. Or both.

That door bothered him. It upset all of his assumptions about therapists. He had thought they had marginal businesses in these days of constant links and modern medicine.

But the door belied that. He was beginning to believe it was made of real wood, because the waiting room itself was upscale. The longer he sat here, the more money he realized the place had.

Two original pieces of art—the actual painted kind, not the kind that rotated on a screen—hung on the wall beside that door. The two chairs across from him matched the blue couch, and looked equally comfortable. End tables beside them had actual lamps on them, with clear artistic bases.

This wasn't the only waiting room either. The designation was waiting room five, which meant there were at least four others, so that clients wouldn't share the space, maintaining that all-important confidentiality.

These therapists had come highly recommended—and not just from Popova. Flint had spent a late night searching, as well as talking to friends, and he couldn't find anything untoward about the place. He believed that if there was something untoward, he had the skills to find it.

So he searched. He searched databases, court records, arrest records. He'd searched through the Armstrong Therapists Association's complaints files, he'd searched the medical licensing boards records, and he'd found nothing bad.

Then he started searching for recommendations: people who felt they got help, organizations that had sent employees who also felt they got help, and discovered several groups that started here. Groups that focused on trauma recovery and daily survival.

Not to mention Popova's transformation.

Flint hoped for that for Talia. He knew he couldn't provide it.

But he had some concerns that he wasn't sure how to address.

He didn't know if Talia could discuss the fact that she was a clone in this place. Flint believed she needed to, because in addition to losing her mother and watching a group of people die at her school, she had lost herself.

She had believed herself to be an individual, with a birthdate, the only child of Rhonda Shindo, with a dad who had abandoned her. Instead, Talia had learned that she was one of many clones of a child who had died, and that her mother had raised her without ever telling Flint about her existence. And then there were her mother's crimes...

The door opened. A tall man, with a pencil-thin mustache and matching eyebrows peered out. The eyebrows were darker than his chocolate brown hair, and Flint wondered if the man had enhancements for the facial hair.

"Mr. Flint," the man said, hand extended as he stepped into the room. "I'm Evando Llewynn. I'm a coordinating therapist here at Armstrong Comfort Center."

Flint took Llewynn's hand. It was warm and dry, the perfect handshake. Maybe Llewynn had enhancements for everything. His face had a perfectly neutral expression, his hands were the perfect temperature, and his voice was modulated to the perfect depth and softness.

Flint felt himself calming, and he didn't want to. He wondered if actively fighting the calmness was worthwhile. Then he realized how stupid that thought was, and had his links search for additives in the environmental system.

"I understand that you would like to bring your daughter here," Llewynn said.

"I have questions first," Flint said.

"Of course." Llewynn seemed unconcerned about Flint's questions. Most people in service industries would have wanted to know if Flint had looked at the data the business provided before coming in, so they would know where to start.

Llewynn didn't ask, didn't even seem to think of it. Instead, he led Flint through a corridor that seemed remarkably empty. The walls were bare, the carpets were just plush enough, and there were no doors.

At least, until they reached a small L in the corridor. There Llewynn stopped at a dark wood door. He opened it, and stepped inside, leading Flint into an office filled with more dark wood and cream carpets. The furniture was the same mixture of dark and cream, and looked incredibly inviting.

Still, Flint slowed as he entered, brushing his hand over the door. It sure felt like real wood, complete with ridges sanded smooth. The expense of having that much wood imported from Earth was staggering. Even using Moon-grown wood, from one of the Growing Pits near Armstrong was outrageously expensive.

When Flint had logged into the therapy office's systems, the quotes he received for Talia's care hadn't seemed outrageous to him. Now he was wondering if the years of wealth had made him jaded somehow, if he even registered the real cost of something.

He frowned a little, not liking that thought.

Llewynn slipped into the captain's chair facing the door. He rested his elbows on the wide wooden armrests. The chair looked like it was built for him, the seat extra long to accommodate his thin legs.

Flint took a seat to the side of Llewynn, not directly in front of him like a patient would. Even though the chair wasn't all fabric, Flint was surprised at how comfortable it was.

Apparently everything in this office was designed for comfort.

"I understand you'll be bringing your daughter here," Llewynn said.

"I'm not certain about that," Flint said. "You come highly recommended, but I'm going to reserve judgment until our conversation has ended."

Llewynn threaded his fingers together. "I was simply going to say that sometimes, when we see a child, we find it necessary to bring the entire family in for discussions."

"My daughter is sixteen," Flint said, "and if you called her a child, she would show you how adult she really is."

Or she would have, before last week. But he didn't add that.

"Sometimes, a child seems adult—"

"Don't," Flint said. "I used to be a police officer. I'm familiar with behavioral patterns. We had to learn them for each branch, and I became a detective. I was a programmer before that. I understand the human brain, and I understand human emotions."

He even understood some alien emotions, which he didn't want to tell Llewynn.

Llewynn's posture had changed ever so slightly. Flint suspected the man believed Flint hostile to therapy. Flint wasn't, but he was concerned.

"My daughter has been through multiple traumas in the past three years. I've been able to help her through some of them, but she watched a group of people die at her school last week during the Peyti Crisis. It shattered her. All that strength she had built up is gone, and honestly, I'm unable to help her."

"Why is that?" Llewynn asked.

Flint narrowed his eyes. He did not want to be manipulated.

Apparently, Llewynn realized his mistake. He separated his hands, raised them, and said in that maddeningly calm voice, "I respect your training and perspective, Mr. Flint. Which is why I am curious that you believe you can no longer help her."

Flint bit back irritation. If there were calming influences in the environment—subtle ones that his links didn't pick up—they weren't working.

"I don't exactly know," Flint said. "It could be because this is a last straw for her, as one of my friends believes."

It was a stretch to refer to Popova as a friend, but he didn't correct himself.

"Or it could be because I was working for the United Domes of the Moon's Security Office when the deaths occurred. I helped find the Peyti clones." He didn't have to say any more. The entire Moon knew what happened next.

Llewynn nodded. "So you believe you might be at fault for your daughter's reaction?"

"No," Flint said. "But I can't summon the warmth I need to be completely understanding. It saddens me that people died that day, but if we hadn't acted, millions would have died. It seems a small price to pay for all those lives saved."

"Each small price—"

"Was loved by someone," Flint said. "I get it, Mr. Llewynn. I know what we did, I know the effects, and I'm seeing some of the devastation firsthand. But if I had it to do all over again, I would do it."

Llewynn nodded. "All of this we could have covered in your daughter's first interview. There's something else you want to discuss."

Here it was. Flint took a deep breath. He had to be careful here.

"I'm a Retrieval Artist," he said. "I was one before my daughter moved in with me. I retired, but circumstances have reinstated me. I deal in confidentiality. I know secrets so explosive that if I reveal them, I will get even more people killed."

"I am aware of the difficulties of your profession," Llewynn said, without indicating if he approved of that profession.

"My daughter has helped me with some investigations, not through my instigation, but her own. I understand therapy. I know that secrets and therapy are incompatible. I have to know this: If I bring my daughter to you people, her secrets—*our* secrets—will never be revealed."

"Are you asking for a guarantee?" Llewynn asked.

"I am," Flint said.

"I'm sure you have already read our documentation that we will sign, keeping any information that we receive confidential."

"I have," Flint said.

"What more do you want?" Llewynn asked.

"It's not enough to be able to sue you and win after information gets out," Flint said. "I need a guarantee that it will never get out."

"No one is perfect, Mr. Flint," Llewynn said.

Flint's heart sank. In other words, Llewynn could not give him that kind of guarantee. It was too much to ask anyway.

He took another deep breath to steady himself.

"Then," he said, "I wanted to ask you this: Can my daughter come into this kind of therapy and retain some of her secrets?"

"Your secrets?" Llewynn asked, obviously trying to clarify.

"Hers," Flint said. Her one big secret. The one that would destroy her with her friends here in Armstrong, especially considering how bad the anti-clone sentiment had gotten.

"She won't get the full benefit of our services," Llewynn said.

"I know," Flint said. "That's not what I'm asking. She's in a bad way. I'd like her to get some kind of help, but if the kind you offer requires her to tell you everything, she can't."

"She knows this?" Llewynn asked. "How your job affects her?"

It's not my job, Flint wanted to say, but he didn't. Because he didn't want to give that away.

"She's very aware which secrets threaten lives," Flint said. "I need your assurance that she won't be forced to choose between those secrets and her mental health."

"I can't do that, Mr. Flint," Llewynn said. "If those secrets are causing her decline, then we will do our best to lift her out."

Flint sighed, and stood up. It had been a long shot anyway. "Thank you for your honesty," he said, and headed for the door.

"Mr. Flint," Llewynn said. "Sometimes, you must trust that others will do the right thing for all concerned."

"And you need to understand that a strict adherence to rules might damage my daughter even more," Flint said.

"Must you be involved in her therapy?" Llewynn asked.

And Flint suddenly understood from that question that Llewynn believed Flint was somehow harming his daughter. He hadn't wanted to lead Llewynn in that direction, but he had.

"No," Flint said. "I'll need to know if there are things I can and cannot do to help her, but this is about her, not me. I wasn't planning to sit in, and I wasn't planning to monitor. I do need to know that she will be safe."

"Do some of her secrets threaten her life?" Llewynn asked. He was still sitting, but his posture was more alert than it had been a few minutes ago.

"Yes," Flint said.

"Can she tell us when we get close to those secrets?" Llewynn said.

"Yes," Flint said.

Llewynn nodded. "Then give us a chance. We might be able to help your daughter."

Flint actually liked the word "might." Certainty disturbed him, particularly in an area like this.

"All right," he said, as he walked back into the room. "Let's schedule an appointment."

37

THE PRISON THAT HAD HELD PIERLUIGI FRÉMONT NO LONGER EXISTED. IT had been torn down thirty years ago, after major riots and an internal fire that no one ever got accused of. For decades, rumors of mismanagement had plagued the place—and Luc Deshin just happened to know that those rumors were true.

Because, even though the prison no longer existed, the black market in the prison's wares still existed.

It had taken Deshin days and a lot of personal reassurances to track down the market. As laws against selling designer criminal clones grew tighter, black markets like this one grew harder and harder to find.

Many had moved to the edge of the known universe. But those that had established themselves in that distant backwater had often died miserably or had lost everything.

Other black markets thrived on the Frontier. Initially, Deshin had been worried that he would have to travel somewhere out there, burning weeks before he ever got any information. And he worried that he would spend all that time getting information that turned out to be useless.

Fortunately, he discovered that the black market he was searching for had changed locations from a space station near the prison to the smallest moon of an uninhabitable planet in the Aebib System.

The Aebib System was one of the first entire systems to join the Alliance. Its governments were old and established, the aliens known quantities.

Deshin found months' worth of data on how to behave with those aliens in every circumstance. He spent the last part of his trip making certain that the assumptions his so-called friends had told him were correct—that there were no alien governments on this particular moon, just a loosely connected group of human cities that pretended to follow Alliance rules.

He was traveling in one of his cargo vessels, along with a security team of fifteen, most of whom did not know the reason for this mission. Keeping things secret was easy for him; his entire business had been built on secrecy.

The ship was transporting cargo, mostly legal, to one of the planets in the Aebib System. The illegal materials were mostly hard-to-find minerals which Deshin had heard were at a premium in this market.

He might have to use them to trade for information on Frémont's DNA.

If, indeed, anyone still had any. Or even knew its history.

The ship remained in orbit above the moon. Deshin had traveled down to the city of Angu in a smaller ship, along with six members of his security team, including Keith Jakande.

Jakande was the best security officer that Deshin had. He didn't even want to call the man a bodyguard. Jakande was too good for that.

Jakande had been with Deshin on Anniversary Day. They'd both watched friends and colleagues die. And then Jakande had accompanied Deshin in his investigation of the zoodeh used that day, as well as the explosive materials.

Deshin trusted no one on his staff more.

He and Jakande had picked nine members of his security detail to go to Angu a day early as an advance team. They had followed protocol: eight members divided into pairs, while a leader remained at all times in the hotel the team had chosen for Deshin.

The pairs had investigated everything from the black market itself to some of the underground clubs. By the end of the night, four team members had heard rumors that Deshin might arrive, but no one had heard *when* he would arrive. And more importantly, no one had heard that any of Deshin's enemies were in the city or even on the moon.

Because of his status in the underworld community, Deshin could not go meet the individuals in charge of the black market. They had to come to him.

That meant he had to have two hotel suites: one he actually stayed in, and one that he did business in. His team had a third suite, one that monitored the business suite.

The expenses of this operation were mounting up. The travel, the staff, the ships, the hotels, all of it cost a lot of money with no return. But he didn't mind. If he succeeded, he would thwart a major attack and be able to continue doing business on the Moon.

But he also spent time on this journey investigating other places to establish his home base.

The business suite that his team had set up for him wasn't as plush as most suites he was used to. Yet the team had rented the two best suites in all of Angu. The entire city—if it could be called that—was shabbier than he expected.

Once Deshin had entered the business suite, his team had sent word that Deshin would like to talk to the person in charge of the Frémont DNA.

Deshin half expected to hear that the DNA was no longer on the market. But he heard nothing, which was standard if a meet was going to happen.

He knew that his suite—both of his suites, the one here and the one in his real hotel—had been vetted by his team, but he still double-checked them. He used his own security chips to scan the unbelievably small bathroom, the bedroom with a view of some remote snow-covered mountains whose names he didn't know (and didn't care to know), and the living room which could have fit thirty large humans without any difficulty at all.

Five of his personal guards were inside this room, but Jakande was not. Jakande ran the entire operation, and he had determined that

Deshin would need five guards, mostly as a show of strength. Living security guards were expensive and much more effective than androids or bots or security monitors. He used his guards to establish his wealth, his power, and his general do-not-screw-with-me attitude.

None of that prevented him from doing things on his own, however. He maintained his weapons proficiency. He had small bone knives in each of his boots, and a laser pistol at his hip. He was also wearing a whisper-thin layer of body armor which could become its own environmental suit. He hated the things. It always felt like his skin was covered in goo, but he had learned the hard way that protection was necessary in uncertain missions like this one.

And he was going to be cautious. Every time he contemplated behaving too aggressively, he thought of the way Paavo smiled at him, of Gerda's worried frown. He wanted to return to them, and he would, if he followed the procedures he had set in place years ago.

He brought his own food, as he always did on trips like this, and used his own dishes to make a small lunch of exotic cheeses and black rye bread. He shared the meal with his team. He drank coffee from a pocket coffeemaker—not the best stuff, but good enough while he waited.

And he did wait.

The rudeness didn't bother him. Black marketeers often felt that being rude gave them power. He saw such behavior as the desperate moves of wannabe tyrants. He also knew that if he didn't act like the rudeness bothered him, he maintained the power in the relationship.

Still, he had an interior clock that told him when a meet was no longer worth his time. He would give the potential seller an extra few hours, but not an entire day.

He gave this meet one hour more than he usually gave someone he was trying to do business with. It was a good thing that he did, because the knock on the door came about an hour after he would have normally given up.

One of his bodyguards, Kaielynn, braced her feet a meter apart, a movement that always made her look even more formidable. She was impressive without the bad attitude: over six feet tall, and muscular, she wore clothes that emphasized her power instead of hiding it. This afternoon, she wore a sleeveless tank top over a pair of skin-tight pants. Only Deshin knew that she also had a layer of armor covering everything.

She gripped her hands together. He recognized the movement. She was checking with the team monitoring the room's exterior to discover what they saw.

Her orders were to open the door to a human only, and to be wary if the human were female. Deshin's information was that his potential supplier was an older man.

Two other guards disappeared into the kitchen area. One more slipped into the bedroom, and another stood just outside the bathroom door.

Kaielynn's gaze met Deshin's. *Shall we?* She sent on their private links.

Yes, he sent back.

His heart was pounding. He was ready for this—beyond ready. He didn't want to seem too eager, but he felt like he had when he first started his business. Every opportunity was exciting.

He bit back the emotion as Kaielynn opened the door.

The man who slipped inside was thick with the beginnings of fat, the way that a former athlete looked before he realized he needed enhancements to keep himself thin. Light shone off his bald head, accenting his white eyebrows and furrowed brow.

"Luc Deshin," the man said in a very smarmy tone. "You're famous all over the Alliance."

Deshin didn't smile or even acknowledge that the man spoke. The man started to step toward Deshin, but Kaielynn grabbed the man's arm.

The man looked at her as if she were violating his personal space.

"No farther until I've had a look at you," she said.

She was not being entirely truthful, since she'd already had a look at him with her various security enhancements, making sure he wasn't carrying known lethal biologicals or hidden weapons.

The outside team had already silently blocked his links, and blocked any warnings he might have set up to let him know his links—including his emergency links—were off.

The man looked at her as if he were measuring his strength against hers. Then he moved his head slightly, a concession or permission, something that kept him in control—or at least let him think he was.

Apparently that movement annoyed Kaielynn because she did an old-fashioned pat down, and she wasn't easy on his private parts. She grabbed hard enough to make him wince.

Deshin let them have their little one-upmanship. He knew that if the man were insecure about his status and strength, he'd try something against Kaielynn now or when they were alone.

Kaielynn could handle herself. The man wouldn't know what he had gotten into.

Kaielynn finished. The man moved away from her faster than he needed to, and cleared his throat, which almost made Deshin smile. Apparently, the man didn't trust his own voice after Kaielynn's little power grab.

"I hope to hell this meeting was worth that," the man said.

Deshin still hadn't said anything.

Kaielynn put her hand on the man's back and shoved him forward just enough to re-establish her dominance.

"You introduce yourself when you're in the presence of Mr. Deshin," she said.

Deshin's desire to grin grew. He loved it when she took control of a particularly difficult potential client.

Deshin kept his face impassive, though, waiting for the man to comply with Kaielynn's request.

"Can you call off the muscle?" the man asked Deshin, still trying to establish them as equals.

"No," Kaielynn answered him. "He will not. And if you are not careful, you'll be leaving before this meeting even starts. This is Mr. Deshin's room, and you're going to follow his rules."

"It's my city, girlie, and you can follow my rules," the man said.

Kaielynn grabbed his arm and propelled him toward the door. Her grip was so tight that the man winced again. Deshin realized the grimaces were involuntary.

"You toss me out and you don't hear nothing about anything," the man said. "I control information here."

Kaielynn grabbed the door knob and pulled the door open, while keeping her other hand on the man. She was so strong that she could keep him under control while handling the door.

The man slammed a hand against the door's frame.

"Look, Deshin," he said, his back to Deshin, "I'm Didier Conte. You've probably heard of me. I used to be a prison guard."

Deshin hadn't heard of him. But that was enough to stop Kaielynn's manipulation for now.

Let him stay, Deshin sent her. *Close the door, keep your hand on his arm, and hold him tight enough to remind him that you could break every bone in his body before he could lay a finger on you.*

I wouldn't have to break his bones, Kaielynn sent. *I just need to squeeze his nuts again. This man hasn't fought in years. He's acting on muscle memory—and not very good memory at that.*

She turned Conte around, "accidentally" knocking him against the door a few times as she did so, bending his elbow backward hard enough to make his skin gray. When he was in position in front of Deshin, Deshin was about to speak when Conte, the idiot, spoke again.

"You don't need to rough me up," he said. "I'm here to do business."

"You'll do it Mr. Deshin's way," Kaielynn said. "You will remember that."

Conte glanced at her, then at Deshin as if Deshin were his friend. Maybe this guy did control the market on Angu. He certainly acted like someone used to being in charge—or convincing people that he was.

Deshin didn't like out-of-shape arrogant bullies. He had never liked them, and he liked them less now that his brilliant little son had been the target of a few.

"I understand you have PierLuigi Frémont DNA," Deshin said. He didn't know that for certain. He had only been told that the black marketeers on Angu had access to DNA from that prison.

"Yeah, I do," Conte said.

That little thread of excitement flowed through Deshin again. He tamped it down.

"But it's only for fast-grow," Conte said.

Fast-grow clones developed into full-sized adults within days or weeks. They were usually designed for one task, and often that task was for disposables. Fast-grows cleared brush on new worlds, for example, and if they went afoul of the aliens there, no one cared. The fast-grows certainly couldn't mount a defense.

Usually, though, fast-grows were for identity shifts, to replace someone who was kidnapped for just a day or so (usually a night, while the original should have been sleeping) to throw off the authorities.

Fast-grows were useless for anything that required brains or complicated maneuvers—things like Anniversary Day.

"Don't play with me," Deshin said.

"I'm not," Conte said. "I have had Frémont DNA since the day the man died, but the DNA was contaminated. I can get you lookalikes, but they're pretty useless for anything else. However, I have DNA from Istvan Uren and—"

"I'm interested in Frémont," Deshin said coldly. "I'm sure you've had other inquiries in the past six months."

"I have," Conte said, "and if I knew who the hell provided the DNA, I'd be talking to that person myself. I could have made a fortune."

If Deshin were a true investigator, he would have wanted the names of the others interested in Frémont clones. But he wasn't. He would let Flint know that a lot of people had been sniffing around Conte, and maybe Flint would tell the right people.

"Frémont's DNA had to come from prison," Deshin said. "The authorities cleaned up Abbondiado too well to make usable clones out of what was left."

Again, he was working on a hunch. Conte's attitude toward that would help Deshin figure out what was going on.

"That's true," Conte said. "For the longest time, I advertised that I was the only source of Frémont DNA in the universe. Then what happens?

Those twenty clones show up, march in lockstep, and good god, they can think. Someone had pure DNA."

Something in his tone caught Deshin's ear. A bit of bitterness, maybe. A tinge of suspicion. Or maybe it was just garden variety envy.

"You know who," Deshin said.

"No, I don't," Conte said. "I'm the one who found Frémont's body. I used to be a guard in the prison, and I took what I needed. I did that for a number of the prisoners, and I was smart. I didn't market the stuff for years. I waited, thinking I'd sell it a decade after I retired. I was just getting ready when the prison fire made it all moot. No one cared what former guards were doing, and no one was tracking the DNA. Especially not fast-grow. No one cares about fast-grow."

And no one cared about DNA that went outside of the Alliance. Deshin knew that much as well.

"You sold a lot before you quit, just not inside the Alliance," Deshin said.

"Are you kidding? No, I didn't." Conte glanced at Kaielynn, who hadn't moved. Then he looked back at Deshin. "I *worked* in max security. No way in hell was I ever going to get interred in one of those places. Patience is the key to getting rich. I'm sure you know that."

Deshin wasn't going to agree or disagree with this man. He wasn't entirely sure he believed him, although that look at Kaielynn made things more convincing. The man wasn't up to defending himself against her; he certainly couldn't handle the kind of prisoners he'd mix with inside a max security—especially as a former guard. A former guard who no longer had all of his defensive and security equipment.

"Then the DNA came from somewhere else," Deshin said, "and you're of no use to me."

Conte bit his lip. Deshin could see every thought cross this man's face. He wondered how Conte ever survived in the black market, especially if he did business with the Black Fleet.

"I may know a name," Conte said.

"A name that's useful?" Deshin asked. He didn't like how tentative Conte seemed.

"I've given out other names, but I received word that they didn't have the DNA." Conte made it all sound so civilized. Deshin doubted that it had been. "There's only one possibility left."

"But you haven't checked the name out," Deshin said.

"I'll be honest," Conte said. "The name makes no sense. But it's the only possibility."

He glanced at Kaielynn. She still had a grip on his arm. It had to hurt.

"I'll tell you what," Conte said. "I won't charge you for the name."

As if he were doing Deshin a favor.

"I don't pay for information," Deshin lied. "So it doesn't matter."

"But you want the name," Conte said.

"I want the DNA," Deshin said. "Someone is clearly supplying it."

"That's the thing," Conte said. "I don't think anyone is."

Deshin couldn't help the look of interest that crossed his face. He was intrigued now.

"What do you mean?" he asked.

"I mean," Conte said. "I haven't heard of any for sale other than my fast-grow DNA."

"Yet there were slow-grown clones of PierLuigi Frémont on the Moon not six months ago."

Conte nodded. "I tried to find records of sales," he said. "I haven't been able to find any."

"So where did they come from?" Deshin asked.

Conte shook his head.

"Then where does your single name come from?" Deshin said.

"A long shot," Conte said. "An extreme long shot."

"So tell me," Deshin said.

And Conte did.

38

SALEHI FELT LIKE HE HADN'T LEFT HIS SHIP'S LIBRARY IN WEEKS, EVEN THOUGH it had only been days. He had been buried deep in existing clone law, most of it cobbled together after some crisis or other. There seemed to be no real thought to the laws at all. They were drafted as reactions to whatever had sparked them, not as an existing body of work. They hadn't been crafted, like some of the laws in the Earth Alliance, and they weren't comprehensive. They hadn't even existed long enough to be chiseled into order by the courts.

They were a contradictory mess.

The library's nanoscrubbers were on full. Bots came in and out, bearing food (courtesy of the staff), coffee, and changes of clothing. Although whenever a bot brought Salehi more clothes, he figured it was time for a shower, and he would leave.

At least the room hadn't developed that law school funk he'd noticed before finals. It didn't matter how many scrubbers were in the law school's systems during finals week, every study area smelled like a gym locker with a broken cleaning system.

Here, at least, the library remained somewhat pristine. A ship had to have better environmental equipment than a law school.

Not that he cared beyond that moment when he returned to the library, saw his staff working, and Uzvuyiten ensconced in his spot.

Uzvuyiten got up every four hours or so, and left the room. Salehi always felt relieved about that. He suspected the others did as well.

The other lawyers and assistants had come and gone from the room. Salehi stopped keeping track of all the players long ago. He simply didn't have enough brain space to handle it all, particularly if he wasn't going to use AutoLearn.

Sir? The inquiry was soft, in his links, which was odd. It came from Lauren Jiolitti, one of the attorneys he had hand-chosen to take this trip with him. She hadn't made partner yet, but she would. She was one of the best he'd seen.

She was sitting only a few meters from him, which was what made the contact even odder.

Yes? he sent.

I just got word from S^3 *about our investigation. I wasn't sure if Uzvuyiten knew about it, so I thought I should contact you first…?*

She sounded tentative. Salehi didn't look at her. She had done well. Uzvuyiten didn't know that S^3 was running its own investigation of the Peyti clone DNA, just to make certain that everything was on the up and up.

Because of his focus, Salehi had forgotten that he had designated Jiolitti as the investigation's contact.

I'll meet you in my quarters in a few minutes, he sent.

He got up, muttered something about a shower break, and headed out of the room. No one paid attention. They were all as focused as he was.

He headed to his quarters which were on a different level. He hadn't used them much. He barely thought of them as "his."

He had the main stateroom on the ship—a large bedroom, a large sitting area, a full kitchen, and a decadent bathroom. He usually loved the main stateroom, but on this trip, it had been little more than a place to change clothes and catch a few hours of sleep.

He had gotten himself an apple of a variety grown especially for S^3, when he heard the chime that announced a visitor. He commanded the door to open.

Jiolitti stepped inside. She was a slight woman with shoulder-length dark hair that usually had another color running through it. Apparently, she had been too busy on this case to add that tint. The lack of it, and the fact that she hadn't matched her eyes to her clothes like she often did, made her attractive.

Salehi hadn't noticed that before.

Of course, it also added a few years to her face, which he appreciated.

She looked around. "No desert?" she asked.

He smiled. "No time," he said, not wanting to explain that the desert spoke of relaxation to him. He probably wasn't going to relax for years now—except on scheduled vacations.

She tilted her head, then ran a hand through her hair. It tumbled around her face. She stepped forward tentatively—"Living room?" she asked. "Kitchen?"—as if she wanted to know her destination before going any farther.

"Sitting room," he said, giving the room the designation it had on the ship's manifest. He grabbed some water for both of them and followed her into the sitting area.

It had no portals. It did have programmable walls that he had forgotten to program. The default program consisted of light paint and dark fake wood lintels, making everything a bit too heavy and a bit too Ancient Earth for his tastes.

He commanded the room to slowly give them sunlight and change the walls to show a country garden. The scenery would change as the conversation progressed.

"What did they send you?" he asked as he stopped in front of his favorite chair. It was large and comfortable, the only thing he never changed when he reprogrammed the room.

He tossed the apple in the air as he began to sit, and caught the apple as he got comfortable. Then he took a bite. He had forgotten how tart the company apples were, and thought—not for the first time—how appropriate that tartness was.

She eased into a straight-backed chair across from him. She watched his antics with the apple with barely disguised impatience.

"So far as our people can tell, the government of Peyla has nothing to do with the clones," she said.

He wasn't sure if that was good news or not. He decided not to react to it. He would hear her out.

"Our investigators split into two groups," she said. "First, we have a group who are retracing the clones' movements beginning with the moment they arrived on Armstrong, and working backward."

He nodded. He knew that. It had been his suggestion.

"Then we have a group of investigators tracking down the DNA." She folded her hands in front of herself. "I thought the second investigation would be simple. Someone had to be selling the DNA after all. But no one is. As far as we can tell."

That truly surprised him. He allowed himself a frown. "Then where did the DNA come from?"

She sighed and glanced at the wall. It now showed a sunrise over some mountains that Salehi should be able to name. Of course, he couldn't. He wished he hadn't reprogrammed the wall, since it was distracting her.

"Where it came from is an actual problem," she said.

He braced himself for something horrid.

Her gaze met his.

"Here's how it goes," she said. "Peyla doesn't have as many identity theft problems as the rest of the Earth Alliance—something to do with the law-abiding nature of the Peyti or something. I think it has more to do with the fact that they're anal about identity in the first place, so they have a lot of double- and triple-checks that make identity theft hard."

He had remembered now why he had assigned this to her. She had an affinity for the Peyti. She always had. She had volunteered to coordinate work with the Peyti lawyers on various cases, and more than once, she had pushed for an S^3 branch on Peyla.

The partners had always decided against it. S^3 had been a human firm for generations, and no one in the firm wanted to admit that many clients appreciated that.

But many clients—particularly some old, staid ones—did.

"Don't tell me," he said. "The Peyti didn't follow Alliance protocols in handling a dangerous criminal when they arrested Uzvekmt after the genocide in Qavle."

"All right," she said with a smile. "I won't tell you. I also won't tell you that they didn't follow protocol when they tried him or when they imprisoned him."

Salehi sighed. "What a mess."

"Well," she said, "to be fair, there was no protocol to follow. Those laws didn't go into effect for another ten years after the capture of Uzvekmt. And the Peyti simply didn't see the need before that."

"So you're telling me the DNA is untraceable."

"That's the odd thing," she said. "It's not untraceable. Uzvekmt was handled by just a few Peyti. From the moment he was in custody until his death, his contacts were limited. So there are very few candidates for the DNA theft."

Yet she had said it would be hard to track the DNA. He took another bite of his apple, still braced for the worst case.

"But?" he asked.

"The company that handled his remains got swallowed up into the Alliance itself. Technically, we should be able to trace that DNA, at least."

"We can't?" he asked.

She shook her head.

"You're telling me the *Alliance* lost his DNA?" Salehi asked.

"Or the record of it, yes, I am," she said.

He set the apple down, happy that his hand wasn't shaking. Then he stood up.

There had been an Alliance connection to Rafik Fujita's death. Salehi had tried to investigate what had gone wrong, only to be told the information was classified.

Classified.

He glanced at the stupid wall. The sun was up over the horizon, turning the sky a delicate pink. Earth somewhere. Made sense. He usually programmed Earth images into his systems.

But it couldn't distract him; it couldn't slow his increased heartbeat.

How could the Alliance lose the records of Uzvekmt's DNA?

He ran a hand through his hair. He didn't like the connections. Usually when he found connections like this in the law, he believed they had meaning, particularly when those connections showed up in a criminal case.

And that's what this was, wasn't it? All of it? The bombings, Anniversary Day, the Peyti Crisis? They were all crimes. He was handling criminal cases.

Only the clones were pawns. They couldn't be full-blown actors in these dramas because they didn't have access. Just by their non-citizen status, he knew they couldn't be at the center of all of this. They couldn't work in the Alliance government, not for any group.

Although, technically, clones shouldn't have been able to become lawyers either.

He pounded a fist at his forehead. Behind him, he could hear rustling as Jiolitti shifted in her chair. His movements were bothering her. Too bad. He didn't have time to take care of her.

If the government—the entire government—was involved in a crime against the Moon, how could he bring anything to court? Was he thinking too small?

And why the hell would the Alliance attack the Moon? It made no sense.

He shook his head.

"Sir?" Jiolitti asked.

He turned around. She was frowning at him.

"It was probably just a clerical error," she said. "Should I have someone in the Alliance track down the DNA?"

That was the logical thing to do.

"No," he said. "Let me handle this part of the investigation."

He wasn't going to lose someone else because he passed off a job. He wasn't going to make Jiolitti or the detectives she assigned into the targets of whoever—whatever—was doing all of this.

For an inexplicable reason that he didn't entirely understand.

"Did the detectives find anything else?" he asked.

"Not anything conclusive," she said.

"Pull them back for now," he said, then stopped himself. He almost asked for a report, but he didn't want them to document anything. "Tell them to be ready in case we need them again."

"All right, sir, but shouldn't they continue? They've found out a lot already."

He shook his head.

"I need to do something else first," he said.

"Would you like my help?" she asked.

He made himself smile before he turned around. He actually struggled to make certain the expression in his eyes matched the one on his lips.

"I have this for the moment, Lauren. You did a great job here."

"I didn't do much." She stood, clearly knowing she was being dismissed. "I'm ready any time you need me."

He nodded, not quite able to answer her.

After she left, he sent a message to Uzvuyiten on a private link. *I need to talk to you in my quarters. It's important.*

I'll be right there, Uzvuyiten sent back.

Salehi wandered back to his chair, then picked up the half-eaten apple. It was turning brown. He cupped it in his hand.

The Alliance wouldn't want to destroy the Moon. Destroying the Moon—or all the cities on it—would cripple the Alliance. So the Alliance itself wasn't behind this.

But he didn't like what he was thinking. He needed to quash the thoughts, if possible.

He needed more information before he made a choice he might regret. Because right now, the information that Jiolitti had given him would force him to choose between his duties to his client, and his duties as an officer of the court.

If he knew that someone in the Alliance was trying to bring down the Alliance, he needed to let the authorities know who that was.

But right now, he had nothing except paranoid speculation, brought on by the death of a friend, an enthusiasm for the law, and a willingness to take risks.

He couldn't take a risk here. He had to be certain.

Or he couldn't do anything at all.

39

ZHU HAD TO GET OUT OF THE OFFICE, IF ONLY FOR A FEW MINUTES. HE HAD hired twenty-five people in the past day, and if he had to repeat their names without using the images on the information chip in his hand, he wouldn't be able. He wasn't even certain he would recognize all of the new people tomorrow.

And he needed to. He needed some form of security in the office, but that required hiring a firm for it, and vetting everyone, and he didn't really have time.

He had been over his head since Salehi had pulled him out of that bar—maybe since he had passed the bar exam—and he was only diving deeper.

It was moments like that—*thoughts* like that—which were driving Zhu crazy. He needed help, he needed support, and he would get some of that when Salehi arrived a few days from now, but Zhu would still be point man on some of this stuff.

Maybe Zhu could become the office manager. Maybe he would tell Salehi to assign him that job.

And maybe the entire Moon would forget that the Peyti Crisis ever happened.

Yeah, right. As if that would ever happen.

Zhu walked around the corner to a deli he had discovered two days ago. The place, named Sevryn's, was keeping him sane. It had real meat, sliced thin—turkey, beef, things you couldn't get far out on Athena Base as well as all of the cured meats he could desire. The cured meats were even better here—he'd never tasted pastrami like they had in this place. The sausages seemed to come in an infinite variety, as did the cheeses.

The place was expensive as hell—even the bread was made with ingredients imported from Earth—and he didn't care. He paid for it all with his S^3 accounts. S^3 was working him to death; they could at least pay for the privilege.

For all its expense, the deli was tiny. It had four tables near the windows overlooking the sidewalk, and those tables were always full. A line formed before the place opened (he knew, because the last two mornings, he had been in that line) and continued until eight, when one of the employees would activate the closing protocol.

Whoever was in line at closing got to stay in line; anyone who arrived five minutes too late was out of luck.

He knew that as well, because last night, he'd been out of luck. Which was why he'd come this morning.

He looked at the types of meats, rotating in a glass cabinet. He knew they were holographic representations of whatever the deli had in its back room, and he didn't care. They looked phenomenal.

Something about all of this work was making him ravenous continually.

Maybe it *was* all of the work.

He was staring at some bluish cheese he couldn't identify when someone bumped him, hard. He scooted to one side. If he hadn't moved quickly, he would have been covered with hot coffee.

He looked up at a woman half a foot taller than he was. She wore an Armstrong police uniform.

"Sorry," she said in a tone that told him that she wasn't sorry at all.

Then someone bumped him from behind. He moved again, but this time he didn't avoid some hot chicken soup slopping on his polished shoes. The soup filtered through old-fashioned laces he had been so proud of, cooling as it did. Fortunately, it didn't burn the tops of his feet, but oh, man, did he feel the warmth—and the wet thickness of the soup itself.

"Yeah," said a man, also in uniform, still holding the soup carton. "I'm sorry, too."

Then a third person bumped Zhu, also a cop, and this time, he got drenched with some kind of cold drink. The drink stank of overripe lemons and it made him instantly sticky.

"Oh, my," said the third cop. "Lookie what a mess you made."

For a moment, Zhu thought he had misunderstood the cop. Zhu thought the cop had said, *Lookie what a mess* I *made*. But the cop had definitely said *you* instead of *I*.

If Zhu had had any doubts this attack was deliberate, they were gone now.

He held up his hands. "Look, guys, I didn't mean—"

"*Guys?*" the female cop asked. "Do I look like a *guy* to you?"

She waved her coffee as she did so, and it splattered on the floor.

"That's enough!" said the man behind the counter. He was older, burly, with a tired air. Zhu had seen him here every day. The older man was probably the owner. "If you four have a beef with each other, take it outside. And don't waste my good food."

"We're not wasting food, Mr. Sevryn," the woman said. "It's coffee."

"I don't care if it's pisswater you brought in from that dive next door," the man—Sevryn—said. "You're slopping it in my place of business, and offending my customers, which ain't allowed. Now, either quit your childish behavior or get the hell out of my store."

"Sorry, Sev," said the second cop. "Didn't mean to offend."

"Well, you did," the man said. "Now get out."

The cops nodded, then headed for the door, bumping Zhu one last time for good measure. He let out a sigh. He was soaked. He smelled of coffee, lemon water, and soup.

The floor was covered in puddles.

"I'll help you clean up, sir," he said to the owner.

"Naw," the man said. "I got bots for that. But I don't want to see your face around here no more."

"I didn't—they—"

"They did, and you did too," the man said. "Don't think I don't know who you are. I didn't lose nobody last week, but on Anniversary Day, I lost a son, two uncles, and my Aunt Marie. So I don't need your kind here."

"I'm not doing anything connected with Anniversary Day," Zhu started. "I'm—"

"The hell you're not." The man had raised his voice. Everyone in the deli was looking at Zhu. "Those clones, they were working with them other clones, and they're all trying to destroy us. Now you're out there, recruiting soulless lawyers to save their asses. You have every right to conduct your business as you see fit, and so do I. And I don't see fit to feed the likes of you. Now get out."

Zhu opened his mouth to defend himself, and then sighed. No one had stepped forward to help him, no one had lifted a finger to stop those cops, and no one spoke up for him now. If anything, the people in line had moved farther away from him.

At first, Zhu had thought that was because of all the liquid splashing around. Then he had blamed it on the cops. But now, he felt vulnerable—truly vulnerable—because he was visible in a very real way.

Did everyone know who he was and what he was trying to do?

"I'm sorry," Zhu said, not sure what else he could do. "I didn't mean to offend you. I didn't ask for the job—"

"Then you shouldn'ta done it, now should you?" the owner snapped. "Now, get out of my place."

Zhu nodded, turned around, and sloshed his way to the door. His socks were heavy with soup, his suit hung on him, and he left little footprints on the floor. As he made his way across the deli, he thought of telling the owner how wonderful the food was, and trying for yet another defense.

But as he thought of the words, he realized he didn't want to say that.

Instead, he put his hand on the door, and stopped.

"For the record," he said in his courtroom voice, "we're hiring more than a hundred people. They'll need someplace to eat. You just screwed yourself out of a lot of business, old man."

The owner chuckled. "I don't need your kinda business," he said. "Have you looked around?"

"You pissed off a lawyer, buddy," Zhu said, "who is hiring a bunch of other lawyers from off-Moon. Think it through."

"Are you threatening him?" a woman asked as she stood.

Zhu ran a hand down his ruined clothing. "Do I look like a man who can make a credible threat?" he asked.

And then he walked out of the building.

He walked until he was past the windows, and then he stopped. He needed lunch, but he didn't feel like he could go anywhere dressed like this.

He sighed, then decided that it didn't matter. No one cared about him here. And he didn't have to look presentable. Theoretically, word would get out—well, actually, it seemed that word *had* gotten out—and everyone would know what S^3 was doing.

Time to embrace it.

He pivoted and walked into the place that the old man had called "the dive next door."

It wasn't nearly as pretty, and Zhu's lemon-filled nostrils couldn't tell if it had much of a good-food smell at all. But it had more tables, and they were full.

He bellied his way up to the counter.

"So you're the guy, eh?" the thin young man behind that counter asked. "I heard what happened next door."

"I'm the guy," Zhu said. "I have an expense account, and I'm extremely hungry. You want make some money?"

"I don't ask what my customers do for a living, so long as their money is good," the young man said. "Whatcha need?"

Zhu hesitated. The food looked a lot less appetizing here. The sandwiches were on bread clearly made with Moon flour, and the meat was the same old stuff that he saw at every other lunch counter between here and S^3's offices on the other side of the sector.

But the sandwiches made from vegetables looked spectacular. He actually perused the menu, saw that this place specialized in Moon food, getting fresh vegetables and fruits daily from the Growing Pits.

Zhu tapped the chip in his left index finger, the chip with S^3's expense account in it, and said, "I'm going to order a couple of sandwiches. If I like what I'm eating, then I'll make a standing order for the office. Do you deliver?"

The young man smiled. "Do I deliver? Absolutely. On everything."

Zhu smiled in return. Maybe this wasn't such a bad day after all. Maybe he just needed to embrace who he had become, and everyone else would too.

Or maybe he just had to learn to ignore the negative treatment.

Like any good defense attorney would.

40

DESHIN STAYED IN THE BUSINESS SUITE LONG AFTER CONTE HAD LEFT. Conte's story had obvious flaws and miscues in it. It was very self-absorbed, like Conte himself, but it also had elements of the truth.

Deshin sat at the built-in breakfast bar with a view of those unknown snow-capped mountains. He could see the faint outline of trees on them—fir trees? He couldn't quite tell, and he knew he wouldn't be here long enough to find out.

He had already spent more time with Conte than he wanted to. Conte hadn't made any money on this meeting—he had probably known coming in that he wouldn't, which was why he had been so late—and he had left bruised. Kaielynn seemed to enjoy twisting Conte's limbs enough to make the man wince.

But from all indications, Conte had told the truth as he knew it. He had found the body of PierLuigi Frémont in his cell. Maybe Conte had provided the drugs Frémont had used to kill himself, maybe not. That wasn't Deshin's concern.

But Conte had taken advantage of Frémont's death to collect DNA in variety of forms. He was a guard in the prison, and he had done it before.

But his usual co-conspirator was off that night, so he enlisted the help of a newcomer, a woman named Jhena Andre.

She had a thing for me, Conte had said, and as he said that, Kaielynn had sent Deshin a message.

A thing? Kaielynn sent. *She probably wanted to kill the bastard.*

Deshin usually liked it when Kaielynn couldn't keep her opinions to herself, but in that instance, he didn't. He wanted to concentrate on what Conte was saying.

And Conte was telling him how the girl smuggled the DNA out of the cellblock, leaving it in an unguarded closet. Conte had come for the DNA when his shift was over. He thought every bag was there, but that was years ago, and he never really checked.

After the Frémont DNA showed up on Anniversary Day in the form of very real clones, and slow-grow clones at that, Conte started looking for the source. If he partnered with that source, he could make a small fortune. Or maybe a large one.

He found some pretenders, people who had modified the flawed fast-grow DNA that he sold, but he never found any untainted DNA. He had investigated others from the prison, but they didn't have it, and some of his black-market friends had talked to the people who made designer criminal clones.

Everyone wanted slow-grow DNA from Frémont, and no one had it.

Except the person who had created the clones for the Anniversary Day attacks.

Deshin had asked only one question in the middle of all of Conte's ramblings: did Conte also sell nonhuman DNA?

Conte did not. He seemed alien-averse.

Besides, he had said, *how'm I gonna know the good from the bad? I don't associate with aliens.*

Good point, particularly since he hadn't known the good from the bad with the Frémont DNA.

Deshin took the name Jhena Andre. While he listened to Conte, Deshin called up the records of Andre's employment at the prison. She had lasted there for nearly two years. The Frémont death had occurred early in her career.

Deshin had mentioned that to Conte, then asked, "Did she ever talk to you about the Frémont DNA?"

Conte had shaken his head. "We never talked about that night again."

"Not ever?"

"I told her we weren't supposed to talk about it. She listened. She was a good girl," he said. "I figured she was just scared. She'd done something that could lose her a job."

"So, you never heard of her selling DNA?" Deshin asked.

"No," Conte said. "She's hasn't broken the law since, either. She's one of those reliable people."

"You know this because…?"

"Because I tracked her down when I couldn't find the DNA," Conte said.

"Did you ask her if she had any for sale?" Deshin asked.

"Of course," Conte said.

"And?"

"She didn't," he said. "The others I sent to her, they couldn't get any from her either. She asked me not to send anyone else."

"Yet you gave me her name," Deshin said.

Conte shrugged. "That's why I'm not charging for it."

A comment which had made Kaielynn snort out loud. Conte had gotten offended at that, and the discussion had ended soon afterward.

Conte left, with two of Deshin's team tailing him, not that it really mattered. They all knew that they were done with Conte.

Deshin had decided to stay in the business suite to use the hotel's network to trace this Andre woman. He did it from here partly because his trace was expected, and partly because he wanted to seem aboveboard with it all.

She wasn't hard to find. Conte hadn't lied. Her career seemed legitimate. In fact, she didn't seem like a person who would ever break any laws for any reason.

She had parlayed her job at the prison into a career with the Earth Alliance. She had moved out of prisons and into other parts of the human-based government, always working in support capacities as she moved up, generally as an assistant.

She had become an administrator a dozen years ago, and was working her way into some part of the Alliance, but he couldn't tell what part. That was classified.

Deshin leaned back from the floating screens and rubbed his chin. As far as he could tell, everything this Andre woman had done had been legal—except for that moment with Conte.

But Deshin had been involved in the fringes of things for a very long time. He knew that people who bent the law, people who broke the law, often repeated the action.

He also knew that very smart people rarely got caught. She hadn't, not with that entire Frémont incident, and she should have. The prison authorities should have investigated everyone associated with Frémont's untimely death. Perhaps they did; but they didn't find Conte—who would have been first on Deshin's suspicion list—and they didn't discover that Andre had helped him.

If they had discovered it, she never would have received promotions. She would have remained in lower-level positions. And she never would have worked in classified areas of the Alliance.

She bothered Deshin. She bothered him a lot.

The little tidbits of information that he kept getting—what he'd been hearing from Flint, and from some of the others, kept coming back to people inside the Earth Alliance.

Maybe Conte had just given him one.

Deshin stood and walked to the windows. He could feel Kaielynn watching him. She didn't like his tendency to stand in front of windows and look outside. She was always afraid a sniper would get him.

Maybe a sniper would one day. But he doubted it.

Deshin hadn't built his business on fear as much as mutual back-scratching. Even though he dealt with some of the shadiest people in the Alliance, they always had a lot to lose if they lost him.

Except here. He hadn't been that kind to Conte.

But Conte had no reason to hurt him. No one did. And no one seemed to care that Conte was giving out Andre's name. She had asked him not to do it again. When Conte had told Deshin that, Deshin hadn't detected a lie.

Then Deshin frowned at the mountains, looming over this small city.

He hadn't detected a lie, but he also hadn't detected any upset.

Andre had asked Conte not to give out her name.

She hadn't come after him, she hadn't been angry with him, she hadn't tried to shut him down.

Given some of her connections in the Alliance, she could have done that.

A generally innocent person, someone who had only made one mistake in their life, worked very hard at covering up that mistake. That person got defensive. That person got angry. That person often got vindictive.

Deshin cursed himself silently. He hadn't thought to ask Conte what her reaction was.

But Conte, in the spirit of full disclosure, would probably have warned Deshin. Conte was a talker who would have said something like, *Be careful when you approach her. She doesn't like hearing my name.*

Conte might have decided to let Deshin walk directly into a mess, but then he would lose any possible business Deshin might bring him.

And the one thing that Conte had to gain was future Deshin business. Conte had even mentioned it on the way out.

We're a backwater, Conte had said, *but I know sometimes organizations like yours find backwaters useful. Now that we've made contact…*

He had let that hang, then he had grinned.

Deshin had nodded, knowing it was always better to leave doors open than it was to slam them closed. He had implied—but never said—that he would continue to do business with Conte.

Even though Deshin doubted he ever would.

So, given that, and given Deshin's assessment of Conte's character, Deshin felt confident in assuming that Conte would have warned him if Andre were temperamental.

All Conte had done was warn Deshin that the woman didn't want to be contacted, which was an entirely different thing.

Deshin clasped his hands behind his back and paced the large room. She didn't want to be contacted, but she hadn't gotten angry. No pure clones of Frémont were on the market, even though someone could have made a fortune from them.

Which explained why the Black Fleet grew angry when Deshin wanted designer criminal clones of Frémont. There were none, at least that the Black Fleet could find.

And Deshin couldn't find them either.

The one person who'd had an opportunity to make them—Conte—had somehow contaminated the DNA, so he couldn't build anything except relatively useless fast-grow. And *he* wanted Frémont clones as well.

In fact, he had the most to gain if he found them. And he had done his research on Deshin. Conte had known that Deshin was worth a fortune. Conte would have offered the clones to Deshin if Conte had them—or even had access to them.

The clones of Frémont, then, weren't on the market at all. They existed for another purpose—and that purpose was pretty clear.

They were soldiers in that war he'd mentioned to Flint. People didn't sell soldiers. They *used* soldiers.

Which made Flint's search of the money even more important.

Deshin sighed.

Kaielynn glanced at him, as if she were wondering what he was doing. She probably was.

He couldn't bargain with a government official for clones that she might or might not (more than likely might) know about. He didn't dare. And he didn't have the capacity to investigate someone with high security clearance in the Earth Alliance.

The other track he could try to investigate was to find Peyti clones of Uzvekmt, and see if he could buy those. But that would look out of character for him, since Deshin's organization only used aliens in their native environment.

The Peyti were so law-abiding that the two times he'd tried to start a business on Peyla, he'd lost a small fortune. He couldn't work with them.

So, he couldn't pursue the Peyti clones either.

He had to give this part of the investigation over to Flint, with suggestions that Flint and his connections see what they could find.

Deshin had other leads to chase, ones he wouldn't mention to Flint or anyone close to the power structure.

At least, not yet.

41

The City of Armstrong had decided to warehouse the Peyti Crisis clones in a prison outside of the dome. Armstrong had several prisons, and this one was considered "transitional," so it didn't follow the rules of the other prisons.

It claimed to be a maximum security facility because it housed criminals of all types who'd been charged and were too dangerous to release while they awaited trial. It had the silly name all of these transitional facilities had: It was called a Reception Center.

Nyquist had been to this particular Reception Center hundreds of times in his career, and had hated it each time. It wasn't clean enough for his tastes. It was also poorly managed, something he had complained about a few years ago. Even then—before Anniversary Day, before these current crises—the response he had gotten was a cold one: *They're prisoners. Why do you care?*

As if that were a personal failing. As if he were sympathizing with them somehow.

He had taken a train to the Reception Center, and arrived through the front doors. Ever since the Peyti clones had arrived, the Reception Center had discouraged visitors. Nyquist had had to go through five layers of bureaucracy to get his visit approved, and even then, he'd had to use DeRicci's name to get final approval.

He ended up telling the prison system that he was trying to see one of the Peyti clones, Uzvaan, because of a case they'd worked on in the past, not because of the Peyti Crisis.

Apparently S^3 had delivered their injunctions here as well. They were making certain everyone knew who could talk to the clones and who could not.

Still, it had taken nearly two hours after Nyquist arrived before he was allowed into the interview area. He felt like the procedures had taken him from cop to suspect to possible bomber. Every part of his person got checked. His identification got run a dozen times. Each time, the procedures became more and more invasive.

He tried to remain calm about it all, but the farther he got into the system, the more he regretted agreeing to this ploy. As the hours went by, and he confirmed his identity as a law enforcement official yet again, he wondered if the clones themselves had been notified of S^3's gambit. Because if they had, then his time with Uzvaan would be wasted.

Finally, after he'd been sitting alone for hours in the strangely set up interview room, he realized the day was lost anyway. Who cared if his interview with Uzvaan was a futile trip? At least he had tried.

He hadn't seen an interview room in the Reception Center like this in years. He rarely had cases that involved interviewing nonhuman suspects. Somehow, his years as a detective mostly focused on human-against-human crimes. That might have been because of a temper tantrum he had had early in his career, before his bosses in the detective division realized he was a cantankerous jerk, not a guy who had hard-and-fast rules about stupid things.

In that temper tantrum, he had complained—loudly—that he hated keeping track of legal murder and illegal murder. He believed then—and still believed—that all murders were the same. What sparked the tantrum had been a Disty Vengeance Killing.

The Disty Vengeance Killings might have been allowed under Alliance law, but Nyquist was a human being first, a member of the Alliance second (or third, or one-hundred-and-fifty-seventh, if truth be told). He believed that murder was murder, especially murder that entailed a gang encircling a single individual, capturing that individual, and eviscerating that individual, then decorating a room with that individual's remains.

He didn't care what the law said; he didn't care that in many instances involving the Disty such things were "justified." He didn't believe they should happen at all.

Someone must have made a note in his personnel file, because from then on, the bulk of his cases were human-on-human. Crimes he could understand. Oh, he still caught a Disty Vengeance Killing now and then—he'd met Miles Flint on one. But mostly, Nyquist investigated crimes he could understand, crimes that made sense, crimes that were crimes—at least in his book.

Which meant that he rarely sat in the part of the Reception Center that housed nonhumans. Even when he visited Peyti criminals here, they had been escorted to the human wing.

This time, Nyquist had been escorted to the Peyti wing. He had been given an environmental suit that he did not want to wear unless he absolutely had to. He draped it over his arm. The authorities also gave him a mask that he could use in place of the suit, rather like the Peyti did, provided he didn't stay in their environment for long.

The mask looked like it hadn't been cleaned in the past decade. He didn't even want to carry it, but he did, just in case he needed it.

He asked for—and received—permission to see Uzvaan in what the Reception Center called "The Tunnels," the area between the human section and the Peyti section. The Tunnels looked like they'd been transported from Mars, narrow little warrens that meandered around equipment he didn't understand.

The tunnels that he went through were narrow little tubes made of a thick, scratched substance that looked like permaplastic, but couldn't be. Permaplastic hadn't been used on buildings since the colonial era. Still, he hated that he couldn't see through what should have been clear.

His links had been shut off, except for his emergency links, and those had been adjusted to the Reception Center's systems, which meant that anything from the outside went through the Reception Center first. But if there was a crisis inside the Reception Center, then he'd be among the first to know.

Not that he could do anything. His weapons were gone. The only reason he still had his badge was because it was part of a chip built into his hand, and not attached to any of his links.

He didn't even have a human guard to take him this deep into the Reception Center. Instead, mouthless android guards with muscles twice the size of his thighs led him inside. He hated the android guards more than he wanted to admit. He found them creepier than some aliens he'd had to deal with over the years.

They deposited him, alone, in a clear round room that looked like it was floating in air. He'd seen the specs for these things but had never actually used one. They were little one-person protective shields. If he knew where the control panel was, he could drive the thing like a spaceship into other parts of the Reception Center—or at least, other parts of The Tunnels.

Instead, he got to sit at a table in what appeared to be a bubble inside an ocean of blue liquid. The table rested on a clear flat floor, that made him feel like he was floating in the center of the bubble—a sensation he didn't like at all.

And that's where he waited for another hour, that was where he decided his day was already wasted and so he shouldn't resent the task, and that was where he felt a small bubble of his own—a bubble of panic. Should there be another attack, should there be some kind of crisis in the Reception Center itself, he was trapped in his little one-person ship, all alone, in that ocean of blue.

After ninety minutes, he found himself wondering if the little one-person bubble was a test of a visitor's resolve. Because he knew if he stayed much longer, he'd go ever so slightly crazy.

Or maybe not slightly.

About the point where he started to weigh the pros and cons of leaving without seeing Uzvaan, another bubble made its way through the ocean of blue liquid. As it got closer, he saw that the new bubble had a single occupant—a maskless Peyti.

Nyquist assumed that Peyti was Uzvaan. He'd only seen the lawyer without his mask once, that day of the Peyti Crisis. And if Nyquist were being honest with himself, he would admit that he had no real idea what Uzvaan looked like without the mask.

That day, Nyquist had simply been focused on the mask itself—and the bomb it contained.

Uzvaan's bubble stopped a few meters from Nyquist's. Uzvaan sat on a chair. Nyquist couldn't tell if Uzvaan's arms were bound to the chair or if he was just sitting with his hands pointed downward.

Every time Nyquist had been with a Peyti lawyer, they'd either been standing or they had been sitting at tables working. He had never seen one just sit before.

Nyquist was grateful for his own small table. He had something to rest his arms on. He used that moment to tap one of his chips, so that he could record the conversation. He wasn't certain if he would be allowed to remove the recording from the Reception Center, but he had to try.

Tiny tubes floated out of Nyquist's bubble and out of Uzvaan's bubble. The tubes met in the middle of the liquid stuff.

"Bartholomew Nyquist," Uzvaan said, his voice as clear as if he were inside Nyquist's bubble. Nyquist started despite himself. Uzvaan's voice had haunted his nightmares for a week now. "I never thought I'd see you again."

And I would have thought that you would sit there quietly, refusing to talk, Nyquist thought, but didn't say. He didn't want to give Uzvaan ideas.

"I actually have to talk to you as a lawyer," Nyquist said, managing to sound put upon.

"Come now, Bartholomew," Uzvaan said in that precise way that once won him cases. "We both know I've been disbarred."

"Well, then one of us was misinformed," Nyquist said. "Surprisingly, none of you clones have been disbarred, at least not yet."

Nyquist couldn't keep the bitterness out of his voice. He told himself that Uzvaan would expect the sarcasm. Nyquist wasn't sure if that were true, but he could only pretend so much.

The bastard across from him had tried to kill him after all.

"Hmm," Uzvaan said. "I would have thought disbarment automatic after the commission of a felony."

Uzvaan was annoying him just enough to keep him on his toes. Which was a good thing; then Nyquist didn't have to focus on the fact that Uzvaan had actually frightened him a week ago.

"I suspect disbarment is automatic," Nyquist said, "but you know how documentation works. Slowly, and sometimes not at all. So, ironically, I need to talk with you about Ursula Palmette."

Uzvaan made that screechy sound that passed for laughter among the Peyti.

"I don't give damn about Ursula Palmette," he said. "Do what you want with her. I'm not her attorney any longer."

"Yes, you are," Nyquist said. "You're the attorney of record."

"For all I care, that dumb woman can rot in prison. Or be killed by the Alliance's lovely death penalty."

Nyquist didn't rise to that. He couldn't. He had to play this one carefully, because he suspected that someone else was recording this. Once they realized that Uzvaan no longer represented anyone, this conversation was not privileged. At the moment, it was protected, but Nyquist had no idea how long that would last.

"You need to release her to find a new attorney, then," Nyquist said.

"How do you propose I do that?" Uzvaan asked. "I have no access to nets here, no way to talk to anyone, and am allowed to interact only with those nameless faceless android guards that even now stand outside my little cell. I see they put you in a cell as well."

"Is this what cells look like on the Peyti side?"

"No," Uzvaan said. "This is a step up. I should probably thank you for the short reprieve. When this conversation is over, I go back to my ugly four walls and three squares per day. Apparently, humans run this prison. Because no one bothered to tell them that Peyti eat one large meal per day, and nothing else."

"Or maybe they don't care," Nyquist said. "I'm rather surprised that you do."

Uzvaan leaned forward, but his wrists—if the joint between his hands and his arms could be called that—remained in the same place. So apparently, he was locked in.

"Why are you really here, Bartholomew?" Uzvaan asked. "It's not to inquire after my health. You do realize that you would have died with me if somehow the Armstrong government hadn't blocked my attack."

Nyquist kept his face impassive. Had no one told Uzvaan that most of the attacks failed? Did he not know that there were hundreds of other Peyti in this prison awaiting trial?

"You aren't the first who tried to kill me," Nyquist said. "I doubt you'll be the last."

He actually managed to sound nonchalant about that.

"And you hold no grudge?"

"I didn't say that," Nyquist said. Hadn't Uzvaan heard the bitterness? Perhaps Uzvaan wasn't paying attention to nuance.

Not that it mattered. Uzvaan had finally opened the door that Nyquist wanted him to open. Nyquist could now say they were having a discussion that Uzvaan initiated, a *personal* discussion, not a legal one.

Still, Nyquist couldn't entirely let the comment about the grudge go. "I can't say I liked you, Uzvaan. I'm not sure I like any lawyers. But I certainly respected you. I'm the one who recommended you handle Palmette's case, remember?"

"I do," Uzvaan said. "I thought it curious, since she was your former partner. I couldn't decide if you thought I was horribly *in*competent or terribly competent. My ego allowed me to choose competent."

"I thought you were damn good," Nyquist said. "I felt a little personal responsibility for Palmette's version of crazy, and I figured I owed her a good counsel. Guess I was wrong about that good counsel thing. You took the case knowing you personally were going to finish the job she started."

"I had no idea what she started," Uzvaan said. "She wasn't part of my mission."

Nyquist suddenly hated the clear table that he sat at. Because he would normally have clenched a fist underneath the table to hide the sudden anger that surged through him.

"It was a *mission*?" Nyquist asked. "Really? Because it seemed out of character to me."

Uzvaan tilted his head slightly. "Some would argue that it was entirely in character. By now you know that I'm a clone of Uzvekmt, I'm sure."

He spoke as if they were having an intellectual discussion, not talking about mass murder.

"Me, and everyone else on the Moon know exactly who you are and what you came from," Nyquist said. "Although, I gotta tell you, I've never been one to believe that biology was destiny."

Uzvaan sighed. Nyquist had never seen a Peyti do that, but then again, he'd never spoken to a Peyti in its own environment, without its mask on.

"What do you really want, Bartholomew?" Uzvaan asked.

Finally, Nyquist had worn him down. That surprised Nyquist. He had expected the discussion to take more work.

"I want help with Palmette's case, but you won't give me that," Nyquist said.

"I have a hunch I can't," Uzvaan said as if he had no choice.

"A hunch?" Nyquist asked. He decided to listen to each word that Uzvaan used. "It sounds like they don't tell you anything in here."

"After I left the Armstrong Police Station," Uzvaan said, "I was transported here with some undesirables, and some old friends. Since then, I've been alone. This is the first time I've left my cell in more than a week."

So S^3 hadn't contacted the clones yet. Nyquist felt his pulse rate increase ever so slightly. That was good news.

"So," Nyquist said, making sure he thought through each word, "they didn't tell you how many people were killed in your attack."

"No one was killed in *my* attack," Uzvaan said, and now he was the one who sounded bitter. "You made certain of that."

Nyquist resisted the urge to smile. Finally, he had gotten an emotional reaction out of Uzvaan.

"I meant," Nyquist said, "has no one told you about the attack by all of the clones of Uzvekmt? Didn't someone in the prison tell you about the death toll?"

"They haven't said anything. I would assume it was quite high. I ran into other of my so-called brothers over the years. There were a lot of us on the Moon. It would have been hard to stop us."

As quickly as that anger had spurted through him, it was replaced by a surge of elation. Nyquist allowed himself a small smile.

"Every one of your so-called brothers was as successful at bombing as you were," Nyquist said. It was a bit of a lie. Some outside the domes had succeeded. But Uzvaan didn't need to know that. "They were also as successful as you were at killing themselves."

Uzvaan leaned back. His wide eyes closed for a long moment.

Nyquist couldn't tell if the news devastated Uzvaan or relieved him.

So Nyquist decided to continue.

"I have to be honest, Uzvaan," Nyquist said. "I never thought of you as a suicide bomber."

Uzvaan opened his eyes. He moved his head forward in acknowledgement.

Nyquist couldn't tell if Uzvaan had taken that comment as a compliment or not. Nyquist wasn't even certain how he had meant it.

"Your life focuses down when you know it will end," Uzvaan said. "I felt very alive at the end."

Nyquist hadn't expected that. "But you don't feel alive now?

"Now, I'm in a legal purgatory," Uzvaan said. "Your authorities know what I am. I have no rights under Alliance law. And yet, I'm a lawyer, with more knowledge than almost anyone about the way things work. I truly did not expect this."

Nyquist wished he understood the tones of the Peyti better than he did. He couldn't quite assume that what he heard was wistfulness or sadness, even though he wanted it to be.

Still, Uzvaan's comment surprised him.

"You didn't consider failure?" Nyquist asked.

For the first time, Uzvaan spoke Peytin. It sounded almost rote. Nyquist hoped the words got recorded, because he didn't know Peytin at all.

Then Uzvaan blinked and looked away for a moment.

Programmed? Nyquist couldn't tell.

"What did you just say?" Nyquist asked.

Uzvaan's eyes closed slowly, then reopened. "It is not important."

Which meant that it had been.

Nyquist wouldn't find out what Uzvaan had said until he listened to the recording—if he could listen to the recording.

Nyquist had to continue moving forward.

"I take that to mean you never thought you'd fail," he said. "Strange assumption for a smart guy like you. Because you had to know that everybody fails the first time they try something."

Uzvaan leaned back, hands still locked in position. "No, they do not."

"You failed," Nyquist said. "*All* of you failed. That can't feel good."

Uzvaan sighed again. "It doesn't feel anything. I did not plan to see the results of our action."

Nyquist let out an understanding "aah." At least, he hoped it sounded understanding. "So," he said, "you felt trapped by your destiny."

"No." Uzvaan raised his head slightly. Nyquist had always seen looks like that on Peyti and thought they were adjusting their masks. He hadn't realized until now that they were raising their heads with pride. "I felt like I was living two lives. The one I wanted, and the one I had been given. Both would end on the same day. I had always known that."

Uzvaan was a lawyer. He knew words were important. He knew admissions were important.

Maybe DeRicci had been right; maybe some of the clones *were* willing to talk.

That was certainly what it seemed like right now. If Uzvaan believed his previous lives had ended a week ago, he owed nothing to anyone—

not his former clients or his former boss, and certainly not the ones who had created him for this mission.

"Which puts you in a bit of a limbo now," Nyquist said carefully.

"I prefer to think of it as born anew," Uzvaan said. "Or perhaps starting anew, since I was never born in the traditional sense."

That spurt of elation returned. Nyquist wished it hadn't. He couldn't let his emotions cloud this interview.

"This new life of yours could be very short," Nyquist said.

"It could," Uzvaan said, "although I don't worry about that at the moment. I am more concerned with the way that my life has become small, and will stay small unless I do something."

He *was* opening a door. There was no mistaking that now.

"What can you do?" Nyquist asked.

Uzvaan tilted his head slightly. "I'm sure you know, detective."

"I'm also sure that I dare not make any assumptions," Nyquist said with more honesty than he would like.

"You came here to bargain, correct?" Uzvaan asked.

"No," Nyquist said. He knew he could not admit that. Uzvaan didn't know that, because he didn't know about S^3, but he would eventually, and if Nyquist didn't play this right, Uzvaan himself might change his mind about what he said. Legally, he could do that. "I came to discuss poor Ursula Palmette."

"Still, you are a detective." Uzvaan was actually pushing this. Nyquist hadn't expected that at all. "I presume you are investigating the attacks of last week. I will wager that you can make deals."

Nyquist didn't agree or disagree. He didn't dare. "What are you interested in?"

"A full pardon in exchange for information," Uzvaan said.

It took all of Nyquist's strength to contain the laugh of derision that threatened to overtake him. Uzvaan was asking the man he had tried to kill for a pardon?

One of the things that Nyquist had always admired about Uzvaan the lawyer was his willingness to take risks. And he just took a big one.

"That's impossible," Nyquist said quietly. "And even if it were possible, I wouldn't tell anyone that you wanted it. Remember, Uzvaan, you were looking me in the eye when you tried to activate your fucking bomb."

"I have not forgotten," Uzvaan said. "But you should remember that I am also a lawyer, and I know negotiation. I will start with what I want."

"All right," Nyquist said. "You want to play it that way? I can do that. Because what I want is for you to tell me everything, and then die according to our laws."

His voice shook just a little. He regretted that. He wanted to sound calmer. But he couldn't.

"Obviously," Uzvaan said, "neither of us will get what we want."

"Obviously," Nyquist said. "And apparently, you're not going to talk to me about Palmette, so I wasted my day."

He stood. Somewhere, there was a button that would notify the authorities that he wanted to leave. He wasn't sure how long it would take them to retract the bubble. He hoped that standing was enough to signal that he wouldn't play games.

"What will you offer?" Uzvaan asked. "Or must you check with your bosses?"

Uzvaan sounded almost desperate. Maybe he was desperate. He probably was. After all, he had said that he had the life he wanted and the life he had been given. Presumably, he had carried that bomb according to the life he had been given.

Presumably, being a respected lawyer on the Moon had been the life he wanted.

He would never get that back, no matter how hard he argued for it.

"They're not going to give you anything," Nyquist lied. He remained standing. "You're part of a plot to bring down the entire Moon. They won't negotiate with you."

"You're portraying them as fools, and I know they're not, Detective." Uzvaan leaned to his left, trying to adjust his right arm. He was pinned in; no doubt about that now. "You need information. I have some. I'm willing to trade it. I'm talking to you because you are my only visitor since I was brought here. I suspect you're the only visitor I'll ever have. I'm not trying to insult you."

Nyquist let out a small snort. "Good to know," he said sarcastically. "I won't take my attempted murder badly then."

Uzvaan bowed his head. "I'm not going to insult you with an apology—"

"Why not?" Nyquist asked. His face had flushed. His heart rate had gone up. This *was* a mistake, a bad one. DeRicci should have sent someone else—anyone else.

"Because," Uzvaan said softly. "It was a condition of my existence."

"*My* murder?" Nyquist asked.

"The deaths on the Moon," Uzvaan said. "They were the price I paid for surviving."

"Surviving?" Nyquist asked.

"Surviving." Uzvaan nodded. "And that is all I will tell you without some kind of negotiation."

42

WHILE HE WAITED FOR UZVUYITEN, SALEHI MADE SOME FRESH COFFEE. He usually wasn't a coffee snob, but he needed something to do with his hands. Besides, his quarters had been stocked with all of the premium foods and beverages blended exclusively for S^3, done to impress the clients. Salehi had no idea if the clients were impressed, but it certainly gave him a lot of choices he wouldn't normally have.

Normally, he would have ordered whatever caffeinated beverage he could find from the bots that kept circling the library. But waiting for Uzvuyiten made him nervous, so he needed something to do.

More caffeine was probably not the best thing—particularly since he couldn't offer any to Uzvuyiten—but Salehi didn't care. The coffee sounded good, so he was going to have some.

He was nearly done using the old-fashioned machine, the one that purists insist he use and which came with the suite, a machine that boiled its own water to the correct temperature and then filtered it through freshly ground beans, when the door eased open.

"Rafael?" Uzvuyiten asked.

"In here." Salehi grabbed a thick mug. He'd nearly burned himself once before making coffee like this, and he had learned his lesson. The air filled with the aroma of fresh-brewed and, as he turned, he realized the scent was wasted on Uzvuyiten.

The Peyti's mask was no different than it had been an hour ago, but now, after the Peyti Crisis, Salehi always found his gaze drawn to the mask first. He wished he could stop it; Uzvuyiten probably thought the glance rude.

Uzvuyiten climbed onto one of the seats near the eat-in table. His movements were jerky—the chair was a little too high for him—and he looked like a child sitting down in a place where he wasn't allowed.

"What's so important?" he asked.

"Has your government found the source of the DNA for Uzvekmt?" Salehi asked. He had decided, while he made that coffee, that he would be as blunt as he could with Uzvuyiten.

Uzvuyiten's large eyes seemed even more liquid than usual.

"I would tell you," he said after a moment.

"Would you?" Salehi asked. "You want this case as much as I do. Finding where the source DNA came from might result in us losing the case."

Uzvuyiten opened his weirdly bent fingers just a bit. He seemed a little uncomfortable. His suit bagged. He hadn't adjusted it like he usually did when he sat down.

"Don't play with me," Uzvuyiten said. "What's going on?"

"We had our own detectives looking for the source of the DNA," Salehi said. "They can't find who made the Uzvekmt clones. But they did find out that the DNA wasn't handled correctly in the first place."

Uzvuyiten's head moved ever so slightly. Then he tilted it sideways. "Laws were different in those days. Peyla makes sure it complies with all DNA laws now."

So he knew that the DNA had been mishandled. Salehi felt his entire body focus, like it sometimes did in a trial. Each movement became theater. He turned and grabbed the handle of the coffee carafe. It creaked from the weight and the hot temperature of the liquid inside.

"Have you found who sold the source DNA to whoever cloned those defendants?" Salehi asked, his back to Uzvuyiten. Salehi only knew how to interpret a few movements in a Peyti, so watching Uzvuyiten's reaction wasn't as important as watching another human's would have been.

"I would have told you," Uzvuyiten said calmly.

Salehi poured the coffee. Steam rose from it. The liquid was a rich golden brown, and it slowly became light tan as the mug mixed in the right amount of cream and sugar.

"Would you really have told me?" Salehi asked. "I thought you might have a few hours ago, but since I got a report from my detectives, I figured you are withholding information."

"What would I be withholding?" Uzvuyiten asked, using a very old lawyer trick. Answer a question with a question, and get the desired response from the opponent.

This time, Salehi didn't mind answering. He cupped the mug, the exterior incongruously cool, given the fact that steam still rose from the liquid inside.

He turned, waited until Uzvuyiten's gaze met his, and then said, "An organization inside the Alliance has had the DNA for decades. There is no record of any sale, at least that we can find. We're also unaware of any trafficking in Peyti DNA."

"You're saying this is an Alliance matter?" Uzvuyiten's voice rose, like a human's might do if the human were showing just a little surprise and distress. But Uzvuyiten was a good actor, just like Salehi was. And Salehi wasn't going to trust any reaction that Uzvuyiten had.

"I've come across the Alliance twice now in relation to the attacks on the Moon. I can't believe that the Alliance would willfully destroy any part of itself, particularly the entrance to Earth, so I have to think something else is going on." He paused, sipped the coffee, and then leaned against the counter, resting the mug on the countertop.

Uzvuyiten studied him for a long time. The silence echoed. It was almost a contest of wills. Most humans would have spoken, would have said anything, to fill the quiet, but Salehi had learned how to use silence as a weapon, apparently just like Uzvuyiten had.

It took nearly ten minutes, long enough for the coffee to cool, long enough for Salehi to get comfortable, before Uzvuyiten finally spoke.

"Why do you think we hired S-Three?"

"We thought it was our stellar reputation," Salehi said, not even trying to disguise the sarcasm in his voice.

"That, yes," Uzvuyiten said, as if he didn't understand sarcasm. Salehi knew better, but he let that slide. "We also hired you because you have few Alliance-based clients. You usually represent corporations which, while they are registered in the Alliance, often sue the Alliance or challenge the Alliance's laws."

"That's the only reason?" Salehi asked.

"You are not afraid of the Alliance," Uzvuyiten said. "And you are the only human firm that we could find that had even a passing interest in clone law."

"Are there Peyti firms that specialize in clone law?" Salehi asked.

"No," Uzvuyiten said. "But that's not why we brought in humans."

"We thought you brought us in because of the tacit discrimination on the Moon," Salehi said.

"We did," Uzvuyiten said. "But humans populate all parts of the Earth Alliance. The Peyti do not."

He let the words hang. Another long silence started.

This time, Salehi broke it. "What do you really think is going on?"

Uzvuyiten closed his large eyes for a long moment, a very human reaction. Then he opened them. They seemed clearer than they had a moment before.

"We think there are traitors inside the Earth Alliance," Uzvuyiten said. "And we do not know how to stop them."

43

Ava Huỳnh stared at the sea of faces and environments before her. She was in the Joint Unit's Major Conference Room, sitting beside Xyven, who wore a mask. The Major Conference Room hadn't been used since he'd become head of the Joint Unit—he'd always held meeting inside his own office—but this time, he wanted everyone to see that he had agreed to place her in charge.

And "everyone" pretty much stunned her.

When Xyven's office meetings happened, she was in her office as well, and all she could see was Xyven's unmasked face, and the face of whomever might have been speaking.

She'd never seen the hundreds of aliens who ran their own units within the Earth Alliance Security Department. She had known that there were hundreds of alien-only units, but she hadn't even met her colleagues.

She was seeing many of them for the first time—and was having trouble processing it all.

First, most of the faces didn't look like faces to her. One, in a tiny floating screen to her left, was simply a bright red eyeball-like thing. Another, in the upper right-hand corner of the room, appeared to be a branch covered with maggots that would stand and wiggle more little appendages that she couldn't see.

Xyven had assured her she would be looking at *faces*, and she couldn't believe that thing in the upper right was a face at all.

Most of the faces blurred. There were too many to process. The room set them all up as floating flat screens, and if someone spoke, its image would enlarge, and a translation would filter through her links.

She didn't have to say much: Xyven was explaining that there would be a Joint Unit Investigation of the Moon bombings and attempted bombings. He was going to assign the aliens who used the port or had suffered losses—his word (at least in Standard)—to the investigation, and now he was asking for volunteers.

She couldn't count the responses. Face-like things would enlarge and make some kind of weird sound which her system would translate as *We shall send a team.*

Before she had even come in here, she had—at Xyven's urging—set up a system for keeping track of the responses, and she hoped her internal network was up to the task. Because her brain certainly wasn't.

All right, Xyven sent to her after forty-five minutes of volunteering. *Your turn.*

She nodded. She was supposed to brief them, and she was supposed to keep it short.

"I have one hundred fifty human teams handling the Moon investigation," she said. "Most are assisting on the Moon itself. A few have transitioned to Peyla to assist in their investigation of the Peyti lawyer clones. We have discovered enough to believe this is some kind of conspiracy that has been active within the Alliance for decades. But that's all we know."

Xyven nodded. She wasn't certain if that was meant as supportive or if he felt uncomfortable wearing the mask, or if he was responding to some action of the other heads of investigative units.

"I think you should fan out throughout the Alliance," she said. "I believe that we will discover some activity far from the center of the Alliance, outside of our usual sphere of influence. Even if something seems small and inconsequential, I want you to bring it to me."

"Please," Xyven added in Standard (probably for her benefit), "make certain you explain the implications of that small thing. We are not as versed in the details of your cultures as you are."

His addition threw her off her stride. She smiled at him, keeping her face away from the camera—she'd been told that some cultures saw smiles as threats.

"The faster you can move on this, the better," she said. "There is the distinct possibility that whatever is attacking the Moon will find another target within the Alliance. We need to know ahead of time if that is the case."

She couldn't tell if anyone in that sea of faces understood the urgency. She hoped they did.

"Thank you for your help," she said. "Xyven will coordinate as best he can, but you're welcome to come directly to me as well."

And if I don't understand what you're telling me, she wanted to add, *I'll make sure someone helps me.*

One by one the images winked out. She leaned back in the chair, nervous sweat dripping down the side of her face.

I'm the one who owes you an apology, she sent Xyven without looking at him. *I had no idea how difficult your job was.*

It's not difficult, he sent. *It requires extreme coordination. This is why I discourage so many joint investigations you all suggest. It is complicated, and generally, you'll do better on your own.*

But not this time, she sent.

Clearly.

To her surprise, he put a bony hand on her shoulder. It took all over control not to jump. She wasn't certain she had ever been touched by a Peyti before.

His hand had a surprising amount of strength.

I hope this works, he sent.

Me too, she responded. *Me, too.*

44

TRAITORS, INSIDE THE EARTH ALLIANCE. SALEHI SANK INTO A NEARBY CHAIR, leaving his half-finished mug of coffee on the counter. The coffee was upsetting his stomach.

He made himself breathe, not caring that Uzvuyiten saw how upset he was.

And then Salehi thought about what Uzvuyiten had said.

There were always traitors—dissenters, people who acted against interest—inside any large organization. That shouldn't have been a surprise, and really wasn't a surprise. Salehi had known that people would work from within to harm the Alliance since his earliest cases.

But these people were often individuals. Or they were saboteurs, who acted alone. Sometimes they were governments who didn't want to belong to the Alliance.

It could be argued—and it probably had been, by someone in S^3—that the Disappearance companies were tiny little traitorous organizations, things that the Alliance itself looked the other way on, because to allow the Disappearance companies was an easy way to prevent internal dissent.

Let the dissidents Disappear. Let them leave. Let them live their lives in peace, even if they are in hiding. Let them move forward, instead of attacking the Alliance itself.

Salehi ran a hand over his face.

"When you talk about treason," he said slowly, "you're not talking about some disgruntled employees inside the Alliance. You're talking about an organized group."

Uzvuyiten leaned forward, pressing his hands together. That movement was creepier than all of his other movements combined because *all* of his fingertips bent in the wrong direction.

Salehi's gorge rose. He swallowed hard against it, hoping Uzvuyiten didn't notice.

"That's what we believe," Uzvuyiten said. "We believe that there is an organized group. We have no proof."

He tapped his fingers together. That movement bothered Salehi less than the others had. He asked, "Your investigators have found nothing?"

Uzvuyiten lowered his hands altogether. He leaned back in his chair. Apparently, he was back in lecture mode.

"The company that handled Uzvekmt's remains," he said, "got folded into the Alliance. It was a Peyti company, but it became part of a large corporation, which does a lot of work with a certain branch of the Earth Alliance Security Forces."

"The Security Forces?" Salehi hadn't expected that. "How can that be?"

"DNA of criminals from across the Alliance filters through the Forensic Wing of the Security Forces," Uzvuyiten said. "You did not know that?"

"I stopped handling big criminal trials years ago," Salehi said. "I focus on criminal cases only when there's legal theory involved. At some point, those cases will go to the Multicultural Tribunals, and that's when my hands get dirty."

As in this case.

The skin around Uzvuyiten's eyes turned slightly blue. Salehi knew that meant Uzvuyiten had an emotional reaction; Salehi just wasn't sure what that was or what, exactly, Uzvuyiten was reacting to.

Salehi decided to move away from his admission. "So," he said, "you believe that the Forensic Wing is filled with traitors?"

"No," Uzvuyiten said. "We found that the only DNA that we could trace from Uzvekmt went into that branch of Alliance government. Which is odd."

Salehi wanted to follow up on the DNA, but Uzvuyiten's word choice stopped him. Uzvuyiten was like many long-time lawyers. He chose his words, especially his words in Standard, with great care.

"Odd how?" Salehi asked.

The color around Uzvuyiten's eyes faded. Had he deliberately distracted Salehi? Salehi didn't know and didn't care. He wasn't really distracted; he just wanted to hear what Uzvuyiten had to say about the Forensic Wing.

"Odd, in that this particular Forensic Wing is human-run," Uzvuyiten said. "We had believed the actor behind these clones, the mastermind as you call him, was Peyti."

Just like Salehi had always assumed the masterminds were human.

"Could the masterminds,"—he was careful to use the plural (he had *always* been careful to use the plural)—"be human and Peyti both?"

"Perhaps," Uzvuyiten said. "The fact that the clones went undetected through law schools all over Peyla suggests Peyti involvement."

Salehi hadn't thought of that. Clones in the same profession, clones of the same *age* in the same profession, clones who looked like each other as well as a famous mass murderer, would have gotten noticed if they were bunched into the same school.

At least, they would have been noticed in human schools.

Salehi silently cursed himself that he had believed the Peyti would be any different.

Every now and then, his own blindness irritated him greatly.

"But the department is run by humans," Salehi said. "Not humans and Peyti."

Uzvuyiten nodded—or tried to. The movement still seemed awkward.

"The Security Department is quite a bureaucracy," Uzvuyiten said. "Each Alliance species has a department and then there are departments that specialize in interactions between the older members of the Alliance, such as a Human-Peyti Relations Department."

Salehi knew that. He also knew what a labyrinth Alliance bureaucracy was. "That Department isn't part of the Security Department. It stands alone."

"It has a branch inside the Security Department. Every aspect of interspecies relations has a branch within the security department."

"But you told me that the Forensic Wing was human-run," Salehi said.

"The Forensic Wing *is* human-run," Uzvuyiten said, "only because humans are more concerned with what you call designer criminal clones. They are generally made by humans for the purposes of disrupting human lives and human systems. Even designer criminal clones made from other species generally have a human overseer."

For oncc, Salehi was having trouble following Uzvuyiten's concerns. Uzvuyiten usually laid out his arguments clearly. This time, he was following a meandering trail.

Because he was trying to throw Salehi off? Off what?

"Yet you thought Uzvekmt's clones came from a Peyti source," Salehi said.

"I still believe that," Uzvuyiten said. "I believe the company brought its resources into the Forensic Wing, which then sold or gave or exchanged or accessed Uzvekmt's DNA to someone—Peyti, most likely—and then that Peyti raised the clones. I cannot believe that the clones of Uzvekmt were raised by humans."

After Uzvuyiten had pointed out what happened, Salehi couldn't believe that humans raised the clones either. It would have taken much too much effort.

"Do you have evidence that the Forensic Wing is selling DNA?" Salehi asked.

"I'm not sure the DNA was sold," Uzvuyiten said. "Remember, there is a Human-Peyti relations department within the Security Division. Therefore, there would be Peyti working in the unit."

"I assume other species would work in the Forensic Wing," Salehi said. "Not every death investigated by the Security Division is human."

"But it is against religions or cultural customs, sometimes against agreements made with the Alliance, for all species to be evaluated forensically.

The human habit of autopsy—of examining the dead—is offensive to many, many cultures, and impossible with some species."

Uzvuyiten pressed his hands together again, probably so that he could proceed into a new lecture, one Salehi didn't want to hear. He'd read cases about some species whose bodies simply disintegrated upon death, causing all kinds of legal problems in human-based murder cases.

"I know," Salehi said. "But the Peyti—"

"Are employees in the wing. I doubt they are the source," Uzvuyiten said.

"Because you've investigated them?" Salehi asked.

"Yes," Uzvuyiten said. "That much we could do."

"Meaning there was something you couldn't do," Salehi said.

"We have been unable to compare the DNA from the arrested clones—our so-called clients—to the DNA available through the forensic wing."

"You believe there would be a difference?" Salehi asked.

"The Wing adds a tiny tag to the DNA that does not change how the DNA works. It's an internal marker, known to very few people."

"Yet you know it," Salehi said.

Uzvuyiten inclined his head. "It factored into a case I worked on as a young attorney, decades ago. I checked: practices have not changed since then."

"I take it, then, that you have the DNA from the lab?" Salehi asked.

Uzvuyiten closed his eyes slowly, a sign of impatience from a Peyti. Salehi wished he had phrased the question differently, because he knew how Uzvuyiten was going to answer.

"I do not," Uzvuyiten said in his precise way, which was exactly what Salehi expected. "However, I have confirmed that the Forensic Unit has Uzvekmt's DNA, and I have confirmed that it has been tagged. Now we just need DNA from the Peyti clones imprisoned on the Moon to test against it."

"No one has sent that to Alliance Security Department?" Salehi asked.

"So far, the case is not theirs. The Moon's security office is handling everything or the local police are, as you well know." Uzvuyiten stared at him, as if Salehi had been stupid.

But he hadn't been. He would have assumed that any law enforcement organization would have sent the clone DNA to the Alliance lab for testing, just to find the source of the DNA. They'd had nearly a week to do anything before S³ enjoined them from acting.

"Huh," Salehi muttered, mostly to himself. "We might be able to find the masterminds before the authorities do."

"Yes," Uzvuyiten said in such a calm tone that Salehi came out of his reverie.

He stood. He obviously wasn't the only one gathering information without the help of the other.

"You knew this when you brought us in," he said.

"Technically," Uzvuyiten said, "*I* did not, but the government officials who hired you did."

"If all the government of Peyla wanted was the DNA, then they should have asked for that, rather than the custody of the clones," Salehi said.

"The problem with you, as both a man and a lawyer," Uzvuyiten said, "is that you often speak before you think."

Salehi's breath caught. He'd heard that accusation before, and he had done his best to make certain that he would change that side of himself. When he had practiced regularly, he had curbed the tendency. But right at the moment, he was thinking aloud, and thinking aloud made him say some things that made him seem incautious.

"If," Uzvuyiten said, "the government of Peyla had simply asked S-Three to help them acquire the DNA, how would you have done it?"

Salehi almost answered that S³ would have asked for the samples to rule out any custody issues with the government of Peyla. But that might have opened the government up to liability. If it had clones of Uzvekmt somewhere or DNA and it hadn't controlled the DNA or the clones, then the government might have been liable for the attacks.

"Now, you're beginning to see the issues. By having the government claim an interest, and enjoining law enforcement from any further work until we arrive, we protect the government of Peyla."

"And if we find the masterminds in the meantime," Salehi said slowly, "we negate the liability before it can be raised."

"Precisely," Uzvuyiten said. "However, we have our fingers in, as you humans say, because we can also claim that these crimes had a negative impact on all Peyti, and so we have an interest there."

Salehi let out an exasperated breath. "Why didn't you just tell me this at the beginning?"

"And point your prodigious brain in a single direction?" Uzvuyiten said. "That would be foolhardy. You have already come up with several different plans of attack that none of us would have ever thought of. Your passion for clone law alone intrigues me, at least, and makes handling such reprehensible clients much easier."

Salehi frowned at Uzvuyiten. Salehi hadn't realized how much the clones disgusted Uzvuyiten until now.

Of course they did. The attempted mass murder, the potential suicides, the crimes were reprehensible enough, but they had been committed by Peyti, who always held themselves to a high ethical standard. More importantly, they had been committed by Peyti *lawyers*.

"Did you know any of these clones?" Salehi asked Uzvuyiten.

Salehi couldn't quite believe that he hadn't thought to ask before. It would be a logical question, particularly after Uzvuyiten's mention of the Peyti law schools.

Uzvuyiten bowed his head just once, an acknowledgement that didn't look nearly as awkward as his nods.

"I met just one of the lawyers, at least that I know of," Uzvuyiten said. Salehi was glad that Uzvuyiten hadn't mocked him for failing to ask the right question first. "We were on opposite sides as junior lawyers on a case involving a major Alliance corporation that had ties to Peyla."

"Did you know this lawyer well?" Salehi asked.

"No," Uzvuyiten said, "and before you ask your next question, I am taking this case personally, but not in the ways you think. I see no reason to defend these clones beyond the legal reasons you and I have already worked through. I do take several things personally. In particular, I am angered that the Moon's authorities are using these events as an excuse to ban Peyti from their ratty little cities. I foresee great problems for my people in times to come if we do not find the masterminds—as you call them—soon."

"The government of Peyla took a risk, hiring S-Three," Salehi said. "It might make the Peyti discrimination worse."

Uzvuyiten stood.

"Perhaps," he said. "But that will only add to our ability to argue the case."

"You think these clones know even more, don't you?"

"I do not know what they know," Uzvuyiten said. "I would not try to guess. I do believe, however, the sooner we can identify who created them, the sooner we can take some of the blame from all Peyti."

"But you believe there's Peyti involvement," Salehi said.

"And human involvement," Uzvuyiten said. "By traitors. As soon as we identify them, then the loyal members of the Earth Alliance, like the citizens of Peyla, will not be targeted any longer."

Salehi bit back his response. Uzvuyiten understood some things about humans but not all. It would be easy for humans to blame only a single human criminal for his own actions and, at the same time, blame all Peyti for the actions of a single Peyti criminal.

"We're not going to the Moon to work miracles," Salehi said.

"Really?" Uzvuyiten braced himself on the wall as if he had momentarily grown dizzy. "Because it seems to me you want a miracle."

"I do?" Salehi asked.

"You want the Earth Alliance to accept clones as equals," Uzvuyiten said. "Which might have been possible two years ago. Now? After all these attacks? It'll never happen."

Salehi crossed his arms. "If the Earth Alliance unifies clone law," he said, "then attacks like the ones the Moon suffered might never happen again."

"Idealist," Uzvuyiten snapped, and walked out of the room.

Salehi watched him go.

"Yeah," Salehi said softly. "We both are."

45

NYQUIST TURNED HIS BACK ON UZVAAN. HE COULD STILL SEE THE BASTARD'S reflection in that weird clear bubble wall or maybe in the blue liquid. To Nyquist's left, the two android guards stood in the tunnel, hands clasped in front of them, eyes watching his every move.

Could they see his distress? Did they understand it?

An apology from Uzvaan would have felt terrible, slight, an insult, like Uzvaan said. But refusing to apologize felt even worse. And putting his own existence above Nyquist's—well, it was a good thing they weren't at the precinct, because Nyquist might have tried to pull Uzvaan out of his chair—not because Nyquist would have forgotten that Uzvaan was cuffed to the chair, but because he would want the strain on Uzvaan's slender twig-like arms.

"It is not personal," Uzvaan said.

"Yes, it is," Nyquist said.

"It was not meant to be. I did not know that I would have relationships with people on the Moon. I did not know that such things were possible."

Nyquist could hear the pleading in Uzvaan's voice. The bastard was trying to tell him something.

The bastard obviously had something to tell.

"I can't make a deal," Nyquist said. He did not turn around. "And I doubt I'll be able to come back, now that you told me about Palmette."

There was a long silence. The sketchy reflection of Uzvaan moved. His head was bowed, his body hunched. He had no idea that Nyquist could see him.

Uzvaan was broken; he was just doing his best to keep up a good front.

"Maybe," he said, his voice still strong despite his posture, "you could argue for better living conditions for me?"

Not a demand any more. Uzvaan was begging. Nyquist hadn't expected that, particularly from the arrogant lawyer he had known.

"I can't do that," Nyquist said. "You're a clone. You're lucky they've put you in a cell."

He didn't have to explain further. Uzvaan knew. He was property, and as such, no laws governed his stay here. He didn't have to be fed or provided a place to sleep or even the proper environment. He had no rights at all.

Uzvaan didn't say anything. His posture didn't change. For the longest moment, Nyquist thought their negotiation was done. And he would leave it at that; he would tell DeRicci that he couldn't get information out of Uzvaan, but he had a sense someone else might be able to.

Then it would be their problem.

"If you change my status," Uzvaan said, "I'll tell you everything."

"I told you," Nyquist snapped. "I can't do anything for you. You're a clone."

"I meant my clone status," Uzvaan said. He had come to the only place that Nyquist could negotiate, and he had done it all on his own. Nyquist wished he could say he had planned it, but he couldn't. He hadn't been able to utter the words first.

He didn't want to offer the bastard anything.

"If I can get you registered in this prison as a Peyti, you'll tell me everything," Nyquist repeated, deliberately misunderstanding Uzvaan's request.

"If you can get my status changed legally," Uzvaan said. "If I permanently become Peyti, a true individual, I will tell you everything."

"I can't do that," Nyquist said, and it was true. *He* couldn't do it. But he had been authorized to do so, and he knew DeRicci could.

Still, he wasn't going to give Uzvaan anything without having Uzvaan work for it.

"Your people can," Uzvaan said. "I'm pretty sure the security chief, DeRicci, can do it without even approaching a court. I can—"

"You can do nothing." Nyquist turned. "You realize that if I can get someone to grant this idiotic request, you'll be tried for attempted murder. You won't get a pardon, and you'll spend decades—however long you bastards live—in this prison. Unless you're put to death under Alliance law. Because every single species is going to want to try you for attempting to kill its people. Every single one. You'll be the representative of the Peyti Crisis. All of the hatred that exists out there toward you clones will be directed at you personally."

Uzvaan raised his head. Not all the way, not that proud look that Nyquist had seen earlier, just a tired movement, then a nod of acknowledgement.

"I have found, oddly enough, that I do not want to die. Your sense of me was correct, Bartholomew. I am not a suicide bomber."

"No," Nyquist said. "You're a failed one. You tried to set off that bomb."

"Yes," Uzvaan said. "I did. It was a condition of my existence."

"You said that before," Nyquist said.

"I'll say it again, and much more. If you can only change my status." Uzvaan was begging again.

Nyquist shook his head. He prided himself on being an ethical man. An honorable man. He had come here to make a deal, one that would exchange information for changing Uzvaan's status, but he could lie and say that Uzvaan had refused. Then Nyquist could destroy the recording he'd made, and it would be his word against an attempted mass murderer's.

But he couldn't do it. As much as he wanted to, he couldn't. Any more than he could have gone into that bubble-cell and broken all of Uzvaan's too-thin limbs.

"I'll see what I can do," Nyquist said.

"You won't regret this, Bartholomew," Uzvaan said.

"It's detective," Nyquist said. "Don't ever presume that we're friends."

"I do not, Detective," Uzvaan said. "I realize what I'm asking of you."

"Do you?" Nyquist asked. "Because I think you have absolutely no idea what this will cost me."

And neither, deep down, did Nyquist.

46

Flint walked out of his favorite coffee shop. The latte he'd had sat uneasily on his stomach. The counselor, Llewynn, had recommended that Flint stop hovering over Talia. Instead, the man suggested that Flint encourage Talia to spend time with others, even if that meant Flint did not see her all day.

The idea sounded so easy, and it was so hard.

He had dropped her at the Security Office. She wanted to talk with Popova, and he thought that a good thing.

He wasn't supposed to return for three more hours. He wasn't certain how he could do that. He had investigating to do, but he was having trouble concentrating, particularly while he was focused on Talia.

The streets were mostly empty. They had been unusually empty since the Peyti Crisis. He wasn't sure if that was because people were staying home out of fear or if so many businesses had closed that no one had any place to go.

Many of the nearby office buildings looked deserted. Only a handful of cars went by, some above him, others using the street itself. Usually there was congestion in this part of Armstrong. The quiet streets felt odd to him.

Of course, there were a lot of law firms in this area. He knew many of them were closed.

He had parked his car on a parking-allowed side street. He was nearly there, when Luc Deshin appeared on his links. Deshin used a hologram so perfect that if Flint hadn't seen it form, he would have thought Deshin was standing before him.

"Is this a good place to talk?" Deshin asked.

"No," Flint said. "I'm on a public street."

"Well, get unpublic and contact me."

Flint almost said that he didn't take orders from Deshin, but before Flint could form the words, Deshin had winked out.

Flint sighed. He was glad for the short walk to the car, so that he could gather himself. He needed to regain his inner balance, or he would start making bad decisions.

He let himself into the car, then quickly swept it to make certain that no one had attached any chips, links, or listening devices. He realized in the last few days that he hadn't been paranoid enough.

Or maybe it was just the image of Luc Deshin, reminding him that anyone could slide through his links.

Flint used the private encoded link that Deshin had set up for them. Deshin appeared before him, looking like Flint had driven the car through him.

Flint shrank the image and moved it on top of the dashboard.

Deshin looked powerful, even at one-tenth his normal size.

"So," Flint said, "you have news?"

Deshin crossed his arms. He looked like a temperamental doll. Flint managed to repress the smile that loomed at that thought.

"I've gone as far as I can," Deshin said. "And I don't have the source of the clones."

Flint's urge to smile vanished. He cursed softly. "Another dead end, then."

"I didn't say that." Deshin seemed to be staring at something over Flint's left shoulder. "I had time to think about this, because I didn't want to contact you until I was certain my ship was clean and no one was able to listen in."

Flint wanted to ask exactly where Deshin had ended up, but didn't dare. Flint also knew the less information he had about Deshin's search, the better.

"I found *a* source of Frémont clones. He appears to be the only one with clones on the market. But they're fast-grow."

Flint started to say that they didn't need fast-grow, when Deshin held up a hand, forestalling him.

"They're fast-grow because the DNA is corrupted. I've hit dead end after dead end after dead end. The usual brokers have nothing. The truly scary brokers led me to this guy. The Black Fleet was nearby as well. Because of the attacks on Armstrong, everyone is now looking for Frémont clones."

Flint sighed. A big event always did this.

"They won't find any useful Frémont clones on the market," Deshin said, "but that means the market in designer criminal clones based on mass murderers will grow, rather than decrease."

Flint closed his eyes for a moment, thanking whatever god he could think of that he was no longer in law enforcement.

"I'll let Noelle know," he said, opening his eyes.

Now, Deshin's hologram seemed to be looking directly at him. "I'd tell you to have her contact the Alliance, but I don't think that's a good idea."

Flint frowned. "So you did find something."

"The guy who is selling the fast-grow clones collected DNA from Frémont on the day Frémont died. This guy had an assistant. Her name is Jhena Andre, and she works inside the Alliance, in some classified position."

"You think she's involved?" Flint asked. "Can't you contact her to buy the DNA?"

"Here's the thing," Deshin said. "My guy already has. He could make millions on Frémont DNA, and she's not selling. She's not saying she has any Frémont DNA either. In theory, she just helped my guy collect the stuff. But he explained the procedure to me, and she had plenty of time to skim."

"And corrupt the remaining DNA?" Flint asked.

"I doubt it. I think that has to do with storage." Deshin had clearly given this a lot of thought. "I believe that she stored hers better than he stored his."

"And this is based on what?" Flint asked. "A theory?"

"Weirdly, yes," Deshin said. "In my world, when there's money to be made, people flock to that area."

In most worlds, Flint thought, but didn't say.

"People have been flocking since Anniversary Day," Deshin said. "They've been trying to buy these clones. They're a proven commodity. They can follow orders. Decades of investment in their upbringing and training have paid off. I don't know if you understand how rare this is."

Flint hadn't understood it. He hadn't wanted to think about it. But it made a lot of sense.

"So," Deshin said, "right now, whoever owns this uncorrupted DNA can make more money than I can even imagine—and I can imagine a lot. *Everyone* has been trying to find this DNA. *Everyone*. That's why I had to wait to contact you. I'm pretty sure once my requests were known, I got followed."

Flint shuddered, and hoped Deshin couldn't see it on their links. To Flint—to any sane human—Anniversary Day was a horror. Deshin knew how the people behind these horrors worked, and could speak of them with complete dispassion.

Flint also knew how upset Deshin was about these attacks, and how he'd been willing to help.

But Flint couldn't entirely understand how a man like Deshin—a man with a family—could delve into these worlds.

"This guy told me about his contact with Jhena Andre, and it wasn't until after our meeting that I realized the significance of what he told me." Deshin made a little bobbing movement, one that Flint finally realized was an apology. "I couldn't contact my guy again, not without making some kind of offer. And then, he might get suspicious."

"All right," Flint said. "Tell me the significance."

"When a good person is guilty of something awful," Deshin said, "someone who has never crossed a line before, that person either confesses or tries to hide the information."

"You think Andre told her superiors in the Alliance that she helped steal Frémont's DNA?" Flint asked, finally beginning to understand.

"It's possible," Deshin said. "But her reaction to my guy's request wasn't the kind of reaction that someone working with the authorities would have. She didn't lead him on and try to get him arrested or anything."

Flint frowned, trying to follow.

"She just told him not to contact her again, and not to give anyone her name." Deshin said this as if it were significant.

Flint thought about that for a moment. "Was she scared?"

"That's what I don't know," Deshin said. "If she was, then it would explain a lot, I suppose."

"But you think something else," Flint said.

"She worked in the prison where Frémont had been incarcerated for two years. Then she moved on, always staying in the prison system and administration, working her way up in the Alliance. Eventually, she became an administrator, and her work—even her job description—is so classified that I'd need to hire someone to break through the classification to find out what she does."

Like Flint could do.

"The Peyti clones also came from a mass murderer," Deshin said, "and he was incarcerated by the Peyti, who are long-time members of the Alliance. If my information is correct, then the Peyti mass murderer's DNA is also in the Alliance system—"

"Where this Jhena Andre presumably had access to it." Flint leaned back, rocking the car. "And she never sold any of it?"

"That I don't know," Deshin said. "You get to trace the money. You have to now. Remember I told you how much it would cost to do the Frémont clones. I have no idea how much it would cost to add in the Peyti clones."

Flint was shaking his head. He couldn't imagine it.

"Was she co-opted?" he asked, thinking of that partner of Nyquist's who had tried to blow up Armstrong on Anniversary Day.

"It's possible," Deshin said. "Then the question becomes how would someone know she had the DNA. And why in the known universe would she keep it?"

"Why do we keep any of this DNA on file?" Flint asked.

"I don't think we do," Deshin said, "but I don't know."

Flint felt cold. He glanced at the street. No one had passed him in all the time he'd been talking to Deshin. The alerts that Flint had installed on the vehicle hadn't gone off either, so he hadn't just missed someone going by.

No one had.

Armstrong had become a ghost town.

He wondered how much of the population had simply fled. And if they had, where they had fled to.

"Could the Alliance be making money off the DNA?" Flint asked. He knew that some governments had made money on arms-brokering in the past. But he had never figured the Alliance for something like that.

"You'd think I would have found the Frémont DNA if it were," Deshin said, "but right now I'm not ruling anything out."

He glanced at something off to his left.

"I'm not able to trace the money," Deshin said after a moment. "My people are good, but not good enough to deal with the Alliance's databases. Besides, if I do something like that, then red flags will go up in every law enforcement agency throughout the Alliance. I've been working very hard since my son's birth to become a legitimate businessman. I don't want to lose that now."

Not even for the sake of the Moon? Flint wanted to ask. But he didn't. Because he knew that Deshin had already gone out on a limb with this investigation.

"You're equipped to do this kind of work," Deshin said. "It would be better if it came from you."

Flint knew Deshin was right. "This investigation won't go quick."

"They're hiding something big," Deshin said. "And they've done so for years. That generally makes someone complacent."

"But the attacks just happened," Flint said. "That usually reminds people to clean up whatever messes they made."

"Are you saying you can't do this?" Deshin asked.

Flint looked in the car's mirrors, thinking of the Armstrong Comfort Center and Talia. He would need something to focus on so that he didn't just concentrate on her. It would make her angry, probably upset her counselor, and frustrate him.

"I can do this," Flint said, hoping he was right.

"Good," Deshin said. "Because I have a bunch of theories and I don't like any of them."

"You already mentioned that these clones might be soldiers in a war we don't know we're fighting," Flint said. "The question is, what war?"

"That's a spectacular question," Deshin said. "Governments have more funds than individuals, and they can hide the tab for creating creatures like these clones in their military budgets. They can also co-opt employees of the places they're going to attack."

"Is that what you think is happening?" Flint asked.

"Every time I come up with a scenario," Deshin said, "I can also come up with a dozen reasons why that scenario doesn't work. So, what I think doesn't matter. But we have to find whatever it is. I've done what I can. We now know what these clones aren't."

Flint let out a small laugh. "I never thought I'd be unhappy to discover that these clones *aren't* designer criminal clones."

Deshin nodded. "I felt the same way. I wanted to be able to buy them. That would have made our jobs so much easier."

"Although," Flint said, "what would we have done then?"

Deshin stared at him. Flint got the sense that Deshin had an answer which he would never admit to.

It was probably an answer that Flint did not want to know.

"We always knew this was big," Deshin said. "I guess we just didn't know how big."

And then, before Flint could say anything, Deshin cut the link.

Flint stared at the empty space on his dash for a long moment. Then he sighed.

"Yeah," he said softly. "We still don't know how big it is. And if we have the ability to bring it down."

But he hoped they did.

Because he didn't want to think about what would happen if they couldn't.

47

DESHIN SANK INTO A CHAIR IN HIS PRIVATE QUARTERS. THE SHIP WAS hurtling toward a nearby starbase, one that Jakande had already vetted for him.

Deshin hated all this vetting, hating being the center of this kind of attention.

But he also wanted to live through this little adventure.

Sometimes he wished he hadn't brought this large security team. He was so used to traveling with *personnel* that he had forgotten until he got to Angu how important being stealthy could be.

He might have to trim the staff and change ships, much as he hated to give up these quarters. They were more comfortable than his bedroom at home. Everything was customized to his taste—the scent, a soft mix of Gerda's perfume and a bit of vanilla; colors that tended toward the brown scale, and a cooler temperature than either his wife or son liked.

The chairs were standard space yacht issue, thick and comfortable, able to mold to his body, which this chair was doing right now.

It didn't comfort him.

He ran a hand over his face, surprised to feel the slight oil of sweat. He had just lied to Miles Flint.

Deshin had just told Flint that he was done with this investigation, that he wasn't going to help Flint any longer.

And that part was true: Deshin wouldn't help Flint any longer.

Flint, and the authorities he represented, were on their own.

Deshin was now going to a place that made him exceedingly uncomfortable.

He was going to find the heart of the government's secret cloning system. He had thought of doing this years ago, when he'd caught a designer criminal clone inside his own organization. Some investigation had shown that clone wasn't made in the usual places.

It was government issue, and it had been put in his organization as a spy.

He closed his eyes and rested his head on the back of the chair. Didier Conte had proven to Deshin that the problem lay inside the Earth Alliance.

Something in Deshin's gut had told him that all along. There simply weren't other governments in known space that were big enough to attack the Alliance, nor were there governments rich enough to fund an attack of this magnitude.

Which meant that the attack was internal.

When he thought of the Alliance the way he thought about his empire, he understood traitors within. He'd found the DNA for Frémont, and it was inside the Alliance. Now he had to find where that DNA was grown into an army of clones.

He had a half-formed plan. He needed to give it more thought before implementing it. Because once the plan was underway, he couldn't turn back.

He felt like he had so few choices. He could ignore what was going on in his home; he could face it head-on; or he could run from it.

He wasn't going to run or ignore.

He was going to solve.

That was who he was, and who he would always be.

"Sorry, Gerda," he whispered.

At least he knew his son was in good hands. Paavo and Gerda would have a good life if this misadventure killed him.

And he had to find comfort in that.

Somehow.

48

Flint sat at the desk in his office in Old Armstrong. He had tracked in a lot of Moon dust, but it was slowly going away. The fact that it was filtering out told him that his new environmental system was working well.

He hoped that meant his security systems were also working well. Because he had decided to do the financial research here. It was the only place where he could completely trust the security.

After he had signed off with Deshin, Flint had driven to the Security Office. He was going to go inside, and start the research.

He'd actually gotten out of the car and was halfway up the block when he realized that searching through financial records in a place with ties to the Earth Alliance probably wasn't a good idea.

If Deshin was right, then someone inside the Earth Alliance was protecting—or causing—these attacks. Flint had hints of that before, but he was even more certain of it now. He had no idea what was being monitored or by whom. He didn't dare trust systems attached to anything from the Alliance, no matter how much he trusted the people in the Security Office.

He had gone back to the car and sat for at least fifteen minutes, trying to figure out where to go next. His usual haunts for dicey research—the university, the Brownie Bar—might put those places in danger. Plus he would be easily traced if someone or something wanted to see who was making those inquiries.

His involvement in protecting the Moon from future attacks wasn't well known, but more and more people knew what he was doing. In other words, it was known by enough people that he could be ferreted out if need be.

It would be easier to catch him on public networks, even with all of the noise surrounding the university and the Brownie Bar, than it would be from the security of his own office.

He needed to protect himself and Talia, but he had to be smart about it. He also needed to protect his colleagues.

He decided, as he let himself into the office, that he wouldn't bring Talia here to work with him.

That meant he was going to need someone to stay with her, someone he could trust. He would impose on DeRicci and Popova as much as he could, but he would need someone else as well.

He just wasn't sure who that was.

He then banished those thoughts. He needed several hours of uninterrupted work.

He started by updating his security, using procedures that even the most paranoid would think paranoid. But he had no real idea what he was up against, so he was going to think of them as all-seeing and all-knowing.

That meant he wasn't going to ever be 100% invisible to them, but he was going to attempt 99%.

Sometimes he stopped and thought about expectations. Criminals—the Masterminds, as he'd been calling them—would expect a Moon-based investigation. They would also expect an Earth Alliance investigation, and probably one from Peyla.

He could spoof the security so that the search looked like it came from Peyla, but he wasn't going to do that right away. He would break the research into component parts. Research into human elements would either come from the Moon or some Earth Alliance address (maybe Earth herself). Research into the Peyti connection would seem to come from Peyla and from a different Earth Alliance address.

He had to move slowly, carefully, and with great deliberation.

And he had to design his searches to meet all the elements that Deshin had set out for him.

Flint needed to find millions, maybe billions, that went to the care and feeding of clones. He needed to investigate this woman, Jhena Andre. And he needed to keep an open mind, to see patterns that he might normally ignore.

If only he were thinking clearly. He was exhausted and a bit unnerved, worried for Talia, and frightened for the Moon herself. For the Alliance itself.

He needed to focus, and he had to do it now.

49

For once, Nyquist didn't bring food to DeRicci's office. He wasn't hungry. In fact, he wasn't sure he'd be hungry for a few days.

He had left the prison, gone home, showered, showered again, and still didn't feel clean. He hated talking with Uzvaan, and knew he'd have to do it at least once more.

That thought made him queasy.

He had tried to banish it on the way to see DeRicci, but he hadn't been able to. He had made a deal with the Peyti who had tried to kill him. Nyquist had made deals with killers before, but never with someone who had tried to harm him personally.

He was beginning to understand—on a very deep level—the wrath of victims who never saw their attackers come to trial, because someone felt some other crime had more importance.

He thought he had walked off the anger until he entered DeRicci's private office.

She turned toward him, her hair mussed, her clothing as wrinkled as he'd ever seen it, and asked, "How did it go?"

It took all of his strength not to snap *How do you think it went?* After all, she had been the one to suggest he go bargain with Uzvaan.

Nyquist took a deep breath to calm himself. In the past, he would snap at employers, and he would take his frustrations out on partners.

But he cared about DeRicci—okay, truth was, he probably loved her—and she was going through hell.

His little interaction with Uzvaan was mild compared to the things she did daily.

"He offered," Nyquist said, deciding not to burden her with the ups and downs of the discussion.

"Offered what exactly?" DeRicci sat at her desk, folded her hands, and leaned forward, as if Nyquist were a supplicant. He wondered how often she had taken that position in the past six months, and whether or not it helped keep her calm.

"He offered to tell us everything he knew if we got rid of his clone status. But the catch is that we can't just wave our hands. We have to really get rid of the clone status. He is a lawyer, after all."

DeRicci nodded, her lips thin.

"We can just declare him legal on the Moon," DeRicci said. "Right now, no one is going to argue with me."

"That's not going to be good enough. He—"

"Wants Alliance approval, I know," DeRicci said. "Popova knows some judges. We'll get that, but it'll take time."

"We don't have time," Nyquist said. "Right now, he doesn't know anything about S-Three, but at some point he will, or they'll learn about him. And then all conversation will cease, no matter what we're discussing."

DeRicci nodded, ran a hand through her hair, and sighed again. "I'll make the declaration on his status tonight, but I'm only going to let the prison know. We'll bury the documentation with the other documents we send to the courts around the Moon, so that S-Three won't find out quickly, at least. That'll have to do as a start. Call it good faith. Because Uzvaan has to know that going through Alliance courts will take time."

"He's probably counting on that," Nyquist said. "He does seem pretty willing to work with us. He didn't expect to live after the attacks last week, so he has no plans for his future, and is rather stunned at his treatment. It makes me wonder how many of the others would be willing to talk as well."

"Hmmm." DeRicci tapped her forefinger against her lips and leaned back. "I'll see what other pretenses we can use to contact them. You might not be the only envoy of this office going to the prison this week."

"Be careful," Nyquist said. "We do too much and everything will come to S-Three's attention."

"God, we sound like they're all-seeing and all-knowing," DeRicci said.

"Right now, they're hampering the investigation," Nyquist said.

"Too bad we can't arrest them for that," DeRicci said in such a clear voice that Nyquist knew she had already looked into it. "Unfortunately, everything they've done so far has been strictly by the book."

"Well, let's hope they screw up," Nyquist said. "Until then, we have to grab the information while we can. Which is why I'm going back."

Something in his tone must have reached DeRicci because she gave him a calculating look. Then her face softened.

"I know I'm asking too much of you," she said. "But—"

"Don't," Nyquist said, putting up his hand to block her words. He didn't want to hear an apology or a rationale, even though he had been angry with her a few minutes ago about this whole thing. "You have no one else to talk to the clones."

"Not with a good excuse," she said. "I suppose I could send one of my people in to see Palmette's lawyer, but that would look—"

"Awkward, I know," he said, "and I had already called Uzvaan into the station to discuss Palmette when the Peyti Crisis happened. It's on the record, Noelle. If anyone suspects I'm doing anything wrong, all they have to do is look at my witness interview from that day."

DeRicci nodded. Every now and then he saw beneath the façade and it worried him. She was so close to breaking apart.

"What I'm going to need from you," he said as gently as he could, "is a list of questions by early tomorrow morning, things that you believe I'm not going to have thought of."

"You're not doing the standard informational interview?"

"I'm going act like we don't have time," Nyquist said, "because we might not. S-Three might shut us down."

DeRicci nodded. She clearly hadn't thought of that.

Nyquist continued. "I'm going to tell Uzvaan that I'm afraid the courts will shut us down eventually. I'm *not* going to tell him about S-Three. But he's sat through dozens of these interviews. He knows what's proper and what's not. He would want to know why I'm not following procedure."

"Do you believe he's thinking that clearly?" DeRicci asked.

"Yes," Nyquist said. "And I have another motive. If I shake up the questions, and don't build like we usually do, then maybe I'll shake some things loose."

DeRicci gave him a tired smile. "I'll put something together. I'm not sure what that'll be. You're a hell of an investigator, Bartholomew."

"I'm sure there are things you'll want to know that haven't yet filtered their way to the Armstrong PD. So give me those. I'll ask what I can."

She nodded.

"I also have one other thing," he said. "Do you have someone on staff who speaks Peytin?"

"Popova," DeRicci said. "But we have translation programs—"

"I know," Nyquist said. "I also listened to one on the way here, and there was a disclaimer up front that said depending on tone, one sound can mean two dozen different things. I'd rather have an actual living ear on this before I go to the programs."

"And before you consult with a Peyti," DeRicci said, with too much accuracy.

"That too," Nyquist said.

The door opened, and Popova peered in. Apparently, DeRicci had contacted her on her links while talking to Nyquist.

"You needed me?" she asked.

"Come in for a moment," DeRicci said. "Bartholomew wants you to translate something from Peytin."

"You haven't tried the programs?" Popova asked.

Nyquist smiled at DeRicci. Once upon a time, DeRicci had hated Popova. Now, they seemed to think in unison.

"I will if you tell me to. I just want my colleagues to hear this. It was weird."

He had the interaction with Uzvaan cued up. Nyquist started a little farther back, so that Popova could hear Uzvaan's speaking voice, and have context.

He hit the chip, and Uzvaan's voice filled the office:

"Now, I'm in a legal purgatory. Your authorities know what I am. I have no rights under Alliance law. And yet, I'm a lawyer, with more knowledge than almost anyone about the way things work. I truly did not expect this."

DeRicci had her head bowed. She was staring at her hands. They were clenched tightly, her knuckles turning white, just another small indication of how much emotion she was reigning in.

Then Nyquist heard his own voice ask the question that had caused Uzvaan to give his answer in Peytin:

"You didn't consider failure?"

Uzvaan's answer came quickly, and it sounded odd, flatter to Nyquist's ears. But he wasn't an expert. Maybe that sentence was something more—a quote, a song, a popular saying.

"May I hear that again?" Popova asked.

Nyquist jumped. He hadn't been looking at her. He had almost forgotten she was here, so deep had he gone into DeRicci's reaction.

Popova was standing near him, a frown creasing her face. He hadn't really looked at her lately either. She had lines alongside her mouth and eyes that hadn't been there before. A few silver hairs mixed into her signature black mane.

"Sure," he said, and played Uzvaan's answer again.

She used her hand to indicate that Nyquist should play it at least one more time.

He did.

Then she said, "What did he say next?"

"I asked him to tell me what he had just said, and he told me it wasn't important," Nyquist said. "I can play that for you if you'd like."

She shook her head. Then she looked at DeRicci, not him.

"I'm fluent," Popova said, "but I'm not an expert. I speak schoolgirl Peytin, the kind you'd speak as a tourist. It's very formal. I can read the language too, better than I can speak it. Peytin has variations all over the known universe, and there are idioms that I don't know."

DeRicci sighed. "So you don't know what he said."

"Oh, I do," Popova said, "and it's weird. It sounds like he was quoting someone or something. The reason I gave you the disclaimer is because I don't know if he said something that every Peyti school child knows."

"All right," DeRicci said through gritted teeth. Nyquist could tell she just wanted Popova to get to the point, and not go through all of this disclaimer stuff. "What did he say?"

"He said, 'You can't have a failure in a unit.'"

Nyquist blinked. He wasn't sure what that meant at all.

"Here's the thing," Popova said. "Peytin has maybe a hundred meanings for 'unit,' because the Peyti work well in groups."

"Yeah," DeRicci said dryly. Nyquist glanced at her. Two minds with the same thought: Last week, the Peyti clones had worked as a unit.

"In this usage, I think, he meant military unit or a group that forms like a military unit." Then Popova shrugged. "It's weird, like I said, and almost a non sequitur."

"Or not," DeRicci said. "If these clones were designed as a military unit, then maybe that would explain it…?"

"I wouldn't guess based on my translation," Popova said. "I'd listen to the translation programs, see what they say, and then maybe bring in an expert. There are several professors of Peytin in the Language Department at the university. Call one of them."

"Are any of them human?" DeRicci asked.

Her words hung in the office. Nyquist wanted to protest. He wanted to say *We can't mistrust the Peyti forever*, but he understood the impulse. Besides, his gut reaction had been the same one. He didn't want to hear a Peyti interpret those words. Who knew what that Peyti's affiliation was and what they were hiding.

"No," Popova said after a moment. Her gaze caught Nyquist's. She, at least, was shocked by the question. Good for her. She was a better person than he was.

"I've got several programs here," DeRicci said. "Let's have each one translate. Isolate the phrase, please, Bartholomew."

He did. Then he played it over and over again.

Each program translated the phrase differently, substituting a slightly different word for the word "unit." Some used military unit, some used "group," others specified "team."

After six translations, DeRicci shut it all down.

Then she nodded, as if this were one more frustration in a universe filled with frustrations.

"We know he was in a group," she said tiredly. "Which we knew before we started."

"No," Nyquist said. He felt a little more optimistic after hearing the translations. He wasn't sure why. "We know that whoever trained the group did not tolerate failure. Uzvaan seemed unfamiliar with the concept of failure as a learning tool at all. My sense is that he's very broken now. I told you that, Noelle."

"Yes, but that could simply be because he got caught," she said.

"Yes, it could," Nyquist said. "But it could also be because he was programmed against failure. That sentence sounded automatic to me. He said it in his native language, and he said it really fast. I don't know if the Peyti are like humans, but sometimes that early training goes so deep that we can't prevent it from coming out our mouths."

Popova was frowning. "It's possible. One reason the Peyti do so well in the Alliance legal system is because our species are a lot more similar than other species in the Alliance. I'll check up on it."

"What good would that do?" DeRicci asked. "It would just help S-Three with their defense."

"It'll help with my approach to Uzvaan," Nyquist said. "We know he was created for this job. If he was trained for it so deeply that he's giving out rote answers to questions—even with his prodigious brain—then we're looking at truly hardcore training."

"So?" DeRicci asked. "We knew they were trained."

"Hardcore training isn't just telling kids to be grateful and sending them on their way. It's true programming, and it takes work. With humans, it also takes fear and a lot of intimidation."

DeRicci froze. "And murder?"

He wasn't quite sure what she meant. "You mean, 'to murder' as the goal?"

"No," DeRicci said. "Fear, intimidation, and murder."

Popova was looking at her. "Do you want me to contact Jin Rastigan?"

"Yes," DeRicci said.

"Who is Jin Rastigan?" Nyquist asked.

"She's the one who discovered the clones in the first place," DeRicci said. "Young ones were being murdered, horribly, in some outpost. Jin thinks they were clearing out the undesirables."

"Undesirables," Popova said. "Like failures?"

"Possibly," DeRicci said. "We're guessing, but possibly."

"My God," Nyquist said. "Yeah, with humans, that would work."

"I'll bet it works for Peyti too," DeRicci said. "We might have some answers without even realizing it."

"I'll contact her right now," Popova said. "She might have answers for us."

"And questions," Nyquist said. "Ask her for questions to ask the clones. On a secure link."

The look that Popova gave him was withering. He felt warmth build in his cheeks.

"Sorry," he said. "I'm used to police department staff…"

She waved a hand at him dismissively, and left. Nyquist wasn't sure how badly he'd offended her.

"She's used to it," DeRicci said. "I did that to her at first too. Or just did it myself. She'll also ask Jin Rastigan what that sentence means."

"I figured that out." Nyquist stood. His knees made a cracking sound that they'd made off and on ever since he survived the attack from the Bixian assassins.

"Noelle," he said, "at some point, we're going to need more investigators that we can trust."

"I know," she said, and this time he heard something in her voice he'd never heard before. Something almost like resignation. "I just can't figure out who they would be."

50

Two frustrating hours. Flint had spent two frustrating hours trying to find out more about Jhena Andre than Deshin had discovered in his cursory search, only to run into firewalls too strong to be Alliance-designed.

Flint had paced his small office, noting with some satisfaction that the Moon dust he had tracked in was gone now. It almost made this space feel like it belonged to someone else.

He had expected the Alliance information on Andre to be as porous as Old Armstrong's filtration system. But it wasn't.

He suspected that was because she had been involved in law enforcement and security. Her job descriptions had never been logged. The methods he usually used to gain information, particularly from government sources, didn't work.

At first, he had thought someone had discovered and closed the back doors he used. Then, the deeper he got, the more he realized that those doors had never existed in the system where Andre's information was stored.

The software designs were different as well, made by someone—or something—that thought differently from the average computer programmer. Flint wasn't the average programmer, and he still had trouble figuring the system out.

He finally had run a weird background search—one that compared elements of the system he was trying to break into with other systems that existed in the Alliance.

He couldn't find anything like that in the human-based programs.

But in one of the Imme-based programs, for the residents of the Imme System, he found a match.

The Imme looked like many other aliens in the Alliance. They had four limbs, walked upright, and had a recognizable face. They also had feathers covering every part of their bodies. The feathers weren't like bird feathers, which fell out or got plucked.

They were more like bark on a tree, an essential part of the Imme. The tips of the feathers brushed against the other feathers, creating links that formed the Imme's brain. Destroy enough feathers, and the Imme's brain function also decreased, just like a human's would if someone damaged one section of the head.

For that reason, the Imme did not mix with non-Imme much. They used the Alliance for protection and trade, but used proxies. And the Imme security systems were based on small packets of data touching other packets of data in a pattern that humans found disturbingly illogical.

Which made Imme systems difficult to hack for groups used to the standard Alliance protocols.

Flint was torn between thinking whoever had designed the security protocols in this part of the Alliance had been utterly brilliant and cursing that person's name. It would take him hours, maybe days, to break into the system, and he wasn't sure he would be able to do it invisibly, like he did with all the other systems in the Alliance.

His pacing reflected his agitation. He couldn't just sit still and work. He needed to move just to keep his brain working.

He needed to go to the Security Office. Maybe DeRicci had access to some anti-hacking information that Alliance Security Officials used.

Flint often used anti-hacking documents as a guide for how to hack a particular system. The people who developed anti-hacking information often revealed too much, and told anyone with a slightly criminal brain exactly where the system's vulnerabilities were.

He was about to return to his main network when he froze in his tracks. His subconscious asked a question so unrelated to the work he was doing he almost felt like another person was in the room.

How do the Peyti pay for law school?

He let out a half-laugh of surprise. His brain had clearly been working on that for some time, and he had calmed down just enough to let that information rise to the surface.

It wasn't just about how the Peyti paid for law school, but how they educated their kids at all.

Unlike the clones of PierLuigi Frémont, each of the Peyti clones had long histories and established lives. They had records, that dated back to law school if not further.

And somewhere, someone had paid money to get those young Peyti into schools that weren't controlled by the Masterminds. Because law firms only hired lawyers from accredited law schools.

Flint couldn't believe that the Masterminds ran all the accredited law schools in the Alliance.

Follow the trail.

If he found the same source of funds—or similar sources—for the Peyti clones' education, then he would have a way to investigate the pool of money they were dipping into.

He grinned like a crazy man. His heart was pounding as if he had run several miles.

Sometimes his brain worked like a cluster of Imme feathers. He had no idea what tiny data packet had touched another tiny data packet.

He just knew he was glad the connection had been made.

Because it felt like a major breakthrough.

Only time would tell if it truly was.

51

Nyquist left DeRicci's office. She wanted to speak to Jin Rastigan alone. He closed the door gently, feeling tired but not quite as dirty as he had felt earlier. Despite his concerns for her, just seeing DeRicci lightened his mood.

Popova sat at her desk, but she wasn't alone. Flint's daughter Talia sat beside her. The girl looked different somehow. She had always been a bit exotic, with her curly blondish-red hair, her pretty copper-colored skin, and Flint's startling blue eyes. Every time Nyquist saw her, he thought she would be a beauty when she grew up.

Her appearance was still startling, but not because she was a nascent beauty. She looked ragged and lost. What had happened to her in the last few weeks?

He threw a questioning glance to Popova, who shook her head ever so slightly.

He wasn't quite sure what she was warning him off: Was he not supposed to say hello? Or was he supposed to keep quiet about Talia's appearance?

He could send Popova a message on his links, but that felt weird. Instead, he said, "Hello, Talia."

She looked up as if she hadn't seen him at all. "Oh. Detective. Hi."

"She's waiting for her dad," Popova said quickly. Apparently, Nyquist wasn't supposed to ask Talia about Flint.

Nyquist wasn't even sure if he should sit down now. And then his stomach growled. Apparently, he had relaxed enough to want food.

"Is it possible to order in these days?" he asked Popova.

"There are a few places whose food doesn't end up looking like it has been crushed by rocks when it arrives," she said. "You want me to order?"

"I want you to order food every few hours," he said, "as long as Noelle's here. She's not sleeping, so she needs to eat."

"She's not sleeping?" Talia asked. The question sounded important.

Popova's gaze met Nyquist's, but he couldn't read it.

"She's working her butt off," he said.

Talia looked down, and nodded.

He decided to venture one more piece of information. "But the stress is taking a toll on all of us."

"We're never going to solve this, are we?" Talia asked. "We're just going to get attacked forever."

He didn't know how to answer that. At his bleakest, he felt that way.

"We're making progress," he said. He had a confidence in his voice he didn't quite feel. Or maybe he did. For all of his disgust, his talk with Uzvaan showed that the clones had answers, and at least one of them was willing to talk.

Several others might be as well.

Talia shook her head.

"I'm sending you a menu," Popova said to her. "I want you to choose something from it."

"I'm not hungry," Talia said.

"And still, you're choosing," Popova said.

At that moment, Flint came down the hall. He was grinning. Nyquist's heart rose. Why would Miles Flint, one of the most serious people Nyquist had ever known, grin?

"Nyquist! You're here," Flint said as if they were long lost friends and Flint hadn't seen him for years. "Excellent."

Nyquist exchanged yet another confused glance with Popova.

"I don't have to brief everyone, then." Flint looked at the door. "Is Noelle available?"

"She's talking to someone," Popova said, "but I think she's almost done."

"What's happening?" Talia asked. She sounded frightened. Nyquist wasn't certain why Flint's good mood would frighten her.

"I think I finally figured out how to wrap my arms around this thing," Flint said.

"What?" Talia asked. She didn't seem to understand. Nyquist had always thought of her as smarter than the average kid, but she seemed dulled somehow.

He wasn't sure why, and Flint didn't even seem to notice, so maybe Talia's behavior wasn't unusual.

"Which thing?" Popova asked.

"Let's wait for Noelle," Flint said.

At that moment, DeRicci's office door opened.

"Did you really just send me a menu?" she asked Popova. "If you were going to order something, you could have..."

Her voice trailed off when she saw Flint.

"Miles," she said, noticing that something was different about him, but she clearly couldn't tell what. "Picking up Talia?"

"Actually, I came to see you," Flint said. "But I can talk to all of you. Let's go in the office."

As if it were his own. Not even Nyquist spoke to DeRicci like that. But she didn't seem to mind. She held the door open.

"Should I order food?" Popova asked Nyquist softly.

"Hold off for a few minutes," he said.

"Me too?" Talia asked her father.

He hesitated for just a minute, as if he were weighing the answer.

"Not this time," DeRicci said. "I have some classified things I need to discuss."

"Order the food after all," Nyquist said softly to Popova.

"Already done," Popova said, as she stood. Then she turned to Talia. "I just ordered food for all of us, and put it on our account. When the delivery arrives, let us know."

Talia nodded. She looked heartbroken.

Flint put a hand on her shoulder, then kissed the top of her head. "I'll tell you what I can," he said softly.

She nodded again, eyes downcast.

Nyquist turned away from her and walked into DeRicci's office. It felt a lot more comfortable in here, despite the clutter and the obvious lack of attention DeRicci had paid to anything this last week.

"What's with Talia?" Nyquist asked DeRicci.

"I have no idea," DeRicci said in a tone that implied she hadn't noticed and she didn't care.

Popova came in next, followed by Flint, who said something Nyquist couldn't hear to Talia. Then Flint closed the door.

He looked almost giddy.

"You have something," DeRicci said.

Flint opened his hands, then folded them together. "Give me a chance on this, because it doesn't sound like much, but I think it's everything."

He hadn't even come all the way into the office. Everyone crowded around him. Nyquist leaned against a desk stacked with empty food containers, some of which he had brought. Apparently no cleaning bot had come into this office for a while. Good thing the containers scrubbed themselves clean after the food became inedible, or this place would reek.

"Deshin kept telling me we had to follow the money," Flint said, "but I didn't even know where to start. That was my biggest hurdle. Deshin himself was tracking the DNA—"

"You've mentioned this," DeRicci said. She clearly wanted him to get to the point.

Nyquist could feel how tense she was, how she believed that each moment wasted was another moment that could lead to an attack.

"I did mention it," Flint said, "but I didn't tell you he found a name."

"A name?" DeRicci asked.

Flint nodded. "A woman who works in a classified area of the Earth Alliance. She had access to Frémont's DNA decades ago. But I can't find much about her."

"I might be able to find out about classified information," DeRicci said.

"I know," Flint said with a curtness that surprised Nyquist. Flint clearly didn't want DeRicci involved. "Not yet. If she is connected to the attacks, she'll be watching for someone in authority on the Moon to track her."

"That's not the breakthrough?" Nyquist asked. Because it sounded like a breakthrough to Nyquist. But he wasn't in on all the planning, and he could tell that DeRicci wanted everything to move quickly.

"No," Flint said. "I was researching this woman, doing what I could, when I realized that we already had an entry point for the money. I don't think I would have figured it out without thinking about this woman's history—"

"*Miles*," DeRicci said, her irritation evident. "I don't care how you got there. I want to know what you found."

"I haven't found anything yet," he said.

DeRicci rocked back as if he had slapped her. He didn't seem to notice her reaction.

"But I know we will," he said, giving her a sideways glance. Then he raised his eyebrows just a bit, as if telling her to calm down.

Now, Nyquist was feeling impatient. He was about to second DeRicci's request for more information when Popova asked,

"If we can find the money, we can find the attackers?"

"That's the theory," Flint said. "The answer isn't on the human side. It's on the Peyti side. In fact, knowing who these clones are—the fact that they failed—gave us a gift. For the most part, they're lawyers."

"Yes," Nyquist said. "That's such a fun—"

"And they went to law school," Flint said.

"Yes, but—"

"They went to *Alliance* law schools," Flint said. "I don't know about Peyti schools, but Alliance schools cost a small fortune. I know; I've been investigating for Talia."

Nyquist took a breath. He was already five steps ahead of Flint. Law school, payments, tracking, applications—there was a wealth of information on these clones that was just out there. Even if there were lies on every single application, the lies would probably match.

"My God," DeRicci said. She'd obviously made the same connections. "We can find them."

"You're sure?" Popova asked. She was the only untrained investigator in the group.

"I'm positive," Flint said.

"I'm even more positive," DeRicci said. "Because we found a clone who is willing to talk."

"Even with S-Three?" Flint asked.

Nyquist nodded. "Palmette's lawyer. You remember Uzvaan."

"I do." Then Flint shook his head. "I never will understand how someone like him could do something like that. Was it some kind of triggered response?"

"We don't think so," DeRicci said before Nyquist could say anything. "He—"

"He told me that he felt like he had two lives. The one he wanted, which he was living, and the one that he had been given, which he had to pay for," Nyquist said. "He also said he knew they would end on the same day. Of course, they didn't, so now he's questioning everything."

"I'm just amazed that he didn't question it before." Flint ran a hand over his face. "And you can talk to him?"

"We're just not sure for how long. When S-Three finds out what we're doing, and they will, they'll figure out how to shut us down." DeRicci sounded disgusted.

"It's an opportunity," Nyquist said, "and it's one I'll be taking advantage of tomorrow."

Nyquist was a bit amazed that he had gone from hating his assignment to looking forward to it. Flint's discovery made Nyquist's job that much easier.

"I have someone who can investigate this on Peyla as well," DeRicci said. "It's a human woman on Peyla who deeply understands Peyti culture. She says they're as shocked as we are by this betrayal, and they're not sure where to look."

DeRicci glanced at Nyquist, then at Popova, before continuing,

"Bartholomew got Uzvaan to speak Peytin to him. This woman, Jin Rastigan confirms that what Uzvaan said is something that some of the clones of Uzvekmt said on Peyla after they were arrested. It's part of the training."

"I knew it," Nyquist said, then, before Flint could ask, he explained, "It's about failure."

He told Flint about the interaction, and then DeRicci mentioned the killings on Peyti, and their theory. Popova added her thoughts as well.

Flint was nodding by the end of it all.

"And Jin confirmed to me that the Peyti brain is similar to the human brain, even in emotional response. So if you take a child and raise him in a world where failure equals death, then he will learn not to fail. And just like humans, the Peyti child will become desensitized to murder if it's part of his daily existence."

"Then I don't understand," Flint said slowly, "how any of these Peyti could have become lawyers."

"They were good at the law," Nyquist said. "They found nuances in whatever was on the books. But their attitudes—Uzvaan's at least—toward their clients was always a bit contemptuous. I didn't like that about him."

"And now we know why it was there," DeRicci said. Then she looked at Flint. "I didn't want Talia in here, because I don't think we should discuss our progress on the Peyti clones with anyone."

"You're right," he said.

"Will she be helping you track the money?" DeRicci asked.

He shook his head. "She's not in any shape to do so."

Nyquist frowned. So there was something going wrong with Flint's daughter.

"I may have found her some help," Flint said. "I'll let you know."

"She can come up here any time," Popova said. "We'll be working, but she's welcome."

"You can work up here," DeRicci said.

Flint shook his head. "Remember what I said about being monitored. If there's a Peyti mastermind as well as a human one, then the

Peyti mastermind will be watching for Moon-based investigations. Better that I do it from my office."

"You have no protection there," DeRicci said.

Flint smiled. "I have no *human* protection there. Otherwise, I'm well fortified."

Nyquist shifted a little. Normally, he would offer his services, but he didn't want to. He wanted to follow the leads now. They actually had a direction. And it felt good.

"Let's get busy on those questions," he said. "I'll find out how early I can get to the prison."

DeRicci grinned—a real, happy smile. "I actually feel hopeful for the first time in six months," she said.

Popova laughed in agreement. Nyquist wasn't sure he'd ever heard her laugh before.

Flint was smiling too. Then he put up one hand.

"Not to darken the mood," he said, "but I want to warn you all that it'll take me a few weeks to find anything. I have to go slow. If I blunder my way into the databases, someone will catch me."

"That's just prudent," DeRicci said. "We need to be careful. But at least we have a direction now. Something to hang on to."

Nyquist looked at her. She seemed more energized than he'd seen her since Anniversary Day. That was what she needed; she needed hope. She had been flailing in dozens of different directions.

Everyone had been flailing. Nyquist too. But he had a purpose now. He wasn't just trying to figure out how to manipulate a suspect into revealing something. He had one who wanted to talk, and he even had questions to ask besides the big one: *Why?*

He might get to that. But he suspected not even Uzvaan knew the answer to that big question. Uzvaan's why—he owed it to his creators—had already been answered.

Now, Nyquist and the rest of the team had to figure out what Uzvaan's creators wanted—what their reasons for the attack were. Maybe Uzvaan knew; maybe not. But the creators themselves couldn't hide forever.

And Flint had probably just discovered how to find them.

"Every investigation has its turning point," Nyquist said to Flint. "And sometimes it's just that moment when everything becomes clear."

Flint's gaze met his, softened, and Flint smiled. "I wouldn't have found it without Deshin. I think he knew all along that the finances were key. We just didn't know which finances."

"I always figured it would be the DNA," DeRicci said.

"I thought it was the choice of mass murderers," Popova said.

"Those are all elements," Flint said. "But we're not going to find our bad guys through those things. If we could, they wouldn't have been so obvious. It's the money."

"It always is," Nyquist said, wondering how he had missed it. "Money finances everything from greed to hatred to wars. Follow the money, and you find who put something together."

"Law schools," Popova said. "It sounds so simple."

"The masterminds expected the lawyers to get blown up with the rest of the Moon," Flint said. "If they had succeeded, we never would have known what caused this round of explosions."

"This was something the masterminds didn't think they had to cover," DeRicci said in wonder.

Nyquist grinned. "And that's their flaw."

Everyone looked at him.

He shrugged. "They didn't plan for failure—because it's not allowed. Uzvaan isn't the only one in new territory. The masterminds are too. I wonder how they'll react."

The smiles faded.

This fight was only just now getting underway. They had a lot of preparation to do.

Because the masterminds would figure out how to react, and this group had to be ready. The *Moon* had to be ready.

And Nyquist would do everything in his power to make sure that it was.

The thrilling adventure continues with the sixth book in the Anniversary Day Saga, *Vigilantes.*

A shocking act of violence...

The looming threat of another attack spurs the Moon's chief security officer, Noelle DeRicci, to uncover the identity of the masterminds behind the Anniversary Day bombings before they strike again. Armed with information uncovered by Retrieval Artist Miles Flint and Detective Bartholomew Nyquist, DeRicci lets herself hope she can put an end to the violence against the Moon.

But then a brutal murder changes everything.

DeRicci must risk everything to launch a secret investigation into the very heart of the Earth Alliance.

Can the next attack be stopped?

Turn the page for the first chapter of *Vigilantes.*

FORTY YEARS AGO

1

The gray door before Claudio Stott had fifteen levels of protection on it. Stott knew because he had actually studied the manual for this part of the Forensic Wing of The Alliance's Security Services. Most of the other candidates had downloaded the manual and used AutoLearn to figure out the massive information contained within.

The problem with that, of course, was that the other candidates gave similar answers to the verbal quiz Terri Muñoz gave them before making her final selection for this job.

Now that Stott stood in the corridor outside the most secure part of the Forensic Wing, he wasn't certain he wanted this job at all. The door stood at the end of several long corridors. The door was buried in the center of the starbase, and the first rooms beyond the door were clean rooms. He would have to use both a sonic shower, and a shower with specialized liquid before entering and leaving the section, something not mentioned in the manual, because, apparently, it irritated everyone involved.

Muñoz told him that several employees of the section actually got enhancements to keep their skin moist and to prevent rashes from the four-to-eight-times-per-day showers. The showers themselves sounded like wasted effort. Stott wanted to know why a decontamination chamber wouldn't work better, one calibrated for foreign DNA.

Then, even as he had the thought, he realized the problem with his question. The Forensic Wing didn't care about foreign DNA. They cared about the DNA that every single human being sloughed off through the course of every second of every day.

The showers, in theory, would prevent the sloughing long enough for the staff to don specially made environmental suits without contaminating the exteriors of those suits.

He should have known all of that; after all, he *had* studied the manual.

He looked at Muñoz. She was slight, her skin tending toward a greenish-olive that made her seem just a little ill. He had seen a holo of her from the days when she was first hired. Then her skin was a creamy brown.

So many people looked different as they aged that he hadn't attributed the change to anything. But now that he was contemplating half a dozen showers just to get to work, take his outside breaks, and eat his lunch, he wondered if that greenish-olive color reflected the beating her skin had taken after decades inside this facility.

This facility sounded so impressive. Special DNA Collections sounded like something positive instead of something scary.

He'd gotten past the scariness of it all by reminding himself that this was where the most interesting work in the Forensic unit occurred. Where real science got done.

He'd initially signed onto the DNA testing unit right out of university, with a newly minted degree in biological sciences. Because he'd been granted admission under the Alliance Poverty Program, he had to spend at least five years working off the cost of his degrees within the Alliance government.

He'd almost decided to move into the private sector when this opportunity came along. The salary was double what he made in the regular DNA testing section of the Forensic Unit, and he got to do actual work, rather than monitor the machines which did the testing almost automatically.

He once told one of his colleagues that he hadn't gotten a degree to babysit computer programs and make sure they ran right. Nor had he gotten one so that he could testify in court, verifying the computer's results.

He had gotten the degree so that he could learn the secrets of DNA, secrets that—after thousands of years of study—human beings still didn't entirely know.

Stott worried about working for corporations. He believed they often acted in amoral ways, particularly when it came to their employees. He knew too many people who had become actual sacrifices for the corporations: sent into newly aligned alien territories, forced to work in uncharted conditions, and then punished for violating alien laws that no human had known about.

Some corporations had Disappearance services which helped employees and their families escape the long arm of alien (and Alliance) justice. But Stott knew from personal experience that the Disappearance Services often came on the scene too late and did too little to save lives.

He shuddered and made himself focus on Muñoz. She was holding a tablet close to her chest. Apparently, the tablet was part of the security system.

Her dark eyes met his. "Are you changing your mind, Mr. Stott?"

He straightened. Double the salary. He didn't have to work with aliens. And he got to do real science. Surely several daily showers and lots of security procedures was worth all of that.

"No," he said, then decided his voice sounded wobbly. So he made himself speak more firmly. "No. I want to work here."

"Good," she said. "Because once you go through those doors, you're not going to be able to change your mind about this assignment."

He nodded. He had heard that warning before. It had been part of the application process at every single step. This was an irrevocable assignment, particularly because he would learn things that would be dangerous in the wrong hands.

"I'm ready," he said. "Let's go."

The thrilling adventure continues with the sixth book in the Anniversary Day Saga, *Vigilantes*, available now from your favorite bookseller.

ABOUT THE AUTHOR

USA Today bestselling author Kristine Kathryn Rusch writes in almost every genre. Generally, she uses her real name (Rusch) for most of her writing. Under that name, she publishes bestselling science fiction and fantasy, award-winning mysteries, acclaimed mainstream fiction, controversial nonfiction, and the occasional romance. Her novels have made bestseller lists around the world and her short fiction has appeared in eighteen best of the year collections. She has won more than twenty-five awards for her fiction, including the Hugo, *Le Prix Imaginales,* the *Asimov's* Readers Choice award, and the *Ellery Queen Mystery Magazine* Readers Choice Award.

To keep up with everything she does, go to kriswrites.com. To track her many pen names and series, see their individual websites (krisnelscott.com, kristinegrayson.com, krisdelake.com, retrievalartist.com, divingintothewreck.com, fictionriver.com). She lives and occasionally sleeps in Oregon.